GOLD, GUNS AND BMW'S

DOUG BIDDLE

America Star Books

.

Hardcover 9781632498090
Softcover 9781632491695
PUBLISHED BY AMERICA STAR BOOKS, LLLP
www.americastarbooks.com

Printed in the United States of America

I have heard it said that a story sometimes writes itself. After finishing Gold, Guns and BMW's and its predecessor, Luster of My Heart, I will have to agree. Not only does the story take its own direction, the characters do so as well. Neither finished the way I thought they would when they were started. However, no matter how I handled the stories or how they took on their own life, without the support of several people nothing would have been on paper.

The support from my family, Pam, my wife, and my daughters Erin and Emily helped push me along when I would hit a stump. Something as simple as 'how's the book coming?' or 'finished it yet?' go a long way to spur me on.

With Gold, Guns and BMW's I took some sound advice from Pam and enlisted the aid of first readers to help find errors that I made. As a West Texan, I will admit a few were made since English is my second language, Texan being my first. Pam, along with our friends Lena and Martha, aided me in finding far more errors than I thought I would ever make. Well, ok, I'm not surprised.

Not having done acknowledgments in Luster of My Heart, I am correcting the oversight here. Wanting to surprise Pam with a published book, I held the manuscript close to the vest until I had an offer to publish. Boy was she surprised. However during the writing of the story I had great advice from Martha. Twice I asked and she delivered. The first was when I was unsure of writing a story she said to me 'why are you worried, you tell a great story, put it on paper.' The other was when I was debating the use of my name or a pen name. Her response to my dilemma was 'are you proud of what you wrote?' Thanks Martha!

Thank you everyone! Pam, Emily, Erin, Lena, Martha and all the fans that have contacted me wanting more…

Doug

March 1945, Bavaria

Holes in his Wehrmacht greatcoat allowed the cold wind to send shivers up his tired back. However he was used to the cold, compliments of the Russian front. Taking a last drag off the harsh Russian cigarette, Captain Maurer tossed the butt, turned up the greatcoat collar and turned to his men.

Taking care not to show emotion at what he saw, Maurer walked among his troops as they unloaded the last of the trucks brought to them by the SS. The SS troops were wearing some type of protective suit like he had never seen. The crates his men were stacking next to the rail spur were marked with SS Runes and Skull and Crossbones. When Maurer asked about protection for his men, the SS Major in charge just glared at him as he fingered the pistol in his belt. Resisting the urge to shoot the little Nazi bastard, Maurer turned and walked over to the last truck.

As Maurer looked into the truck he saw scared eyes staring back at him. The man looked worse than his men who were unloading the crates. Remnants of a Wehrmacht infantry uniform stuffed with paper in an attempt to keep warm made the man look just like his own men. Nodding at the man, Maurer turned as he heard the whistle of the train that was to pick up the crates and his men.

Perhaps he will be able to treat his men to a real meal as well as a warm bed when they reach Nuremburg, Maurer thought as he boarded the train. If they reached Nuremburg, he thought with a cynical smile on his face.

CHAPTER 1

6 SEPT, 1977 NEW MEXICO

She gazed at him with wide innocent eyes, unsure how to react to his advances and statement he just made. He was handsome, standing there with the slight breeze blowing through his dark hair. His hazel eyes gleaming and his lips carried a slight smile while he stood there, waiting for her to speak.

He couldn't believe his eyes when he saw her. Crystal blue eyes, peering through long blonde hair as it blew across her face, froze him in place. Standing only three feet away, it was all he could do to keep from reaching for her and holding her forever.

Finally she smiled, stepped to him, kissed him on the cheek, turned and ran to her mother. Holding his hand where her lips touched, he turned and ran to his.

"Your son has already found his first girlfriend." Soledad said with a smile as she watched him run to us.

"Yep, I saw the kiss but I don't know what prompted it." I said picking him up. Holding him in my arms I leaned over and asked, "What did you say to the pretty girl who kissed you?"

Grinning ear to ear, he answered, "I told her I want our babies to have hair like hers and she kissed me."

Lupe, his 9 year old sister chimed in, "Mom, Dad, I told you, the reason he hangs around my friends when they come over is to flirt! That's why I have to keep running him off, he's so annoying!" All Soledad and I could do was laugh. Lupe shrugged at us, shook her head and went to join a group of the annoyed friends as they headed to their class room.

Rebecca, his twin sister, looked up at him with a gleam in her eye and asked, "Why would anyone want to kiss you? I'm the pretty one!" With that comment she took her mother's hand and led us into their new school.

Looking over at the girl and her parents as we headed into the school, they were smiling and shaking their heads as they were led inside by our future daughter in law. The first day of Pre School was going to be interesting.

After our little man and his mischievous sister met their teacher, a nice older lady who he liked instantly, but she was studying, they told us goodbye. They entered the class with all the enthusiasm the two of them gave everything else, that is to say they took the bit in their teeth and went in full speed ahead. Soledad touched my arm to get my attention and pointed. Kyle was holding out a chair for the little blonde girl to sit. Sitting, she smiled up at him and motioned for him to sit next to her.

"I am proud of our little man's manners. He is such a gentleman, much like his father." Soledad said as she held my arm and looked up at me.

It took me a minute to respond, every time I look directly into Soledad's eyes, my heart melts. Before I had a chance to reply, the girl's parents joined us.

"Your son seems to be quite the lady's man. He sure caught our darling's eye." Her mother said as the two walked up beside us.

"The boys out West seem to be more polite than boys in New York. I do not believe I have seen a boy hold a chair for a girl." Her father said as he extended his hand. "I am Joseph Latimer, this is my wife Janet. Our little darling over there is Jennifer."

Soledad laughed and said, "Kyle has mastered that move, with style."

After introductions and a short visit the couple offered to take us to lunch to get better acquainted. They had just moved from New York and we were the first couple they had met. We had to decline for we already had plans. However we did decide on dinner Saturday night.

Saying goodbyes we went our separate ways. With our backs to the couple, we did not see the stare they gave us and the glance between the two as they watched us walk away.

As we pulled out of the parking lot, Soledad reminded me she wanted to stop at her mother's on the way to meet Lae and Gregor for lunch. This was quite amusing since we were five minutes from the restaurant and her mother's was a two hour round trip from the school. Oh well, she's the boss and we have plenty of time to kill.

I never mind the drive to her mother's Hacienda. The scenery is beautiful and when Soledad is digging into her work, as she is now, it gives me time to ponder, as my grandfather called thinking. Gregor and Lae's trip to Laos brought back a flood of memories.

The last five years have been an interesting. After Thailand, Soledad and I settled in New Mexico, close to her family. Lae and Gregor joined us after Naval Intelligence finished with them. Lae and Soledad started a business utilizing Soledad's love of flying. L and S Flight School has been a success and I was their first student.

Gregor and I have a very successful fishing-camping guide business, anything this much fun can't be called work. We have turned down several offers to guide hunters. However, I agree with Gregor when he got into a jerks face that would not take no for an answer. Gregor extended to his full 6'4' height, leaned over the shorter man and growled, "We will not be KILLING GUIDE. Now go away before I do to you what you want to do to Bambie and I hang your hide on my wall." I tried unsuccessfully to keep my laughter down as the poor guy ran from our office.

Pulling into the parking lot of our favorite restaurant, Soledad looked up, smiled, and said, "Right on time, as usual. Glen, it still amazes me how we are always on time to things. Before I met you I was always late, well most of the time."

Smiling at her, I got out, went around and opened the door for her. There was no way I was going to say anything about her old habit of being late.

Lae and Gregor were already seated and had drinks for all of us in front of them. Sensing there was something up, Soledad and I sat down, took a long drink of our beer and waited for them to spill the beans.

Lae could not hold her excitement, "We are going to Europe on vacation! Gregor wants to show me things he has seen when he was on holiday when he was young. Want to go?"

Gregor and I locked eyes as the two women went into planning mode thus preventing us from getting in a word edgewise. We just sipped our beer and watched our women with the amusement that is born out of love. As our food hit the table, the ladies had the trip planned. Lae and Gregor are going to Laos first so Lae could see her family. This will give Soledad and me time to get things ready for us to meet them in Germany in two weeks. The kids can stay with their grandmother, she will be thrilled. Our staff at both businesses can handle things for a while since we are going into fall and things slow down a bit. Finishing the meal, while the ladies settled down to a more mundane chore of planning who will do what while they are gone, Gregor and I made plans of our own.

"Why do you want to hook up in Munich in two weeks?" I asked as I drained my beer.

Smiling, Gregor said, "I want to buy a new BMW as it rolls off the assembly line. I want to be the one to drive it for first time. Why don't you pick one as well?"

"Never thought about it, but it sounds like fun. Count me in!" I replied as we stepped out of the restaurant and headed back to school to pick up our little Casanova and his sister. We better pray the class is intact after a full morning of Rebecca's attention.

Neither of us saw the small man leave the restaurant behind us and head to a parked car on the next block. The car was occupied by a man and a woman with whom he had a quick conversation.

This was all taken in by a young man wearing an L & S flight jacket. Sitting on his Harley across the street, Kurt Creager watched as the small man finished his conversation with the couple. As they pulled away, the small man started walking down the street toward his car. Removing his flight jacket, Kurt stuffed it in his saddle bags and climbed aboard the motorcycle. The deep rumble of the Harley idling by got the other man's attention. As he looked up, Kurt cut in front of him, blocking his path.

"What do you want? Get out of my way." Bob Pearson said in his high squeaky voice.

Smiling at him, Kurt pushed the kickstand down on his ride, dismounted, walked up to Bob and said, "Of course, but I do have one question Sir."

Frowning, Bob asked, "Why should I tell you anything?"

"It is simple Sir, if you do not, you will be dead in two minutes." Kurt replied with a smile that did not reach his eyes.

The cold look in the young man's ice blue eyes scared Bob to his bones. He couldn't speak fast enough, "They paid me to snoop and tell them what I heard. That's all. Please let me go, I didn't hurt anyone."

"What did you hear, what did you tell the people in the car, and what was their response?" Kurt asked, smile unchanging.

Shaking uncontrollably, the small man told Kurt all he knew in a matter of minutes. Still smiling, Kurt remounted his Harley, nodded and rode off. As the young man disappeared around the corner, Bob realized his pants were soiled. Looking around quickly hoping no one saw, he ran to his car.

As he rode back to the office, Kurt knew he had to call his superiors. Not Lae or Soledad, who he has grown to hold in high esteem, but his superiors in West Germany's BND.

CHAPTER 2

Sitting on a bench just inside the foyer of the church, Sister Anna surveyed the chapel. The wedding that afternoon had filled the church and the mess left behind attested to that fact. Even with a lot of work needed to get the church ready for Mass, Anna was in great spirits. Her favorite niece was now married to a wonderful man with a bright future ahead of her.

Joining the other Nuns in cleaning, Anna started gathering paper along the wall. Halfway along between the door and the opening into the chapel she hit her head on a shelf that was hung a little too low for her 5'11" frame. Rubbing her head at the point of contact, she held her tongue less a not to lady, nor Nun, like exclamation would pass her lips. If that happens she would be in trouble with the Father, again. Looking up at the offending shelf, the occupants made her smile. The brightly painted figurines and statuettes always made her smile.

Angels with spread wings, Nuns in full habit, Mary and Joseph sat in the front of the shelf. Various Saints, miniature copies of the statues for which the church is famous, and of course, St John, for which the Church was named, filled the rest of the 12' long shelf. The over thirty handcrafted and painted figurines, along with another sixty or so scattered about the church, were the pride of the Father. All were made by wounded German soldiers that were recovering at the Schloss just outside of the village in the spring of '45.

As a young Priest, Father Aaron was awed by the men and the spirits they projected during their recovery. The men, mainly

Wehrmacht, knew the war was over for them and would soon be over for everyone. That alone lifted their spirits. Several were artisans, painters, sculptors, and were quite good. They would bring figurines every Sunday before Mass and present them to the Father as gifts to the people of the Church. Unfortunately, there were times when the Father presided over their funerals when they died of their wounds.

The Father held the Mass, yes, but not the burial. The men insisted on burying their own, including carving of their stones and the placement of the graves. None of the villagers were invited to attend the burials and none knew the location of the graves.

Reaching as far along the shelf as she could, Sister Anna dusted it as well, taking care not to disturb the figurines. Upon finishing the foyer, she proceeded into the chapel looking for more to clean. The others had finished the rest and the Church was ready for mass later in the evening. As she turned to go to her quarters to prepare for the service, she had to pause and admire one of her favorite pieces in the collection.

The soldiers had brought a heavy, sturdy built oak table with a circler recess in the center. They told the Father it was for a very special Baptismal basin they were working on. The table had to be strong to support its weight since they were using special clay to make the vessel. Not questioning the gift, the Father made a special place for it and instructed the Sisters it was not to be moved. Using shades of bright blues, the men painted a beautiful basin that was known throughout the area as a prime example of fine German artistry. Even after over thirty years of use, it was as lovely as it was the day the men placed it there. According to the story, the last soldier who touched it, as it slid into place, died. Apparently the only thing keeping him going was the Baptismal and seeing it in the church. Not able to resist the urge, Anna touched it and said a quick prayer for him before continuing to her quarters.

10 SEPT, NEW MEXICO

I have to hand it to my friends, they picked a great spot to build their house, I mean log cabin. Well, outside Gregor got what he wanted, an American log cabin. Hand cut timber, precision cut corners, large overhangs, massive porches and a stone fireplace made their home ideal for the cover of Rocky Mountain News. Add all that to the location, damn nice job. They placed their home on a mountain north east of Santa Fe with a view of the city. Pine forest surrounded their home giving it a real mountain home feel.

Inside was another story. Lae did a fantastic job finishing the interior. Light earth tones on the walls, leather furnishings in their den, living area and eat in kitchen. Subtle hints of the orient combined with Native American art tastefully finished out the décor, all but their master suite. Laos was represented beautifully in their master. Bamboo and hand carved wood furniture, hand carved statues, and rice paper wall art among other decorations imported from Bangkok filled the room with a pleasant representation of her native home.

Gregor sat quietly, considering his response to the question I had just hit him with. He and I were out on their porch drinking coffee while we waited for the ladies. We only had a few minutes until we had to head for the airport so they could make their flight.

Cupping his hands to warm them against the cool morning air, he finally looked up and said, "I know there are risks going there, but she is homesick for her family. She wants the trip, she will have it."

"Even with the Vietnamese occupying a major part of the country, with their Soviet advisors?" I asked, and then continued, "Gregor, they think you're dead and not looking for you. Do you really want to chance being spotted? You and I stick out there like wolves in a hen house."

Smiling, Gregor said, "Ah my friend, the saying is 'fox in a hen house.' Even I know that American idiom."

"Yea, but you're more wolf than fox. I'm serious Gregor. I worry about this part of your vacation. In fact, I am thinking of going with you." I said, exasperated at my friend.

Reaching over, Gregor grasped my shoulder and said, "Not to worry Glen, Lae will make sure I get to Germany to collect my BMW." Looking over his shoulder he continued in a loud voice intending for the women to hear as they stepped on the porch, "here she is now, ready to see the world and eat her mother's cooking also."

Soledad held my hand and leaned into me as we watched their plane take off. Standing there in silence until it disappeared. Finally she said, "They will be fine Glen, besides we will see them in Germany in two weeks. Now come on, we have things to do before our for our dinner date."

Dinner was interesting. The food was great as we went to one of our favorite restaurants, the company was strange. They were nice enough but something bothered me all evening. I couldn't put my finger on it until we were leaving and our new friend said, "We will not be able to wear our clothes if we continue to eat like this."

After we got in the car, I turned to Soledad and said, "I don't trust them. She may be an American but he isn't and he is trying hard to make us think he is."

"What makes you say that?" Soledad asked with a serious look in her eye. We learned long ago to trust each other's instincts.

"How many Americans do you know that don't use contractions?" I asked back.

"Well hell." She replied.

CHAPTER 3

Otto Klaus studied the cable from one of his operatives in the U.S. Even though West Germany and America were allies now, one sometimes spied on friends in order to find out what ones enemies are up to. By its self, Kurt's report could be nothing, but when added to three others, which are on his desk, a very interesting picture comes to light.

Picking up one of the reports from Georgia, he reread the section which dealt with his old friend John Kirkpatrick. Five years ago John had resurrected his belief that he knows where Nazi gold was hidden, in Germany of all places. Everyone knows the Nazis were outstanding when it came to stealing and smuggling. There is not any evidence of gold still in Germany, only theories.

However it is better to err on the side of caution. Young Kurt was sent a year ago to watch one of the Americans to which John had mentioned his theory and has stayed in contact with. Looks like that decision would be paying off. The American is headed to Germany, to the very area John says the gold is hidden.

Apparently others were interested in John and his antics, as two of the other reports reflect. Over the last few days, after the American bought tickets to Munich, the Stazi, East German Intelligence, and the Mosad, Israeli intelligence, both have teams watching John and the other American. Things might get interesting over the next few weeks, especially if everyone who is showing interest descend on the same village in Bavaria.

Picking up the last folder, Otto read about the American in question, Glen Williams. The photo was one Kurt sent last year. Williams, his wife and another couple were seated in a restaurant, facing the camera with glasses raised. Looked like a celebration of some sort. The photo showed a handsome young man with, what appears to be, a quick smile. But after reading the report, which included his time in Thailand, and studying the photo further, especially the eyes, Otto knew this young man would be a tough advisory, therefore he would do everything possible to make him an ally. With that thought echoing in his mind, he turned off his lights and started home.

12 Sept, New Mexico

Lights also turned off a half a world away. The smell of fresh coffee filled the kitchen as Soledad stepped onto the rear deck. After Glen made love to her, she usually collapsed into a deep sleep, last night was no different, and damn he could light her up. But tonight she did not stay asleep, her eyes snapped open and worry flooded her. Not for herself nor her immediate family, but her extended family of Gregor and Lae.

Lae had a plan on how to keep Gregor safe while she visited her family. Soledad had sat there in silence when Lae told her in detail the plan she had set into motion the week before. Soledad held her tongue while her friend filled her in because she knew Gregor will be furious at Lae but, as Lae put it, he will be alive. Wondering if she should tell Glen the plan Lae had hatched, Soledad was deep in thought when Glen came up behind her and scared her half to death.

I woke and reached for my Heart, ready to begin round three, but she was not in our bed. The faint whiff of the coffee she prefers told me where she was. But the kitchen was dark so I headed to the only place she could be, this early and with coffee, the rear deck. Since our home faced east our rear deck was a perfect place to watch the Sun and the Moon set in the west.

Looking out the window, I saw her wrapped in a blanket leaning on the deck rail. With her hair up and pulled away from her face, the moon light caused her face to have a soft glow that was both soft and sensual. As she raised her coffee cup to her soft lips, a frown creased her brow. Wondering what caused the frown, I decided to join her and find out.

Softly opening the door, I stepped on the deck, my bare feet silent on the wood decking. Just before I reached out to touch her I realized she had not heard me at all and didn't know I was there. I was in a dilemma. The four of us had taken several self-defense courses, Gregor and I to stay sharp and the girls to learn. And learn they did! Lae and Soledad were the best in their classes and were quick, very quick. Here I am, within striking distance of a woman who could put some serious hurt on me, and she doesn't know I'm here.

Deciding to back track and get out of her reach I stepped back, but on a different board. The creak was soft but she heard it. Jumping from fright, she turned quickly on one heel and struck out with the other. Her tendency had been to punch when frightened, which we had been working on improving. Well our hard work paid off, sort of. I was watching for the punch I thought was coming when her foot caught me square in the solar plexus and knocked me out of breath and on my ass. I'm so proud of her, she didn't stop there. When she completed the kick she spun around and stomped on the unprotected place my legs come together doubling me over in pain. As she stepped back she realized the withering mess on the deck was me.

Sunrise found us in the kitchen where Soledad was preparing breakfast. Kyle and Rebecca were up early to go on a school field trip. Lupe helped her Mom with the cooking. Kyle sat down his glass of juice and studied me. After a few moments he slid out of his chair and walked over to me.

"Dad, did Mom hurt you again?" He asked with a smile on his face and a gleam in his eye.

Soledad stifled a laugh and glanced over at Lupe who was having a hard time not laughing out loud. Soledad must have told her about our early morning encounter.

After glancing over at our two cooks, I looked at him and answered, "What makes you ask that?" Pointing to my lap he answered, "You have a bag of frozen peas in your lap. The last time you had them in there you and Mom had been wrestling."

That did it, Soledad and Lupe cracked up but their laughter increased when we all heard Rebecca.

"He has two bags in his lap this time, Mom must have won big." She said as she climbed out from under the table laughing.

I tried to act indignant, but all I could do was laugh with them. "Yep, she won big. One of these days I may win."

With an expression of deep thought, Rebecca said, "Naw, she's too good." Then kissed me on the cheek and sat back down to dig into the omelet Soledad had sat on the table.

The rest of the meal was filled with fun and laughter. As I put the TWO bags of peas in the freezer I couldn't help but think how lucky a man I am.

An hour later we pulled out of the drive, headed for school. We did not see the blonde couple down the road watching us through binoculars. Nor did we see Kurt sitting on his motorcycle to the blonde couples left. They didn't see him either but he saw us all.

As we drove out of sight, Kurt's full attention was on the couple. He knew two other teams were in the area. He had been briefed on both and was prepared, if necessary, to take steps to remove any threat to the family he had been assigned. Those steps would not be needed today, he thought, as the blonde couple drove away, not following the Williams family.

Kurt went back to his Harley and swung his leg over the gas tank and sat down. As he got ready to kick the starter a flash of light, to his right, got his attention. Reaching into his saddlebags to retrieve the binoculars he had just placed there, Kurt studied the area from which the flash came. In a matter of seconds, Kurt spotted the cause of the flash. The Sun was at the right elevation to reflect off the rifle scope that was pointed at him. Not worried about getting shot, the rifle was over a mile away, but he knew no one used a rifle scope just to spy. Kurt fired up his Harley and headed to the location of the rifle. Besides, if shooting started he had to get close. All he had with him was a .380 Walther.

Standing in the spot where the rifleman had lain, Kurt was disappointed in the gunman not being there. Looking the grounds over in the manner of a trained agent, Kurt found nothing of value. Stepping back to his motorcycle he missed a clue, almost. Kneeling beside a flat rock, half hidden under a juniper, Kurt noticed tobacco. Looks like the man had put out several cigarettes on this small rock. But he was careless and left residue behind. Picking up the leavings Kurt first smelled then tasted the tobacco. Spitting it out, he frowned, Russian.

Standing up, Kurt studied the area from the rifleman's vantage point. Slightly below where Kurt stood, roughly 800 meters to the east, lay Glen and Soledad's home. The view of the rear deck was perfect to observe and if good enough, to take a shot. Studying the area further Kurt knew he needed help, but who can he ask without risking his cover and his mission? There is no scenario where he can tell any American what he is doing here. They would have him arrested then sent out of the country leaving the Williams family vulnerable. That must not happen.

Looking around one more time, Kurt took the time to admire the Williams placement of their home. To the west stood Redondo Peak and Cerro La Jara, to the east was Santa Fe Baldy and Elk Mountain. The Rio Grande River was only a couple of miles west. These are not the Alps, Kurt thought, but he liked it here and wanted to stay.

As he turned toward his motorcycle, it came to him where to go. There is one man he could turn to for help, hopefully.

CHAPTER 4

Lae sat on the edge of the bed watching Gregor sleep. The last few days of travel were exhausting to them both. First the long flights to Bangkok then the boat ride up the river to the Chief's place where Laos, Thailand and Burma come together. The Chief, a retired Chief Petty Officer of the US Navy, Ronan Macleod, had helped the couple in the past. Lae hoped he would do so again. She was not disappointed. Not only did he welcome them with open arms, he went along with Lae's plan.

Leaning over and placing a soft kiss on her man's forehead, Lae paused for a moment to make sure the drug Ronan had given her was effective. Gregor's deep breathing confirmed the mickeys strength. Turning to go, she caught a glimpse of herself in the dressing mirror by the door. Pausing for a moment she studied the woman staring back at her. Even the native dress Ronan provided could not dampen who she had become. The last five years with Gregor in America had changed her in more ways than she realized. Nodding at the woman in the mirror, she turned to go. The two men Ronan insisted on accompanying her were waiting at the boat he had given her. Stepping out of the room, Lae's excitement at seeing her family for the first time since leaving with Gregor, took command of her emotions. With bright eyes and a dazzling smile she all but ran to the boat.

The current on the Mekong River was flowing rapidly due to the rains upstream making travel upriver slower than normal. However the boat Ronan loaned Lae had a new motor, fresh from the States, allowing them to make good time. By nightfall they were at a small village where they would spend the night and proceed on foot in the morning. Late evening the second day found them in Lae's village having dinner with her family.

As the sun bid its farewell, Gregor started to stir. Wanting to know the instant Gregor awoke, Ronan had posted a boy just outside Gregor's room. Kimo was 12 and he loved the Chief. Always hanging around, he was quick to do anything to please Ronan. After hearing Gregor stir, Kimo ran to fulfill his duty. Pride in the honor of doing such an important task for the Chief, he had to calm down and catch his breath so he could report. Smiling at the boy, Ronan thanked him and patted him on the head. Kimo's beaming smile lit the room at the praise bestowed on him.

Slowly Gregor's befuddled mind cleared. After what seemed like an hour, Gregor's eyes finally focused enough for him to understand his surroundings. As his feet hit the floor, his head landed in his hands, trying to stop the room from spinning. He was in that position when Ronan entered his room.

"Had a rough night son? You've slept the clock around. " Ronan asked in an innocent tone.

Looking up at him out of bloodshot eyes, Gregor asked, "What does that mean?"

With a broad smile he got his answer, "It means you slept almost 24 hours. You look like hell but food in your belly should help." Ronan answered with a bigger smile.

Gregor nodded in agreement, looked around then asked the question Ronan was waiting for, "Where is Lae?"

"On the way home with two of my best men." noting Gregor's surprise, Ronan continued, "she wanted it that way son, she is concerned with your safety. And quite frankly it didn't take much to talk me into helping her, because she is right."

Gregor's face flushed bright red, you could see the anger build in him. As quickly as the anger built, it was gone and a smile spread across his face. "Lae would think like that and there is not anything you or I could have said to change her mind. But, it will not keep me from worrying about her."

"Didn't think it would, however I have a proposition for you that might just help pass the time until she returns next week." Ronan said with a slightly crooked smile.

Eyeing the Chief closely, Gregor asked, "What might that be?"

Sitting in a chair across the room, Ronan laid out his plan, "I have business back in the States that needs my personal attention. All told it would take a week there and back so the time frame isn't too bad. My problem is I don't have anyone to leave in charge while I'm gone. Don't get me wrong, I have great people here but they look to me for security and guidance." Pausing for Gregor to interject, he waited. But Gregor just sat there and listened, finally he continued, "I want you to take charge and take care of things while I'm gone."

Gregor sat there in shock. After a few moments he replied, "We do not know one another very well. However it does seem I have a week to spare."

"I like to think that I am a good judge of character. We know each other well enough for me to be comfortable in asking this favor." Ronan replied with a slight smile.

"I would be honored." Gregor said with a smile of his own.

"Come on then, let me introduce you to my men, I'm packed and ready to go." said Ronan as he headed out the door leading a smiling Gregor, who slowly shook his head in amusement of how his trip had changed.

14 Sept, Berlin, East Germany

Utilitarian walls and décor made Stasi headquarters a dull and depressing place to work. The black multistory building was an eyesore compared to the old majestic buildings that did not survive the war. Manfred Wagner's small window was the only saving grace to a work environment as boring as his personal life. Boring yes, but Wagner was mean to the core. His cruelty even surprised his superiors, who were evil in their own right. His enthusiasm for ordering arrests, torture and killings had earned him the nickname "Little Himmler", after the Nazi Gestapo leader of the Third Reich.

Reading the reports from his teams in the US, Wagner started forming a plan to put the information to good use. John Kirkpatrick, his old American advisory, was up to something involving Nazi gold. An American contact of his in New Mexico is apparently going to the area John thinks the gold is hidden. Both men have CIA operations in their past, therefore Wagner deducts, mistakenly, this must be a CIA approved operation. Interestingly the American in New Mexico has a family he will be leaving behind. Perhaps leverage may be needed in the near future. The family may provide what he will need.

Wagner's aid noticed the smile on his superiors face and knew it meant trouble for someone. He hoped it was not meant for him, it wasn't.

18 SEPT, BAVARIA

As the church emptied, Sister Anna had a chill run up her back. Looking quickly around, she spotted a strange little man sitting in the back. She noticed him the night before and thought his interest in the church was curiosity, like many new comers. Again he sat alone, eyeing everyone as they filed past.

As the last person left the chapel, the man reached into his jacket pocket. Anna half expected him to pull a weapon and make demands. Thankfully he pulled out a note pad and pencil instead. After sitting a few minutes taking notes, he stood, stretched, and with a slight limp, walked around the room taking more notes. As he walked into the foyer, Anna kept an eye on him from the chapel. She saw him spend several minutes in front of the shelf that holds the figurines of which she is so fond. Had she been able to see his face, the trail of tears running down his aged face may have surprised her.

Feldwebel Willie Storch, retired, stood in front of the figurines he had helped create so many years ago. They were as bright and vibrant as when they were presented to the Church. If only the others could see them, their pride would be as great as his. However, most of his comrades from that time in his life are dead. Only he and two others are still above the grass that he knew of.

Having worked many years as an analyst with the BND, Willie was continually hearing rumors and theories. After hearing rumors of the BND's interest in this area and stories of lost Nazis gold he contacted his two friends. The conversations were short and to the point, damage control. He was not a field agent by any means, but he would do what he could to make sure their secret is not revealed.

Smiling over his shoulder at the nervous Nun, he walked into the night.

18 SEPT, NEW MEXICO

Kurt sat quietly in the small dark room, patiently waiting for the meeting that took almost a week to set up. Time was growing short. Soledad and Glen will be leaving on their trip Saturday and nothing was in place to help him protect them and the children from the danger he knew they were in. Tired was not strong enough word for Kurt's condition. Working all day at the airfield and watching the Williams home at night left him exhausted.

His superiors at home placed agents in Bavaria to await Glen and Soledad's arrival. This left him in New Mexico to keep watch on the family. But it also kept him alone. Hoping he had not made a mistake coming to the Reservation to look for help, Kurt waited in silence.

Finally the old door creaked open. Standing to greet the arrivals, Kurt extended his hand. The gesture was ignored by the three old Navaho who came in and sat down in front of him. Sitting, Kurt waited for them to speak first.

Minutes seemed as hours to Kurt as he sat in front of the three. The deep lines on their faces made them seem as old as the rocks around them, and just as immobile. One finally moved, digging out the fixings to roll a cigarette he asked Kurt if he wanted one, in Spanish. Kurt smiled and politely declined. The shock on their faces lasted only a second. They were not expecting him to understand. Nothing else was said until after the old one lit his smoke.

Blowing a ring of smoke into the air, the old one said, "You speak the language of the Conquistadors, but look nothing like them. This is good, for the three of us do not speak the White man's tongue, by choice." Reaching for the floor, he put out the cigarette, sat back and asked, "Why did you seek us out?"

Getting to the point, Kurt said, "I am Kurt Creager, an employee of Soledad Garcia's company. I think she and her family are in danger and I need your help."

"We know who you say you are. We also know you and others are watching the family of Soledad and Glen. Our question is why." said the man to the right of the smoker.

Studying the faces of the three men, Kurt decided, correctly, he must be honest with these men if he is to receive the help he so desperately needed. The full story took ten minutes. As he finished telling them every detail he knew, including who he really was and what he was doing there, Kurt sat back and waited.

When he finished, the three looked at each other and had a private conversation in their native tongue, which Kurt did not understand.

The three stood as one. The smoker extended his hand and said, "I am the one known as Sani, it is I you seek. We have protected the Garcia family for over three hundred years and will do so as long as the water flows in the Great River. We welcome help from the land of the Teutonic Knights. Be warned, we do not recognize the White man's law, nor are we bound by it, and will deal with threats in our way, is this acceptable?"

"Yes." Is all Kurt could say.

"Come, we have plans to make, but first we eat." Sani said with a smile.

At the mention of food the others smiled with him. As he followed his new friends out of the shack, Kurt was somewhat surprised the smiles did not make their faces crack and fall off.

CHAPTER 5

Lae was having a wonderful time with her family. Things had settled down and returned to an almost normal state after the war. The Pathet Lao ran the country in a fairly organized manner. Instead of Warlords, the Pathet Lao turned into bureaucrats and became like the government officials they replaced. The Vietnamese and Soviet occupiers were more in the way than they were helpful, however it did not stop them from strutting around as if the wellbeing of every Lao depended on them. With her days growing fewer, Lae packed as much into every minute as possible.

Meanwhile, Gregor was actually enjoying the responsibility the Chief had placed on him. That is right up until Burmese pirates decided to visit.

U Zeya traveled the rivers of the region in hopes of finding easy prey. Almost 40 years of doing so have netted him very little. He robbed enough all right, but spent all he took. The authorities in four countries want his head, but he has stayed one step ahead of them all.

When word got to him that McLeod had left the country for a week or so, he was ecstatic. Hatred for the Chief was too mild of a word to describe what U Zeya felt. MacLeod cost him men, money and, most hurtful of all, his pride. He now planned on taking what MacLeod had, his home and fortune. Contacting his lieutenants and then his associates, U Zeya started planning his revenge. But time was of the essence, the destruction had to be completed before MacLeod returned.

The half Moon on the 20th would aid his men by shielding their movements with enough light to move into position without giving them away. It seemed to U Zeya that nature itself was on his side. Confident his men would wipe everything MacLeod had built off the face of the Earth, U Zeya celebrated by having two local women join him in bed.

They say the best battle plans go out the window when the first shot is fired. U Zeya's was no exception.

19 SEPT, NEW MEXICO

I got home before Soledad and the kids. Opening the refrigerator I grabbed a beer and went out on the deck to watch the sunset. The view was breathtaking. Soledad, Lae and Mi Ling did a fantastic job picking the placement of our home. Going over everything I had to do to be ready for our trip, I lost track of time. Hearing Soledad's car coming up the drive I finished the beer and went to greet my family.

Eight pair of eyes watched the door close behind me. Roughly 800 yards due west lay two men, watching through spotter scopes, not touching the rifle next to them. Leaving the rifle on the ground saved their lives, for now.

Unknown to us, Kurt and Sani had placed riflemen at all four points of the compass. They also placed extra men on each side of the spot Kurt had seen the rifleman. The big difference between the unknown riflemen and Kurt's new friends was Kurt's men were all but invisible. The aggressor team didn't know they were being watched.

Gunther and Steiner were the two best men the Stasi had in the U.S. Both were excellent marksmen and cruel as hell. Neither had qualms about harming women and children much less shooting an unarmed, unsuspecting man. Every time they watched the American, Steiner wanted to shoot him and get it over with. Gunther had to keep reminding him about their orders from Wagner, observe but be ready to strike. The last order from Wagner gave them the prospect of a new direction, kidnapping. Wagner may want the children. If so, they had to wait until the parents left for Germany on Saturday. In the meantime, they watch and wait.

Packing up their gear after the sun disappeared below the mountains, the men headed into Santa Fe and their hotel. Dark eyes watched every move they made, right up until their hotel door closed. Even then, three men rotated watching them throughout the night.

On the mountain range east of our home, higher than the rest, two pair of eyes watched everyone. Having spotted three of the Navaho teams and the Stasi team, the two people smiled at each other. While the East Germans concentrated on us and the locals kept track of the East Germans, they were free to operate with impunity. And operate they did, having been in the area for about two weeks the Latimers knew movements, habits and most important of all, weaknesses of everyone involved, or thought they did.

As they packed up and headed to a house they had rented, Sani smiled to himself as he followed them home. He had not had this much fun since he played cat and mouse with the Army when they were trying to gather Navaho to fight in their war. That thought gave him pause, for just a second, as he remembered the young Navaho who fought the White man's war and did not return home.

20 SEPT, GOLDEN TRIANGLE

U Zeya moved the last of his men into position just before dawn. Being a river pirate, he didn't think of terms of an infantry assault but a water bourn attack. Six boats with ten men each should give him an overwhelming force in which to raze the Chief's dreams off the face of the earth. Not having a subtle bone in his body, his orders were simple, burn every building and kill everyone, no survivors.

His revenge was to start as the first rays of the sun made their appearance, six boats sweeping in, two upstream of the docks, two on the docks and two downstream. Every boat carried two, two man demolition teams armed with enough C4 to level everything in sight. The other six in each boat were marauders, armed with assault rifles and orders to kill, just kill.

As U Zeya waited the arrival of the Sun, Murphy's Law made its appearance. North of the village on the Thai side of the river, Kimo was walking along the river bank. He and several of his friends were meeting for some early fishing. Kimo was hoping for a good catch, enough to bring home and some to take to the Chief's friend. He wasn't too sure of the big white man but the Chief likes him and trusted him to take care of things while the Chief was gone for a few days.

As he walked round the bend of the river, he spotted the boats full of men. Dropping to the ground, Kimo worked his way close so he could hear what they were saying. What he heard scared him into action. Leaving his fishing gear where he lay, Kimo jumped up and ran through the trees, taking a short cut to the village.

The hot steaming brew in Gregor's cup was called coffee, what it really was, Gregor wasn't too sure. But the men who had joined him needed the strong brew. They had talked Gregor into drinking and gambling with them into the wee hours of the morning. When they called a halt to both activities they were all very drunk and broke. Instead of risking the wrath of their wives, while in a compromised condition, they stayed in the Chief's bar to sleep it off.

Smiling at the condition of his new friends, Gregor was thankful for the habits he picked up while a soldier. Vodka can cause a vicious hangover if not handled correctly, if nothing else the Red Army taught Gregor how to control the liquid fire, and the ability to rise at the same time every morning without an alarm clock. Too bad the men in front of him could do neither. He almost felt sorry for them, almost.

He had however, planned to return the money they had lost to him. While they sat there with their heads in their hands he counted out their losses and slid the money to them. Smiling through their pain, the men gathered the gift and started home.

As the first man reached the door, Kimo almost ran him down. The young man was so scared he spoke rapidly in his native tongue. Gregor had trouble following him. One of the men got him to slow down, take a deep breath and tell them what has him so frightened.

"Six boats with many men, perhaps ten or so in each are around the bend in the river that comes from Burma. They have many weapons and plan to attack us when the sun comes up." Kimo finally said in an understandable way.

Gregor instantly became a soldier again, not only a soldier but an officer. Taking a look at the quickly sobering men in front of him, he knew what they had to do.

"Gather everyone in the village and take them to the other side of the lake west of the village. We can't fight that many men and hope to win therefore we don't give them anyone to fight. Now GO! HURRY! We haven't much time." Gregor yelled at them to spur them on.

As they went about their task, Gregor went to Ronan's office and tripped the latch that gave him access to the weapons locker where the Chief had given them arms years ago. As he gathered Claymores, grenades, two AK47's and a bag of loaded clips, he noticed a new addition to the Chief's collection. Pulling it down where it was displayed on the wall, Gregor tried it on. It was a little tight but not a bad fit. Placing it in the bag, Gregor thought the new style body armor may come in handy. On the way out, he grabbed an M-14 with scope and a few clips.

Rushing to the dock, Gregor studied the layout of the buildings, docks and piers. He had to plan for the worst case scenario. If he were attacking by river and planned on killing everyone, he would split his forces. Half of his men would hit the pier in the middle of the village while one fourth would hit the shoreline to the north and the rest would hit the shoreline to the south. This would give him overwhelming forces in the center of the village while the others flanked the village in a pincers and kill everyone trying to escape the onslaught.

"Dear God in Heaven" he thought. If the bastard leading the assault had military training this is exactly what he would do if he planned a massacre. He had to divert the pincers back into the center of the village to give the escaping people more time to get out of harm's way in case this is their plan.

Four of the men came back to inform him the evacuation is underway. Studying the faces of the men, Gregor saw fear, but something else was in their eyes, anger. Fear for their loved ones and anger at the men who were coming to put those loved ones in jeopardy. Gregor knew these men had not been in any army, but Ronan would have worked with them since they are his right hands in running and protecting the village.

With these four men, Gregor would mount a defense to save the lives of the people who put their faith in the Chief, and now in Gregor. As they completed the defenses, the first rays of a new day brightened the landscape around them and they heard the motors of six boats coming their way.

Standing on the bow of the lead boat, U Zeya gave his best "On to Victory and Riches" speech. As he sat down and motioned the operator to lead out, he smiled an evil smile thinking of the onslaught he was about to bring upon everything McLeod holds dear.

Watching the incoming boats, Gregor knew they were in serious trouble. The enemy forces deployed the way Gregor thought they might except they are hitting the flanks with more than he thought they would. Twice as many men were coming ashore to the north and south of the pier than they were prepared to defend against. But this also meant the center force was smaller. Another defensive option came to Gregor as the invaders feet touched dry ground.

The pirates hit the ground running, yelling and firing at the buildings. By the time all sixty were aground and the leading men got to the edge of the village their momentum had slowed to a stop. They were puzzled to a man. There was no resistance, no people running in fear, nothing. It was as if the villagers had vanished.

Stepping in front of the men who charged up the pier in the middle of the village, U Zeya eyed the village with a critical eye. Motioning his men forward he took the lead. When he was 100 meters from McLeod's main building he saw movement on the large porch of the building. Too late he realized what he was looking at.

Gregor knew he was taking a big chance with his new plan. With no one to fight, the pirates had lost their momentum, just like he hoped they would. The loss of momentum may bring the leader out to urge his men forward. It worked. What he planned next would bring the entire invading force against him.

As Gregor pulled the trigger of the M14 he had braced on one of the columns of the porch, he couldn't help but notice the look of surprise on the man's face. When the man went down, Gregor went from man to man until the clip was empty. With the rifle empty, Gregor went into the building, picked up an AK47 and opened up through a window.

Firing of the AK was the signal to Gregor's men to fire the Claymores they had placed at each end of the village. While the blasts echo faded, Gregor's helpers followed his orders and melted into the brush and headed to defend their families if Gregor's plan went awry.

The heavy .30 cal round went through U Zeya's heart without slowing down and into the man behind him. Dead before he hit the ground, U Zeya didn't know who had killed him. The last thought that went through his head was McLeod had returned early and bested him again.

The pirates that survived the Claymores couldn't find anyone to retaliate against so they proceeded to join the center force since they were engaged with someone. The center force took a few minutes to shake off the shock of losing their leader and was doing so as the survivors of the flanking forces joined them. With their numbers reduced by about one third they were tempted to abandon the assault. However, one of U Zeya's lieutenants stepped up and took charge. Prodding the men forward he had thoughts of grandeur at taking over all U Zeya controlled. Those thoughts were going through his head as more Claymores decimated his forces further.

Dropping the detonators, Gregor picked up the AK's, ammo and grenades and started firing through the windows as he passed them. He hoped it would make the attackers think there were more defenders in the building than there were.

The new pirate leader shook his head trying to clear it after the multiple explosions that went off around him. Looking around, anger started to build in him as he surveyed the results of the Claymores.

His force had been cut in half. Dead and wounded littered the street while the survivors checked on their comrades.

Gathering his wits, then his men, he charged the building where the firing came from. Twenty or so assault rifles tore into the building ripping the walls to shreds. Motioning the remaining two men who had C4 charges forward, he ordered them to set the fuses and throw them in the windows in the front of the house while riflemen went to the back to kill anyone trying to escape.

Gregor knew he had hurt the attackers, but not enough. He saw the men circle the building and the force gathering out front. Moving to the center of the building he entered the dining room, opened a bottle of vodka and took a long draw. Placing fresh clips in the AK's, clipping several grenades on his clothes and belt, Gregor got ready to repeat his favorite scene from his favorite American movie. Butch Cassidy and the Sundance Kid were surrounded by the Bolivian Army they charged a superior force side by side. Too bad Glen is not beside him in his last fight. But then, he is glad his friend is not with him now. Glen will take of Lae for him. Picking up the rifles, Gregor turned and looked straight in the eyes of Kimo.

With his men in place, the new pirate leader ordered the charges thrown. The explosions tore off the front third of the building. Before the debris settled he attacked the building front and rear. Running throughout the building, firing into every corner, they covered the area in short order. They found nothing, no survivors and no bodies.

Anger turned into concern as the new leader heard something bounce off the wall. Staring at the grenade in disbelief he turned to warn his men. But they had their own trouble. Grenades were raining in every broken window. Diving for cover, a few of the men survived the multiple blasts. While still stunned, the men found themselves disarmed and pushed outside.

The six men who survived the attack on the building were joined with their wounded brothers. Of sixty men who started the attack just a short time ago, twenty-one still lived and most of them were wounded, some seriously. The men of the village, armed with M16's, herded them to the pier where they were loaded onto two of their boats. The pirate dead was loaded onto two more boats and were tied behind them. Several of the armed villagers boarded and started the boats upriver. The other two boats were loaded with armed villagers as escorts for the flotilla, and transportation for their brothers after they left the pirates deep in Burma.

A muddy Kimo stood proudly next to a muddier Gregor, watching the boats disappear around the bend. Kimo had remembered the tunnel the Chief had started as an escape route in case something like this might happen. It was dug but not finished, the walls in over half of it was still dirt and with the rains, the bottom mud. It was a miracle Gregor was standing in the dining room where the trap door was placed when Kimo opened it.

Gregor looked down at his rescuer and smiled. Looking around he started sizing up the damage and what it would take to put things back to normal. The hotel, restaurant and main building of the Chief's complex were a total wreck. The outlying bungalows were relatively intact. Ronan would be back in two days, not enough time to completely rebuild, but he could get started making calls for building supplies and men to use them.

After receiving reports from his four lieutenants, Gregor said a prayer of thanks to all that is Holy. All the villagers were unhurt, not as much as a scratch. Turning to one of the men, Gregor said, "You and your men did well, thank you."

The man smiled, shrugged and said as he walked away, "It is what the Chief would want us to do."

Kimo helped him remove the body armor, which was scratched up but took no direct hits. Free of the restrictive weight, Gregor turned to the young man and asked, "Are you hungry? I could eat a water buffalo."

Frowning, Kimo replied, "I do not think anyone would let us do that, but on the river bank is my fishing pole and lunch my mother made me. If it is still there I will be happy to share."

Rubbing the top of the young man's head, Gregor smiled and replied, "Thank you. I would be honored to share a meal with a warrior such as you."

Smiling an even bigger smile, Kimo led the way.

Taking one last look at the village, the biggest concern going through Gregor's mind was how to explain the mess to Lae.

CHAPTER 6

22 Sept, New Mexico

We had several late season fishermen plan trips with us at the last minute. Finally the trips were planned, supplied and ready to go. With this behind me, I didn't have anything to do the rest of the week. Well, other than finish getting ready for our vacation. With that in mind, I headed home to finish a few last minute chores that I had promised Soledad I would get to before we left.

As I made the last curve leading to the house, I saw a man run from our deck into the brush. Flooring the accelerator, I was at the front of the house in seconds. After grabbing a Python out of the glove box I jumped from the car, ran full circle around the house checking for signs of a break-in. Seeing nothing, I eyed the brush where the man had disappeared. Liking the feel of the Colt in my hand, I proceeded after him.

A man running full speed is very easy to track. Dirt kicked behind his tracks told me he was not trying to be subtle nor quiet. Roughly 400 yards from the house I spotted him in front of me. Well, the back of his head any way as he went over a rise and into an arroyo. He was running as if he knew exactly where he was going. This gave me pause. Since building our home, we made it a point to know the surroundings intimately. About 400 yard from where I stood is a knoll that commanded a great view all the way to our home. If the running man had a partner on that knoll with a rifle, and was so inclined, I might not be taking a vacation if I continued pursuit.

Squatting down, I used the dirt as canvas to review the area from me to them, if there is more than one. There are two arroyos, one on each side of the knoll, that run east to west toward the Rio Grande. The knoll has a great view of both so they aren't an option. The side of the knoll that faced our home had heavy brush to where I stood. Heavy brush it is.

Working my way past the arroyo where the man disappeared, I tackled the brush. Moving carefully as possible, I made better time through the mess than I had first thought. Game trails weaved back and forth under the growth thus giving me ease of movement without giving my position away.

As I got to the edge of the brush a mere 25 yards from the knoll, I heard an engine fire up and the sound of a vehicle driving away. Not taking a chance on them leaving a rifleman behind, I continued to crawl. In a matter of minutes I was standing where the men had been waiting. From the sign they had left behind, in their haste to flee, there were two men, two men and a rifle on a bipod if I read the imprints correctly. Looking at the rifle imprint, a chill went up my spine. Directly in the path the rifle had pointed was our home.

Walking home, Navaho eyes watched my progress. Unknown to me, four rifles had been trained on the two men in case they decided to do me harm. Luckily for them, they packed up and high tailed it out of here. That night my Navaho guardians were all smiles as they told each other their version of my pursuit of the two men. After food, several beers and long tales, they decided I was worthy of a Navaho name. I would forever be known to them as Klah.

22 Sept, East Berlin

Wagner had finished his last report of the day. Smiling at the folder as he put it away, he wished he could be there when the object of the file was arrested. He would love to see the expression on the face of his old history professor when he was told he had been found an enemy of the State and would spend the rest of his life in jail.

As his light over his desk went dark, his phone rang. Tempted to ignore it, Wagner picked up his briefcase and turned to go. The phone did not stop, after several rings Wagner couldn't stand it and picked up the hand piece.

Steiner gave Wagner his report crisp and concise. They had been discovered and needed instruction. Wagner's response was to the point as well.

22 Sept, New Mexico

Turning to Gunther as he placed the hand piece in the cradle, he smiled. Gunther knew the smile and knew what their instructions were without Steiner saying a word. Sitting on their hotel bed, Gunther picked up the rifle and cleaned the dirt off it that their hasty retreat had caused. The next time he would lay eyes on the American it would be through the scope with his finger on the trigger.

They may have been the best the Stazi had in the country, but they got sloppy, Steiner did not need to explore the Williams home. Gunther tried to prevent him from approaching the house but Steiner was insistent. He had it in his head that after they killed the family he would rob the house. This was not protocol for agents and Gunther was against it. Steiner kept talking about retiring upon their return to East Berlin and money from the robbery would aid in that goal.

As Gunther cleaned the rifle, he understood his duty. The last round fired from this rifle would take the life of his erroneous partner.

While Gunther cleaned his rifle, I pulled up to Soledad's office at the small airport. Sitting in the truck for a few minutes, I took the time to run through my head what I know verses what was theory. Soledad is very fast to grab a situation and make heads or tails out of it. I hope this was no exception.

Looking up as I came in, she asked, "Hey big boy, what cha doing here? Is it time for lunch already? She said as she eyed the clock on her wall.

"No, not yet, Soledad we need to talk." I said in a stern voice, which was unusual for me.

Her head snapped up when she heard my reply. "Glen, what's wrong?" She asked as she came around her desk and stopped in front of me.

Explaining what happened this morning in a crisp monotone, I relayed everything I knew in a matter of a minute or so.

Soledad paled for a moment then turned a deep red. I have seen this before. The color change is not from fear, but anger, anger at someone, unknown, who seems to want to do harm to her family.

"We can't go home Glen, not until this is settled. I will call my mother about picking up the kids after school and taking them home with her. She will lock down her home better than any military installation when she hears this. She has some very capable men, as you well know, that will keep them safe." After catching her breath, she continued, "Who is the target? You, me, the kids, all of us and why?"

As I started to answer, we heard a scraping noise at the side door that goes into the hanger. Turning as one, we saw one of Soledad's employees standing there. Out of instinct, I pulled the Colt out of my waist band, where I placed it after the chase in the brush, had the hammer back and pointed at the young man's belt buckle. Slightly paling, he stepped fully into the office with his hands slightly raised.

"I did not mean to intrude. When I saw Mr. Williams rush to get into your office, I came to make sure all is well." Kurt said in a soft voice.

Noticing his color returning, even as I held a weapon on him, I took another long look at him. This man has sand, I thought, as Soledad moved over to me and placed her hand on my gun arm.

"Glen, this is Kurt Creager. You have met him and he has been to our home several times for parties. He's one of my best pilots and is a friend." Soledad said in her soothing voice. She knows I can't resist her when she uses it.

Lowering the hammer on the Colt, I placed it back in my waistband, stepped forward offering my hand. "Sorry about the reception." I said as we shook hands.

Locking eyes with me as we release the handshake, Kurt said, "I understand Mr. Williams. I overheard the problem."

"Call me Glen, Mr. Williams is my father." I said with a smile.

Nodding a reply, Kurt turned to Soledad and said, "Perhaps I can be of service?"

Soledad and I locked eyes for a moment, turned and asked as one, "How?"

Kurt smiled and said, "This will take a while, let me explain over lunch."

Always ready to eat, I quickly agreed, Soledad only took a few seconds longer replied, "OK, give me a couple of minutes and I will be all for it." Looking at Kurt then me she said, "Our usual place?" With that she picked up the phone and called her mother. When she finished, Soledad turned to us and said, "Mom would like for us to be there this afternoon to plan our next move. I told her we will be there."

After agreeing, I turned to go saying, "I will get us a table. See you there in a few." Looking straight into my Hearts eyes I said, "And I mean a few."

Smiling, Soledad nodded her surrender. With that I closed the door behind me and headed to my truck. Not totally convinced Kurt could help, I couldn't wait to hear what he had to say.

After I left the office, Kurt turned to Soledad and said, "I did not know your husband had a weapon much less knew how to handle one. He and his partner never take hunters into the mountains, just fishermen and campers."

Smiling at him, Soledad answered, "Oh Kurt, don't let him fool you, my man can shoot. He and Gregor have a firing range that would put most military and police ranges to shame. They each shoot, oh I would say about 1,200 to 1,500 rounds per week. All kinds of weapons in all kinds of situations, they are both very good. "

"Shooting at targets is different than shooting at a man, especially a man that is shooting back." Kurt said with a slight smile.

Soledad turned to him as they walked out the door, "Kurt, some day over a beer, if you can get Glen to talk about it, ask him about

Thailand a few years ago." Seeing his surprise, she continued, "Many have tried to take my man's life, he is here, they are not."

Not saying a word, Kurt followed her out the door. His thoughts were of his superior's omission of Glen's combat experience in his briefs. Lunch should be interesting.

Sitting at our favorite table, looking out at the beautiful Santa Fe Plaza, I couldn't help but wonder how much history this place has seen. For almost 400 years this was a place of commerce, politics and social gatherings. From where I sat, to my left, was the Palace of the Governors, built in the early 1600's. Its front, a long covered walkway, was filled with sitting areas that softly spoke of the history it has seen. Directly in front was the main Plaza with tree covered walkways to its heart. Surrounding the rest of the Plaza are buildings almost as old as the Palace, their architecture as varied as the times they lived through. Pueblo, Territorial and Spanish styles completed the Plaza with character that spoke of, no, screamed history.

Taking another sip of the sweet tea our server had brought, I decided this table was not suitable for the forthcoming conversation, much too open and public. As Soledad and Kurt walked through the door, I stood and motioned them to follow me to a table in a more private area. We walked past the long counter that sparkled with the chrome of the Fifties, past the open dining areas across from the counter into one of the tables in the back. After seating us and bringing more tea, chips and salsa, the server faded back giving us time alone.

Soledad sat next to me on my right with Kurt sitting across. As the server faded back I said, "Let's cut to the chase. Who are you and what are you doing here?"

"Glen, don't beat around the bush, get straight to the point." Soledad said with a mischievous smile.

Glancing her way, I couldn't help but smile and replied, "I will work on being more direct my love." Looking back at Kurt I said, "Well?"

Kurt never broke his composure. He sat there with a neutral expression, taking in the banter between Soledad and me. At my direct question he replied, "You know my name, and it is my real name. I work for your lovely wife as a pilot and mechanic, I am from Austria, thus my accent, I overheard talk among the Navaho about outsiders stalking you and your family."

Slowly I raised my left hand and sat the Colt Python on the table, pointing it directly at Kurt. I could see Soledad frown out of the corner of my eye but I continued. "Try again Whistle Britches, you smell like a spook to me. You have one more chance to convince me I don't want to blow a very big hole through you."

Seeing the confusion on Kurt's face as to my terminology, Soledad said, "Kurt, Whistle Britches is Glen's way of saying you haven't impressed him enough for him to use your name. When he says spook, he means government agent. Sometimes I am able to take the sting out of Glen's words, but since the safety of my family hangs in the balance, you might want to tell us the truth before he makes a mess."

Without as much as a flinch, Kurt looked at Soledad, then me. Smiling he said, "I believe he would. Again, you know my name, however, I am what you call, a spook. I am an agent with the BND, West Germany's version of your CIA. My superiors sent me here when they got information of your involvement with a man named John Kirkpatrick. It seems Mr. Kirkpatrick has a fixation with Nazi gold and has mentioned the gold to you in the past. Word of your upcoming trip to Bavaria has sparked multiple agencies into action. Stazi, Mosad, and the BND have agents in play because of your trip. The men watching your house, I believe, are a Stazi wet team. I also believe I have identified the Mosad team."

Looking at Soledad with a question in my eye, she nodded and said, "I know who the agencies are and what a wet team is. But why would anyone want to hurt any of us over a trip and the rumor of Nazi gold?"

I gave a nod to Kurt, he continued, "East Germany could use the money, West Germany the positive press, Israel a victory over Nazis and the return of property illegally seized, and the men involved, riches and notoriety." pausing for a moment, Kurt continued, "Then there are the fortune hunters who may hear of this and go after the money. They can be the most dangerous."

As Kurt finished the last sentence, I caught movement on my left. Caught up in our conversation I let another get close. I didn't feel too bad though. Most people don't know Sani is around until he wants them to.

As he sat down beside me, he patted the hand that held the Colt and shook his head. Looking him in the eye, I saw amusement, not concern. I placed the weapon back into my waist band, sat back and waited for what I knew was coming. I was right, what ensued was a long winded conversation in Spanish, which I understand very little and was a bit surprised that Kurt spoke. As the three discussed the situation, I took the initiative and ordered fajitas for four, sat back and enjoyed my tea.

The conversation slowed only when the food hit the table. Slowed, but continued until the plates were cleared and coffee was served. Finally, as one, they sat back, sipped their coffee and nodded all around.

Not one to be quiet for this long, I asked, "Well, what are we doing?"

Soledad spoke up as Sani left the table, "We are going to go after them, after we pick the children up from school and take them to Moms."

"I guess you will fill me in as we go?" I asked quietly, thinking to myself, "what's this 'we' crap girl."

Before Soledad or Kurt could say anything, we were joined by the Latimers.

As they walked up to the table, Joseph said, "We hate to interrupt, but we find ourselves in a bit of a bind and was hoping you might help."

"You are the only people we know here. We have no one else to ask." Janet interjected in a worried voice.

Soledad spoke first, "Of course, sit and tell us what we need to do. We will be happy to help."

As Janet start explaining, Kurt and I each grabbed a chair from an adjoining table and gave our seats to the couple. As we sat in the newly acquired chairs, Kurt and I locked eyes for a moment. His expression and eye movement gave me the impression he was trying to tell me something. Before I could act on that impression, Soledad drew me into the conversation.

"Glen, what do you think? Since we are going on a trip this Saturday and the kids are staying at my Mother's, it should be ok if Jennifer joined them for a few days while Janet and Joseph make a quick trip?" Soledad asked, looking me dead in the eye.

Knowing that look means her mind is made up and the question was, in fact, a statement, I said the only thing I could, "Sure, the kids would love it and your Mom won't mind a bit."

Joseph then said, "Great, it is settled then. Where and when do you want us to bring Jennifer to her?"

Soledad replied, "How about Friday night about 6pm. We are going there to drop the kids off and have dinner. You would be more than welcome to join us."

With that, we stood as one, and said our farewells. As the Latimers turned to go, I felt a tug at my shirt and a picture on the wall, directly over my shoulder, shattered, the sound of broken glass mixing with the muted report of a silenced pistol. Everything after that happened very fast.

As I pushed Soledad with my right hand, my left grabbed the Colt in my waist band in a cross draw. Bringing the Colt around to follow my eyes, which has locked on a gunman, I shot the bastard through the heart and then quickly looked for another target. None were found.

Standing next to me was Joseph and Kurt, both with Walters in their hands, surveying the room as I had just done.

Kurt stepped next to me and said, "It is you they want, not Soledad. There is more to come. They never work alone, there are always two."

Looking quickly around, I turned to Soledad and said, "We have to get you and Janet out of here, NOW." Turning to Kurt and Joseph, I continued, "Get the women out of here. I will take care of this. If they are after me, you four should have save passage." Locking eyes with Soledad I said, "Go to the Sheriff, tell him everything, but have our friends here stick to their cover stories."

Turning to Joseph I ask, "Yours is a cover, right? If so, who do you work for?"

Turning to go, Joseph smiled and said, "It is dear boy, MI6."

Watching them walk past the long counter to go out the front door I thought, "Oh great, now the British are joining the West Germans, the East Germans and who knows who else, in on our little situation."

The manager walked up to me and asked, "Other than clean up this mess, what can I do to help?"

Gripping his shoulder in thanks, I asked, "Do you have direct roof access?"

Smiling with a twinkle in his eye, he said, "Oh yes my friend, there is a metal ladder attached to the wall in our store room. The hatch at the top has a lock. I will get you the key."

While he went to get the key, I went to our assailant's body. After a quick search of his pockets I only found a hotel room key, which I pocketed. Looking down at him, it dawned on me, I have seen him before. Well at least the back of his head and the side of his face, I chased him through the brush this morning. I also noticed something else, a total of five bullets were in our unlucky gunman. I knew they fired but didn't know if they hit him. Kurt and Joseph can handle themselves. Good, we may need them.

Taking the offered key, I headed into the store room as I heard distant sirens. I had to hurry, if the second man is out there waiting for me to put in an appearance the police my scare him off.

With the lock removed, I slowly raised the hatch. Taking a quick look around the roof of the building, I didn't see anyone. Staying low, I crawled to the edge where I could get a look at the buildings that could see the front of the restaurant. The top of the Palace of the Governors that I could see looked clear. Nothing looked out of place along the street in front of the Palace. The buildings across the Plaza from the Palace looked clear as well. Trees blocked the view from the buildings directly across the Plaza so they were out of the picture. Taking a fast look on the roof on both sides of the restaurant, I was relieved when they were clear too.

Where the hell is he? I may not be able to see him but I can feel him. He's out there ready to put large holes in me where God didn't intend holes to be. Wishing I had a rifle instead of the Python, I moved into position to study the street. Sitting where I was gave me a great view of the three Police cruisers and a Sheriffs car as they pulled up out front of the restaurant. Smiling, I watched the officers approach the building with weapons drawn and ready for bear. I know these guys, which made it even funnier when one tripped over the curb and fell on his face. Jumping up, after looking around to see if anyone saw his fall, he continued on as if nothing happened.

Still laughing at his fall, I caught movement out of the corner of my eye. Looking in the direction of the movement, what I saw took a second for it to sink in. Sitting to my left, on the corner of the Plaza in front of the Palace, sat one of the big Ford Country Squire station wagons. It was only 60 or so yards away so I didn't need a scope to look it over. Not seeing any more movement I looked away only to glance quickly back at it. Damn, it's backed into the parking place! It then hit me what I had seen. The movement I had seen was the back window rolling up.

This morning I did not see the vehicle as it drove away. This could be it. Sitting there, backed in, a rifleman would have an easy shot and a quick getaway. The windows look to be tinted as they were too dark to see inside the car. Perhaps he will decide to stay put for a while so he won't draw attention by leaving soon after Police arrive.

Hurrying to the hatch, I all but slid down the ladder. After placing the Colt at the small of my back I grabbed a case of something and came out of the store room and walked past the officers as they questioned witnesses. Several of the people saw me and just smiled, they didn't say a word to the Police as I walked out the front door.

Using the case of food to block my face from the Ford, I walked across the street into the Plaza. As soon as I was out of sight of the Ford, I made a sharp left turn and walked into a group of tourists that were headed to the Palace. There was a musician playing a guitar under one of the large trees so I gave him the case of food that I had used as a shield. I couldn't help but laugh when I saw what it was, a case of lard.

When we got to the side walk I departed my escort of tourists and headed for the car, which was still parked. Thirty feet away I reached for the Colt only to hear the big V8 start up. Pulling the weapon I ran toward the car. With only ten feet to go the rear tires spun, got traction and the big wagon sped away leaving a black trail on the road and the smell of burnt rubber in the air. Even as I pointed the pistol at the car I knew I would not fire, too many people around to chance it. DAMN!

Beside me, Sani appeared. Looking down at him, I stashed the Colt in my waist band and waited for him to say something. Which he did, in Spanish, he then turned and walked into the crowd. Checking the location of the police, I decided I better make myself scarce as well. Turning, I too got lost in the tourists who were gathering at that end of the Plaza. As I reached my truck I remembered the hotel keys I had taken from the unlucky assassin. The fifteen minutes I devoted to searching his room revealed nothing. It was clean as a pin. These guys are professionals, no clues whatsoever. Perhaps the Sheriffs forensics team may have better luck.

When the witnesses had been interviewed and the police were comparing notes, one thing stood out. When the lone gunman fired one round, three men returned fire in the blink of an eye hitting the gunman multiple times. Then the three men disappeared. The coroner's report would state the first round killed him, a heavy magnum round through the heart. All the others were .380's from two different weapons. The coroner thought he knew who fired the magnum, which he would never mention to anyone, the man he suspected had helped him numerous times, but who fired the .380's?

Meanwhile, Gunther was turning onto an old narrow road heading north. Hoping this old road was little used, he was determined to put as many kilometers between Santa Fe and himself before nightfall, without being seen.

He should have not let Steiner talk him into changing their plan. Sitting down range and taking out a target was more Gunther's style, not walking up to a target in a public place and shooting him face to face. As the morning drug on, Steiner was convinced he could pull off a hit such as this. Hell, he even knew the location of the American, thanks to their many days of following him.

The more Guenther thought about it, a solution to his problem of eliminating his partner materialized. Let Steiner go in and kill the American. When Steiner walks out of the building, Guenther will kill him and make a fast getaway. Instead of Steiner walking out of the restaurant and getting a bullet from Guenther, Guenther almost took a bullet from the American. It was close, much too close. Ten miles out of town the wagon started swaying and he heard the thump of a flat tire. Cursing his luck, Gunther pulled over and proceeded to try and change the tire. Never one to be mechanical in nature, he couldn't make the jack work. His frustration was peaking when he heard another vehicle approaching from the north.

An old, beat up pickup slowed down and came to a stop beside the wagon. Inside were three Indians with three more riding in the back. After stopping, they sat in the truck, smiling at Gunther.

"Can you help me with this?" Gunther asked in frustration.

Nodding, the Indians piled out of the old truck and changed the tire for Gunther. The smile never left their faces. As they lowered the jack and started putting the tools away, another old pick up drove up.

As he climbed out of his old truck and looked the situation over, Sani smiled.

A beautiful New Mexican sunset found us in Senora Garcia's dining room. The view out the wall of windows that faced the west was stunning. The mountains were lit with hues of gold and red that cast a glow on the trees that is, in a word, breathtaking. Not wanting to turn away from such beauty, I had to force myself to do so.

Turning to face the room, I had to smile at the eclectic group of people sitting around the table discussing our situation. Soledad and her mother, the Latimers of MI6, Kurt of the BND, Rolando Garcia, County Sherriff and Soledad's cousin and the Chief of Police of Santa Fe, Fred Ortiz. Then there was me, which according to many at the table, of the CIA.

Just before I sat down, one of the young ladies that helped around the house came in and whispered something into the Senora's ear. After thanking the girl, the Senora said, "Rolando, Fred, would you join me in my office for a moment?"

They looked at each other, nodded and followed her out of the dining room. I went ahead and sat down, picked up the cup of coffee that was placed in front of me by the same young lady and took a sip. What I wanted was a beer, but we all decided we needed to keep our heads clear if we were going to get anything accomplished tonight.

After a moment of silence, Joseph said, "Your German friend is correct. Your friend Kirkpatrick's insistence on finding Nazi gold has started an incident with international ramifications."

"Why now? John mentioned this to me five years ago." I asked, puzzled.

"Simple, since your exploits in Thailand and Laos a few years ago, you have been under the eye of several intelligence agencies around the world. Your purchase of tickets to Munich, the general area Kirkpatrick claims to have knowledge of gold hidden by the Nazis, set things in motion."

"We met you before we bought the tickets, why were you here?" I asked.

"This was to be a simple observe and report assignment, deep cover of course, approximately three years in length. I talked my superiors into letting my wife, who was MI6 and our daughter tag along." Joseph replied with a sigh. "So much for simple."

Looking at Joseph then Janet, Soledad asked, "I guess the trip you are taking is to Munich? And, you came to us about our family keeping your daughter while you were gone. Doesn't MI6 have something in place for such emergencies?"

"We were planning to beat you to Munich. As to our Jennifer, we never planned on having to take "business" trips. And, we had much rather leave her in your mothers care than MI6." Janet said as she looked over at Joseph.

Soledad turned to Kurt and asked, "So, you have been here a year, what was your mission?"

"Much like our MI6 friends, who I thought were Mosad, observe and report." Kurt said, but after a moment, continued, "And to protect. We knew the Stazi would make an appearance if anything developed into a trip to Bavaria, which it did. They are cruel, mean and resourceful at being underhanded, as today proved. Normally they are only concerned with happenings in West Germany and would not bother with a U.S. situation. I guess your trip to Germany increased their interest. However I do not understand their willingness to kill so quickly. We also know there is a Mosad team out there and we are still unsure as to the KGB becoming involved, not to mention your own CIA."

"You mentioned fortune hunters earlier, will they become dangerous?" Soledad asked Kurt.

"Gold is one of the few words that can bring out the worst in people." Kurt answered with a slightly crooked smile.

While we thought about Kurt's statement, two things happened. The Sun disappeared below the mountains thus ending a marvelous display of God's talent and the Senora led the two peace officers back into the room.

Chief Ortiz spoke up first, "This is the first time I have been on the phone with the State Department, much less the Secretary of State. I knew your family was connected, but wow."

Sherriff Garcia responded, "Yea, it takes some getting used to. Who would have thought we would be asked to quietly close this incident as solved by the Secretary of State."

Turning to us, Chief Ortiz looked Kurt, Joseph and me over thoughtfully. After a moment he said, "There were five shots fired in my town by you three. All went where you intended and no innocent people were hurt. Had there been innocent causalities, a call from the President himself would not have kept you out of my jail. Understood?"

As one we said, "Yes Sir, we understand."

Walking up to me, he paused and said, "Glen, the witnesses said you had a revolver and fired first. Two of the witnesses are old friends of mine that were in the First Calvary and served in South East Asia.

They told me a story about a Glen Williams. Said in '72 he had a reputation for having an uncanny sense of situational awareness, was fast to shoot when needed, hit what he shot at and knew when not to shoot, even when others might have. Today others saw you in the Plaza, said you aimed but did not fire. In their minds you didn't shoot for fear of hurting civilians. I have one question, are you that Glen Williams?"

All I could say was, "Yes Sir."

Looking around the room, he rubbed his chin, looked back at me and said, "In that case, I am glad you are as good as they say you are. However, if at any time, your actions cause harm to an innocent, you will spend time in my jail. Understood?" Turning to Kurt and Joseph he repeated, "Understood!"

"Yes Sir." I said looking him straight in the eye.

"Yes Sir." They said in unison.

Smiling, he said, "My Medical Examiner said the first bullet did the job and the other four went in as the man was going back and down. He also said two bullets from the right that were only an inch apart and two from the left almost matched the spacing." Smiling bigger he continued, "You boys are very good, but maybe MI6 and the BND need to take shooting lessons from a good ol' New Mexican."

Saying his good byes to the Senora, he was still laughing as he walked down the hall. I didn't have the heart to tell him I'm from Texas.

Turning to Soledad, I asked, "By the way, what does "Klah, dispone uno, esta lamia" or something like that mean?"

Smiling at me, Soledad said, "You mean "dispone de uno, esta es la mía"? It means roughly "you got one, this one is mine." I am not familiar with Klah. Why do you ask?"

"As the station wagon disappeared around the corner, Sani walked up to me, said that, smiled and vanished into the crowd." I answered.

The Senora smiled and said, "Klah is the name the Navaho have for you Glen, it means left handed."

As one, everyone in the room turned and looked at the Senora. She just smiled and said, "We have rooms prepared for all, please stay the night. As to the other man, we can all sleep well."

As we headed to our rooms, I thought, damn, this woman knows everything.

CHAPTER 7

23 SEPT, NEW MEXICO

The full moon put a magnificent gleam in her eye as she walked toward me. The white silk gown picked up the moon light in a way that made it glow as if from within. She was an angel sent from heaven, here to give me undying love, love which I will return for an eternity.

Smiling up at me as she stopped just out of reach, I could see love glowing with luster so bright it caused the moon to dim. It penetrated me and wrapped my heart in a glow as pure as the love we share. Smiling into Soledad's eyes, I took a step and bent to wrap her in my arms.

It then hit me, this was a dream. I had this dream the first time I stayed in this room. She will vanish just before I can wrap my arms around her, just like the other times this dream haunted me over the last five years. But what the hell, I reached out and got a pleasant surprise. Her cheek was soft and warm, her smile grew bigger and her eyes glowed with their mischievous gleam.

As I started to express my surprise, Soledad placed a finger on my lips. Smiling she took my hand and led me out onto the balcony that overlook the grounds. The cold mountain air felt good against my skin, helping to control the fire her touch builds in me. Motioning for me to set in one of the chairs that lined the wall, she moved another to face me. Sitting in front of me, she leaned over and removed my shorts. Shaking her head at my tightie whities, which she always teased me about sleeping in them instead of pajamas, she tossed them into the room.

Sitting back in the chair, she arched her back to the point her gown opened slightly, revealing a wonderful bosom. Shifting slightly, her gown slid open further, giving me a moonlit glimpse of the valley between her breasts, down her stomach to her crossed fantastic legs. Her smile drew my attention, her tongue slowly, softly running over her full lips threw fuel on the fire her touch had started. Slowly her hands when up her legs, across her body and stopped at her breasts. Sliding her hands under her gown she started massaging them, a job I sorely wanted. The white gown absorbed the moonlight in a way that made her glow, accenting her natural beauty.

Starting to rise, her bare foot stopped my progress when she placed it in the middle of my chest and pushed me back. Taking the opportunity to place both feet on my chest, she slowly opened her knees giving me a quick view of her inner thighs, her sweet spot still hidden from the moonlight. Reaching her knees, she slowly ran both hands up her thighs, moaning as they reached the smooth, sensual area of her upper thighs.

The moonlight, her scent, her movements and my inability to touch her drove me crazy, well crazier. My breath was deep and quick. Blood burned like liquid fire as my heart forced it to race through my veins. The shine in her eyes caused the almost full moon to dim. Smiling, she stood, took the one step that separated us, opened her gown and sat with her feet touching the deck on each side of me. Sliding forward, she took me in her hand and guided me into her. The antics she used to drive me nuts worked on her as well, as I found out as I slid deep into her. Draping the gown over us, she leaned into me and kissed me deeply. Her tongue teasing mine in a dance that increased tempo as our kiss deepened.

In a matter of a few minutes, her eyes widened, her pulse raced and her face flushed with heat that radiated around us. Throwing her head back she found her release and all but howled at the moon with pleasure. Her heat overwhelmed my reserve and I exploded deep in her and I DID howl at the moon. That is until her lips covered mine in an attempt to quieten me. Riding the wave of pleasure, she relaxed into my arms as our breathing and heart rate slowly returned to normal. Sometime during the night, the cold forced us back into our room and bed.

Rebecca looked out the window of the room she shared with Lupe and her new friend. Turning to her sister she said, "Well, Mom and Dad were wrestling again. I hope she doesn't hurt him much."

Jennifer looked over at her and said, "Your Mom and Dad wrestle and they get hurt? Wow."

Lupe just lay in her bed and tried to keep her laughter from the younger girls.

Across the grounds, sitting in the shadows rolling a smoke, Sani smiled to himself. He was glad his instinct five years ago were right. This man the Granddaughter of the Patron fell in love with is a good addition to the Garcia family. He and Soledad will provide generations of the family for his people to love and protect.

24 SEPT, GOLDEN TRIANGLE

As Sani finished his smoke, on the other side of the world, Ronan stepped out of his truck and shook his head. Looking quickly around, his pulse raced in fear of his friends and the people of the village. The main building of his hotel, restaurant and bar was gone, completely. Other buildings showed signs of a battle. Bullet holes and blast damage were evident along the water front and into the edge of the village.

"Chief, you need to be briefed on what happened. But first, rest assured, everyone is well. There were no casualties among the villagers." Gregor said as he walked up behind Ronan.

"I need a drink." Ronan replied.

Gregor smiled and said, "All that is left is a bottle of vodka in my bungalow. It is cold and I have two glasses."

Nodding to Gregor, Ronan followed him to his quarters without a word. Two hours and most of a bottle of vodka later the Chief knew the story, the whole story. Along with Gregor and Kimo, it seemed every man in the village and a few women paraded in and told their version of what happened.

When the last man left, leaving Gregor and Ronan alone, the Chief said, "It's a miracle, a bloody miracle no one was hurt much less killed. I knew U Zeya was crazy but not stupid. Well, ok, maybe a little stupid, but to attack the Triangle area while I was gone is insane. I would have hunted him down and killed him in his sleep for doing something this stupid. Are you sure you killed him?"

Gregor took a folder off the top of the dresser and sat it in front of Ronan. Opening the folder, McLeod was greeted with several Polaroid pictures of the pirate and his men, on the ground and in the boats as they were sent back to Burma.

After studying the pictures for a few minutes, Ronan said, "Tell me something Gregor. The tactics you used to defend the village and keep everybody safe, were you taught them or did you improvise?"

Gregor thought about the question for a moment before saying, "The Red Army trained me well, however not that well. They do not like independent thinking. I asked myself how I would attack the village and kill everyone then planned the defenses accordingly. We were lucky."

Ronan smiled, looked at the pictures and said, "Or they were unlucky. But I have a feeling it was a bit of both, along with a very brave man commanding the defense. Thank you for saving the villagers. Buildings can be replaced but these people are my life."

"I was here for them, it was my duty." Gregor said stiffly, slightly uncomfortable with the praise and gratitude Ronan was displaying. Then to change the subject Gregor continued, "Tomorrow there will be trucks arriving with building supplies. There are contacts in Bangkok with more. Use anything and everything you need to build a grand hotel."

"There is only one way I could possibly accept." Ronan said in all sincerity.

"Which is?" Gregor asked.

"Partner!" Ronan said as he held out his hand.

Gregor's smile was almost as big as when Lae accepted his hand in marriage. They toasted their new partnership with the last of the vodka. As they downed the last shot, they heard the rumble of a small outboard motor. Looking at each other, they both said out loud, "Lae."

Lae's boat touched the dock as Gregor's hand went out to help her out of the small craft. After planting a huge hug and kiss on him she hugged Ronan and kissed his cheek. The smile on her lovely face turned to a frown of concern when she looked past the two men and saw the village.

She immediately turned back to Gregor and searched his body for injury while talking up a blue streak, "Gregor, are you okay? Chief, are you okay? Was anyone hurt? What happened? Who did this?"

Letting her have her head and get her questions out, Gregor finally said, "I am fine, Ronan is fine, and no one in the village was hurt. Now, how was your trip and how is your family?"

Starting to calm down, Lae answered, "Everyone is great. Things are so much better than when we left." pausing to look at more of the damage to the village. When she started to continue, Gregor interrupted her.

"Lae let us get you settled in and we will tell each other our tales over dinner tonight. We have an early day tomorrow to get back to Bangkok in time to catch our flight to Munich."

Nodding her head in agreement, Gregor escorted her to their bungalow. Along the way she asked every villager she passed if they and their families were okay. Ronan stayed a step behind the couple with an amused look on his face. Amused but proud, their actions and concern for the people of this village confirmed to him the man he chose as partner was the right man.

With dinner over, stories told and the plans for departure in the morning settled, Ronan said good night as he closed the door behind him, leaving the couple alone. Gregor watched the door close behind his friend and new partner with anticipation of what is to come. Turning back to the room, he saw Lae as she stepped onto the deck that looked out at the river.

Moonlight reflected over the water lighting up the area in a magical glow. Ripples in the river cause by current and the slight southern breeze caused the moonlight to dance as if alive. Laughter coming from several dwelling in the village added to the setting as Gregor walked up behind Lae and wrapped his arms around her.

Leaning into him, she sighed and said, "When I saw the village my heart tightened with fear. Fear for the people, for Ronan and for you my love."

Gregor started to speak but she continued, "That fear made me realize my mother was right when she said life is uncertain and we must take chances at achieving happiness and contentment."

Turning in his arms, she leaned up and kissed him deeply. Holding her tight, the passion in his return kiss took Lae's breath away.

As their lips parted, Lae looked deep into Gregor's eyes and said, "Gregor my Love, make love to me as never before. Give me a child tonight."

Softly kissing her on her forehead, Gregor replied, "Yes my Love, the first of many."

Scooping her in his arms, Gregor carried the love of his life to their bed. The moonlight was brighter, the ripples bigger and the jungle came alive with calls of the night, seeming in celebration of the new life tonight promises.

CHAPTER 8

As our plane disappeared in the distance, the kids turned and ran to the car, ready to go to Grandmothers and pig out. Promises of their favorite foods, including desserts, put huge smiles on all four faces.

Smiling at the children as they ran by, Consuelo turned to go and found her way blocked. Her smile turned to a frown then right back to a smile as she recognized the man standing in her way.

Embracing him, which he returned with vigor, Consuelo said, "John, it is so good to see you. I knew you would come."

Stepping back to give her polite space, John said, "Connie I couldn't stay away. Not after what has happened here the last few days. The reports I have read said everyone here is unhurt, but you have one dead scoundrel and another captive."

Smiling at the last part of his statement, she replied, "One dead and one missing is more like it. Reports are he tried running and ended up on the Reservation north west of here. Come to dinner tonight and we will catch up. Your favorite room will be ready for you, as always."

"Lead on Connie my Love." John said as he followed her out of the airport and to her car. As his rental car pulled up beside them, two capable looking men already inside, he asked, "Would you have room for a couple of my associates?"

'Of course, we have plenty of room for anyone you want to bring. See you at 7." she said.

Nodding and waiving, John stepped into his car and said to the driver, "Gentlemen, at 7 pm tonight you will have a most wonderful dinner in one of the most beautiful settings in the world. In the meantime, let's have a chat with one of my old and dear friends. Proceed to the south end of the airport and look for a C-47 that has seen better days."

Aaron Samuel Snider, the 5th stared in silence at the worn out tires on his beloved airplane. Parked in the shade outside the hanger Myrtle, as he called the old C-47 needed new shoes but Sam didn't know where the money would come from. Sitting on a coke case in dismay, his ample rear end overhanging in great proportion, he turned as a car drove up beside him.

Squinting into the sun, trying to see who was getting out, Sam sat there and let the man come up to him. Recognition put a smile on his face as he stood up quickly and grabbed John in a bear hug. The two men with John slid their side arms back in their holsters when they saw a smile on Johns face as well.

"Damn John, you look great!" Sam said as he put John's feet back on the ground.

"You look smashing Sam. I see you have not forgotten to eat." John said with a grin.

Patting his abundant midriff, Sam said, "I have a lot of time and money invested in this and it's coming along fine."

Small talk went on for a few minutes until John turned the discussion to a more serious subject, "Sam, I need information. I need to know what is going on here that is not in stuffy, dry reports. I also want to get my hands on the Stazi agent, if that is possible."

Smiling, Sam replied, "It's possible, come on in and have a seat."

Three hours later, John walked out of the hanger with a determined look on his face, while Sam called his tire man. The newly acquired credit card in his hand didn't have a spending limit.

Seven o'clock, on the dot, everyone was sitting in Consuelo's dining room with a feast before them. John's associates were not disappointed in the view or the meal. The grounds were well lit with lights contrasting the Spanish arches, trees and the full flowing fountain. The wall of windows displayed the view in a way that was breathtaking.

Knowing John loved Fajitas and all that came with them, that is exactly what Consuelo served. The look in John's eye, as he helped himself to the platter of beef strips, confirmed Consuelo made the right choice. The two associates, introduced finally as Bill and Joe, having never had fajitas, got help from the children on how to eat the food before them. Getting the hang of it, they made a dent in the meat, rice, beans, salsa, onions, peppers and tortillas before them. Right after finishing their meal, John's associates excused themselves and retired for the evening, moaning a satisfied moan as they stood.

Eight o'clock found John in a room full of children's laughter. The smile on his face was genuine and came from his heart. Living alone as he does, he had forgotten the simple joy of a child's laugh, the warmth of a child's smile and the love in a child's embrace. Looking past the children, his eyes locked on the woman who owned his heart and had for years. Connie was smiling at something one of the children had said, her smile broadened when she looked up and saw John's expression of joy.

"What do you think Mr. Kirkpatrick? Should the children be allowed to eat their dessert on the patio in the cold night air? It seems the portion they want may melt before it is eaten." Connie said through her laughter.

Through his own laugh, John said, "Why not? Let them have as much as they want where ever they want."

Rebecca turned to him and said with a gleam in her eyes, "Thank you sir, we won't let any go to waste."

Kyle pitched in his two cents, "That's right Sir, with two girls eating it, the cake doesn't stand a chance."

The girls voiced their comeback and challenged Kyle to an eating contest. As the children paraded outside with two of the Senora's helpers in tow, Consuelo caught the expression on John's face. Did she see regret, pride or a bit of both, Consuelo couldn't decide which.

As the door closed behind the children, Consuelo asked, "Care for a stiff drink? I could use one."

"I thought you would never ask my dear. Pick your poison and pour me one to match." John said with a smile, the earlier expression gone from his aged handsome face.

Sitting at a small table by the windows, the longtime friends sipped their brandy in silence as they watched the children devour their dessert. Two drinks later the children went off to bed. Coming through for hugs and kisses, they left Consuelo and John laughing in their wake.

Pouring their third brandy, John said over his shoulder, "Connie my dearest, I will be off tomorrow night for points around the globe. I would ask you to come with me, however I will be going places you do not belong." Handing her the brandy, he sat across from her and continued, "At any rate, I know you would not go at this time due to the happenings here of late."

"And the children are in my care." Consuelo said as she took another sip.

Looking deep into her eyes, John stated, "If only I were in your care, even for one evening."

Standing, a smiling Consuelo took his hand in hers.

25 SEPT, OVER EASTERN EUROPE

With both having stories to tell, Gregor and Lae talked every waking moment. Lae had a wonderful visit with her family and plan to return every two years, unless family activity like births, weddings or funerals, called for visits in between. This was all good news to Gregor, after all he has a new business to occasionally check on. Ronan planned on sending him updates regularly as to the reconstruction and operation of their new hotel.

Needless to say, Gregor's story scared the hell out of Lae. When Gregor got to the part about how he and four men held off sixty, she almost climbed the wall. It is a good thing you can't put a speedometer on a person's mouth, Lae would have wound it completely around and broken it. She was definitely talking faster than a hundred miles an hour.

Several hours out of Bangkok, Gregor had her calmed down from livid to angry and she got quiet, then after a while went to sleep. Looking out the window, his thoughts turned to the fight. As he took the shot of vodka, standing in Ronan's main dining room, he knew in his heart he was dead. Kimo's sudden appearance renewed his spirit and saved his life. One way or another he will pay the young man back. Gregor's thoughts went to Soledad and Glen. He again wished Glen had been with him and, at the same time, was glad he was not. Knowing his friends had a busy two weeks getting everything ready to operate without them, he was glad the weeks were safe as well. A few minutes later he went to sleep, his thoughts of his new BMW.

25 SEPT, OVER THE ATLANTIC

It had been a long night, in more ways than one. Layovers in Dallas and in New York before the trip over the Atlantic made for a very long flight. Couple the flying with apprehension of what we will face in Germany made sleep scarce. Soledad finally succumbed to Fatigue and fell asleep about an hour out of New York.

My Heart has carried my name for five years and I still can't get enough of looking at her. The curve of her cheek, the shape of her lips, the color of her hair, all perfect. I fell in love with her the day we met and my love has grown with every sunrise and tempered with every sunset. With all I feel for her, I couldn't come up with an argument strong enough to talk her out of coming with me on this trip. I tried.

The rumor of Nazi gold had to be settled or they will never leave us alone, she said during one of our discussions. Unfortunately, I think she is right. But the thought of taking my Heart into harm's way scares the hell out of me, not to mention Gregor and Lae. We plan to fill them in on everything at dinner tonight. Blunt and to the point, not leaving out the dangers we know we will face and the dangers that we fear. However, knowing them, Gregor and Lae will stand by our side, no matter the danger. I am so glad they had a peaceful trip to Laos before we hit them with a ton of bricks, even if the bricks are gold.

Just before Soledad fell asleep she said a prayer, smiled at me and said God will give us the strength we need to come through. Kissing her on the cheek, I agreed. God will give us the strength, the brace of Colt Pythons, checked in our luggage with Gregor's 1911's, the fire power.

25 SEPT, NEW MEXICO

Sunrise gave Consuelo's bedroom a slight glow as it peeked around the dark turquoise curtains. Just enough light made it through to highlight the curves Consuelo made as she lay sleeping. John was tempted to open the curtains and admire the mountains in the early morning light. However, the infrequent chance to watch the woman he has loved for years stayed his hand. Her hair, tossed from their lovemaking the night before, was draped across her face, giving glimpses of the beauty beneath. Though covered completely, other than her head and face, the outline of her body spoke of a woman who takes care of herself and is very fit, especially for a woman her age. Their antics in bed the night before gave testimony to how fit she is and spoke to John, painfully, on how out of shape he had become.

The steady rhythm of her breathing told him she was still fast asleep, but he could not resist touching her. He started to touch her cheek with the tips of his fingers but decided his lips needed to taste her cheek. Gently moving her hair aside, he leaned over, as his lips made contact with the love of his life she laughed and scared the hell out of him. Jumping back, his feet got tangled in the ruffled bedding and he fell flat on his ass.

"John, are you okay?" Consuelo asked through her laughter.

"A bruised ego and a sore derriere my dear, nothing more." He said with a laugh of his own as he got untangled. Climbing into bed beside her, he continued, "Connie, you take such joy in making me jump, fall, and dodge, thus landing in inexplicable positions."

"You are just an easy mark and your reactions always make me laugh." She said with a gleam in her eye.

"I live for your pleasure my lady." He replied as he kissed her shoulder.

Out of the blue, Consuelo changed subjects on him, "John, you aren't staying are you? In fact you are probably planning on leaving today as you stated last night. Am I right?"

"Yes my Love." John whispered.

"Your men are staying behind?"

"Yes my love."

"May I go with you?"

His lack of an immediate response caused her to turn over and look him in the eye. After a few long moments searching his soul she asked, "You are going to kill him aren't you?"

Looking deep into her eyes for forgiveness, John said, "Yes my Love."

Rolling over, Consuelo hid the tears running across her face.

Not saying another word, John held her close until a knock at the door told him it was time to go. Dressing without a word, he stepped into the hall where his two associates waited. After John issued last minute instructions on protecting this family, he took another look at the closed door before walking down the hall. His pace was that of a man on a mission, one that he prayed was his last.

As his steps echoed into the distance, Consuelo went to her dresser and picked up her favorite Rosary. Opening the curtains, she knelt by the window and said a very long, heartfelt, prayer.

John's first stop was a three hour drive from Consuelo's hacienda. Following the old pickup down a dirt road deep in the reservation, John was weighing his options. He wanted to meet the Stazi agent for one reason and one reason only. John wanted to know who gave their order to hit Glen. His plan of action came to him as he stopped beside an old log and adobe building.

Sani climbed out of his pickup and motioned for John to follow him. Stepping into the building, it took a few minutes for his eyes to adjust to the dimly lit room. Sitting in the middle of the room, tied to a chair, was a dirty white man with terrified eyes.

John's plan was simple as was his execution. As he walked up to the man, John pulled a Smith and Wesson Model 39, 9mm automatic, pulled the slide thus loading the chamber, pointed it in the man's face and said, "You have five seconds to tell me who gave you your orders."

Gunther's eyes almost bulged out of his head at the sight of the Smith and the sound of Johns voice. He quickly stammered, "Maann, maan, Manfred Wagner."

"He is all yours." John said to Sani as he holstered the Smith and walked out of the room without another word.

John knew the answer before he asked the question, but confirmation was essential.

CHAPTER 9

Anna could see the entire sanctuary from where she sang in the choir. Her height allowed her to see over the others quite easily. During the third song of the evening, she wished her view was not so good. Sitting in the last row was the small man that scares her so. Beside him sat two other men of approximately the same age. They were not paying attention to the music but had a lively conversation among themselves. Distracted, she missed a short duet that her friend, Sister Karen, turned into a successful solo. Embarrassed at the lapse, Anna put everything into the remainder of the song.

Later, as the service ended and the Church emptied, Anna tried desperately to keep the three men in sight. It was not hard to do, the men stayed in the foyer studying the statuettes. Their concentration so great, they paid no attention to the people passing them. Anna decided to control her fear and ask the men directly what they were doing there. As she stepped out of the sanctuary, the men turned toward her. What she saw froze her in place. They were laughing, huge smiles lighting up their aged faces. Then Anna saw something else, something that melted her heart, tears. The men were crying.

Stepping out, Anna greeted them, "Good evening gentlemen, may I help you?"

The smallest man of the group, the man who scared her, stepped forward and said, "Perhaps you could give us a tour? We understand there are many such statuettes in the Church."

Hesitating for only a moment, Anna agreed. "Certainly Gentlemen, if you will follow me, I will be more than happy to do so."

Two hours later, with broad smiles and many thanks to Sister Anna, the men left the Church. Watching them disappear into the darkness, Anna wondered why the little old man had scared her. They were all so nice and very respectful, to her and to the Church. With joy of helping them in her heart, she sang as she headed to her quarters.

The men were quiet as they walked down the street to a small guest house where they had rooms, each lost in their thoughts of the past. Willie kept glancing at his two friends, trying to read their thoughts, concentrating his efforts on Hans. Frederic was always the calm one while Hans was more volatile. As they got to the guest house, Hans turned and walked straight into the small bar. Frederic and Willie followed with raised eyebrows, Hans never drank before.

Turning to his friends, Hans said, "Tonight I am glad we made the statuettes. They are in the correct place for people to see and enjoy them. I thought they would have been looted by the Americans when they came through here, but they were not the criminals the Nazis painted them to be."

Willie spoke up and said, "In fact, they did not damage the village in any way, no bombing or ground fighting took place in the area."

Frederic smiled and said, "I remember when an American jeep came up the road to the Schloss with three officers carrying a white flag. Old Doctor Weiss met them on the lawn with a rifle in his hands. The American Major walked up to him with his arms raised and asked if the Doctor needed any medical supplies, which he was offering to bring to the Schloss."

"Yes, I remember, the American was smiling the entire conversation. He did not seem worried at all, which I thought was peculiar." Willie said with a smile, and then continuing said, "That is until Dr. Weiss turned around and I could see the rifle, the old Mauser did not have its bolt. The only way the rifle was a danger to the American was if Weiss tried to club him with it."

That brought laughter all around and brought the attention of the bar maid, who asked for their order.

Hans turned to her and said, "Three Schnapps followed by three more please." Nodding she turned to fill their order.

Willie then said, "I often wondered how they knew the old castle was used as a hospital."

As the bar maid place the first of their order in front of them, Hans laughed and said, "Do you not remember the sheets that were painted with big red crosses and placed on the roof?"

That brought laughter from Frederic as well. The old friends spent the evening reminiscing and drinking schnapps until they were helped to their rooms by other guests, led by the bar maid. After making sure they were tucked in, she went to the house phone and called a number that was given to her by an old friend of her family.

When given the number she was told to call it any time anyone showed interest in both the Church and the Schloss. Knowing of others in the village that had the same instructions over the years, she was glad to be the one who got to use the number first. The report of what she heard only took a few minutes and the instructions she received took less. Locking up for the night, she started planning on how she was going to spend the one hundred American dollars she was just promised.

As she placed the phone back in its cradle, the stately old woman was flooded with long forgotten memories. Looking out her window, she noticed the weather mirrored her mood, dark and damp. She had hoped the call she just received would not come in her lifetime, but it had. Picking up the phone, Frau Elsie von Beitel made a call of her own as lighting flashes of an upcoming storm lit the Schloss, which she could see out of the southern windows of her estate. The effect was quite lovely she thought, as someone answered her call.

CHAPTER 10

The hotel Gregor booked for us was not much to look at on the outside, a big white building on a corner near the old rail yards, but inside it was beautiful. The staff was friendly and very helpful, the décor modern with a colorful flair. The rooms were spacious and, in Soledad's words, quite lovely with their bright walls and rich wood trim and doors.

Tired from the flight, we planned to grab a shower and catch a nap before meeting Gregor and Lae for dinner. Soledad was quick to get in the shower while I unpacked. Listening to her singing as I put the last of our clothes in the chest, an ornery thought ran through my head. In five years of marriage, I have never been able to shower with her. She just won't allow it. For some dumb reason I thought today was the day.

Quietly slipping out of my clothes, I eased the bathroom door open and quickly stepped into the shower. Well, today was not the day.

"Get out." Soledad said with a frown.

"But." was as far as I got.

"Get out." She said again, pointing.

Her back was now to me so I couldn't see her face, but I could hear the tone in her voice. Sheepishly I stepped out, grabbed a towel and vacated the room with my tail between my legs. One of these days I said to myself, one of these days my plan will work. Well, maybe.

As soon as she finished I grabbed a fast shower, shaved and came out ready to try a little romance on my Heart. She had pulled the covers back and slid under the sheet. Her deep breathing told me the romance was out of the equation, at least for now. Sliding between the sheets I spooned her and settled in, my mind still running full speed about other ways to pass the time. However, my fatigue must have been as great as hers, the next thing I knew something was making a dreadful racket. By the time I had found the radio/alarm clock we were both wide awake, but without the time for pursuits other than dressing for dinner. Damn.

I was dressed in ten minutes, slacks, button down shirt and sports jacket, all in shades of gray. Soledad took a bit longer, but man was she worth the wait, as always. Make up, or what she calls War paint, was perfect, hair exquisitely draping loosely across her shoulders, fingers and toes glistening, and her dress, WOW. She wore a shimmering ensemble that highlighted her best features, that is to say, all of her. She had taken a simple, satin black dress, knee length, form fitting with just a touch of cleavage showing, added accessories in the form of a simple silver necklace with matching bracelets and earrings. Open toed high heels in black and matching purse finished the masterpiece before me. Saying a silent prayer of thanks for having her in my life, I smiled at her, opened the door and followed her out of our room.

The restaurant was not a disappointment. The décor was modern, linen table clothes covered every flat surface and the staff very professional, all smiles. Finding Gregor and Lae was simple to say the least. Lae's long black hair stood out in a room full of blondes and brunettes. With Gregor's habits like mine in many ways I knew we would not be able to sneak up on them, he would be facing the door. He was.

Gregor and I shook hands while the ladies hugged and started telling each other how great they looked, at a hundred miles an hour. I swear those two talk faster than I think. After hugs all around we sat down to drinks freshly brought to our table. In front of Gregor and I sat rock glasses that sweated from the cold liquid fire they contained. The ladies had a drink they both liked, beer. It looked light for a German beer but I doubt they would like the heavier brews.

Picking up his glass, Gregor proposed a toast, "To friends, family and a new BMW!"

We all laughed, clicked our glasses and said as one, "Here, Here!"

Gregor sat his glass down and said, "I took the liberty of ordering for us. I hope you do not mind me doing so." When no one objected, he continued, "Caesar salad, braised pork served with potato dumplings and for dessert a six layer cake filled with chocolate buttercream."

"Sounds wonderful, especially the cake." Soledad said as she looked over her glass at Lae, who nodded in agreement.

The meal was superb and the company better. Lae told us about her visit with her family and how she left Gregor asleep when she went into Laos. The story had me laughing so hard others in the restaurant took notice and a few of the older diners gave me frowns that any mother would be proud of. But I could not help it and Gregor added his laughter to mine when Soledad told them why I thought it was so funny, she had drugged me in Thailand to make me rest an extra day after I was banged up. After the waiter cleared the dessert dishes and brought us coffee, the discussion turned to more serious matters.

"You and four men fought off sixty and lived to tell the story. Damn, I knew I should have gone with you." I exclaimed as Gregor finished his story of the pirate invasion. But, I would not have been home to help with the situation there. We then told our friends about what happened and what we think may happen.

Gregor and Lae sat there quietly as we went over the last two weeks, not leaving anything out. Soledad finished our narrative and sat back in her chair, waiting for the questions we thought would come.

Gregor said to Lae and Soledad, "Ladies go home while Glen and I resolve the situation."

Both women jumped on him at the same time with the same comeback. When the tempest died down and the two ladies had made their point, Lae looked at Gregor and smiled, with that he got the waiter's attention and held up four fingers. The waiter nodded and brought us four chilled shots of vodka.

Picking up his glass, Gregor said, "A toast, to two remarkable women and true friends, may we have grand adventure and live to tell the tale."

Raising our glasses and shouting, here, here, we tossed down our drinks and slammed the glasses on the table. I couldn't help but notice the older crowd in the restaurant and their stares of displeasure at the loud Americans. Several of the younger people raised their glasses in salute to Gregor's toast.

Gregor and I both noticed a table in the corner with three men sitting quietly watching everything and everyone. Every time we tried to make eye contact with any of them, they immediately turned away. After a survey of the rest of the diners, we knew they were alone. Catching my eye, Gregor stood and I followed suit.

Soledad spoke up as she glanced at Lae, "Don't you two get us thrown out of this hotel, we like it here."

Smiling at her, we turned and walked to the three men's table. They were in a corner table, one man in the corner and one on each side. The side of the table a fourth man would have sat, with his back to the room, is where Gregor and I stopped. Their placement gave them a great view of the dining room, however it turned into a less than advantageous placement when Gregor and I stepped up to the table. We had them boxed in with limited space to move.

Stopping in front of them, we placed both hands on the top of the table. I said, "Gentlemen, you seem to have a keen interest in our little group. We would like to discuss the interest, however before we start, please place your hands on the tabletop as well."

The man in the center smiled and nodded to his two men, he seemed to appreciate our maneuver. After all three had their hands where we asked, I continued, "I am John Wesley Hardin and this is Sam Bass, perhaps you have heard of us."

Lae and Soledad's laughter could be heard throughout the room. Perhaps identifying ourselves as two old West outlaws was a bit out of line, but what the hell.

The boss man, which I figured was the man in the center, smiled bigger and said, "We know who you are Mr. Williams. You have been under our surveillance since 1972, due mainly to your association with a mutual friend who currently resides in Georgia. It was amusing though, we only know those names in history books. Perhaps you can tell us more about the men, at a later date of course.

I liked the man immediately, which could be dangerous, especially before I find out who he is. So I replied, "You have us at a disadvantage sir. Who do we have the pleasure this evening?"

Reaching into his coat breast pocket, he tossed me a leather bound wallet. After reading the credentials inside, I passed it to Gregor.

Gregor handed it back and asked, "What business could the Mosad have with us?"

"We are only observing, I assure you," he said as he placed the wallet inside his coat, "However, should you come across gold that was taken from our brethren by Nazi criminals, we shall become actively involved in the recovery and dispersal."

"You do realize there are several factions interested in our trip, some watching, like you gentlemen, and some taking a more preemptive role." I stated as I studied the faces of the three men. "We will remember your faces and your claim of observation only. I would hate to make a mistake and harm a friend, should things turn ugly."

His smile never leaving his face, the man replied, "We will not get in your way, nor should expect help from us."

"Fair enough, good night gentlemen." I said as we turned to go.

On the way to our table we kept our eyes on our wives, knowing they would be watching everyone in the room for aggressive moves. Sitting back down, we noticed two more shots of vodka awaiting us. Smiling, we nodded our thanks and slid them to the middle of the table, thus saving them until this was settled. Soledad and Lae returned our smiles and nods, understanding our passing on the drinks. As one we stood and left the room, some diners smiling at our departure, others lifting their glasses in salute.

As the elevator door closed, Gregor said, "I feel, how you say? Naked?"

That's how you say it my friend, but stop by our room and pick up some old friends." I replied with a smile.

"Ah, nothing like old friends to make one feel clothed." Gregor said with a smile.

The three of us laughed loud and long at the turn of phrase our friend used, leaving him looking at us trying to determine what he said that was so funny.

As I stuck the key to our room into the lock, the hotel manager stepped off the elevator just down the hall, pushing one of the room service carts. Stepping aside, we gave him room to pass, instead he stopped beside us.

"Good evening, I have a delivery for you." He said with a pleasant, practiced voice.

We glanced at each other and before I spoke up, Gregor asked, "What kind of delivery is so important that you, the manager, had to deliver?"

"One from an old and dear friend." He said as he parked the cart beside us. Standing up straight, he dipped his head in a salute and continued, "If you need anything further in your quest, feel free to ask. Good Evening." With that he walked to the elevator without looking back.

Looking at Gregor, I asked, "How did you decide on this hotel?"

Watching the managers back as he walked away, Gregor answered as he shook his head and smiled, "Mr. Kirkpatrick recommended it when I told him we were going to Munich. You know he checks up on all of us from time to time and I did not think anything of it when he told me about this hotel."

Lae patted him on the shoulder and said, "None of us would Gregor. Let's see what he sent."

"Well, hotel has good food and great shower!" Gregor said with a smirk.

My expression and Soledad's smirk led our friends to the wrong conclusion about the shower. Then Soledad whispered something in Lae's ear that made her laugh out loud while Soledad continued to smirk at me. Gregor caught it all, looked at me and gave me thumbs up. I let him think that we had fun in the shower too, I'm not about to tell him otherwise.

Inside our room, we unloaded the cart. Six boxes of files, photos, notes and a journal, John Kirkpatrick's journal, were spread out before us. Soledad picked up the phone and ordered two pots of coffee. It was going to be a long night.

26 SEPT, NEW MEXICO

The two associates John had left behind were having an early breakfast in the kitchen. Quiet, capable and unresponsive to questions or attempts at dialog, they ate quietly, savoring the food before them. The quiet was shattered when the children came in for their breakfast.

Lupe caught the expressions on the men's faces and tried to keep the younger children in line. She was partly successful. Jennifer sat by her and ate in silence. Rebecca and Kyle sat on each side of the two men. The twins would take a bite and stare, first at one and then at the other.

Kyle finally spoke up, looking at the man next to him, "Are you any good? Are you strong? Are you fast? Can you shoot straight?"

Before the man could say a word, Rebecca chimed in, "I think this one by me is better than the man by you. He looks smarter and smart makes up for a lot of things."

Both men held their tongues and let the twins continue their bantering back and forth, an amused look on both faces. Finishing their meals, they thanked the cook and started to leave the room. A statement from Kyle stopped them.

"Our Dad is better than you guys." Kyle stated as a matter of fact.

Smiling they turned to go when Rebecca said, "Our Mom is better than you."

Taking the bait, one of them asked, "Why do you think that young lady?"

Smiling, Rebecca answered as Kyle nodded in agreement, "Because she is better than our Dad."

The two men looked at the twins then each other and laughed. One of them spoke up, "I don't doubt that little lady. I don't doubt it at all."

Consuelo and Sani entered the room and motioned the men to join them. As they approached, Consuelo said, "What are your names, I don't know what to call you."

Shaking her hand, one replied, "My name is Richard, my friend is Rick."

Smiling, Consuelo said, "I'm sure you are dear, I'm sure you are. I'm not going to ask you what happened to Bill and Bob. Do either of you speak Spanish?"

Rick smiled and answered, "Yes ma'am, we both do, as well as three other languages, besides English."

Upon hearing this, Sani spoke up, "Are you planning on staying until the danger is past, to aid in the protection of this family?"

Rick said, "Those are our instructions. We will be here until Mr. Kirkpatrick tells us otherwise."

"In that case, I want to show you our defenses. I do not want you to wander into the wrong place in the night and get hurt." Sani said with a stern look on his aged face.

Richard smiled and said, "We will be happy to see what you have set up, however I doubt there could be anything out there that could harm us."

Sani just turned and walked away, expecting the two to follow him, which they did. Ten minutes later, the three men were standing on a rise about two hundred yards from the main house. From there they could see all the grounds and surrounding area. It was quite a view.

"We took a route that would give you the most visibility to my men. I want them to see that you are friendly so they won't shoot you in case you are out and about." Sani explained.

"What men?" Rick asked.

Smiling, Sani spoke into a small walkie talkie. In the matter of seconds, men with rifles started appearing in key positions around the main house, in the barns, the field behind the house and along the mountain ridges on both sides of the Hacienda, twenty five in all. Standing on the veranda was another fifteen or so men, heavily armed.

Richard whistled and said, "Damn, I would hate to try and penetrate that perimeter."

Rick said, "That makes two of us." Turning to Sani, he continued, "Can they shoot and hit what they shoot at?"

"They are Navaho. They live off their rifles from time to time. One hundred of my best riflemen will be ready to rotate every four hours to keep their minds sharp and their bodies ready. We have protected this family for centuries and will continue to do so. The men on the veranda are as good as any of my best men. They have the family's blood flowing in their veins. The man in the front is Carlos. He is a retired Green Beret, even though he does not speak of it and refuses to speak English since his return. " Sani said as a matter of fact.

Richard and Rick gave each other a glance, turned to Sani and said as one, "Prove it."

Sani gave a few instructions in his native tongue and sat back and waited. In a matter of minutes four men came out of the barn with eight gourds about the size of a dinner plate. The men walked north of the main house until they came to a draw at the base of a mountain. After hanging the gourds on four pine trees they stepped out of the way and waited.

Turning to Richard and Rick, Sani said, "Pick the man you want to test."

Richard pointed to one of the men across the grounds from the targets and said, "The man on the ridge to our left, that has to be a 500 yard shot. Let's see what he can do."

Sani radioed the request and waited. He was not worried about his cousin's ability. Since he was one of the men higher and further from the house, he was one of the better shots. He was using a 7mm magnum rifle with a variable scope, a great long distance weapon.

While they were watching the shooter, he knelt beside a tree and steadied the rifle against it. Seconds later he jerked as he fired the high velocity round. Just as they laid eyes on the gourds, one exploded in a cloud of spray as they were full of water.

Rick and Richard looked at Sani and said, "What would happen if we said everyone but the last shooter takes a shot at the same time at the remaining gourds?"

Sani spoke in the walkie talkie again and smiled. Without warning the area erupted in gunfire that lasted no more than a second. The gourds disappeared entirely and so did the shooters.

Richard and Rick looked at each other again, smiled, shook their heads and headed back to the main house.

Consuelo watched from the courtyard. Her hands in the light jacket she wore were clenched in anger, anger at the men who brought the need for such violence to her door and to her family. Her prayers tonight will, again, be for the young people going into harm's way as well as John to be successful and his safe return to her arms.

A little over a thousand feet above the ridges manned by the Navaho, two men with spotter scopes took in the entire demonstration. Packing up their gear they started the long hike to their vehicle, a 4x4 rented in Denver. Four hours later they were on Highway 285 heading back to their hotel in Alamosa. During the trip, the passenger wrote a report they would file with their superiors. Both men were professionals and did not care what their orders would be after the report was read.

CHAPTER 11

Manfred Wagner shook visibly as he read the report detailing the death of one of his men and the disappearance of another. His anger was flowing freely, which did not bode well for his secretary or any of his staff. Had the man who wrote the report been standing in front of him, Wagner would have shot him. The man, who wrote the report, happened to be a low level attorney in the US State Department and on Wagner's payroll. Unknown to Wagner, the man did not send out anything not approved by the CIA, in the business, he was known as a double.

Shouting and throwing things, Wagner made a spectacle of himself. The tantrum lasted over an hour. Finally he got quiet and called his secretary. Timidly, she slowly walked into his office and stood by his desk while he gave her instructions. Staring straight ahead, anger barely in check, he gave her only one order, find a Frenchman named Caron and bring him before Wagner. He then threw her out of his office with curses and threats.

Wagner sat there staring into space, thinking of how the bastard Caron was the only man he knew that could complete any mission given and show no mercy or remorse. He didn't know he sent the poor girl on a Snipe hunt. Caron was in a shallow grave in Northern Laos and had been for five years.

26 Sept, Munich

A stray ray of sunlight found its way past the curtains of our room and right into my eyes. Squinting at the light, I sat up and looked around, what I saw made me smile. From the overstuffed chair where I sat, I could see Gregor stretched out on the floor using a cushion from another chair as a pillow, Lae curled up next to him using his arm as a pillow and Soledad stretched out on the couch, one arm over her eyes. All over the room, in orderly fashion, lay papers from the files. On the bed lay blueprints and drawings of several buildings that were of an interest to John. All the buildings were in and around a small village approximately thirty kilometers southeast of Munich.

One of the buildings in question was a Church in the middle of the village. From the notes it was five or six hundred years old but was rebuilt only a hundred years or so ago and was still in use. There were several smaller buildings of interest around the Church and on the northeast side of the village.

The building that really caught our attention was a Castle, or Schloss, that is about a mile northeast of the village. Its history goes back a thousand years and is now a school for girls. There were also blueprints of underground bunkers and other modifications made by the German government over the years. Soledad and Lae found a document that tied the Castle to the Nazis, evidence that part of the castle was used as a Wehrmacht hospital during World War II.

John had obviously done a tremendous amount of research over the years and accumulated a large amount of information. Unfortunately he has not found the Nazi gold for which he has been looking.

My thoughts returned to the occupants of the room, well, Soledad. The stray light beam that woke me up had expanded and was growing across her chest and was almost to her face, which was now exposed as she had moved her arm. Thinking I would prevent this from happening, I tiptoed across the room and grabbed the curtain in an attempt to close it. To my surprise and everyone else in the room, my tugging on the curtain caused the rod to jump from the bracket and hit the floor thus flooding the room with light.

Gregor jumped up with a curse in Russian, reaching for a weapon that was not there, thank God. Lae rolled away from Gregor, giving him room to reach for the phantom weapon, then peered over the coffee table looking startled. Soledad sat up, stretched, smiled at everyone, not the least bit surprised.

"Good morning everyone, everyone sleep okay?" Soledad said with a smile.

Lae laughed and stood up and leaned over to help Gregor to his feet, then said, "You were not startled at the noise and light?"

Before Soledad could speak up, not knowing who Lae was talking to, Gregor blurted out, "No, I was not. Nothing startles me my love." He then looked around and said, "Most of the time nothing startles me."

Soledad and Lae cracked up with that confession and then turned their scrutiny toward me. Eyebrows raised and arms crossed, they tried to look like they were mad at me. Gregor tried to mimic them but failed miserably, his expression made me laugh.

Breaking the glare first, Lae turned to Soledad and said, "You didn't answer my question, you were not startled by the noise and light?"

Laughing, Soledad said, "I have lived with the man for the last five years, you get used to sudden and strange happenings."

"Sorry guys!" Is all I could think to say. Then I thought to divert attention from the happenings of the last few minutes with, "Who's hungry? Let's go grab a bite of breakfast." It worked.

Lae spoke up first, glancing at Soledad who nodded, "I, for one, am starved. Gregor, let's grab a shower and meet Glen and Soledad in an hour for brunch."

Gregor said, "An hour? I can shower and be ready in ten minutes." He then saw the look in her eye, started stretching his back and said, "Oh, it might take longer to work out kinks in my back after sleeping on floor."

Soledad laughed and said, "Nice save there Gregor." then looking at Lae she said, "An hour it is."

As our door closed behind them, Soledad ran for the bathroom yelling, "Me first!"

The click of the lock sounded final as I heard the water running in the shower. One of these days I said to myself, one of these days.

Looking around the room, my thoughts returned to the problem at hand. Several people think our trip is to find Nazi gold, not to buy cars. Some of those people do not mean us harm, others do. Circumstances are dictating our actions. To stop the danger to our family, our best option is to find the gold. Therefore we will find the gold. Before me lay the clues we needed to get started on, as the manager said, our quest.

The bathroom door then opened ten minutes later and a towel wrapped Soledad said, "Your shower awaits my Love."

Thirty seconds later I was wet, ninety seconds later I was shaved, two minutes later I was dry and wrapped in a towel, four minutes to shower and shave! Must be a record!

I opened the door, stepped out, stripped off my towel, swung it over my head and said, "Here I am with forty six minutes to spare."

We were not alone. Soledad had dressed and was sitting with a very old woman who had a very surprised look on her face. Soledad was trying to hold back her laughter but was having a hard time doing so.

I had let the towel fly across the room so I had no choice but to dive back into the bathroom, slamming the door behind me. Looking quickly around the room, I could only find one more bath towel. Wrapping it around my waist I opened the door and walked straight to the closet, picked out a shirt and a pair of pants, went to the dresser and retrieved socks and underwear. Looking at the women I smiled, nodded and went quietly back into the bathroom to get dressed. As the door closed, I heard both women break out in laughter.

Well, I have always said I want to be remembered as a guy that made others laugh. I never said how I was to accomplish it. As I combed my hair, after finishing dressing, I couldn't help but wonder two things, who is she and how am I going to be able to look her in the face.

The two women were deep in conversation as I came through the bathroom door. Soledad extended her hand and motioned me over, without interrupting the older lady's dialogue. As I approached the couch she stopped talking, looked up at me and smiled, with a slight blush.

Trying not to laugh, Soledad introduced us, "Frau Hartmann, this is Glen, my husband the streaker."

Holding her hand over her mouth, trying to hide her smile, Frau Hartmann said, "It is so very nice to meet you Glen I have heard and seen so much about you."

Smiling back at her, I replied, "Nice to meet you too Frau Hartmann, however I must say you have me at a disadvantage, I know nothing of you."

"I am just an old woman who is lonely and likes to talk, when I can find someone to talk to." She said as she looked at Soledad with a knowing smile. Soledad nodded and she continued, "I think I can talk to you, you are such a nice couple. After meeting you I can see why John likes you both."

With that, I glanced quickly at Soledad. Frau Hartmann caught the glance, sat back and got a serious look on her face.

"I also had these files brought to you. But, I wanted to meet you and tell you something that is not in those boxes." She said in a low voice.

Soledad leaned forward and asked, "What do you want to tell us?"

"I know the gold exists, I watched the men unload many boxes several nights in a row. One night, one of the boxes fell. When it hit the ground the side broke open and small golden ingots fell out. After the men gathered them up and finished unloading they drove into the night." She said, sitting back as she finished.

"You are sure of what you saw?" I asked.

Smiling she reached into a pocket on her dress, pulled out an object and tossed it to me and said. "I went down, searched the area and found one."

Looking at the heavy gold ingot, I turned it over in my palm. Two things stood out, stamped into the ingot was "100g" and a Swastika.

After tossing it to Soledad, I called Gregor and Lae to come back to our room after they shower, and then called room service to bring brunch for five. The food got to our room as Lae and Gregor returned. Both were still a bit flushed after hurrying to shower and dress, well, that sounds good anyway. After eating everything on the cart, we sat back with some great tasting coffee while Frau Hartmann continued her story.

"December 1944, I got word that my husband of twenty years had been killed in action near Bastogne. When he was killed, his Wehrmacht pay stopped and I had to find a way to feed myself. The Wehrmacht had been using part of the Schloss as a hospital so I became an orderly, then by default, a nurse. Most of the men we treated lived, thank God, but quite a few did not survive. The staff became very close to the men, almost like family, so it hit all of us hard when they died." She paused for a moment to take a sip of coffee and to wipe away a tear.

"One night, in January 1945, a SS Colonel and a company of his goons came to the Schloss and commandeered the old stables and blacksmith's shop. They worked on the shop for a week before the first shipments started arriving. We did not know what they were receiving and they threatened to shoot anyone who came near them. After a few weeks they forced some of the patients to work for them. The SS threatened them with death if they talked about what they were doing." Lae filled her cup while she caught her breath.

"Some of the men were true artists. They molded clay figurines, in their spare time, and painted them beautifully. It became a ritual for those men to take their work and give to the Church in the village. The Father loved the gesture and proudly displays their work to this day. As to the gold, the last shipment arrived in late March, which is when I found the one you now hold." She said, pointing at Lae who was studying the ingot.

"What did they do with the gold?" Soledad asked.

"I do not know. As the war news worsened, there were a lot of people coming and going. I do remember the SS Colonel and his men left in several trucks that were loaded with crates. Perhaps the gold was in those crates." Frau Hartmann replied.

"Was there anything on the sides of the crates?" I chimed in.

"In fact, there were several symbols on them, the SS Runes, the Skull and Crossbones, and one that I had not seen before." She said while deep in thought, and then she said, "It looked like a three bladed boat motor propeller."

Gregor and I looked at each other and smiled. The ladies noticed the look and Soledad asked, "OK, spill it, what do you two know that we don't."

"They probably cast the gold into whatever shape their A-bomb program was using for their fission material, painted it, packed it and drove it right out of here, no one the wiser." I replied.

Gregor spoke up and said, "Hollow spheres, if they were uranium they would be hollow, but gold could be solid spheres. With the SS markings and radioactive signage no one would come near the crates."

Turning to Frau Hartmann, I asked, "Do you have any idea how much gold might have passed through there?"

Looking through a stack of papers in front of her on the coffee table, she found a small brown notebook. Thumbing through the pages it only took a few minutes to find the page she was looking for, smiling she handed it to me saying, "Those are our calculations based on how many creates each truck could carry and how much gold could be in each crate."

Reading the notes in German, I reread them several times to make sure I was correct in my translations. The good thing about numbers, they are the same in both languages, which made it easier. I passed the book to Gregor. While he read the notes, I called the front desk and asked for the current gold price. That is one of the great things about staying in a nice hotel, they will help with anything. It only took a moment to get it for me, jotting the number down I thanked him and placed the phone on the cradle. Sitting down at the small desk in our room, I took paper and a pen and calculated the value of the gold in today's market. Damn.

Sitting back, I handed the paper to Gregor, who read it and passed it to Lae and Soledad. Both women paled slightly and handed the paper to Frau Hartmann. She read it, nodded, smiled handed it back to me.

Looking down at the calculations again, I asked, "You are sure of the amount, as far as you know?"

"Yes." She simply said.

Currently the value of a troy ounce is $147.84 US. There are 14 troy ounces in a pound. That makes a pound of gold worth about $2,000.00 US. A metric ton has about 2200 pounds which makes a metric ton worth about $4.4 million. According to the note there were FIVE metric tons involved with a current value of 22 million American Dollars. Double Damn. No wonder people are paying attention to what we are doing. I can understand trying to take it away from us, if we find it, but why try to stop us?

Soledad said, "Let's order more food, looks like we will be here a while."

"You got that right." I said to her, then turned to Frau Hartmann, "Who knows about the gold and the information you brought to us?"

"The only living person that I know of, besides the five of us, is John Kirkpatrick. However, I do not think he knows about the third symbol on the crates. I did not think it to be important so I never mentioned It." she said.

"Unfortunately there are others, dangerous others, that have some knowledge of the gold. They tried to stop us before we got started." Soledad told the older woman.

"Tried to stop you? How?" she asked.

"Deadly force, they tried to kill Glen, had they succeeded, I could have been next." Soledad told her.

"Will the men who tried to kill you try again?" Frau Hartmann asked as she looked at me.

"No ma'am, they won't, but the people who sent them will probably send more. Are you sure you want to be involved with us? It could be dangerous." I told her.

Smiling at me, then all of us, she said, "I am seventy seven years old, out lived two husbands, in ill health, and have no children. What is there to be afraid of? Dying? Do not make me laugh," She then leaned over in my direction and continued, "besides, I want to know what happened to the gold as much as anyone, it has intrigued me for over thirty two years. John said if anyone can find it, you four can. Can you?" smiling at Soledad and Lae she said, "John said you were smart and tough. I thought he meant you girls were the brains and the boys would be the brawn, but after meeting you, I realize you are all smart and tough. I think he is right, if it can be found, you four will find it."

Gregor picked up his coffee cup, held it up as if giving a toast, and said, "Here is to successful mission! Find Nazi gold, then we drive our new BMW's."

After holding our cups high and a round of hear hear's, we went to work on the rest of the files. It looked to be a long day.

CHAPTER 12

Cognac is truly the nectar of the gods, John thought as he swirled the amber liquid in the sniffer. He then placed the unlit end of his cigar in the liquid gold, letting it soak for a moment before taking a long flavorful draw of the Cuban Otto had given him. The office was full of overstuffed seating and heavy dark oak furniture, typical of expensive offices of the day. The view they were enjoying, sitting in overstuffed chairs in the sitting area of Otto's office, added to the experience. Pullach, while still under reconstruction in some areas, was a beautiful, modern city. Otto's view took in the Isar River, a great view of Pullach and to the north, Munich, which was beautiful in its own right.

Sitting several long minutes, enjoying the quiet, both men waited for the other to speak his mind. They had been friends for over thirty years and know each other as they know themselves. Otto knew he did not have the patience of John so he gave up and was the first to speak.

"So my friend, what brings you to our lovely corner of the world?" Otto said around the Cuban he was enjoying.

Looking at his friend over the rim of the snifter, John smiled and said, "I wanted to personally thank you."

Acting surprised, Otto said, "My dear friend, I am afraid I do not know what you are talking about."

"I doubt that. There is very little that you do not know and nothing going on in your agency that you do not have a hand in. Officially, we don't know anything about Kurt and his actions in the United States. Unofficially, the young agent was a Godsend. Thank you for sending him." John said with all the sincerity he felt deep in his heart.

Leaning forward to look John in the eye Otto replied, "John, we are more than allies, more than friends, we are family. I would do no less to protect your family than my own." Taking another puff of the Cuban, Otto continued, "Does she know?"

"No, she does not. Connie felt it needed to stay our secret." John said with a sigh, and then said, "However she is very intelligent and may grow to suspect something if the quest they are on turns ugly and our involvement grows."

"They are treading into still waters that do indeed run deep. If they find the gold, they may not live to tell about it, or, the tale, as you Americans say. John, is there anything we have missed over the years that they could discover thus leading them to their goal?" Otto said as he finished his cognac.

"Otto, if I knew the answer to that it would not be missed." He replied, smiling at his friend, "However, Soledad, Glen, Lae and Gregor are a very talented group. If anyone can find the missing gold, it is them.

"You may have to add another name to the group. Young Kurt asked permission to follow them to Germany and participate in their mission. It seems he has grown quite fond of them and wants to do what he can to protect their group." Otto said as he clipped the fire end of his Cuban to save it for later. "Of course I will consider his request."

"Indeed? Getting emotionally involved while on assignment is not a good sign, if the young man wants to remain an agent." John replied a little astonished. Like the CIA, the BND prides itself in the professionalism of its agents.

Shaking his head with a smile on his face, Otto said, "I fear we will lose him when this is over. It seems not only is he fond of our little group, but has found a local girl that has also found him. There may be a wedding in his future. If so I plan to attend and see New Mexico for myself."

"In that case, see if you can manage an invitation for me." John said as he sat the empty snifter on Otto's bar.

"Naturally, you will be at the top of the list." Otto replied, and then said, "Are you staying close, just in case they need you?"

"I have business in Berlin, however I can return at a moment's notice, should the need arise. Please keep me abreast of things." John asked as he extended his hand.

Shaking his friends hand, Otto said, "I will, Gods speed my friend."

Otto watched the door close behind John, the click of the lock had a sound of finality that Otto did not like. Picking up his phone, he placed two calls, one to Berlin and one to New Mexico, Kurt will get his wish.

Placing the cognac in its resting place on his bar, Otto opened the lower cabinet and grabbed a bottle of American bourbon. Pouring himself a shot in a decorative glass from the US, Otto toasted the health of his friend and downed the amber fire.

27 Sept, Munich

It had been a long day, then a long night, then a long day. We finally had to stop and rest. Lae and Gregor had gone back to their room, Frau Hartmann to hers. The sound of running water slowly woke me. Checking the alarm clock on the night stand, I was surprised at the time. It was almost 9PM. I had slept for five solid hours and felt great, hungry but great.

Soledad stuck her head out of the bathroom to let me know the shower was mine. I took another fast shower, ready to go to the restaurant and eat everything in sight. But when I stepped out of the bathroom, something got my attention. Soledad sat on the couch with just one of my shirts covering that fantastic body. She was finishing her makeup when I sat on the coffee table facing her. Smiling at me, Soledad stretched, holding her arms over head, arched her back and flexed her toes is such a way that lit my fuse. Picking up her hair brush, she started brushing out her long, dark hair while smiling at me.

After taking a few minutes to admire her loveliness, I got on my knees and kissed her legs, first one fine leg then the other as I worked my way up her soft, smooth thighs. As I kissed my way up her legs, she spread them slightly, thus giving me more access to where I was going. Upon reaching my destination, I ran my tongue over then into her. The second my tongue touched her, she moaned and dropped the brush, right on the top of my head. Since it is hard to see when your eyes are rolled into the back of your head, I quickly forgave her.

Spreading wider, she gave me full access to her womanhood. Her taste was wonderful, her scent intoxicating, and her light breathing got heavy. Suddenly she grabbed the back of my head and pulled me into her. I knew what was fixing to happen and I promised myself I would ride out the reflex she has when she has an orgasm. I tried. However when she exploded and tried to roll to the right, I held fast. I held fast for all of thirty seconds. Did I ever mention how strong she is? Well, she is very strong. Rolling me over with her, she tossed my full 225 pounds around like I was weightless. Releasing her before she really did break my neck, I sat back and enjoyed watching her ride the wave of ecstasy while I stroked her legs and feet.

Reaching for me she pulled my pants down around my knees thus giving her access to me. As she touched me there was a knock at the door. Damn. Pulling my pants up while she sprinted into the bedroom, I went to the door and looked through the peephole. There stood two men in Hotel uniforms with a food service cart, but we hadn't ordered anything.

"Who is it?" I yelled through the closed door.

"Room service, Meine Herr." One of the men answered.

"We didn't order anything." I replied.

"Compliments of the hotel." The other man said acting irritated.

I couldn't help myself so I did a comic routine from one of my favorite comic teams and said, while trying not to laugh, "Dave ain't here man. Go away."

The first man reached in his jacket and shifted a shoulder holster, frowned at the other man and said, "What we have is not for Dave, we do not know Dave."

During our little exchange, Soledad looked out of the bedroom to see what was going on. When we locked eyes I motioned for her to bring me the Colts. She brought them, handed them to me and stepped back to the bedroom door, holding her Walther we had picked up a few years ago.

"Hey man, Dave ain't here." I yelled back.

That did it. All presence was gone as both pulled pistols out of shoulder holsters, pushed the cart aside. One of the men had a key and used it. The chain was on the door but it did not hold them off, one shoulder to the door and it came loose. As the door banged against the wall they rushed in. I don't know what they were expecting but what they got was a view of the business end of three pistols.

We had them dead to rights, pistols pointed center mass on both. They were professionals, thank God and knew when not to buck a stacked deck. I motioned for them to lower their weapons and place them on the coffee table and step back. They were more than happy to oblige. Well, happy may not be the right description of their mood.

After sitting on the couch, side by side, I moved a table chair directly in front of them, about six feet back. Sitting down with a Colt pointed at both, I said, "I told you Dave ain't here. But you insisted on finding out for your selves."

The first man answered, "We do not know a Dave. We came for you."

Nodding, I asked, "To kill?"

With an indignant look, he said, "We cannot get information out of the dead. Our orders were to take the four of you in for questioning."

Soledad and I locked eyes and for a terrible second at the same thought, Lae and Gregor! Just as Soledad got to the phone, two men walked, or I should say, staggered, through our broken door, Gregor and Lae in tow. One of the men was holding a bloody handkerchief to his nose. The other had a pronounced limp and was holding his ribs. I motioned for them to join their cohorts on the couch. It was a bit crowded but at that point I didn't care. I looked over at our friends with a questioning expression.

Gregor said, "These men used pretense of bringing food. Lae is hungry so it made her angry when cart was empty. She pushed cart into one while using the momentum to put force into her kick, which caught other one in face. She has learned much from her lessons, I am very proud of her. I gathered their weapons and we came to make sure you are ok."

Soledad and I looked at each other and broke out in laughter. It was a great stress reliever. Gregor and Lae smiled at our outburst, then joined in when Soledad told them how I made them mad before they came in.

As the laughter died down, I asked the men sitting like sardines in a can one question, "Who do you work for?"

They glanced at each other before the man I pissed off through the door answered, "We are BND. Our orders are to bring you to our headquarters in Pullach for questioning."

"Why the strong arm tactics? You could have asked." Soledad told them with disgust.

"We were told you were dangerous and to be careful in our approach. As team leader it was my decision on how we accomplished our mission." He answered.

Turning to the man with a bloody nose, Lae said, "You should have been team leader, perhaps you would not be in pain had you approached us differently."

Gregor then said, "I say, shall we take a drive down the river and meet with their superiors?"

Looking at Gregor, I asked, "We have been in Europe one day and you sound like you are turning British on us."

"I am trying to perfect my English. As you point out, I have long way to go and after all, they invented the language." Gregor smiled at me.

"Son, you live in New Mexico not London. We will work harder together to get you sounding like a Westerner and then who knows, like a Texan." I said in a mock stern voice.

Lae and Soledad rolled their eyes at us, as usual, while Soledad ordered room service so we could eat before our road trip.

As she made the call, Gregor and I unloaded their weapons, all four were carrying Walthers. After searching them for more clips, we emptied each clip, placed them in the pistols and gave them back to the men. They holstered them while glaring at us, unhappy at being unarmed.

Soledad ordered enough food for everyone so no one was left out. With a full stomach the four agents relaxed a little and started to converse.

Getting Soledad's attention, the team leader said, "Thank you for the meal, it was unexpected."

Soledad smiled at the man and said, "You are welcome, after all, we are all on the same side. Aren't we?"

Looking at first her, then Lae, the man with a broken nose said, "I certainly hope so."

As the laughter died down, Gregor made arrangements for a van to pick us up and take us to Pullach. The trip was quiet, everyone was tired, and after all it was almost midnight. The only talking was the team leader giving our driver directions to his headquarters. Upon our arrival, we walked in the front door like we owned the place. The receptionist sensed the unease in the men and alerted security with the touch of a hidden button. Expecting such a move, none of our group was armed, unknown to our four traveling companions. When armed men appeared from every door, we held our hands over our heads and did as we were told while they frisked us. One of the men got a little too friendly while frisking Soledad and got a broken nose for his trouble. As he rolled back and away from her in pain, one of the others took a step toward her and ended up beside his friend.

At that point the team leader shouted at the men to stand down and stop the harassment. As things settled down an average looking man stepped out of an elevator down the hall and walked up to us with a slight smile on his face. Upon seeing him, everyone but us snapped to attention.

Walking up to Soledad and Lae, he stuck out his hand, shook their hands, then Gregor's and mine while saying, "I am Otto Klaus, I asked my men to invite you to my office for a short visit. It seems my request was misinterpreted. Please accept my apologies of the inappropriate treatment and the ungodly hour of the day." Turning to the armed men in the area, he said, "You may return to other duties." Turning to our traveling companions he said, "We shall discuss your methods later."

With that, we followed him to the elevator and to his office. Upon entering his office, he offered us all a drink, which we all accepted. Gregor and I took the cognac while the ladies drank wine. When all were seated in his plush office, drinks in hand, tired bodies in overstuffed chairs, our host started the conversation ball rolling.

"I want to start with an apology. Kurt, as you well know, is one of my agents. He was sent to keep an eye on you and to inform me of any rising interest in Bavaria. I think we all know why, after all, we are all acquainted with my good friend John Kirkpatrick." Otto said as he leaned back in his chair. "Please accept my apology for the subterfuge in sending Kurt and for the mismanagement tonight."

Soledad looked over at me, I motioned for her to speak up and she said, "Kurt is a good man. It does hurt a little to know he was spying on us. As to tonight, I think your men got the short end of the stick." Looking at us, we all nodded, and then she said, "Apology accepted on both counts."

Otto leaned forward and said, "Thank you. He did not spy, as such. The weekly reports he sent in were empty of personal information. The only information he was to pass had to do with Nazi gold, nothing else."

"Still, he is a spy." Lae spoke up.

"I pray you are not too hard on him, he certainly likes you, all of you. In fact he plans on resigning after your return trip. He has found a woman and wants to make New Mexico his home." Otto said around the cognac snifter.

Soledad looked a little surprised and said, "I didn't know he had a girlfriend. He never spoke of his personal life."

I had to speak up, "Any man who will stand beside me while I'm being shot at is welcome to our house anytime. It would be nice to have an extra man right about now." Everyone nodded in agreement.

Otto smiled and said, "It is wonderful that you all feel that way, Kurt is a good man."

"What do you know of our trip and the reason we are here?" Gregor asked.

"Everything." Otto answered.

That one word drew looks of astonishment from all four of us. We didn't realize how anyone could know everything, until Soledad started laughing.

Looking at the rest of us, she said, "John and my grandmother, that's how he knows."

Cutting to the chase, I asked, "Why did you want us to come to your office? It wasn't to drink and talk about home."

"No, it was not. I want to help you all I can, therefore I will turn over all files and documents we have on the gold in question and wish you good hunting." Otto said with a straight face.

"Damn, I think he is serious." I said.

Thirty minutes later, Gregor and Lae were in a library office in the basement of the building and Soledad and I were in one on the third floor. Before us sat a three foot stack of files that we needed to go through. Leaving us to our research, Otto told us he would be back at 7AM and we would have to be finished and gone by 8AM.

Somewhere around five, we had gone through almost all of it and had several pages of notes. There was one file that had gotten wet or something, all the pages were stuck together and the ink seemed faded. After several attempts at separating the pages, we gave up and added them to the stack. Both of us were wired and wide awake at what we found and were ready to get back to the hotel to compare notes with the information we received from the Frau. Soledad gathered her purse, the notes and looked up into my eyes. She shouldn't have done that.

Looking into my Hearts eyes, my heart melts and my soul soars. She smiled up at me, leaned up and lightly kissed me on the lips. That did it. I picked her up and set her on the folding table we had been using. Wrapping my arms around her I kissed her deeply letting my tongue tease hers. This built a fire in her to match my own. The kisses intensified to a point I had to have her, no matter where we were.

She felt the same, helping me remove her panties under her dress was a definite give away, as well as her unzipping my pants and releasing me from the constraints. Shifting and raising her knees, she guided me into her while our kissing continued. I almost exploded from the contact but was able to restrain the impulse. My mind embraced the lovemaking to its fullest to the point everything else around us faded away until all that existed was my Heart.

Our lovemaking intensified, our thrusts built in power, our kisses deepened, and our embrace entwined us into one. Suddenly our lips parted as Soledad placed her cheek against mine and whispered.

"Oh Glen, I'm going to explode, I can't hold out any longer." she said with the deep husky voice she gets when we are joined.

Before I could respond, she threw her head back, grabbed my rear, pulling me even deeper into her, and had a wonderfully intense orgasm. The heat from her rush set me off as I joined her in not being very quiet. I am surprised no one upstairs heard our love play and came to check on us. Slowly our breathing returned close to normal, and our senses expanded our knowledge of where we were. Giving her another kiss, I stepped back and helped her to her feet. After making a quick restroom break we went back to work gathering the files to take back upstairs. Files in hand, we looked at each other and grinned, the glow of our lovemaking still showed in our flushed cheeks and glassy eyes, but we had to meet with the others.

Taking the stairs instead of the elevator gave us an excuse, we thought, for our appearance, and perhaps no one would notice. We also missed the maintenance worker go into the room we just vacated, nor did we see the puzzled look as she noticed one of the folding tables was out of place. Shaking her head, she couldn't figure out how it got pushed six feet until it was against the wall. Oops, we missed that little detail.

Gathering in the conference room with the rest of the researchers, Soledad and I were the last to put in an appearance. Soledad sat next to Lae while I sat across the table. Sitting where I was, I did not miss the look and smile that passed between the two. Damn, Lae knows by just looking at us. Glancing at Gregor, he was as impassive as normal, I thought. Turning his head toward me, he winked. Damn, he knows too. Well I don't care who knew, I started to get up, get everyone's attention and declare our lovemaking to the world, but Otto spoke up first. That probably saved me from Soledad's wrath at doing such a thing.

"I think your time was wisely spent ladies and gentlemen. You seemed to have obtained multiple clues to aid you in finding the missing gold. I will have my staff make copies of everything you found and have the copies delivered to your hotel by nightfall. Is that acceptable?" Otto asked.

Soledad spoke up first, "Thanks for your assistance and the information you are sharing. I do, however, have one question. What, if any, participation will you or your agency have in aiding us further?"

Gregor and I locked eyes and waited for the answer. We both knew this will probably be the extent of their help. We got a surprise.

Smiling at Soledad and then the rest of us, Otto answered, "Kurt will be joining you this evening. It seems he feels the need to come to your aid here in Germany. His report on the security in New Mexico leads me to believe he may be correct. Mr. Kirkpatrick put in an appearance and left two of his operatives to boost the formidable forces that have been brought to bear to protect the household of Consuelo Garcia. Frankly, I would not want to attempt an assault on the Hacienda with anything less than a combat brigade." Pausing for effect, Otto continued, "We have also been contacted by my counterpart at MI6. He is asking for permission to send two operatives to Bavaria to assist you as well. I have recommended the request be approved. I believe you know the agents in question."

Sitting there dumbfounded at the friends that were coming to our aid, it took us a moment to find our voices. The idea of attacking the problem with seven heads instead of four appealed to us all, however it was humbling to have someone put themselves in harm's way on our behalf.

Surprisingly Gregor spoke up first, "The men, as well as the woman, are talented, capable agents as well as valued friends. They are most welcome. I do have a question. Will we be allowed to arm ourselves, for defense of course?"

Otto shook his head, but smiled, "The public do not carry weapons in Germany. However, you are not German."

Gregor started to push for a clearer answer when Lae put her hand on his arm and said, while looking at Gregor, "Thank you Herr Klaus, we understand. May we bother you for a ride back to our hotel? I believe the van that brought us has been sent back?"

"Yes it has and it is no bother. I will have my car brought around and will take you personally. I have one of your American Chevrolet Suburban's, plenty of room for everyone." Otto said with a smile, "Besides, my wife expects me home at some point, no matter how late, or in this case, how early."

Gregor stood, walked over to Otto's desk, placed a paper sack in front of him and said, "Please give this to your men, they probably have to account for every round."

Otto looked into the sack, smiled as he shook his head and said, "I most certainly will. Perhaps they will live longer if they remember tonight and learn from their mistakes."

Soledad then remembered the file we could not read, handing them to him she said, "Otto, maybe someone here can get these apart without destroying them."

Looking at the stuck mess, he said, "We will see what we can do. In fact we have a new agent that came over from Archives. Perhaps she can help us."

The ride to the hotel was entertaining at best, a little boring at worst. Otto gave a running history of the areas we passed as if he were a tour guide. The information was interesting, the delivery monotone and almost put us to sleep.

Just before I dozed off, Soledad leaned into me and whispered in my ear, "Glen, I just realized something. Where are my panties?"

Suddenly awake I said, "Crap, I thought you picked them up, I forgot all about them."

"I can't believe I just now missed them. Not only that, where are they?" she said in as soft of a whisper as she could manage.

"They must be in that file room where we worked. I don't remember what happened to them after they cleared your sexy as hell foot." I said with an idiot grin on my face, for another thought had passed through my mind.

Seeing my expression, "No, we are not making love now! Gregor and Lae are right in front of us and Otto is giving us a tour, so wipe that look off your face."

"I can't help it if the thought of you panty less gets my attention, in more ways than one. Besides we are in the very back and it's still kind of dark." I responded in my attempt at a husky voice.

Soledad held firm and said, "You always tell me I light you up with just a look. Right now that is not the look you are getting, now hush before we wake the others."

Right in front of us in the middle seat, snuggled into a sleeping Gregor, Lae had a huge smile on her face.

Knowing I was butting up against a brick wall, I sat back and wondered about the lost panties. I tried to doze off, but thoughts of Soledad's panties do not induce sleep in me.

Two days later while studying some old files, a secretary from the fourth floor got a surprise when a pair of black lace panties slid off the light fixture and landed on top of her head. Being an old busybody, she immediately went on a hunt for the owner, wrongly assuming they belonged to a co-worker.

CHAPTER 13

28 SEPT, NEW MEXICO

Consuelo sipped her coffee while studying the men in front of her. After a few moments of silence she sat her cup down and looked across the veranda at the glow of the rising sun. The diversion of the sunrise gave her time to digest the information the two men from the FBI had presented her. Turning back to the men, Consuelo eyed them closely and said.

"Gentlemen, the information you brought to us is disconcerting. After the Stazi team was removed, we, or I should say I, was hoping that was the end of threats to the children. Now you tell me there is information that another Stazi team is sure to be on the way and a KGB team is already in the United States."

The senior agent sat back and responded, "I am sorry to bring this to you, but we felt you need to know everything we know." Looking at his partner, he continued, "We don't know the orders of the KGB team but we are certain the Stazi team will be ordered to kidnap the four children."

Richard leaned over and whispered something to Rick, Rick nodded. Richard looked at the FBI senior agent and asked, "What brought this situation to the Bureau's attention?"

Everyone noticed the quick look between the two agents. Sighing, the agent answered, "Our Director got a call from your Director," he said looking at Richard and Rick, "and here we are. Frankly we both thought this was a bullshit assignment until we saw the armed camp upon our arrival here."

"You should see these boys shoot. When this is over I'm planning to recruit several of them." Richard said with a laugh.

The other FBI agent spoke up and said, "We expect the CIA to stay out of the picture, after all, you can't legally operate inside the States."

Rick grinned at him and said, "Boy, we are on vacation. I can't think of a more beautiful place to kick back and relax."

A hand placed on his arm kept the young FBI agent from responding. The senior agent shook his head and said, "We don't want a turf war when there are lives on the line, do we?"

Shaking his head, the young man sat back and was quiet.

Turning to Consuelo, the FBI agent said, "We will stay in touch and keep you abreast of everything we turn up. I expect you to do the same."

Consuelo nodded and said, "Of course we will stay in touch with the Bureau, thank you for the help."

Saying their goodbyes, the FBI agents were shown out by one of the maids.

Sitting at the far end of the table, Sani had been quiet. One of the bilingual maids had sat with him and translated the discussion in a whisper. His dark eyes burned with anger, anger at the men who wanted to do harm to this family, as well as anger at the infighting among the white men. He had come to respect the men Senior Kirkpatrick had left behind, but these new white men he did not trust.

The phone rang in the foyer. Moments later, one of the maids came to the veranda and told Consuelo the FBI was on the phone requesting to speak to her. After taking the call, she returned to the veranda and her guests.

"I had an interesting conversation with the Special Agent in Charge in Denver. He would like to send two men to brief us on the situation as they know it as this time. The men will be here tomorrow in time for lunch. The description of the men he is sending does not match the men who were just here."

As the maid finished translating, Sani stood and said, "Senora, with your permission, I must attend to my men."

As the old Navaho walked past Consuelo, she said to him in his native tongue, "Do not kill, information is more valuable than their lives."

Smiling at her, Sani walked across the veranda and headed to his old truck. His smile took on a vengeful look as he planned out his capture of the two white men.

As Sani walked away, Consuelo's thoughts went to Soledad and the group in Germany. Should she fill them in on what may be happening at home? No, she decided that would distract them from what they have to do. She would keep everything to herself when they make their nightly call to the children.

Fifteen miles away, on Hwy 285 North, one man wrote his report while the other man drove.

28 SEPT, BAVARIA

Elsie von Beitel lived to entertain. She loved parties, luncheons for the ladies of the area and any excuse to show off her home. Her cook had been a chief from one of the more famous hotels in Berlin, therefore the food was exquisite. The manor was well taken care of, clean and bright. Tapestries, paintings and statues, some famous, others not, filled the foyer and the main hall. Furnishings were what you would expect from a wealthy German estate, beautiful heavy woods and tasteful fabrics. The grounds, well-manicured and rich in trimmed evergreens and sculptured shrubs put the finishing touches on her lovely home.

With all her beautiful surroundings Elsie lived with fear, fear of what would happen should her past come to light. One of the reminders of that fear sat at her dining table, much to her distaste, drinking her wine and eating her food. Having known him for thirty three years, she knew he was a minion, not a leader. However he answered to a leader, one that he was there to represent after the phone call she had made a few nights ago.

With the food gone and the wine bottle empty, the minion sat back, smiled, and scratched his mountain of a belly before fouling the air with a belch that all but echoed through the room.

"That was pleasant. Why don't you try and be more disgusting, I am sure you can if you put what little mind you have into it." she said with a frown, unable to hold her tongue.

"Watch what you say to me woman, I will not be talked down to." the minion said as he stood, knocking over her upholstered chair, the sound echoing down the hall.

Suddenly the door to the hall was filled with two large, concerned men. The cook and the grounds keeper both lived in the main house in case of situations such as this, unruly guests. Each man owed the lady of the house a debt of gratitude they will spend a lifetime repaying. Part of the repaying was keeping her safe. Neither man liked the guest that made an unexpected appearance and would be more than happy in removing him, preferably by force.

Waiving them off, for now, Elsie turned to the man and said, "You have my information, in full, about the situation at the church. Now please go and report everything to the Sturmbannfuhrer. He will have instructions for you and me after he hears what I have to say."

Not liking his chances with the two men present, the minion grunted, nodded and walked out of the room and, with a two man escort, proceeded to his car.

Watching from a window, she made sure he left her property. As his lights disappeared into the night, she thought of the first time she saw him and his master. The night air was cold thirty three years ago when a staff car pulled onto the Schloss grounds almost running Elsie down. Hurrying from behind the wheel stepped this minion in a SS Rifleman's uniform. Upon opening the rear door of the car, he stepped back and gave room for an SS Major to emerge. The Sturmbannfuhrer that glared at her was a distinguished, good looking man, however his evil eyes made her shiver more so than the cold Bavarian winter night. Over time she got to know him and ended up doing his bidding, until she betrayed him. Her betrayal was so well done, he still is not aware of it, not yet anyway.

28 Sept, Munich

The Sun disappeared minutes before we took another break to let our eyes and minds rest. After returning from BND Headquarters we all took a four hour nap and dug into the files after grabbing a bite of lunch. Seven hours later we felt no closer to the gold than we had been last night.

Lae sat back in her chair, rubbed her face and said, "Everything shows shipments coming in but only a few going out."

"And the strange things about the outbound shipments, there were fewer but with large quantity of crates, crates that two men could carry." Soledad said as she mimicked Lae, showing her fatigue.

"The men carrying the crates were wearing rubber suits with breathing gear, not unlike modern radiation suits." Gregor said as he poured more coffee.

"Damn it, there are zero indications that any radioactive materials were brought to the Castle. Could they have created any?" I asked, already knowing the answer but my tired brain wanted someone else to say it.

"Not with equipment they used and not without any fission materials." Gregor said profoundly.

Soledad stated the obvious, "That leaves the gold leaving in those crates."

Lae continued her thought, "Disguised as radioactive material to keep others away."

It suddenly hit me. I had another stack of files Otto had given us. Railroad schedules and bills of lading for those trains did not, at the time, seem to tie in. Scrambling through them it only took minutes to find a correlation between the trucks leaving the Castle and shipments of dangerous materials, in crates, being loaded on a train in Munich. But, the rail yards had been destroyed by Allied bombing, why a train? At that point in the war the Allies controlled the air, any train in operation would draw unwanted air attacks. Unless it ran at night, but even then it couldn't go far. Unless that was the plan, make a show of leaving the area on a train then switching modes of transportation away from prying eyes.

A small note was written in one of the margins, diese Oranienburg, 15. Marz 1945.

Turning to Gregor I asked, "Gregor, in one of our discussions about WW II, didn't you say the Germans may have tested a nuke in early '45? Near a town named Oranienburg?"

With a thoughtful expression he replied, "Yes, they did, according to one of the instructors at our academy. He said the Americans bombed the area extensively to keep its secrets away from the Red Army. I think the date of the bombing was 15 March. Why?"

Handing him the note, I told the ladies what was written on the file.

Soledad spoke up, "Do you think the note means the crates were bound for Oranienburg and they were departing on March 15th?"

"I certainly do. And if the area was under bombing attack that same day then the crates never arrived." I answered.

Lae, who had been quiet up to now said, "First things first, we need to confirm there were no radioactive materials at the Castle. If there is not any there then we know the gold was in the crates and not bomb making material. We need a Geiger counter and a drive to the Castle tomorrow."

Soledad and I looked at each other, smiled and said, "Road trip!"

28 Sept, New Mexico

Kurt was at the airport and anxious to get to Germany, but before him was a lovely young lady with tears in her eyes. Not quite as big as Gregor or Glen, Kurt was none the less a big, good looking man and drew attention from the ladies. His size is what got her attention. One rainy afternoon almost a year ago she was shopping at the local grocer and could not reach an item on a top shelf that had been pushed back. Having seen her dilemma, Kurt stepped over and got it for her. After placing the item in her cart, she turned to thank him.

When she turned and looked into his eyes her heart melted. Stunned at her reaction to the young man, she muttered a thank you and walked away, trying to get her breath back. Kurt watched her walk away while wondering what had caused the expression on her face. Over the past year, he learned what had caused the expression, for he has the same look on his face every time he looks into her eyes. After kissing Mai one more time, Kurt turned and walked to his awaiting flight. His heart was heavy at leaving her behind, but he knew when he returned she would become his wife.

Mai's thoughts were almost the same as Kurt's, but she had a wedding to plan. Her mother wanted a traditional Navaho wedding but she was leaning toward a "white man" wedding as her father calls anything involving a Church. Thoughts of the wedding filled her head to the point that she didn't notice the eight men who were watching her walk by. After she walked past them, two of the men went to the windows and watched Kurt's plane take off.

One of the men walked to the bank of pay phones and placed a short call, notifying his superior of the BND agent's departure. The voice on the other end was a little high pitched with excitement mixed with a little insanity. That voice gave him the orders the man was expecting, kidnap the four children or die in the attempt. Placing the hand piece on the cradle, the man turned and looked at the rest of his team. They were capable, professional agents and were not the least bit sloppy as Steiner and Gunther had been. Gathering his team and their luggage, he thought this was going to be a short trip. He had planned everything based on the previous teams Intel and was not expecting any problems, after all, the CIA and BND agents were out of the way. Unfortunately for him, he didn't know about a very pissed off old Navaho and one hundred warriors under his command.

Wagner's reaction to the call was a little different than his agent's had been, he did a dance he called The Hitler, after his beloved Fuhrer, one clenched hand in the air while quickly picking up one foot then the other in rapid succession and turning in a circle. Finally, Wagner thought, something was going his way after the inability of his staff to find the French bastard Caron.

The Stazi team rented two cars and drove to their hotel on the outskirts of Santa Fe. After settling in, they gathered in the team leader's room to make preparations for their mission. Studying the pictures of the Hacienda and its grounds, he made the same observation that had been made five years ago by a killer for hire. Only this time there will be two snipers on the mountain ridge 300 feet above the grounds providing cover for a five man assault team. The plan was simple.

The two snipers will be in place by 3AM while the assault team works its way to their demarcation point north of the Hacienda by 5AM. The full moon will aid in their positioning. They would take the children by force Friday morning at sunrise. The assault will begin at 6:58 AM. The eighth man will arrive at 7:05AM in a small bus they had acquired and cart the assault team and children to a rallying point where the snipers will join them for their escape. Hidden in an old barn sat four different sedans of various types and conditions, ready to take a divided force in four different directions. They would meet up in Juarez, Mexico by the next morning.

Looking over the plan one more time the team leader stepped onto a balcony outside his room to get some fresh air. For the life of him he could not understand why they were here and why they were going after children. Every bone in his body screamed at him to abort and return to East Germany before it's too late. He should have listened.

Across the street from the hotel, two men sat in an old pickup truck waiting for the new arrivals to show themselves. Having relieved the two man team that had followed the white men from the airport, these two Navaho were more experienced in the art of surveillance, having served with the 5th Special Operations Group in Vietnam. Of the hundred men working with Sani, over half were veterans. Marines, Air Bourne, Calvary, Air Assault, Green Beret, and three SEALS made for a diverse force that, if properly equipped, could take on any battalion in the world. On top of the military experience, the men are Navaho and these are their Mountains.

CHAPTER 14

The restaurant at the hotel started serving breakfast at 6AM. We were the first to be seated and I guess our hunger showed. The hostess took one look at us, said she would take care of us and turned away heading to the kitchen. Less than a minute later we had coffee and juice in front of us. Within minutes we had a traditional German breakfast before us. There were different varieties of Brötchen (bread rolls), marmalade and jam, chocolate spread, a variety of cheeses, hams, salami, ripe tomatoes, Schwarzwälder and honey. The four of us ate everything she brought except for the napkins and plates. Lae and Soledad frowned at Gregor and me when we acted like we were going to lick the plates. At least the waitress thought it was funny.

We were on the road by sunrise with full stomachs and resolve in our step. Gregor had rented us a BMW to drive and it was a blast, can't wait to get our own. As we hit the open road southeast of Munich, Gregor and Lae spread the maps and files we brought with us and started studying them again hoping they would catch something we all missed. They had the full back seat to use and they used it all, paper was everywhere, I don't know how they could find anything. But they did.

Lae read and reread a page several times before asking Gregor to translate the German file. She did not trust the translation into English the BND had provided. Gregor read the German original, then the English, grunted and read it all again.

"Glen, do you remember the German words for horse?" Gregor asked from the backseat.

"Sure, pferd is the only one I remember." I answered.

"Yes, that is the most common, but there are others. If I remember correctly, Ross is another. I think you need to read these pages with me." Gregor said in a soft voice.

Pulling into a gas station, we changed drivers. With Soledad driving and Lae riding shotgun, we hit the road again. Soledad didn't have far to drive. We stopped in the outskirts of Neubiberg, which put us only twenty kilometers from our destination.

Gregor and I read the pages in question several times apiece. Every time we read the pages we got something different out of them. Words like "Ross", "Reiterei", and "Kavallerie" were used as proper nouns making them names, not unlike Williams or Garcia. But the strange thing is the sentences they were used in made no sense, they rambled as gibberish. All three words meant horse and when we placed horse in the translation instead of those three words, the sentences changed drastically.

Gregor and I sat there staring at the translation we had just finished, not really believing what was before us. Could it really be this simple? Or this complicated? We had narrowed the clues to just four. All involved a word for horses and all mentioned gold in one form or another. Taking each clue one at a time, we reviewed the source, looking for irregularities.

Of the four in front of us, two came from John's journal. There were references of Calvary horses being taken care of and groomed where they "rested on mountains of gold". Another clue in his journal spoke of "cave lined with gold that reflected on the horses polished bridals". Both of these supposedly came from diaries of men who were at the Schloss and died of their wounds. John seemed to think they were ravings of feverish, ill men.

The other two were from dispatches that were decoded by the OSS (father of the CIA) after the war. Horses and trains play a prominent role in both. According to the notes in the margins, John thought these documents were the most credible he had found. Everything we had found interesting about our search was contained in just five pages. Horse, trains, hazardous material, gold, March 15th bombing raid were all there. One other item had our attention, a rail bridge that was damaged by American P-47's, a bridge on the line to Nuremburg.

Gregor spoke first, "The gold did leave the Castle and made it to Munich, however, it did not get to where it was going, American fighters made sure of that. I think it is hidden somewhere between Munich and the destroyed rail bridge."

After rereading one sentence, I replied, "The report said damaged, not destroyed. I believe the train got past the bridge but something happened to it and the gold was either hidden or stolen."

Soledad spoke up, "Guys, we are here."

"What a lovely village." Lae said as she took in the scenery.

She was right, the village and surrounding country side was indeed beautiful. Fall colors in the trees and scrubs, houses and buildings were laid out orderly in a typical German fashion. A Church steeple could be seen well outside the town, a beacon of invitation to all.

Driving through the village, looking for a place to park, we noticed some activity in front of the Church whose steeple we had been admiring. Lae spotted empty spaces across the street so Soledad pulled in. Gathering at the rear of the car, we watched the drama that was unfolding on the Church grounds.

There seemed to be a disagreement between a tall Nun and, from the looks of him, a teenage boy. A Priest held the boy while another Nun held back the tall one. From the looks of the tall Nun, she was royally pissed off. The Priest was doing a good job of shouting them both down for his was the only voice we could hear. Several minutes later, the boy handed the Priest a candle and stopped resisting. Turning him around so he could look the boy in the face, the Priest said one more thing to the boy and turned him loose. Once free, the boy hit the road on a dead run and did not look back. The tall Nun was now pissed at the Priest. The poor man can't win for losing. Noticing us, he handed the candle to the mad as hell Nun and walked over.

As one, the four of us crossed the street and met him on the front lawn of the Church. He greeted us with open arms and a smile that lit not only his face but seemed to brighten the area around him. It is rare that my heart and my head tell me the same thing where people are concerned, they both said 'here comes a good man'.

"Guten Morgen." He said in a truly heart felt way. But seeing Soledad and Lae look at Gregor and me, he quickly switched to English and said, "Good morning, welcome to our village. Can I be of service?"

Soledad stepped forward and took lead, "Good morning Father, I hope we didn't interrupt anything."

"No, nothing serious anyway, some of the local boys find it fun to steal a candle when Sister Anna is on duty in the chapel. She can have a bit of a temper and they bring it out with their pranks." He said trying not to laugh. I think he knew Sister Anna was walking up behind him.

Sister Anna has good hearing for she said as she walked up, "Pranks indeed, they steal from God's house, it does not matter the value of the stolen object, and it belongs to the Lord. But I do like to put a little spark under them when they see me." Her smile went to her eyes, another good person my inner voices whispered.

Soledad introduced each of us and told them she and Lae were in the area to buy a BMW for each of their spoiled husbands and are sightseeing while the cars were built. Wow, I thought, the truth, except for the Nazi gold thing, and maybe the spoiled husband thing. The Father, whose name is Aaron, said he had put coffee on before the young man started the excitement and invited us in for a cup.

The Church was simple in design but beautifully built. The steeple was at the very front of the building with the chapel opening up behind it. The double front doors went into the base of the steeple and opened into a foyer. Along the wall to the left was a large shelf full of fantastic figurines and statuettes. The ladies went to the shelf immediately and among ohs and ahs, commented on the beauty of the art. Sister Anna lit up like a thousand watt bulb at the mention of the art works in the Church and went into tour guide mode. The three of us watched the three women disappear into the Chapel, Sister Anna talking excitedly. Father Aaron smiled, shook his head and motioned for Gregor and me to follow him to the promised coffee.

The walk to the back of the Church was interesting in its self. Father Aaron gave his own short tour telling us the long and eventful history of the Church. The original Church was destroyed during the Thirty Years War and a new church was started in the late 18th century. Finished in the early 19th century it could use some renovation. His office was simple but functional with a bit of elegance. Sitting in plain but comfortable chairs, we enjoyed the coffee, much to our surprise.

Noting the look on our faces Father Aaron smiled, sat back and said, "I acquired the taste for American coffee during the occupation after the war. Your army was more than generous to us and the local people. Our food resources were dangerously depleted by the Nazis by the time the war ended. The Nazis may have hated the Third Army, but we were never Nazis. General Patton's men saved us." He finished with glassy eyes, trying, unsuccessfully, to hold back tears.

Holding up his cup in a toast, Gregor said, "To General Patton!"

Smiling at Gregor, the Father said, "You do not hear many Russians toasting Patton."

Gregor replied, "Patton was a warrior. No matter nationality, my toast is from one warrior to another."

The Father had a surprised look on his face at Gregor's proclamation. He glanced at me as if asking a question. Catching the look, I smiled at him, took another sip of the coffee.

"Father, sometime I will tell you a story about how one man lead an army of four against an invading force of sixty and won the fight without a single friendly loss." I said as I pointed a finger at Gregor.

Father Aaron raised an eyebrow and said, "I would be very interested in hearing that story, anytime you want to tell it."

"Perhaps before we leave Germany we will come back to your lovely village. May I use your restroom? The coffee I drank on the way here wants out." I asked.

After getting directions, I found my way to the restroom, taking note of the décor along the way. This Church is a true work of art.

Not only was the building and grounds beautiful but the alter art was classic and, from the looks of it, very old and expensive.

Upon leaving the restroom, I wandered about a little, looking for the women. I shouldn't worry about them, since they were with a Nun, in a Church, but old habits die hard. They were just outside the building at a side door, looking at the grounds. Everything looked good so I headed back for more coffee.

Stepping back into Father Aaron's office, I nodded at Gregor. He relaxed a little, knowing what it meant. Helping myself to another cup, I sat down and listened to Gregor and the Father's conversation.

Father Aaron looked at me and said, "Gregor and I share an interest, skiing. We have been telling stories of our near misses with serious injury over the years. He said you do not care for the sport."

Shaking my head, I replied, "Father, the fourth time I went down a slope flat on my back and my feet stuck straight up in the air, I packed it in and now watch our families fly down the mountains from the warmth of the lodge."

Their combined laughter drew the attention of the ladies. As the three women started toward the Father's office, another lady came in the side door and caught up with them. After a short discussion, Soledad stuck her head in the office and told us they were going across the street and sampling a new recipe for muffins, which they would bring us a bite. After the women left the building, Father Aaron got up, walked to his door and closed it. He then turned the thumb lock to secure the door. He then poured another cup of coffee and sat down.

Sitting his cup down after taking a sip, he said, "Gentlemen, there is more to you than meets the eye, including picking up new cars," leaning forward he continued, "I have seen treasure hunters come here for the past thirty years looking for lost Nazi gold. You however, do not fit the mold. Would you care to tell me why you are here, drinking my coffee and reconnoitering my Parish?"

Gregor nodded at me so I leaned forward and said, "Father, you won't believe us but here goes."

I told him everything. Well, almost everything.

He didn't interrupt me, not once. I finished and sat back, waiting for his response.

"Thank you for your honesty. I will help you all I can. What do you need?" he asked in a soft voice.

"We need access to the Castle north east of here, at least the old stables and blacksmith shop." Gregor told him.

"The Schloss is now a school. I can get you uninterrupted access but it will be Sunday afternoon when none of the children or the staff is on the grounds. Will that suffice?" he asked.

"Father that will be perfect, I don't know how we can thank you." Gregor said, meaning every word.

"Thank you for what Father?" Sister Anna said from outside the door.

"I knew these doors were not thick enough." Father Aaron said as he opened the door letting the women in the office.

Lae spoke up and said, "We were not eavesdropping, Gregor's voice carries even through doors." Soledad was nodding in agreement.

Soledad took one look at me and laughed, turned to the other two ladies and said, "I told you guys I can read him like a book, that's why we are so good together." Looking at me she said, "You told the Father the truth about why we are here, didn't you?"

I smiled and nodded, not saying anything because I knew she wasn't finished yet. But I did reach for the plate of muffins, which I passed to Gregor and the Father after taking two.

"That's okay, we told Sister Anna everything too." Lae said with a smile, "she is going to help us, if the Father lets her that is."

Sister Anna took one look at the Father and said, "I can read the man in my life as well, he has already agreed to help, right Father?"

Noticing the look that passed between Gregor and me, Sister Anna swatted me on the arm and said, "He is in my life in every way but that!"

Our laughter echoed down the hall, heralding the start of friendships that will last a lifetime.

After planning our next move at the Schloss, we spent most of the morning getting to know our new friends and the Church that is so important to both. The story of the soldiers and their art was heartwarming. The figurines the men made were beautiful and very detailed. We all could see why they are so important to the Father. After a very tasty lunch, we finalized the time table for Sunday and headed back to Munich.

Gregor smiled at me as we got in the car, wondering what the look was for I asked him as we pulled out of the village, "Ok, what's on your mind?"

"You did not tell the Father about the intelligence community's interest in our venture. You may need to tell him in case they come into the picture here?" Gregor asked with concern in his voice.

"He knows, didn't you see the skiing picture on his credenza? Our good friend Otto Klaus was sitting next to the Father. He knew we were coming, probably before we did." I answered as we pulled out of the parking space.

None of us saw Willie sitting in a car down the street. The pictures he took were pretty good. Good enough for his friends at BND headquarters to identify all four of us, he hoped.

CHAPTER 15

Breakfast at the hotel was another feast, not unlike the previous meals. Our fellow diners were a mixed lot of tourists, locals and spooks. The Mosad team was across the room, they toasted us with their juice. Three tables to our right, next to the door, sat the four BND agents that we greeted so warmly earlier.

Two tables to our left sat a couple of men that looked vaguely familiar. One turned in our direction, made eye contact and nodded. When he did I knew exactly who they were. Even though I had not seen them in five years, I knew they were John Kirkpatrick's men that gave Lae, Gregor and me a ride in Thailand when we went after Soledad. Gregor saw my expression and followed my eyes. His smile told me he recognized them too.

Out of the corner of my eye I saw Soledad smile and wave. When I turned to see who she was waving at, I had to smile. Kurt, Janet and Joseph came in together and headed to our table. Looking around the room I tried to figure out who might be KGB and Stazi, everyone else was present and accounted for, CIA, BND, MI6 and Mosad. An idea hit me that made me smile. After greeting the late arrivals, I went to the manager's office to ask for a favor, which he quickly granted.

Fifteen minutes later, the manager came to our table, nodded and handed me a key. Soledad, Lae and Gregor gave me a funny look but then they all smiled when they saw the mischievous grin on my face.

Standing, I grabbed a water glass, a table knife and used them to get everyone's attention. "May I have your attention? We all know why we are here, or I should say, we think we do." Pointing at the tables in question I continued, "I want to invite you, you, you and you to a short meeting in a conference room just outside the restaurant. If I have missed anyone who has an interest in our venture, feel free to join us."

With that, I turned to our table and motioned for them to join me. After every one stood, I turned and motioned for the rest to join us and we walked out the restaurant door into the conference room. Holding the door open, greeting each and every person who took me up on my proposal, I was surprised that everyone came to hear what I had to say.

As she walked through the door, Soledad whispered to me, "You are crazy!"

Lae smiled up at me and said, "She is right you know."

Gregor said, "May I go to my room for clothes?"

"I hope we won't need them my friend, not yet." I answered, knowing he was referring to his pistols.

I am not sure how the staff did it in fifteen minutes, but the room was perfect. At the head of the room was a long table with four name cards with our names on them. In front of our table were six tables with one name card on each, no one was left out, MI6, BND, MOSAD, CIA, STAZI and KGB.

Several of the men had amused smiles on their faces, a few had scowls, but they all went to their tables as labeled. We sat at our name cards and waited for them to be seated.

Soledad leaned to me and said, "Now what Sherlock?"

Smiling, I motioned her, Lae and Gregor into a huddle. "Simple, lets tell them why we are here and that we will keep them in the loop with briefings every three days. What do you think?"

Lae and Soledad looked at each other and said as one, "Yep, crazy."

Gregor smiled and said, "I like it. Straight and to the point, it will mean less people looking over our elbow."

"Shoulder my love." Lae whispered with a smile.

"Yes, thank you, shoulder." Gregor said as he squeezed her hand.

With agreement all around, I stood and said, "Thank you for joining us. We don't know what your respective agencies have told you about us or why we are here, or for that matter, what your orders are from those agencies. Therefore we decided to cut to the chase and fill you in."

Those comments started several of the tables stirring. A couple of minutes later they had settled back down, so I continued, "Some believe we have knowledge of lost Nazi gold and are here to find it. We are actually here to buy two BMW's and take them home." That started them muttering again and several more moments to settle down.

"However, others think we know something and tried to stop us at home, where two men made the mistake of shooting at us. When we arrived, files came in to us that got our attention. So, long story short, we are going to look into the myth. Also, we will meet in this room every three days and brief you, if you show up, on our findings, any questions?"

You could hear a pin drop.

One of the BND agents asked, "What happened to the two men who shot at you?"

"One is dead and the other wishes he was." Soledad answered.

"Who killed him?" the same agent asked.

Smiling, Gregor pointed at me and said, "He did."

Silence again.

"Can we trust you to keep you word? What is to stop you from taking the gold and running?" one of the Mosad agents asked.

Lae answered him, "Simple, we don't want, or need, the money."

Several more moments of silence ended when one of the CIA agents stood and said, "We will see you in three days." Then he and his partner walked out.

The rest of the spooks followed them, all but our friends, Kurt, Janet and Joseph.

When the door closed behind the last man, Janet said, "Glen, I have never seen anyone get our four agencies to agree to anything, congratulations."

"Thanks Janet, I'm not worried about the four agencies who just left, but the two who didn't show." I said, pointing to the tables marked KGB and STAZI.

Kurt spoke up and said, "None of our brothers know the seven of us are working together, let us keep it that way, including my friends in the BND. We will leave separately and take different cars everywhere we go, agreed?"

With agreements all around, we split up and headed to our respective rooms, only we all ended up in ours. Seven pairs of eyes went over every file, scrap, note and binder at our disposal. It was a long day.

By 6 pm we had a plan. Kurt was going to get us a small airplane and a cleared flight plan for tomorrow that will take us over the area we want to focus, thus speeding up our reconnoitering. While we are in the air Kurt will go to BND headquarters and look for a few items we all have questions on. Janet and Joseph will be at the British consulate doing the same thing, as well as checking in.

That settled it was time to have dinner and that's a good thing, I'm starving. The dining room was almost full, but we found a table close to the wall of windows. Gregor gave me a look as we sat down, I don't think he liked my seating selection. Normally I wouldn't either, too exposed.

Smiling, I said, "No one is going to take a shot here, especially with the room half full of competing spooks."

He just grunted and sat down. Soledad and Lae were whispering back and forth, laughing to themselves. I could tell by the looks in their mischievous eyes they were laughing at Gregor and me. That didn't bother me, they laugh at us a lot. Several of the diners had been present that morning and raised their glasses in salute.

As usual, I surveyed the room as we walked in. Across the room sat a distinguished looking old gentleman reading a newspaper while enjoying the marvelous food in front of him. What I could not see was the SS Runes tattooed on the inside of his arm.

30 SEPT, NEW MEXICO

Ten minutes till one, three sedans, a van and a 4x4 pulled out of the hotel parking lot. The team leader was in the last vehicle, which was the 4x4. He was taking the snipers on a direct route to set up their shooting stations. The five drivers stayed within sight of each other as they left the city behind and drove into the mountains. Phone calls went out immediately to Sani, the Senora and an intricate system of keeping tabs on them went into play.

The only route to the Hacienda was a narrow paved road that connected to US Highway 285 about twenty miles north of Santa Fe. Along the path they took were Navaho at key points to track the agents. Using old Army surplus walkie talkies, the Navaho stayed in contact with each other and passed current information along to the next station the agents would pass. It all worked perfectly.

After reaching the turn off, the agents slowed to a crawl as they approached their demarcation points. The first to pull over and stop was the van. It and its driver would not be needed until the others had the children. With his cohorts tail lights disappearing in the darkness, the driver stepped into the night to make a call of nature. Finishing his business, he walked toward the front of the van and was surprised when the headlights came on and blinded him. In reacting with the normal instinct of blocking the sudden light with his hands, he effectively raised his hands away from his sidearm. As his vision returned, he left them in the air. Six Navaho with rifles pointed at him convinced him it was the right thing to do.

One bend in the road stood between the convoy and the turn off for the 4x4. Suddenly the night exploded in front of and behind the agents. The team leader reacted far faster than his men in the other cars. Turning quickly to the right, he accelerated the 4x4 and darted between two large pines and fled into the night with several Navaho in pursuit. The others were not as lucky.

Both explosions fell large pine trees and blocked the road at each end of the convoy. The quiet night was further ripped apart with search lights and rifle fire as the Navaho who sprung the trap fired into the ground around the cars. The men inside made themselves as small as possible and never returned fire. Sani called for a cease fire after two minutes of salting the earth around the agents with high velocity rounds. It was more than long enough to convince the agents that surrender was in their best interest.

With the agents unarmed and secured, two of the retired Green Beret supervised the search of the vehicles. They did not find what they were looking for.

"Sani, there are only side arms and assault carbines with these men. The 4x4 that darted into the trees must have their long range assets." One of the Green Beret reported.

Sani looked up the mountain and said, "We need to know how many men are in that truck and how they are armed." Looking directly at the Green Beret, Sani continued, "Take one man into the trees. You know what to do."

"Yes sir, I do." The man said as he motioned to the other Green Beret.

The two big ex Special Forces NCO's made a big show in selecting a man, effectively scaring the hell out of most of them. Finally picking a man, they marched him into the trees, not quite out of sight. When they were in position Sani and a German speaking ex Green Beret walked among the prisoners glaring them in an attempt to intimidate them. It worked.

Sani motioned for the Green Beret to begin, he said in a booming voice, "How many men are in the truck who escaped and how are they armed?"

Silence, so he repeated himself three more times, still no response. Sani motioned to the men in the trees. One pistol shot echoed through the night as a body fell in the trees. Turning back to the prisoners, Sani picked another, one with scared eyes. Two Navaho had to pick him up, his knees too weak to carry him.

Half way to the trees and the body of his cohort, the man screamed, "There are three men in the truck, three men but only two rifles. Please do not kill me! I have answered your question."

"Who among you is the leader?" The NCO asked the scared man.

"He is driving the truck! Please let me live." The man whined.

His brethren cursed him and yelled threats until the Navaho presented them with the business end of several rifles. He sat, sullenly, away from the others, hanging his head in shame. He was very surprised when the body of his fallen comrade was placed next to him. It took a few minutes longer for him to look at the fallen man. Several more minutes passed before he realized the man was breathing.

Sani had been watching the man and smiled as the man realized his comrade had been knocked unconscious instead of shot. Turning his gaze into the night, Sani knew it would be a long night. However he was not worried at the outcome of the upcoming man hunt. By dawn there would be over one hundred riflemen combing the mountains for these three men. Sani was confident, but not overly so. He had no desire for any of his men to get hurt. The men they are going after are some of the elite of their country, and one is the team leader. You don't command a team of this kind unless you are the best at what you do.

Five miles away the Stazi team leader checked his watch. Sunup is only thirty minutes away but they were in position and well hidden. The Hacienda was just below them and they had a commanding view of it and the surrounding area. He tried raising his men by radio, until the batteries died, without success. Going with his training and the assumption that some escaped the ambush and are proceeding with their mission, he waited for his men to make their assault.

His wait was in vain. By 7:28, thirty minutes after the assault was to start, the grounds below him were quiet, with no activity what so ever. Lowering his binoculars, the team leader wished he was back in East Berlin, the thoughts that he and his men should not be here went through his mind, again. Sitting beside his two men, he started planning on how to remove them from the predicament they found themselves.

At the Hacienda, everything looked quiet for a reason. The eight women and six children who live there were on the Reservation and had been since the children got out of school the day before.

Sani reviewed the preparations he had made and the deployment of his men. Every road, trail and stream was guarded by at least a four man team. Another thirty men were deployed on the north side of the Hacienda, high in the mountains with observation posts watching all points of the compass. The men had high power scopes supported by long range rifles. They could spot a flea on a coyote's ass at a thousand yards.

The remaining men, approximately forty, will act as drivers to attempt to push the three agents into the open where they can surrender or not. At this point Sani did not care which. They were planning to start the drive at midday when the drivers would not create shadows thus highlighting their positions. The Navaho had a major advantage besides numbers, knowledge of the terrain. Sani knew every position that a sniper would use to cover the Hacienda. His men would be watching those areas very closely.

Looking at the sun, Sani decided to check the prisoners and grab a bite to eat before the fun starts in about an hour.

Across the mountains, the Stazi team decided to stay put until dark. Between sundown and moon rise the night will be at its darkest. They will put those few hours to good use to egress over the mountains south of their position. Their goal is the main road where they can steal a car for their run to Mexico. Sounded good and looked good on paper.

At 12 Noon, Sani uttered a command in one of the walkie talkies. An orchestrated series of shots echoed across the mountains. Every Navaho position fired one round into the air, letting Sani know they were in position and ready. Sani also used this unorthodox method to mess with their advisories minds. The shots told the Stazi agents they are surrounded and greatly outnumbered. Hopefully surrender would run through each man's mind. Sani had no desire to kill these men or get any of his hurt. That said, he would be damned if he let them escape.

By 3pm, one hundred and fifteen Navaho had tightened the circle around the Stazi agents. Every man knew exactly where the three

Germans were hiding. Sani looked the situation over and decided a little conversation might go a long way to resolve the situation.

Turning to the German speaking Green Beret, Sani said, "I want to talk to the leader before someone gets hurt. Find something to use as a white flag and lets you and I go for a walk."

The man smiled and said, "My pleasure Old One, but if they do not honor the flag, we will be the first to die today."

Looking over the area, Sani said, "The Lakota in the north have been credited with saying, "It is a good day to die."

The Green Beret smiled and said, "I like the saying, "Live to fight another day."

Sani laughed and said, "Well said my son, now get a flag and let us find out what kind of day this turns out to be."

Fifteen minutes later the two men started walking to the Stazi position, white flag waiving in the breeze.

Lowering his binoculars, the team leader let out a stream of curses. For the life of him he could not understand how the men found them. He had been careful and not left a trail for them to follow. They made no noise, no smoke from a fire, not even from a cigarette. After taking one more look, he turned to his men and gave them instructions in case he did not return. He then stepped out and walked toward the two men walking down the mountain under a flag of truce.

Stopping ten feet apart, the three men stood in silence for a few minutes. The Stazi agent was the first to speak.

"It seems you may have us at a disadvantage." He said in English with a bit of a smile.

The Green Beret translated what the man said into the Navaho tongue. Sani smiled and said, "More than you know, you have over one hundred rifles aimed at you."

Sani could see the man's expression change as the Green Beret translated to the agent. Sani had to give the man credit, there was not an ounce of panic in him, nor was there anxiety.

Finally he said, "I would never be so bold as to call you a liar. However you will understand if I asked you to show me."

As Sani got the translation, he smiled, took the white flag and walked about thirty yards and planted the flag. Speaking into a walkie talkie as he walked back, his relayed his orders to his squad leaders.

Stopping next to the agent, he raised his right arm, grinned and quickly dropped his arm. The flag disappeared under a hail of bullets. Sani said something to the Green Beret and looked up at the agent with a big smile.

"The old One said that was three fourths of our men, one forth are at an angle the ricochets would pose a danger to the three of us. He also says he does not want your blood, only your surrender." the Green Beret said.

The agent looked at Sani for a moment before saying, "It appears you do have the men and we would have a difficult time winning a fight and escaping. However we may not have a choice, as East Germans we find it almost impossible to surrender to the American government."

The Green Beret smiled for the first time saying, "We are Navaho, it is our nation to whom you would be surrendering."

After a long moment, the agent made a big show of presenting his side arm to Sani. He then turned to the position held by his two men and motioned for them to join him. Well trained, his men joined him in a matter of minutes, weapons presented to the Green Beret.

With an over the head wave, Sani signaled his men to come out of their positions and join the party which they did, smiling and laughing among themselves. The Germans could not believe how close to their position the Navaho were, the number of men, nor how they were armed. At least ten of the Navaho had military grade sniper rifles, including two .50 calibers. The Stazi team leader consoled himself with the knowledge he made the right decision in surrendering. Had he chose to fight, he and his men would now be dead instead of tied up in the back of an old pickup truck on the way to an uncertain future.

1 October, East Berlin

The sun was not yet up when Wagner walked to his favorite Saturday morning retreat. He had a ritual of walking from his apartment to a small coffee shop for a modest breakfast, relax and read the morning paper. No reports, no files, nothing what so ever that has to do with his Stazi work.

The coffee shop had outside seating on the walk as well as indoors. The morning was cool but comfortable thus Wagner chose to sit outside at the north end of the establishment. The walkway to the main entrance divided the tables sitting outside. Three tables north and four tables south of the doorway. He did not notice an elderly man sitting at one of the four tables to the south. He would not have noticed a naked lady sitting at one of the tables. His was an old attitude that small men with power have had throughout the ages. Nothing mattered but themselves and their power over others. He should have paid more attention.

As the waiter walked away after pouring his third cup of coffee, Wagner folded his paper and reached for the cup. His hand froze midway. Sitting across from him was a man he would recognize anytime and anywhere. The food in his stomach turned into a brick as his blood ran cold.

"Good morning Manfred, I was hoping you would be here today enjoying this wonderful mild weather." The man said in a neutral tone, his smile never leaving his face.

Finishing the reach for his cup, Wagner replied, "Yes, it is quite lovely this morning. It is unfortunate the view has been spoiled."

"I hadn't realized I had grown that ugly in my old age." The man said with a laugh.

Sitting his cup down hard enough to break the handle, Wagner demanded, "WHAT do you want?"

"I want you Manfred, just you." The man replied.

"Why?" Wagner asked, sitting back, looking around for help, but there was none to be found, the waiter was even absent.

"Because you went after my family." The man answered.

"Your family, who, who is your family?" Wagner stammered as real fear gripped him.

"Soledad Garcia Williams is my granddaughter." The man said in a monotone.

Too late Wagner noticed a folded newspaper sitting at the man's right, his hand under the paper. Three shots rang out so quickly the witnesses could not be sure of the number when they were interviewed by the Police. All three went in and around the heart and were devastating. Manfred Wagner died without uttering a sound.

John Kirkpatrick stood and walked away leaving the pistol under the paper.

Two blocks away a car waited that took John to the airport for a flight to Munich. His appearance slightly altered with a fake moustache peeled away and the sweater he was wearing replaced by a light jacket. The gloves he wore, as well as the sweater, were already on the way to a burn bag at a CIA safe house, having been tossed out the window and retrieved by another CIA agent.

With his plane banking toward Munich, John's handsome face broke into a smile at the thought of the pistol he left behind. The Police are going to have fun running down what is left of the finger prints on the weapon, clip and bullets. John had relieved an SS Major of this Walther PP at the end of the War. As a member of the OSS, John was always thinking ahead during every aspect of his job. This Walther had gone under wraps and had not seen the light of day for over thirty years. It was a perfect drop weapon with no ties to him or anyone but a long dead Nazi.

CHAPTER 16

1 OCT, MUNICH

A small sliver of sunlight made its way past the heavy hotel drapes in our bedroom, dancing across Soledad's cheek as she lay on her right side, sleeping. Leaning on my right elbow, I watched it slowly move across her lovely face, hoping it would not move into her eyes, waking her. After all, waking her was my job.

It was not quite 7, thus giving me two hours to properly make love to the woman of my dreams. I have heard by the fifth year of marriage the luster has gone out in most relationships. If anything, the luster for my Heart shines brighter now than it did the day I proposed. Normally, this situation of studying the light as it danced toward her eyes would bring my blood to a boil and I would proceed to ravish the goddess lying beside me.

I don't know if it was everything we were going through, the danger, or the uncertainty we were facing, but all I wanted to do was hold her close and soak myself with her essence. Just before the light made its way into her eyes, I leaned over and buried my face into the nape of her neck. Using my left hand, I reached around her and cupped her right breast. Only when she stirred did I pull her into me and held her tight. An hour later we were still in that position, and it was time to get ready to meet Lae and Gregor for our outing.

By 9:30 we were at a small airfield southeast of Munich. Kurt out did himself with the aircraft he reserved for us. It was a twin engine Beechcraft, almost the same aircraft that Soledad had at home. This Beechcraft was a BND aircraft and had special modifications such as high resolution cameras. With a crash course under our belt on the use of the cameras we were on our way.

We had decided to follow the railroad tracks so we would have a better chance of seeing every crossing and bridge. Thirty years had passed and we know the landscape had changed, to some degree. Our flight plan, provided by the BND, let us go anywhere we wanted, which we did. Soledad made it a point to gain elevation when flying over villages and farm houses, trying to be thoughtful of the inhabitants.

After three hours in the air and over a hundred pictures we had not found the spot we were looking for. Banking to the right as we turned for home, Lae called our attention to a small rail spur that we had missed. The spur left the tracks under some heavy trees and stopped immediately. Flying directly over it, we could make out remnants of an old line, long unused.

Gregor marked it on our map for our return on the ground. We all had smiles as we headed back to Munich, confident we had found the right spot to start our search for the lost gold.

Kurt met us at the airport right after we landed. He had a smug look on his face that said he found something. Sitting in the coffee shop at the airport, he explained what he discovered.

"Do you remember what the Frau Hartmann said about a symbol on the crates that looked like a three blade boat propeller?" Kurt asked, trying to keep the excitement out of his voice.

We all nodded and motioned for him to continue.

"That symbol was adopted as the universal symbol for radioactive material well after the war. In fact a group of students at Berkley came up with it in 1946." Kurt stated.

"Damn, she lied to us, but why?" Soledad exclaimed.

I sat back and said, "Let's go ask her. We know her room number."

The ride to the hotel was not quiet, not in the least. All of us expressed our theory as to why she would bring all the information she brought and then lie about this one detail.

Three minutes after our car stopped, we were at her hotel door. No one answered. Three minutes later we stood at the front desk and found out more disturbing news. There was no record of a Hartmann, Frau or otherwise, having stayed at the hotel, in fact the room in question had not been used in several days. Surprised and a little perplexed, we went to our room and hit the bar.

Gregor looked at his beer after taking a long draw and said, "You do know these drinks will cost three times what they would downstairs."

Looking over at him, "Yep, but here no one will over hear our discussions. Right this second I don't know who we can trust, everyone in this room excluded of course." I said, looking at Kurt.

Soledad and Lae were standing by the small desk where the files and documents that Frau Hartmann provided us were stacked. Lae picked up one, thumbed through it then tossed it aside.

Turning to us, Lae said, "You do realize we probably can't trust any of this, not one document, not one word."

Soledad said, "She is right as rain, Damn it."

"What about the rail spur we found? Should we investigate it anyway?" Kurt asked.

"Why not?" I asked, "We have gone this far and it does look as if no one has bothered it in years."

Looking at her watch, Soledad said, "If we hurry and with the way Kurt drives, we could get there with about two hours of daylight to work with. I'm game."

"Yeah, let's check it out. Tomorrow we go the check out the Castle with the Father and Sister Anna. That lead originally came from the BND, not Frau Whistle Britches." I said with a grin as I looked over at Kurt.

Raising his beer in salute and smiled at my use of Whistle Britches. Standing, Kurt said, "I will meet you out front in three minutes."

He then downed the remainder of his beer and sprinted out of the room. Knowing how fast he is, we had to scramble to beat him. Three and a half minutes later we pulled out of the hotel parking lot and headed north at a brisk pace. Two and a half hours before sundown, we sat at the end of a dirt road, roughly two hundred yards from where the spur split from the main line. Kurt's driving is fast, but the man is not reckless. Apparently the BND does as good of a job training driving techniques as it does everything else.

The main rail line went beside the copus of large trees we had seen from the air. The trees were in such a position to hide the spur from where it branched off the line and for about a hundred yards afterword. The rails had been removed from under the trees and for as far as we could see. As one, we started following the old spur. Roughly three hundred yards from the trees, the trail stopped, abruptly. It did not disappear into the side of a mountain, at the edge of a river or gorge, it just stopped.

"Gregor, is the metal detector we rented in the back of the car?" I asked.

Smiling, he replied, "Yes, it is."

Kurt nodded at us and took off at a dead run. Not only can he drive, he is fast on his feet as well. In a matter of ten minutes Kurt was back and we had the detector operating.

"What are we looking for?" Lae asked with a puzzled look on her face.

"Yeah, what's up?" Soledad asked as well.

"We will know it when we find it." I answered with a grin.

Soledad turned to Lae and said, "Glen has that look on his face, he knows something, or thinks he does."

Lae looked at Gregor, elbowed Soledad and motioned to Gregor and said with a laugh, "Gregor thinks he knows the same thing."

We had the laughter tuned out as we listened to the metal detector and its weird screeching it makes. First Kurt used it for fifteen minutes, then Gregor, then me. After almost an hour going over the area, in and around the old spur, we had nothing. It was getting late so we started back to the car. Soledad and Lae wanted to carry the detector and check it out on the way. They said the boys didn't share well so it was their turn. We let them take the lead so we could laugh at the way they squealed every time the unit screeched in their ear.

Lae held the unit as we went into the trees. She held it across her body, the disk to her right about two feet off the ground. When she got within a few inches of one of the trees the thing went nuts. Turning to us for guidance the look on her face was priceless. Gregor went to her and showed her the way to tune it in, letting her do the honors.

She ran the detector up and down almost every tree. A pattern started to appear. The trees on the north and east side of the copus had some kind of metal in them at various heights and concentrations, the rest did not. Soledad motioned to Lae and made a sweeping motion along the ground under the trees, nothing,

When she completed the search of the trees, we gathered at the edge for a little discussion. We tried to keep our excitement in check. After all we don't know what we found.

Turning to Gregor, I said, "If I read this right, something happened here and a thorough job of cleanup took place. They policed the entire site but forgot the trees."

He replied, "Either the trees had to stay to keep from drawing attention to the spur or they did not think they would matter."

"What would the trees matter? Where did the metal in them come from?" Lae asked, but then answered her own question with Soledad nodding in agreement, "Shrapnel! Shrapnel and bullets! That is what is in the trees, evidence of a fight."

Kurt stepped to the car and returned with a Kbar knife and proceeded to dig into one of the trees that gave off a strong return signal. A few minutes later his efforts paid off. In his hand was a .50 caliber, full metal jacket bullet that could only have come from an American machinegun.

Turning to me, he said, "I believe the American P-47 had eight of this type of weapon."

With that, we all knew the search for answers in this area will resume. However when he made that statement the Sun disappeared below the mountains and darkness set in.

1 Oct, New Mexico

The Stazi team leader was surprised to see the sunrise. Every bone in his body told him the Navaho would kill him and his men out of hand. Instead he and his men have been treated with respect. Just as he started to set on his bunk, there was a knock at his door. After bidding them to come in, the door opened and one of the big Navaho that he knew was ex-military filled the door way.

"Excuse me sir, Sani would like for you to join him for breakfast." the man said in a voice that sounded deep as a well.

"I would be happy to join him, provided I am assured of my men having breakfast as well." He said in a tone the Navaho understood and respected.

"Of course sir, they are being served food as we speak. You can look in on them if you like." The Navaho said.

"Yes, I believe I would." The Stazi leader said in an even tone.

The Navaho nodded, backed out of the door and motioned for him to follow. As the Stazi stepped into the small hall, two men stepped in behind him, effectively boxing him in. Smiling at his inability to attempt escape, he followed the big man without hesitation. As they came to another small door, one of the Navaho on guard opened the door to allow them to look in the room. What the Stazi leader saw amazed him. The room was large enough for a dozen bunks and a table in the middle large enough to seat everyone, including a man he did not recognize. Before them were several platters of food served family style. There was more than enough to feed his men, several times. A ghastly thought crossed his mind as they closed the door, a last meal. The thought made him shiver.

Several minutes later they entered a well lit room with a table set in the middle. There were eight guards, stationed in pairs, on every wall. Standing as they entered the room, Sani offered the Stazi a seat beside him. As the Stazi sat, the big Navaho sat across from him. On platters before him were several types of meat, fruits and flat bread. He later found out it is called a tortilla.

Sani said something to the big Navaho in a language the captors had used earlier. The big man turned to the Stazi and said, "The Old One said eat, then we shall talk of you and your men."

"I speak English." The Stazi said in an indigent tone.

Smiling, the man said, "I know, but the Old One does not. Sani speaks only Spanish and our native tongue, by choice. Sani does, however, want to know what to call you, besides White Man."

Smiling, he said, "Schultz, my name is Schultz."

Laughing, the big Navaho said, "I'm sure it is, but hey, it will work. You can call me Mike, this is Sani." Mike said, pointing to Sani.

Turning to Sani, he explained what he was laughing at. Sani laughed as hard as Mike had seen since he met the old man years ago. Still laughing, Sani motioned them to eat, which they did in silence.

Finishing off the last of the gravy on his plate with a piece of tortilla, Sani sat back and spoke to Schultz as if the German could understand. He knew eye contact was as important as what he was saying. Finishing, he motioned for Mike to translate.

Mike turned to Schultz and said, "Sani said to get the boring stuff out of the way first, so here goes. You and your men are prisoners of the Navaho Nation and will be treated with respect. However, such treatment will be suspended if you harm any Navaho or attempt to escape, both transgressions will be punishable by death. Do you understand and will you relay this to your men?"

Stiffly, Schultz said, "I fully understand and I will make sure my men understand as well."

"Sani wants your word as a leader that neither you nor your men will do harm or try to escape." Mike said in a crisp voice.

Standing, Schultz came to attention, clicked his heels and bowed at the waist in the purest form of a German Officer and said, "You have my word."

Mike explained to Sani what had just happened. Sani smiled, stood and offered Schultz his hand, which Schultz shook, thus calling a truce between two forces that were ready to kill each other 24 hours before.

The table was cleared of food and coffee was served. Schultz was surprised at the quality of the coffee, it was excellent. The three men talked for four hours, passing information back and forth, much to the satisfaction of both. Schultz was relieved that the Navaho were in contact with the American State Department concerning him and his men. They were to be held where they were until transportation arrangements are made. However, Sani would not turn the East Germans over until his demands are met. That bit of information caused concern in Schultz and it showed.

"What are your demands, if I may be so bold to ask?" Schultz asked anxiously, too tired to keep the tone neutral.

Smiling, Sani answered and Mike started laughing. Turning to Schultz he said, "All of Sani's demands have been met but one. We are getting items needed for our schools and for our elderly. You and your men must be worth a lot, we are getting a lot. The last thing, and the hold up, is Sani's new pickup truck. He wants a bright red extended cab and they are scrambling to find one with the options he wants."

Mike and Sani broke out laughing. Laughter that was so genuine that Schultz couldn't help but to join. As the laughter died down, Sani got serious for a few minutes. Mike listened intently to understand what Sani wanted him to relay to Schultz. Finally silent, Sani sat back and motioned for Mike to begin. Sitting there, sorting in his mind how to translate Sani's words, Mike was amazed at the depth of the wisdom of the Old One.

Turning to Schultz, Mike began, "Evil men control most of the world, control how people act, how people survive. However, they control only as long as men let them. The men who sent you here are evil. The men you will be turned over to may be evil as well, but, all white men are not evil. I have looked into your eyes while you were angry, while you were relieved, and more importantly while you laughed. You are not an evil man, you serve them. You serve because you want to serve your country, however the evil men are in control. Go home and take control of your country. When you do, come back under the name your father gave you and we will talk again."

Schultz was stunned. This was not what he had expected from the old Navaho. Sani's words stayed with him for years. On 9 February, 1990, three months, to the day, after the fall of the Berlin Wall, a polite, well-dressed white man came to the reservation and asked for Sani. Konrad Frederick sat and talked to Sani's grave, as the Navaho tell the story, until tears could fall no more.

1 Oct, Bavaria

Elsie sat in her parlor, reading and re reading the note she just received from the Sturmbannfuhrer. There are Americans interested in the Schloss, the Church and Nazi gold. They were coming to the village tomorrow. He wants her to keep an eye on them and report everything they do and everyone the talk to.

Folding the paper over, Elsie was at a loss of what to do. She can't be seen snooping around, it would harm her reputation. Showing interest in tourists is far beneath her station in life and is unacceptable. She hated to ask her two men to do it in her stead, but she saw no alternative. Calling them into her parlor, she explained what she needed. Loyal to a fault, they accepted her instructions without question. After they left, she drafted a response for the Sturmbannfuhrer and gave it to the courier who waited in the foyer.

Picking up the phone, Elsie called the bar maid and gave her instructions to be watching for tourists asking about the Schloss and the Church. Her promise of two hundred American dollars guaranteed the girls vigilance. Having set everything in play at her disposal, Elsie sat back and prayed for the outcome of this turmoil to be in her favor.

1 Oct, Munich

The Sturmbannfuhrer, that drives such fear in Elsie, sat back and read her letter. The old woman is scared out of her mind he thought to himself. Good, scared people tend to do as they are told. If she does not, her future will be dim indeed. Putting the letter away, he dove into the wonderful dinner in front of him. He must thank the American fools for staying in this hotel, the food is excellent.

We finally made it back to the hotel, better late than never. Gregor and I were starving. The ladies were more concerned with freshening up. Promising to meet us in the restaurant, they headed to our rooms while we headed to food and a beer or three.

As we walked into the restaurant, I noticed the same distinguished older gentleman I had seen before. Seeming to sense my interest, he looked directly into my eyes. I had seen those eyes before. Just before I shot the timber rattlesnake they belonged to. We better watch him, the little voice in the back of my head said very loudly.

Upon seating and ordering our first beer, I told Gregor about the man and how he set my radar on full. Casually looking over my shoulder at the man, Gregor agreed with my assessment. Our list to watch and not trust is growing, again.

Looking around the dining room, I didn't see any of our favorite spooks. Since we called them out and promised regular briefings, they seemed to vanish. Out of the corner of my eye, I saw Gregor stiffen. Turning slowly, as to enjoy the décor, I got turned around to see what caused the reaction. Sitting across the room sat two men, looking at nothing but seeing everything. Damn, two more spooks, unidentified spooks.

"Those men are KGB. One of them I have met." Gregor said as he sat his beer down.

"Are you armed? I'm not." I asked, as I sized the men up saying, "They looked tough and very capable and you can bet your ass they are armed."

"No." was his only response.

"Do you think he will recognize you? How long has it been?" I asked as I checked the silver on the table for a suitable weapon.

"Three months before I was sent to Laos. He was one of the interviewing officers that determined my assignment." Gregor said as he turned his head away from the men.

"That means it's been almost six years and he only saw you for a short time. He probably will not recognize you at all." I said, trying to put a positive light on this mess.

At that moment, the ladies walked into the dining room, man oh man is Soledad beautiful! So is Lae but that is for Gregor to express, not me. I don't want to be picking myself up off the floor. However, we were not the only red blooded men to notice the two lovely ladies.

Every man in the room stopped to admire our wives, including the two KGB agents. Standing as they approached the table, Gregor and I presented our ladies with chairs and seated them. Returning to our seats, Gregor looked at the men as we sat down, mistake.

"Glen, he has a puzzled look on his face. I do not think he recognizes me as of yet, but he is thinking." Gregor said in an anxious voice.

That comment brought interest from the ladies. After a quick explanation, we decided to act normal and not draw attention. We had a great meal and nothing happened. We finished our meal and retired to our rooms, after deciding to meet for breakfast at 7.

Watching the four Americans leave the dining room, the two KGB agents let them go without following. They thought they knew everything. After all, they got their information from the mother of one of the women. After leaving the Hacienda, they made a fast drive to Denver, turned in their rental and caught a flight to Munich.

They did not realize how close behind Sani's men were. Three minutes made the difference between Munich and capture. Sani was livid when he got the news. The four men he sent were his best. He was assured of their capture, he thought. Now he must tell the Senora about his failure, which he hated to do that more than anything in the world.

The Senora was calm when he told her. She promised to tell Glen and Soledad when they placed their calls to the children. Sani shook his head as he left the room. She is truly an amazing woman, he thought as the door closed behind him.

CHAPTER 17

Breakfast was great, the morning clear, the car fun and the women beautiful! What more can a man ask? We pulled out of the hotel at 8 sharp, putting us in the village by 9:30. Watching for a tail, we took a little more time driving through Munich in case we were followed. Even though we can't go to the Schloss until the afternoon, we wanted to get there in time for Mass. Soledad and Lae promised Gregor and me that we would not have to translate for them, just being there was enough.

The Father was pleased to see us in his congregation, as was Sister Anna. When the Mass was over they whisked us into his office where they had brunch prepared for us. After a delicious meal of assorted cold cuts, cheeses and breads the Father got down to business.

"We have a 2pm appointment with the grounds keeper. We will meet him by the old stables and will start our search there." The Father said in a whisper.

Leaning over the table, Soledad, in a whisper, asked, "Why are we whispering?"

Sheepishly, the Father smiled and said, "Do not know, I guess the excitement of the quest is the most excitement I have had in years."

Sister Anna laughed and said, "We need to get you out more Father."

Soledad laughing, said, "Come to New Mexico after this is over and we will make sure and keep you entertained, in the air and on the ground. In fact, why don't you both come?"

"The trip is on us. I know you have other Priests that can come and fill in so you don't have an excuse not to come." I interjected.

Sister Anna and Father Aaron looked at each other and immediately agreed, with huge smiles on their faces.

Gregor leaned toward me and whispered, "We just have to make sure they survive the next few days."

Whispering back at him, I said, "Us too."

Following the Sister and our ladies in the rental, Gregor, Father Aaron and I rode in the Fathers car. With only three kilometers behind us, Gregor and I decided the Father needs a new car. Gregor looked at me and mouthed "new B M W" and pointed to the Father. I nodded in agreement. I have ridden in junk cars but, DAMN this boy needs a car.

Five minutes until 2, we arrived at the old stables, behind the main grounds. A stately older gentleman met us with smiles and a firm hand shake. I liked him on the spot. Father Aaron introduced us all around, identifying the man as Vati, a German version of "dad". Leaving us to our research, Vati said he would return at sundown to lock everything up.

When I think of a castle, I think of a big stone fortress, not what I see here. This place is massive. There are multiple buildings north and west of the main structure, which in its self is huge. You can tell parts of it are very old with new additions adding to its function. There are two schools here, a Kindergarten and a school for girls. They have a soccer field, tennis courts, a track field and horses, not many but a few. On top of all that, this place is beautiful. Sitting on top of a mountain, for which it is named, the view in all directions is fantastic.

Still in awe of the beauty of the place, it was old hat for Father Aaron and Sister Anna, we headed to the stables. They are at the north end of the grounds. Part of the original castle, the stable was mainly rock with a wooden roof. As a stable it is pretty standard, rows of stalls running down each side with a tack room at one end and small living quarters at the other, which was not in use. A large door off the living quarters opened into a blacksmith shop that had not seen use in decades, from the look of it.

Gregor and I went along the north wall opening shutters and letting in much needed light. The room did not have modern lighting. While Gregor and I checked out the shop, the ladies found a door that led outside. They were in the forest to the north of the shop, looking back at the shop to give them a different angle.

"Glen, look at this and tell me what you think I see." Gregor said in a soft voice.

Stepping over, I looked around him and studied the back wall of the shop. At first I didn't see much. Centuries of soot build up, cracked mortar, nothing special. But when I stood by him and saw the wall from his angle I knew immediately what he saw. Evidence of small arms fire, multiple bullet impact points, one machinegun burst placed seven bullets in an evenly spaced line about three feet long. Gregor and I locked eyes and headed out side.

We walked away from the shop to the edge of the forest and looked back. The north side of the shop looked like it was the site of a major fire fight. Impact points covered the rock structure with concentrations around all five windows. We found the window there the seven bullets entered. It appeared like the gunner started at the windows edge and ran straight across with a very controlled burst.

"I was under the impression there was no fighting in this area. The Third Army went straight for Munich and left the outlying farming areas to the south alone." I said to Gregor as the ladies walked up to join us.

"That is my understanding also." Gregor said in his thoughtful voice.

Father Aaron said, "I was in the village the first time an American soldier passed through. Three men were in a small truck. I think they are called Jeeps. They waved and smiled at us, no shooting, and no fighting at all. I don't understand."

"What's going through that Russian mind my friend, I have seen that look before?" I asked Gregor.

Looking at us, Gregor said, "I will get metal detector. Perhaps my theory will be confirmed."

As one the five of us said, "What theory?"

We had to wait. Our big Russian friend didn't even look back as he sprinted for the car. Five minutes later he returned with two shovels, a few cloth sacks and the detector. Sweeping the area along the shops north wall he immediately got hits. We all looked at each other as if saying, oh, that theory. Our excitement grew along with his. Soledad and I grabbed the shovels and started digging. Lae, Father Aaron and Sister Anna went through the dirt as we spread it in a small area. In the matter of fifteen minutes we had a collection brass, spent bullets in a multitude of conditions and unfired cartridges. By the time we had been at it for an hour we had two hundred or more artifacts.

While we continued to dig, Lae and Gregor took the metal detector to the forest. They didn't find anything at the edge but when they moved into the trees, the detector went nuts. Soledad and Sister Anna joined them and started digging where Lae was marking the hits Gregor was getting. They started finding objects similar what we were finding by the shop.

The sunset snuck up on us as we were engrossed in our quest for clues. Just before the forest went black, Gregor held the metal detector against several trees. He got several hits but ignored them because of their lack of strength. Giving up on the trees, he turned and bumped into one causing him to drop the detector. Bending over to pick it up, Gregor noticed a large scar about a foot off the ground on one of the older large pines. The detector let him know immediately that what caused the scar was still present.

Gregor called to me, "Glen, do you have a knife? We need to perform surgery on a tree."

"You bet I do, I grabbed your Kbar out of the car when we got here." I answered as I walked to him.

He was standing by a large old pine that had a large blemish just above the ground. I handed him the knife and got out of the way. Gregor can make those fighting knives look like an axe the way he makes wood fly. About two inches into the tree he found a metal plate with an engraving of an Iron Cross. Using the knife as a pry bar, he popped the plate off the tree. Behind the plate was a carved cavity. It was four inches tall by six inches wide and about six inches deep. Inside was a small leather pouch. In the pouch were thirty six small gold crosses. Each cross had engravings on both sides. But our light died with the disappearance of the sun preventing us from studying the engravings.

We gathered our work and walked back to the car where we found Vati waiting to escort us off the property. He didn't say anything about the sacks and shovels we carried. We didn't offer explanations either.

Twenty minutes later we sat in Father Aarons office with our artifacts spread on two tables and his desk. The items found along the shop wall were kept separate from the forest finds. The gold crosses and cover plate were on the Fathers desk.

Sister Anna picked up several of the bullets from the shop, looked them over and asked. "Some of these are almost intact, others flattened out, but some are torn to pieces. Why?"

Gregor and I looked at each other before Gregor said, "Sister, the more intact bullets were fired from far away, the flattened ones closer. The bullets that are torn to pieces were fired point blank as the shop was overrun."

Paling, Sister Anna placed them on the table and said, "Oh, I see. In other words the defenders were probably all killed."

Nodding Gregor said, "Probably, or they may have surrendered."

Sister Anna crossed herself, walked over to Soledad and Lae who were studying the crosses and joined them. They had determined the engraving were names and were alphabetizing them. By the time they had the thirty six in order, their meaning struck them. They whispered among themselves for a few minutes before turning to us, without a dry eye among them.

Soledad asked in a low tone, "These represent men, who died here, don't they?"

Father Aaron answered, "I saw a few of the inscriptions, one of the names I remember. He died in early May, 1945."

"My question is where did the makers of the crosses get the gold? The tools are not a problem, but the gold?" I asked. All the while a little voice in the back of my head whispered the answer.

Gregor caught my expression, smiled and said, "Stolen from thieves perhaps?"

"That would be my guess. Somehow they pilfered enough from the SS to make the crosses. That took smarts and not a little courage." I said, shaking my head, a smile of admiration on my face.

Father Aaron said, "The SS were ruthless in their dealings with the patients of the hospital, most of which were Wehrmacht. In fact, several were executed by the SS for very small infractions such as stealing food and blankets."

Gregor looked at his watch and said, "It is getting late, we need to head back to our hotel. When should we meet again?"

While the others figured out our next meeting, I took my time sacking the artifacts in different sacks. We had decided to leave the gold crosses with Father Aaron and Sister Anna so they could research the names. As I sacked the second pile in a separate sack, something kept digging at the back of my mind, but I couldn't put a finger on what it was.

Father Aaron checked his schedule and found his only free day to be Wednesday. He and Sister Anna would join us in Munich for the day, if his car could make the trip. Gregor and I both had doubts but Sister Anna told us we must have faith.

They walked us to our car, and after handshakes and hugs all around, we loaded up and headed to Munich and a good night's sleep.

To the north of the Church, two men in a parked car watched us drive off. They were tempted to follow us to see where we went, but Elsie's orders were to watch and report. To the south, a man and a woman did the same. The man was a loser the bar maid had promised things if he gave her a ride. After we drove off, she got out of the car, deciding she didn't need a ride after all. The loser tried to protest her change of heart, but her flashing a knife changed his mind.

Two others sat under the trees across from the Church, watching everyone. Two old friends looked at each other and shook their old heads.

One said, "Why, after all these years, are people interested in old stories and fairytales?"

The other answered, "My friend, one word sums it up, gold."

The two old friends helped each other up, steadied their tired aching legs and walked toward their apartments. Shaking their heads in amusement, they disappeared into the night.

The drive was uneventful. The ladies dozed in the back while Gregor and I recounted the day and our discoveries. The gold crosses proved there had been gold at the castle while it was a hospital. They also pointed to the resourcefulness of the soldiers being treated there.

Pulling into a parking place at our hotel, I turned to Gregor and said, "For the first time since John mentioned lost Nazi gold at our weddings, I am getting a little excited at the thought. Not just that it existed, but that we may actually have a chance to find it."

Gregor looked at the ladies asleep in the back and said, "No amount of gold will replace our cargo."

Smiling at the sleeping beauties, I said, "You got that right. The first sign of serious trouble, we ship them home."

In stereo, the ladies said, "Like hell you will!"

That particular discussion ended right there.

CHAPTER 18

Strawberries, oranges, cherries and grapes were everywhere. Oranges were rolling from wall to wall in a small room where I stood. The cherries and grapes rolled around each other in a large bowl in the middle of the floor. The strawberries started coming apart as if slicing themselves. Suddenly ice started falling from the ceiling.

When the ice hit me, I awoke. Laying there for a minute, getting my bearings after such a strange dream, I reached for Soledad. She was not in bed. Then the aroma of the strong Sangria wine that Soledad likes filled my nostrils. Along with the wine, the aroma of cheese and strawberries filled the room with promises of a delightful moonlit encounter with a beautiful woman.

Rising to start my quest, I didn't bother with a robe and since I had showered right before bed, my tightie whities were nowhere to be seen. The soft carpet padded my footsteps as I went from the bedroom into the living area of our suite. The first thing I spotted was the drapes on the south wall, they were open and Soledad had moved the chaise lounge that we had yet to use, in front of the windows. My Heart was sitting on the edge of the lounge with a glass in her hand and a bowl beside her. Thinking of romance all the way, I approached her with plans to kiss her on the neck.

"Hi." She said, spoiling my stealth approach.

"Hi yourself." I said with romance still in my head.

Smiling at my nudity, she patted the lounge next to her. Quickly joining her I was surprised at the heat she radiated. Her motions were smooth, her touch soft and sensual as she moved into my arms. My blood boiled within seconds.

Surprising me once again, Soledad picked up an old book from the table next to the lounger and said, "I was thinking of the situation we face and couldn't sleep so I picked up this book from the bookshelf and started thumbing through it." Looking deep into my eyes she continued, "Glen, I found you."

Opening it to a marked page there was an illustration of a Knight, blonde hair flowing, sword in raised hand, shield blocking a blow from another Knight, his mounts nostrils flaring, teeth bared as he reared to match their opponents horse in the ferocity of battle.

I started to speak but she placed her finger to my lips. Turning the page she pointed to another picture. This one was of the same Knight standing in front of a beautiful Lady. Her dress was flowing from head to foot in regal purple, her jewelry was of diamonds and assorted gemstones. Even in the dim light, love radiated from them brighter than the brightest day.

Starting to speak, Soledad stopped me with a finger on my lips, again.

Turning the page back to the picture of battle, Soledad said, "The look I have seen on your face in combat is the same as on this Knight." Turning the page, she continued, "This look on the Knights face I have seen as well, every time you look at me."

Pointing to the caption below the illustration, she said, "I can't read German, what does it say?"

Looking at the words in the dim light, I read the inscription out loud, "A warrior is fierce in battle because he knows the value of life, he is tender and giving in love for the same reason."

Standing, she placed the book on the table, turned to me and said, "Glen my Love, my thoughts are of you, my heart is filled with you, my blood boils for you. Come my Warrior, kiss me.

Kiss her I did, softly. As our lips melted together in a slow sensual kiss, I found the tie on her robe, opened it. Slowly I backed up, not wanting the kiss to end but other thoughts passed through my head and took control of my hands. Reaching up with both hands, I slid the robe off her soft shoulders and let it fall around her sexy as hell feet. Under the robe she was wearing the same thing I was, nothing. The moon light caused her skin to have an effervescence that made her glow from head to toe. At that moment, right then, it seemed all the love and beauty in the world was wrapped up in the woman before me.

Dawn found us in each other's arms, the glow from out lovemaking on our cheeks.

3 Oct, East Berlin

Erich Mielke, Minister of State Security, Stazi for short, was a ruthless, driven man. Unfortunately for his adversaries, he was also highly intelligent. He knew everything that happened in his agency. From Administration 12, electronic surveillance, to Felix Dzerzhinsky Guards Regiment, the Stazi's armed force, to the Main Administration for Reconnaissance, which Wagner was an officer, Mielke held full control of everyone under his command. After reading a disturbing report, Mielke called one of his department heads into his office and all but crammed the report down the man's throat.

Dieter Koch reread the report in front of him which told him of the loss of a team in the US and the assassination of one of his officers six blocks from where he sat. The lack of urgency demonstrated by the staff who compiled the information infuriated him to no end. He will not show the same lack of concern. Also, he must handle this and keep Mielke out of his hair. His secretary knocked on his door and reminded him of his next meeting. Staring first at her, then the folder, he muttered something under his breath and walked out. His devious mind started working on a response to the Americans capture of his men and, if they were involved, the murder of one of his officers, even if the officer was a hated little bastard.

Three hours later he sat, alone, studying the folder further. How could things have gotten so out of hand? Wagner should have been the perfect man to oversee this small enterprise. He was ruthless, a pro at this type of operation and had the full cooperation of Koch's department, the Main Administration for Reconnaissance.

Picking up the phone on his desk, Koch called his counterpart in the Felix Dzerzhinsky Guards. Thirty minutes later he had a Spetsnaz trained team at his disposal. The team leader would meet with Koch that evening for orders. If the fifteen man team could be ready to infiltrate into the West in two days, Koch should be able to avert a disaster.

Not wanting to place the next call, Koch decided to place the call from a pay phone for security reasons. Telling his secretary he would be out the rest of the day, Koch left his office and walked to a small café where he could get a beer and place the call he dreaded. Sipping the beer as the waiter walked away, Koch thought this setting looked familiar. A chill went up his spine when he realized he was sitting at the table where Wagner was killed. Shaking slightly, hoping it was not a sign of things to come, he decided to drink another beer before he called the crazy old SS bastard. The money he received from the old man was fantastic. The thought of the old man holding his life in his hands scared the hell out of Koch.

3 Oct, Munich

Soledad and I grabbed a quick shower, separately damn it, and met Lae and Gregor in the restaurant. It was time to meet with the spooks and fill them in on what we found. The manager had the meeting room set up and ready for us so right after breakfast the fun could start.

Everyone was there enjoying the marvelous food while keeping an eye on us. The Israelis sat next to our table and started a conversation about the gold and what it represented.

"I must apologize for my behavior earlier, however, you must understand, the gold means more to my people than to anyone else. Also, I know who you are but you do not know me. My name is Dov, I am the senior agent assigned to this case." He said with a smile.

Soledad looked at him then the other men and asked, "What are their names?"

Dov maintained his smile and answered, "Their names are not important, all you need to know is mine."

Gregor got my attention and mouthed "asshole" and smirked.

Dov didn't miss the exchange between Gregor and me. Smiling again he shook his head and said, "No, my name is Dov, not Aaron, although it is a fine Jewish name."

I couldn't help myself. Leaning over toward him I said, "No dumbass, he called you asshole, not Aaron. Apparently you are not as good at lip reading in English as you thought."

The man's face turned so red I thought his head was going to explode. The looks on the faces of his team were quite different. They had a hard time not busting out laughing. Apparently their boss wasn't well liked.

Lae spoke up and defused the situation, "Dov, if we find the gold and turn it over to you, what will become of it? There is no way to determine who it belongs to, what makes you think it came from Jews?"

The question calmed Dov down. Staring at Lae and then the rest of us for a moment, he said, "True there is no way to identify gold as to its origin, however there are millions of dollars of Jewish gold that has not been recovered."

Soledad interjected, "Let me see if I can sum it up, you lay claim to all gold recovered from Nazis in the hopes of retaining some of it."

Dov sat back, clasp his hands and said, "My dear lady, not at all, not at all. The Israeli government would do no such thing. We merely want to make sure Jewish gold is recovered by us. We will put it to good use building schools, roads and securing our safety as a nation."

Gregor then stated, "All gold stolen by the Third Reich was not stolen from Jews. The Nazis stole from everyone they could, French, Poles, Italians, and Arabs of all nations where they occupied. Every occupied nation in Europe and Russia were pilfered in historic fashion. Also, not just gold was taken. They took art, jewels, other precious metal, anything and everything of value."

The discussion and arguments went on throughout our meal. As they cleared the dishes and we sat back with coffee, the manager motioned to me. It was time for out meeting. Standing, I got the attention of our spooks and motioned for them to join us. Everyone stood and paraded to the meeting room, all but the two KGB agents. They just sat there and watched in puzzlement. We knew who they were from Gregor's revelation earlier and the description the Senora had given us the night before.

Walking up to them, I said, "You might as well join us, we have a table just for you."

After glancing at each other, the older of the two said, "Come Comrade, we might as well play along. This should be interesting."

The other man nodded, stood and followed the older man to our meeting. As I watched them walk in front of me, I chill went up my spine. These two killers were in the Hacienda posing as FBI, under the roof where our children were thought to be safe. The Senora filled us in on everything that had happened to date, the visit by these men, the capture of a Stazi team and John leaving two men behind to bolster the defense of the Hacienda. Even though these men caused no harm, we will have to watch them like a hawk. They are professionals, like the rest, and will do anything to accomplish what ever mission they were given.

When the three of us walked into the meeting room we walked into a whirlwind. Finger pointing, threats and angry voices filled the room. I guess Janet was right, getting these agencies to agree to any thing for very long is almost impossible. But the arguments this morning started over something really stupid, seating arrangements. The BND agents started it by demanding the Mosad be moved to the back of the room because they will try to dominate the conversation like at breakfast. The Mosad had sat first and refused to move for the wanna be Nazis and stayed in their seats. Infuriated at being compared to Nazis, the BND agents threatened to move them by force. That is where things stood as I walked into the room.

Gregor, Lae and Soledad were at the head of the room at our table trying to quieten things down, to no avail. Just as I started to pitch in my two cents, Kurt walked in. He didn't say a word, only glared at the other BND agents. They took one look at his face, sat down and shut up. That seemed to stop the arguments and things got quiet. It made me think, Kurt is by far the younger of the BND agents involved. How high is his rank? How much power does he have?

The two KGB men found their assigned seats and were observing everything while being stone silent themselves. The jackets they were wearing had a little size to them telling me they were armed. Looking around the room, I decided everyone was armed, including the four of us. Well, so much for trust among spooks.

I decided to get started, "Ladies and Gentlemen, let's get this meeting rolling. For our late comers, "I said as I pointed to the KGB table, "I'll recap why we are here."

Five minutes later, Soledad told them what we found and did not find at the rail line up country and at the Schloss. For now she left out the gold crosses, which I thought was smart. She opened the floor for questions as she sat down.

"How do we know you are telling us everything?" one of the unnamed Mosad agents asked.

"You will have to decide for yourself wither to believe us or not. We are through trying to persuade any of you. Attend or do not attend, it is your choice." Gregor said with a bit of a growl.

Janet spoke up, "Our superiors in London have agreed to take a back seat and let our four American friends here lead the investigation. They also instructed us to aid them if called upon in either of the two situations, aid in the search or prevent interference by anyone."

Dov stood and said, after Soledad motioned for him to speak, "It appears our instructions are the same as our British colleges, standby but assist if called upon." Then as he sat down he said, "I, of course, have the authority to act as I see fit under those guidelines." Smiling as he sat back.

Kurt spoke for the BND, glaring at his fellow agents as he stood, "We feel this is a German investigation, on German soil, dealing with German citizens. However our orders are almost an exact copy of our British and Israeli brothers. However in this situation, I have full authority to assume command of the investigation and everyone involved."

That settled the question of Kurt's power and authority. It also caused a stir, but the announcement was not unexpected since we were on German soil. Things settled down quickly because everyone had been expecting the BND to lay such a claim. During Kurt's announcement I was watching the KGB and CIA agents. Elbowing Gregor and nodding in their direction, he saw the same thing I did. They were not interested in our proceedings, but each other. At least we knew where those four agents stood. They will be out of our way.

Soledad took the floor as Kurt sat. Pointing at the only empty table in the room she said, "The only agency that has shown interest in this little enterprise and not attended our meetings is the one I worry about. As you all know, except perhaps our KGB guests, the Stazi have made two attempts on our family. Thank God and a strong group of friends both were stymied. I fear they aren't finished and we all must be vigilant. You of all people know they will kill anyone to accomplish their mission, whatever that mission is. Be careful everyone and keep the rest of us informed if they make their presence known."

With that, we ended the briefing. As the agents left the room, I noticed the KGB agents were still seated. As Gregor and I approached them they motioned for us to join them.

As we sat, the senior of the two took a sip of his coffee, sat back and said, "Thank you for including us in your briefing, it was most informative. Now we would like to brief you on a development that is pertinent to your enterprise. Please call your women over so we may tell it only once."

Motioning to Lae and Soledad to come and join us, Gregor and I slid two more chairs to the table. Noticing the looks on our faces they hurried over.

After the ladies sat, the man said, "Saturday morning a Stazi senior agent was killed a few blocks from their headquarters in Berlin. This agent was the one who sent the teams into America to do his bidding. With both missions failing and their men either killed or captured, we do not know who killed him. However, it could have been the Stazi themselves as punishment for the failure, or another agency for some other reason than gold. Either way, we are certain another senior agent will be assigned to take his place. Involvement in your mission could disappear, or increase, based on his whim.

"Why are you telling us this? Isn't the DDR and the Soviet Union allies?" I had to ask.

The younger of the two spoke up for the first time, "Allies yes, trusted no. The information our government received that sent us to America was full of half-truths."

The older interrupted and said, "My young comrade is correct. Without going into detail, I will say this, the KGB does not like to be tricked into doing others bidding. If we want someone killed, we do it ourselves. The Stazi will use anyone and everyone to accomplish their missions. Be careful my American friends, they are demons in men's clothes. Now, we will say goodbye until Thursday. We will look forward to your next briefing."

As they reached the door, the older man turned to Soledad and said, "Your Grandmother is quite lovely. She is a remarkable woman and one I could, perhaps in another life, call a friend." With that he turned and walked away, without giving Soledad a chance to respond.

As he walked out, Gregor turned to our group and said, "The KGB calling the Stazi demons? Isn't that like the kettle calling the pot dirty?"

Lae smiled at him, shook her head and said, "Gregor my love, it's the pot calling the kettle black."

Frowning, Gregor said, "Forgive me my love, these American idioms are difficult to master."

Soledad said, "Come on, let's get a move on. The offer for the use of the BND lab to study our finds is for today only."

She's right," Lae said, "We want to know everything about these items by tonight."

Pushing Gregor and me to the door, the ladies took control and got us to the BND headquarters right at lunch. The onsite cafeteria was pretty good and the servings were large, which suited Gregor and me. While we ate, Otto introduced us to the research assistant that will help us in the lab, a nice young lady named Maria. After lunch it was off to the lab with three boxes of scrap metal.

Spectrometers, XRF Analyzers, scales, microscopes and a varied number of machines filled the tables in the lab. I'm not sure what they all do so I am happy to let Maria take the lead. Well, Maria, Lae and Soledad took the lead. Gregor and I sat out of the way. We had studied the scraps as much as we could, while the ladies had a blast.

Two hours later, Soledad came to me and said, "Glen, take a look at this and tell me what you see."

Gregor looked over my shoulder and read along. After reading the report twice, I turned to Soledad and said, "I am not going to ask if this is accurate because I know who compiled the data, but damn, are you sure?"

Lae and Maria had joined us and all three women said, "Absolutely."

Gregor said, "This is saying Germans fought Germans at the Schloss and the rail spur."

The three said, again, "Absolutely."

Looking the report over again I couldn't believe it. The small arms bullets we found were all 7.92mm, German rifle ammo, and 9mm submachine gun ammo, not any .30cal that would mean American combatants. The heavy machinegun rounds were not .50 cal American but 13mm German. All of the metallurgy tests came up as German alloys, not American, in every sample.

"I didn't expect this, not at all. Every theory we have had just went out the window. Damn." I stated, exasperated.

Soledad then turned the page and said, "Keep reading you guys, it gets better."

Continuing to read over my shoulder, Gregor said, "Multiple damn."

Cracking up, I looked over at him and said, "Double damn."

"Thank you," Gregor said with a smile, "but this will need more than two damns, several are in order."

The ladies looked at each other, then at us and said, "Absolutely."

"Which sample did this come from?" I asked, continuing to read.

Soledad answered, "The tree line at the Schloss. These were the defenders bullets."

"We have work to do, things are getting interesting." Looking at the four of them I continued, "I need a beer."

Gregor added, "And a shot of vodka."

The three ladies said, together, "Absolutely."

Soledad slid the report in her purse and we filed out of the lab. Maria said she knew the perfect Guesthouse to attain our requirements so she took the lead. As we entered the bar, one word in the report kept running through all our heads, Radioactive.

3 Oct, East Berlin

With dinner over, Dieter Koch retired to his study, well away from his family. His wife had the children in their rooms preparing them for bed. Deep wood paneling, oil paintings of various Middle Ages battles and two suits of armor adorned the dark room. His thoughts were as dark as his furnishings and deep into the problems at hand when there was a knock at his front door.

Opening the door, Koch thought he knew what to expect, after all he wanted this meeting. Much to his surprise, instead of a commando before him stood an elderly gentleman.

"Pardon the interruption Mein Herr. May I have a few minutes of your time? It will only take a moment. I was a friend of Manfred's." the man said in a nervous voice, hat in hand.

Not trying to keep the annoyance he felt out of his voice, Koch said, "He had friends? Extraordinary. You have two minutes." Koch said, looking into the night past the man.

"I have a report for him but since he is out of the picture, my instructions are to give it to you." The man said as he stepped into the foyer.

"I will be taking his cases for now, what do you have?" Koch asked.

Reaching into his coat the old man pulled an envelope from a front pocket and handed it to Koch. Not waiting for a reply, he turned and hurried out the door, almost running down two men coming up the walk.

As the man ran into the night, Koch looked at the package and paled when he recognized the handwriting on the outside of the envelope. Inside the envelope was written instructions how this operation should be handled. Quickly dropping the package in a drawer, he stepped out to meet his two expected guests. After a quick introduction they retired to the study.

Koch sat at his desk, brandy in hand, and studied his guests. These men had the look of commandos, unlike the running man. Almost two meters tall, they were muscular to the extreme and all business. Koch, even with his authority and power, was a bit afraid of them.

"Hauptman, how much did your superiors tell you about your upcoming operation?" Koch asked the senior of the two.

"Not much, only that we were to report to you and to follow your instructions to the letter, without question." The Captain answered.

"Outstanding," Koch said with a smile, "I will be short and to the point. Southeast of Munich is a small village that has a Schloss a short distance away. This Schloss was a field hospital during the late war. The SS also used it for clandestine operations involving many things, among them handling stolen gold. There is a group of Americans investigating the Schloss looking for the gold. Your orders are simple. We want the gold and anything else they find."

"I assume we are not to interfere in the investigation, only relieve them of their find, if they find anything that is." The Captain responded.

"You are correct. I have prepared a brief with all pertinent material and information you will need. Please take time to study the information while you are here so I can answer any questions you may have." Koch said as he handed the Captain a briefcase. "Would you care for a drink, perhaps a brandy?"

"No, thank you, we prefer water while we are working. Perhaps after the operation is over we can have a celebratory drink." The Captain said with a slight smirk.

"Of course, of course, you are quite right. Planning the operation will require a clear head. My study is yours gentlemen. I will be across the hall if you need me." Koch said as he closed the door behind him.

The two men looked at each other and almost broke out laughing at the little scared bureaucrat. Opening the briefcase they dug into the material and studied it closely, in silence, for over two hours. After placing all the material back in the briefcase, they went looking for Koch.

They found him in a small office across the hall, drink in hand. It appeared he had partaken in more than one during the time they were studying the information. Leading them back into the study, Koch staggered to his desk and fell into his chair.

The two commandos looked at him in disgust, debating asking him anything. However they had a couple of questions they wanted answers to before leaving.

"Herr Koch, we only have two questions. One, why are you sending us, a highly trained 15 man strike team to interdict the investigations of four American operatives, two which are women?"

Koch looked at the men through drunken eyes and answered, "Because the other two teams we sent after them did not return. The first was a two man wet team, the other an eight man team lead by one of our best commanders."

The two men looked at each other, shook their heads before the Captain asked the second question. "Are we to terminate the four Americans?"

His question fell on drunken ears. Koch sat head down, out to the world.

As the two men walked out of Koch's home, the Captain said, "Lieutenant, it appears the answer to the second question is up to fate."

"Yes sir, it does. Hauptman, why are we going into the West to clean up a mess made by the Main Administration for Reconnaissance? Can they not clean up their own mess?" the young officer asked.

"Orders son, orders, that is why we do what we do. As to our sister agency, they are all dumb shits." The Captain said as he clasped the shoulder of the young man walking beside him. In the back of his mind he prayed the young man would survive the operation, after all he is soon to be his son-in-law.

CHAPTER 19

Koch was a nervous wreck. He didn't remember much of anything that transpired the previous night. He remembered the two officers but not much about their orders. On his desk sat the box with all the files, right where the Hauptman sat it after going over the information it contained.

Not the type to leave anything to chance, he called the Regimental office and asked to speak to the Hauptman. The three minutes that passed seemed like an eternity to the man. Finally the Hauptman came to the phone.

Koch went straight to the point, "Hauptman do you understand your orders?"

Amused at Koch, he replied, "Of course I do, you made it very plain that we are not to interfere with the American's investigation but are to take everything they find and bring whatever it is to you."

Relieved, Koch said, "Very good, I expect a status report when you cross over and when you have the items and are returning to me, is that clear."

The amusement was wearing thin at the attitude Koch was displaying, "Yes sir, I understand completely." The Hauptman answered.

He started to ask his second question from last night, but realized he was talking to dead air, Koch had already hung up. Staring at the hand piece for a moment, he placed the hand piece softly on the cradle. Shaking his head at the stupidity of the men he served, he wondered how any of them could hold so much power over so many others. In his mind the answer to his second question, are they to terminate the four Americans, was his call. Satisfied with the resolution to that detail, he turned on his heel and returned to his men and their preparations for a night incursion into West Germany set for tomorrow night.

4 Oct Santa Fe

With the Stazi team in custody of the U.S. Marshal's office and on their way to Denver, everyone breathed a sigh of relief, everyone but Richard, Rick and Sani. The three men sat on the veranda, enjoying the outstanding view, and discussed their concerns. Richard and Rick were surprisingly good with Spanish so no interrupter was needed.

After setting down his coffee cup, Sani started the conversation with, "The evil men across the waters will not give up after losing only a few men. They will send others. I have seen it in dreams."

Richard and Rick glanced at each other before Rick said, "I haven't dreamed it but my operational experience tells me they are not finished."

Richard agreed saying, "Rick is right, we don't think they are finished, not by a long shot."

Sani said, "Good, we agree. I will keep my men on lookout but I will have to let them spend time on their jobs and with their families. However I have more than enough to stand guard in the mountains, at the airport, the rail station and the bus station. If more strangers show up, we will know within minutes."

Richard was pleased with Sani's preparations and said, "Well done, we can work with that. However I would like to add a 10 man squad on site, under our command in case someone gets through your outer defenses."

Sani smiled and said, "You would make a good Navaho, I will furnish three such squads so they can rotate and stay fresh."

The three men poured more coffee, sat back and looked across the courtyard and soaked up the view.

"Go get our daddy and Uncle Gregor. They will make the bad men stay away." Rebecca said out of the blue, scaring the crap out of the three men.

Turning as one the men saw, not only Rebecca but Kyle, Lupe and Jennifer. The four children used the dumbwaiter to sneak into the kitchen then it was easy to sneak out on the veranda. All four had a serious look on their faces, not scared, concerned.

"I'm sure they could little lady but they are not here at the moment. We will be able to protect you, don't worry." Richard told them.

Kyle threw his two cents worth in by saying, "Can we go back to the reservation? I had fun playing with the boys. Here I am surrounded by girls."

Consuelo came in at that moment, smiled at Kyle and said, "There is no need for you us to go back, not yet anyway. I want to show all of you a little secret. Follow me please."

Leading her procession upstairs and to a closet at the top, Consuelo opened the door, reached in and pulled one of the clothes hanging bars, right in the middle. When she pulled it they all heard a soft click and a door opened at the back of the closet. Motioning for everyone to follow, Consuelo went through the door into a dimly lit room. After everyone was in the room and out of the way of the closing door, she pressed a button on the wall. The door closed by itself and they could hear a click when the door locked. As the door locked, lights came on and everyone was surprised at the size of the room.

Becoming a tour guide, Consuelo gave them the nickel tour. "This room connects to all three of our bedrooms as well as the closet we came through. You open the entrances the same way we got in here, pull the center of the lowest bar and it will open. Be sure you close it behind you, or whoever is after you can follow you in here.

Small walkways came into the main room from four areas, all led to the main room where they stood. In the middle of the main room was a twelve by twelve steel room.

Consuelo continued the tour by entering the small room, "Here we have a self-contained hideout. The walls are one inch steel plate, the roof an inch and a half. There is a ventilation system as well as a remote start generator and water supply. All are separate from the main house and well hidden. This is where I want each of you to go in case of an attack."

The children nodded and said, as one, "Yes ma'am."

Richard asked, "Why didn't you show us this before?"

Consuelo smiled and said, "The reservation is much safer and the children have friends there. Besides this is meant for a short stay, we could live on the reservation forever if needed."

Richard and Rick saw the logic in what she said. They spent a few minutes looking the room over. The technology they saw surprised them, closed circuit television with cameras at key locations around the grounds and in the main house. A fully stocked pantry, stocked refrigerator and bunk beds for 6 finished out the contents of the room. Almost, underneath one of the bunk beds sat a locker. At Consuelo's nod, Richard and Rick pulled it out and opened it. Inside was four M-16's, four Israeli Uzi's, four 1911 Colts and plenty of loaded clips for each of them.

Rick looked over at Richard, then turned to Consuelo and said, "One thing for sure, if you have to defend this room you have almost everything you need."

"What are we missing?" asked Consuelo.

"Phones and grenades." Rick said with a smile.

Smiling back at him, Consuelo said, "What do you think us under the other beds?"

She leaned over, grabbed a handle of a drawer under the next set of beds and pulled the drawer open. Inside was twenty or so fragmentation as well as ten or so flash bang grenades. Closing the drawer she stepped to a small counter, opened a drawer, reached in and produced a phone.

Richard turned to Rick and said, "Never underestimate this lady."

"Amen!" Rick said with a smile.

Consuelo closed the drawer and said, "I am sure breakfast is ready. Let's go see what the ladies have prepared for us."

She didn't have to tell the men nor the children twice, the food is always fantastic.

As they left the room and headed to the dining room, Rick turned to Richard and said, "I am glad to see the arms. We may need them if Sani's dream comes true."

Richard replied, "Before we came here I would have blown off a dream, but that old Navaho is probably right."

Thoughts of defending the Hacienda stayed on their minds as the aroma of smoked bacon filled their nostrils.

4 Oct Munich

The room service cart sat beside the door, picked clean by the seven of us. It had been a long day going over every bit of information we had in our hands. Some contradicted others, some sounded unbelievable, others sounded too good to be true. By the time we were ordering a fresh meal a new theory emerged. New, but it was full of holes.

"At least we can take American forces out of the picture." Soledad said as she picked through the platter of food room service brought moments before.

Lae replied, "That is true, in fact there were no other allied forces in the area so that leaves Germans fighting Germans."

Gregor added while making a sandwich, "I think we all agree that the fight at the blacksmiths shop was over stolen gold. The patients were discovered taking gold and the SS went after them. The fight ended up being their last stand."

"That has to be what happened at the Castle, but why would a German fighter strafe a German train. And who went to all the trouble to scrub the site clean leaving no evidence behind, well almost none." I said between bites of the sandwich Soledad fixed for me.

"Why do you think the fight was their last stand? Couldn't some of them have gotten away?" Janet asked.

"Remember how some of the attackers bullets were almost intact while others were torn to pieces?" Joseph asked.

Nodding, Soledad motioned for him to continue.

"The bullets that were torn up were fired at point blank range. In fact the attackers could have been in the room with the defenders." Joseph somberly replied.

Lae and Soledad said "Oh" at the same time. The looks on their faces changed as the implications set in.

"You are saying the defenders were wiped out? Could none have escaped?" Lae asked in a soft voice.

"It does not appear that way, however anything is possible." Kurt answered.

"One more detail, why were the defenders ammo radioactive? Was there radioactive material being handled at the Castle and no one from the outside knew about it?" I asked, mainly thinking out loud.

"Apparently so, and if that's the case, Frau Hartmann was telling us the truth, at least about that. How much of the other files are real and how much is a red herring?" Soledad asked.

"Soledad, herrings are not red." Gregor said with a straight face.

Lae leaned over and kissed Gregor on the cheek then said, "My Love, red herring is a phrase meaning not real."

Looking at me, Gregor asked, "How many more American idioms have I not heard?"

Soledad and I answered simultaneously, "Thousands."

Lae laughed out loud as Gregor rolled his eyes.

Soledad summed up our theories and the unsolved areas, "The fight at the blacksmith shop was between SS and Wehrmacht patients over gold. The train was strafed by German warplanes and destroyed at the spur. That's all we think we know, as to the big questions it's any body's guess. The questions remaining are, where is the rest of the gold, why were the defenders bullets radioactive, where is the radioactive material, who did the cleanup at the rail spur?"

Lae said, "It appears we do not know as much as we thought."

"That sums it up, I think. How about your thoughts Glen, you have been very quiet today." Gregor asked.

"There is something bothering me since this started. Why is the Stazi so anxious to kill over theories? There has to be something we are missing." I answered.

The other three looked at each other before Soledad said, "Glen has a point, why are they so eager to kill?"

That question stayed on our minds as we packed up the files and headed to bed. Unfortunately bed it was, everyone was beat, including me.

4 Oct Munich

John Kirkpatrick sat in a borrowed office at the American Consulate in Munich. Across the desk from him sat Frau Hartmann. However Frau Hartmann's appearance was drastically different than the woman Soledad and company had met. The young CIA agent was beautiful, auburn hair, green eyes and a knock out figure.

"Did they accept your story? Or did they just give you the idea that they did?" John asked.

"Oh, they believed me alright. That is until they tried to find me after I left. They talked to a desk clerk that is not part of my contacts. He told them I was never there. Those four are pretty sharp. They will start doubting all I gave them. This little exercise may have been in vain." She replied.

"I don't think so, everything you gave them are in our files. They will weed through and find the real stuff. That's why I wanted those files in their hands, to weed out the truth." John said.

"We haven't been able to find anything in over thirty years. What makes you think they can do better? She asked.

Leaning over the desk, John said, "Sometime we can't see the forest for the trees. They will bring four new intellects into the picture and may find something we have been missing."

"What about the Stazi threat to the children?" She asked.

"I have resolved that issue." John said in a flat tone.

Small talk lasted a few more minutes before the agent said goodbye and gave John a hug.

On the way out, she turned and said, "It was nice working with you Uncle John, perhaps we can do it again sometime."

"That would be nice dear, take care." John replied with a smile.

4 Oct. Buenos Aries

The phone rang three times and stopped. Then rang again, this time it was answered by a clean shaven blue eyed blonde. Paul Franz waited for the people on the other end to speak first, as was their signal. He didn't have long to wait.

"Paul, how are things at the other end of the world?" an old voice asked.

"Fine, it only snows when it wants." Franz answered thus completing an exchange of passwords, confirming who they were speaking to.

The old voice got straight to the point and said, "I have a mission for you. I believe your generation call it a snatch and grab. I want you to take possession of four children and hold them until you have further orders. You will receive a packet with all the information you will need to perform your duty."

"Yes sir, we are at your disposal." Franz said with poorly hidden excitement.

"Yes, remember that." The old voice said, followed by a click.

Franz looked at the hand piece, shook his head and placed it on the cradle. His thoughts were all over the place, trying to imagine what challenges the mission would have in store for him and his men.

Across the world, the old man placed his hand piece in its cradle and smiled one of the most evil smiles imaginable. Thinking to himself, "The idiot Stazi better take notes, they are going to see how professionals handle things."

CHAPTER 20

5 Oct Munich

Father Aaron and Sister Anna were to meet us for bunch at the hotel around 10am. They were right on time. With a flurry of hugs and handshakes we escorted them to the restaurant. After a wonderful brunch and loads of conversation we sat back with fresh coffee and got down to business. It took fifteen minutes to bring them up to speed on our discoveries and theories.

"It still amazes me that Germans were fighting Germans as the war was coming to an end." Father Aaron said in disbelief.

Sister Anna said, "I have read stories telling of SS units shooting any soldier they thought were deserting. It really does not take much of a stretch to believe there could be fighting between the Wehrmacht and the SS as Nazi Germany crumbled around them."

"There are multiple accounts of that happening. However the fighting we are talking about seems to go far deeper than politics. Somebody had an agenda that went well into the millions of dollars." I added.

Soledad sat in silence for a moment, then said, "What if is its not "had" but "has"?

"That could explain the Stazi's hard core involvement and the lack of hesitation in killing. If, that is, the person who has interest in the gold has ties to the Stazi." Lae stated.

"It would also mean we must step up our security measures." Gregor said.

Nodding in agreement, I said, "We all go armed from now on, no one goes anywhere by themselves, not even to the restroom."

Gregor added, "This includes Father Aaron and Sister Anna, you must never be alone."

"We will not carry a weapon Gregor, you should know that." Sister Anna said, in a voice an octave higher than normal, her eyes a little bigger as well.

"Sister Anna is right of course. We are servants of God and will not do harm to another person." Father Aaron said in a normal voice.

Soledad offered a solution, "If there is a hotel close to the Church we can move to, we can stay close to Father Aaron and Sister Anna and watch their backs. I think we would be better off there than here. After all, the Castle is where the answers are."

"We can do better than that. There is a Guesthouse across the street at the rear of the Church. The owner is a close friend and is a large contributor to the fund arising activities of our youth." Sister Anna stated, her voice a little more normal.

That settled our living arraigments. We will move there tomorrow and stay until this is settled. The rest of the day was spent showing Father Aaron and Sister Anna all the files and evidence we had. It made since, Lae said, to have them look at everything, especially the items in German, after all it is their native tongue. Perhaps they will spot something we missed.

The manager of the hotel let us use one of his meeting rooms, thus giving us more than enough space to spread out everything we had. It was a God send, as were our Church friends. Almost immediately Sister Anna spotted a translation mistake. By itself it didn't make much of a difference, but as we went along, a few more mistakes were found.

Gregor and I were right in most of our translations. What we missed, as it turned out, was the direction a shipment from Munich went. We assumed north, as it turns out it was south and west was the correct heading. That opened huge holes in our theory about the train. If it went south, why the diversion to the north and the rail spur we found? We spent the afternoon going over every document we had. By 7pm, my stomach thought my throat was cut since I hadn't put something in it since brunch. We called a stop and went down to dinner.

As we entered the dining room, I looked the diners over. None of our friends were in attendance, making me wonder where all of them were. However, in his usual spot sat the man with rattle snake eyes. I watched him out of the corner of my eye trying to catch him looking at us. He never bothered to look up and ignored us completely. I thought that odd in itself.

Dinner was exquisite and the company entertaining. Father Aaron and Sister Anna are great at telling stories, of which they had many. All of us had a fantastic time and the evening flew. We finally paid attention to the time when we saw the wait staff stacking chairs on the tables so they could clean the floor. We bid our farewells to them and apologized for staying so late. Gregor and I made sure we left them a nice tip for the trouble.

Since it was too late to book rooms, we decided the men would take our room and the ladies would sleep in Lae and Gregor's room. Gregor, Joseph and I decided we would stand watch outside our hotel for a few days. It was a good decision on our part.

It was just before midnight as the private plane landed, fifteen men off loaded and walked straight into a hanger. The man who greeted them was a bit nervous, and it showed. On tables along one wall sat several shipping crates. The men wasted no time in opening the crates and distributing the contents, MP5 submachine guns, P9 pistols and enough 9mm rounds to start a war. Within thirty minutes the men were loaded in three vehicles and on their way to their hotel, down the street from ours.

6 Oct, Munich

Sitting across the street in the shadows, I had a clear view of two sides of the building. Just after 4 am, two men walked to the corner, stopped and lit cigarettes. Their movements were not of tourists, they had the bearing of soldiers, ramrod straight posture and when they walked up, they were in step. Soldiers, but whose? Not one to sit back and wait, I ambled across the street like a tourist coming in late.

As I got to them, I said, in German, "Good morning, how are you?"

One, elder of the two said, "Who are you to ask, leave us alone and move on."

That's the kind of response I was hoping for, "Excuse me, I only asked a polite question. Why are you so rude?" I asked as I squared up to him.

The younger of the two tried to step in between us and defuse the situation but the elder man pushed him out of the way. When he pushed the younger man, his foot slipped and fell against me. Perfect, with the younger man now several feet way and the elder against me, it gave me the opportunity to pick his pocket. Unfortunately there was nothing to pick but an automatic pistol, which didn't surprise me. Slipping the pistol into my pocket I gave the man a push, creating space between us.

As the man got his balance, he threw a punch aimed for my throat. He missed. My counter punch landed square on his jaw. He must have had a glass jaw because he fell like a ton of bricks. The younger man and I locked eyes and both laughed. Shaking his head, he leaned over and checked out his friend.

"I am afraid my friend is out. He may sleep for hours." He said as he pulled the man out of the gutter and laid him on the grass.

Turning to me, he extended his hand, which I shook. As we let our hands drop to our sides he held out his hand again, smiling. Smiling back at him, I pulled the pistol out of my pocket, popped the clip and cleared the chamber before handing it to him.

"Thank you, he would be in serious trouble without his sidearm when we report for duty in a few hours." The young man said.

In English, I said, "I have no doubt about that."

Nodding, the man said, "Ah, American, I should have known. What Division are you with?"

"What makes you think I am a soldier?" I asked, very curious as to his response.

"The way you handled my sergeant and his sidearm tells me you are, or were." He said with a smile.

"Just a tourist, here to buy new BMW's in a few days." I said in all sincerity as I turned toward the hotel entrance. Over the man's shoulder I saw my relief take his place in the shadows, Joseph nodded and gave me a slight salute. Waving goodbye, I left the two men behind and headed upstairs.

We met for breakfast at 6AM. The ladies looked fantastic for the early hour. Soledad made the simple tourist shorts and flowered top look like high fashion, Lae and Janet were right there with her.

As we sat at our usual table, Joseph said, "The two men you met earlier did not linger after the man you put to sleep woke up. The younger man is a Lieutenant and really gave the sergeant a tongue lashing."

Gregor asked, sad that he had missed the fun, "A Lieutenant in what?"

"That is the question, isn't it?" Soledad stated.

"They are not regular army." I said, "Soldiers are not allowed to walk around armed. Gregor, does the Stazi have a combat arms side?"

Gregor, Kurt and Joseph all answered at once, "Yes."

Laughing, Gregor and Joseph bowed to Kurt, who said, "Yes they do, it is the Felix Dzerzhinsky Guards. They are like the palace guard of old. They do have commandos that are trained by the Spetsnaz, tough bunch."

"Do you think that is who our mystery soldiers belong to?" Father Aaron asked.

Before I could say anything, two men walked into the restaurant and took a table close to the windows. One was the lieutenant from earlier, the other was older but not the same man that was with him earlier. This man looked like he was in charge, at least a Captain perhaps a Major.

Kurt picked up his coffee, sat back, took a sip and said, "The Stazi have arrived. It seems our cast of players is complete. Ladies and Gentlemen may I present to you Captain Ernst Lange. I have never met the man, but I have read about him. He is tough and no nonsense.

Cut from the same bolt of cloth as Rommel, orders are orders and he will follow them to the letter."

One of these days I need to learn to curb my impulses, but today isn't the day. Gregor caught the look in my eye so we stood together and walked directly to the Stazi inhabited table.

Coming to a stop directly in front of the Captain, I awaited his acknowledgement. He did not make us wait.

Looking directly into my eyes, he said, "Good morning, may I help you?"

Smiling, I said, "Good morning Captain Lange, let me make introductions, this is Gregor, I am Glen. We would like to invite you to a meeting in the main conference room here at the hotel at 8AM. I think you will find it informative."

"No last names?" he asked with a smile that didn't reach his eyes.

Smiling back I answered, "They are not important. What is important is the meeting."

Lange said, "In that case, we shall attend."

The rest of breakfast flew and 8 o'clock arrived quickly. By exactly 8, everyone was in the room and seated at their designated table. Lange and his Lieutenant were amused that there was a table marked Stazi. Sitting, playing with the name card, Lange had a thoughtful look in his eye. He definitely bears watching.

Soledad pulled me aside and asked, "Are we going to tell them everything? And I mean everything?"

"Yep, I want to see who is surprised and who is smug when we tell them about the radioactive bullets and what is in Frau Hartmann's papers. We all agreed Honey, are you having second thoughts?"

"No, yes, no, oh well, let's get it over with." Soledad said as she sat down next to Lae.

"Let's get the ball rolling!" I said and then proceeded to tell them what we knew. Papers came to light about radioactive material passing through the Schloss in early '45. Gold was recast in the blacksmith shop and was shipped, as it turned out, to the south, we think, destination unknown. A train thought to be carrying gold was attacked by the Luftwaffe and destroyed. The site of the attack is a rail spur north of Munich. The site was cleaned and evidence of the attack was removed, all but expended bullets in the trees around the spur. The fight at the blacksmith shop where we think the SS wiped out a group of patients who were relieving the gold shipments of its contents. The defenders bullets in the blacksmith shop fight were slightly radioactive.

When I made that last statement, several people shifted in their seats, the Mosad, CIA, and the KGB. Our new friends in the Stazi had no reaction.

After a moment of silence, Dov spoke up, "You have evidence of this? Are you willing to share such evidence?"

Soledad fielded that one, "Yes, we have evidence and will make it all available when this investigation is over."

Dov nodded his agreement.

Captain Lange spoke for the first time, "Who put your group in charge of the investigation? You are not part of any of the intelligence agencies."

I took that one, "Captain, it should be very simple. In fact it is so simple I just now figured it out." That drew looks from everyone, including my partners, so I continued, "The Agencies represented in this room did. Every Agency in this room knew of the files, rumors and myths surrounding the gold, and as it turns out a little radioactive material as well, for over thirty years. None of you found anything. But, one of you figured out a way to get us interested. Now that we are involved, we will find the damn gold and radioactive material. We have no interest in keeping any of what we find so we will get out of the way and let you fight over the spoils. We will continue these briefings and will have another Sunday morning at 8AM, right here."

After everyone but us filed out of the room, I had some explaining to do.

Soledad asked the first question, "Have you lost your mind? Why don't we turn over the information we have, buy the damn cars and go home?"

Gregor threw his two cents worth in, "His mind has been gone for years. But I understand why we must find the gold. We know too much, they will never let us leave."

"What do we do now? Keep looking for the shipment?" Lae asked.

"Yep, let's take a drive to the south. I marked some rail crossing that looks promising. We will be back by night fall." I said, ready to hit the road.

Father Aaron and Sister Anna were quiet while we discussed our next step. When another road trip came up, Father Aaron said, "I am afraid we will not be able to follow you, my car will not, in all probability, make the trip."

As he said that, Kurt, Joseph and Janet came back in the room. Kurt spoke up, "Father we have a van, come with us." Noting a look from me, Kurt continued, "That is correct, we are going, someone needs to keep you four out of trouble."

"All our gear is still in the rental." Gregor said, seemingly as ready to hit the road as I am.

Thirty minutes later we were headed south, south west, in a last ditch effort to find which way the gold went.

CHAPTER 21

Paul Franz and his eight man team didn't waste any time after getting their package from Buenos Aries. Their equipment was air freighted overnight by a friendly owner of a freight company and was waiting for them in the freight terminal of the Santa Fe airport. This allowed them to use their own weapons and gear which any operator prefers to do.

Just before noon they left the Santa Fe airport in a rented van while Navaho eyes watched every move. The nine men fit the profile Sani had given his men. However, these men did not follow the expected route upon leaving the airport. Instead of going to a hotel or north toward the Hacienda, they proceeded to Interstate 25 and headed west toward Albuquerque. Ten miles out of Santa Fe their tail dropped off and reported the men were out of the picture.

Fifteen miles out of town, Franz pulled over and double checked their back trail. Reassured they were no longer followed, Franz proceeded to Albuquerque, covering the fifty miles in less than an hour. Waiting for them were three hotel rooms, a new van and a sedan, provided by another friendly citizen. After preparing their weapons and gear, the men ate a meal at a local restaurant, went back to their rooms to sleep and wait for nightfall.

In a room to himself, Franz studied the grounds, the house and the people whose world was going to be turned upside down by his visit. After over two hours of concentration, Franz came to the conclusion the Hacienda was a fortress, he wasn't sure a Brigade could take it.

One of his strong suits was tactical planning, therefore a new plan hatched in his devious mind. After calling his men in their rooms with a new departure time he was ready for some much needed sleep. Reaching up with his right hand to turn out the lamp, the SS Runes were noticeable on his inner arm.

6 OCT, BAVARIA

Elsie wanted to hide from the man coming up her drive. Her heart was racing and fear gripped her with such force it threatened to choke the life out of her. As the Mercedes Benz stopped at the front door, the minion jumped out and ran to the passenger rear door, opening it quickly. As the man inside stepped out, the minion snapped to a Nazi salute and said "Heil Hitler."

Nodding to the man and giving a halfhearted salute back, the passenger stepped onto the porch and rang the bell. Elsie opened the door herself, putting the best smile she could muster on her terrified face.

The Sturmbannfuhrer looked around the entryway, nodded his acceptance and acknowledged Elsie saying, "Good evening Frau von Beitel, I trust you are well."

"Oh yes, thank you for asking, and you?" Elsie asked with all the voice she could find.

"I am well, thank you. You are probably wondering why I have graced you with my presence." He said in his usual manner, condescending to say the least.

"I am sure the Sturmbannfuhrer will tell me when he is ready." She said in almost a whisper.

"Quite so, quite so." He said as he continued to study the inside of the home, "Are you going to offer me refreshments or is that old fashioned tradition gone by the wayside here in Bavaria?"

"Of course, tea and scones will be here shortly." Elsie said, "It is being prepared as we speak."

Grimacing, the man smiled an evil smile and said, "I am afraid I shall not be here long enough to partake. I have a job for you that is of the utmost importance and I did not trust anyone to deliver the details."

Slightly relieved that he was not here to kill her, Elsie said, "I am here for your will Herr Sturmbannfuhrer, just ask."

"Ask? No dear lady, demand." He said as he stared into her eyes, "You will prepare a place to hold four children captive. They will be here in two days. The length of time they will be here will be determined by circumstances beyond our control. No one is to know anything about this or I will take your life. However, if you do as I say, I will forgive your past transgressions and will not vent my anger over those transgressions. Do you understand dear lady?"

It took Elsie a moment to gather a voice, "Yes, I understand." She said, holding her head down.

As he stepped by her, on the way to the door, he stopped, placed his hand under her chin and lifted her head up to look directly into her eyes. Staring into her eyes for a moment, he finally nodded, turned her loose and proceeded to his car. His tail lights were well past her main gate before breath returned to Elsie. Stepping to a window, watching him disappear, fear caused her to shake uncontrollably. The few moments she had locked eyes with him, she felt she was looking into the eyes of Satan's serpent. Hell had touched her soul.

6 Oct, Outside the Church

Sitting across from the Church, Willie, Frederic and Hans passed schnapps back and forth to hold the cold at bay. It wasn't working. All three knew trouble was coming to the Schloss, they were an observant group. The three were undecided on what they should do and to who they should tell their story. Finally Hans stood up and started walking toward the Church. Willie and Frederic jumped up and followed him as fast as their tired cold legs allowed. Pausing for a moment as he reached the door, Hans grabbed the handle and pulled. The door opened, much to his surprise, Hans was not a Church going man.

The three friends walked in side by side, the warmth welcome to their cold old bones. One of the Sisters met them in the foyer and bid them welcome. They told her they came in to pray and light a few candles, the Sister smiled and motioned for them to help themselves. Admiring the figurines they helped make so long ago, they proceeded into the chapel and the magnificent statues that lined the Church walls. They lit candles, talked among them and prayed. After an hour, they stood as one and walked out the front door, their step full of purpose and determination.

6 OCT, SOUTH OF MUNICH

We had stopped at four rail crossing of the river the road followed, to no avail. According to a local map, we had only three more before we were out of Germany. Gregor unloaded our gear for the fifth time and walked to the edge of the water carrying the metal detector. Where we were standing we had a good view of what happened next.

Gregor was walking slowly, messing with the sittings on the detector when he took one too many steps. One second he was walking, the next he was gone. Rushing to where he disappeared, I stopped just short of joining him. Looking into the hole I was relieved to see Gregor looking up at me with a smile on his face.

"Glen! Join me. You will not believe what we found." Gregor shouted at me.

Kurt tied a rope to a tree and I repelled into the hole. Kurt and Father Aaron tossed us flashlights and we got a good look at where we were. It was obvious where we stood, inside a buried rail car. It was on its side and half filled with crates. Most were three feet square and about four feet tall. There were smaller ones about half that size, mixed with the larger crates. Kurt and the Father joined us, bringing pry bars and hammers with them. It's a good thing Gregor packed the tool kit, he remembers everything.

Some of the crates had the Swastika. Others had writing that had faded with time. Picking one of the larger crates with the crooked cross, Kurt pried it open. The contents was shiny, but not in the right way. The crate was full of machined metal, coated in grease. Wiping some of the grease away, Kurt figured out what we had, weapons parts. After opening three or four more crates, we decided we needed to report our find to the Army so they could recover the contents of this car and any other that may be buried with it. Machined steel, not cast gold, what a letdown this was.

Thirty minutes later we had cleaned up, put the tools away, marked the hole with roadside reflectors to warn others and continued to the remaining crossing we wanted to check out. Strikeouts don't just happen in baseball, that's what we did, struck out. The rest of the sites were a bust. Since we had to pass the rail car we found on the way back and there were several hours of daylight left, we decided to look at the site further.

Lae had a blast showing the Sister how to use the metal detector. Their laughter echoed across the stream and put a smile on everyone's face. Soledad nudged me and motioned toward Father Aaron. He was watching the two women as they worked with the detector, laughing as much as they. It only took me a minute to figure out what Soledad wanted me to see. There was only one way to describe the look on Father Aarons face, love. Leaning toward Soledad, I started to ask a question but she cut me off.

"He can love, but not in the physical sense." She said with a smile.

"If I were him and had that look, I would see what it would take to become a Lutheran." I said, smiling back.

Gregor walked over to me and said in a low voice, "We have visitors, three men in the trees due north."

"I wonder if they are with the four men sitting at the side of the road to the south." I ask in response.

Soledad saw the concerned looks on our faces but she did not give us away. She is a real trooper, continuing to watch the fun as if nothing amiss was going on.

Gregor got Kurt's attention and the two of them started walking with a purpose toward the trees. I tapped Father Aaron on the shoulder and had him follow me to the road. I guess none of our observers wanted to chat, before any of us got halfway to the men, they loaded up in their cars and hauled ass.

Meeting at our rides, Gregor said, "One of the men I have seen before, he is the Stazi Lieutenant we met at the restaurant."

"I don't know the men on the road, but I bet they are related." I added.

Suddenly, a squeal made us turn to the women. Soledad and Sister Anna had hammers in their hands while Lae was aiming a flashlight at the ground. They were motioning for us to come to them, jumping up and down like kids. The four of us rushed over to them, anxious to see what they found. As we approached them, Soledad held up her hand to stop us.

"Easy guys don't fall in, here is another car and you won't believe what is in it." Lae said with a gleam in her eye.

From the looks of it, the ladies had found another car that was as close to the surface as the other. Using the hammers to beat a hole in the side of the car, about the size of a basketball, the ladies hit the jack pot. The flashlight reflected off bars of gold scattered among several unopened crates. Trying to hold out enthusiasm, Gregor, Kurt, Father Aaron and I started widening the hole to allow entrance.

We retrieved the rope we had used to repel into the other car. Tying it to a tree, Kurt repelled down first. I was starting to follow him when he stopped me.

"Wait, let me check something." Kurt yelled up at me.

Nodding, I stepped back and watched as he went from one open crate to another. He was careful to keep what was in the crates away from him. Finally he pulled himself up out of the hole.

"Something is strange down there. There are gold bars scattered around, but not enough to fill the open crates. Also, there is a fine ash everywhere. It is coating everything down there. Some of the open crates are half full of the ash as well. I do not want anyone going down there without some type of dust mask." Kurt told to us.

"Obviously we don't have the right equipment with us to explore and remove whatever is down there." Soledad said.

Lae said, "We do not want to leave an open hole for someone to fall into, do we? Not to mention all it takes to see the gold is to look down."

Father Aaron said, "I know where we can get what we need without going back to Munich. There is a hardware store not far from the Church where we can get everything we need, including more lights."

Since the Church and promised hardware store is not far, as the crow flies, Gregor and I volunteered to stay while the others went for supplies. Besides, we had our weapons and, since we hadn't eaten since lunch, were in no mood to be disturbed by anyone. We did have something to talk about to spend the time, our new BMW's, which we are looking forward to if we ever finish this quest.

In less than an hour the group made it back. They brought plenty of rope, lights and thankfully, food. We ate while we plotted our assault on the buried box car. Everyone had their idea on how we should proceed, unfortunately we got preempted.

"Glen." Soledad said in a voice I recognize as her "oh crap" voice.

Quickly looking up at her, I followed her eyes until I was looking eye to eye with the Stazi Captain and fourteen of his closest friends. His friends were also carrying some nice specimens of H&K submachine guns.

Well hell.

When they got all of our attention, they motioned for us to come together as a group. I recognized the ill-mannered sergeant from earlier. He was eyeing the ladies in a way I did not like.

The Captain finally said, "If you do as I say, everyone will be able to retire to their comfortable hotel beds tonight. If you do not, you will find yourself sleeping in this hole for the rest of your short lives. Do you understand?"

"We understand. What are you planning to do?" Kurt asked.

"We are going to relieve you of your find. Afterward, if you behave, we will leave and you will never see us again." the Captain replied with a smile.

Three of his men started rounding us up so they could keep a close eye on us. Gregor and I both had our shoulder holsters on but knew we didn't stand a chance against so many, especially with the ladies present.

Apparently we weren't moving fast enough for the Sergeant, he grabbed Soledad's arm and gave her a push. Needless to say, I didn't like that. Three of the men drew their machinegun bolts back as I took a step and got between the bastard and Soledad. The Sergeant sneered at me and drew his finger over his throat in a slashing motion.

Turning from him I faced the Captain and said, "If he touches any of the women again, I will kill him. Do you understand?"

Smiling a mischievous smile, the Captain surprised me by saying, "We might as well get this over with. I cannot control his actions to that degree." Turning to his men he said, "Shall we have some fun before we work?"

The men cheered and started placing bets, well a few. It seemed no one wanted to bet on me. That is until they let Kurt and Gregor place bets. While they were busy, I took off my jacket, being careful to take the shoulder holsters off at the same time, concealing my pistols in the jacket and placing it in the front seat of our car.

Across the way, the Sergeant stripped his gear, removed his outer shirt leaving a skin tight tee shirt. He then stepped away from his cohorts and started flexing his muscles in some kind of weird dance. His men cheered him on like this was a prize fight, not a fight that could end in someone's death. Physically, we looked pretty evenly matched. I have him on reach, being a couple of inches taller. He had a few pounds on me so things should balance out.

After a minute of watching him, I turned to the Captain and asked, "What are the rules?"

"My dear fellow, there are no rules." He answered with a smile on his face and a gleam in his eye.

I turned back toward my opponent as my group yelled a warning. While my back was turned, he had picked up a fallen limb and was coming behind me at a rapid pace, planning on laying me out with the first blow.

As I turned, taking it in instantly, I ducked the blow. Since he was swinging right to left, catching his right arm in my left I gave him a push. With his momentum and my push, he stumbled forward and to the left, trying hard to keep his balance. He tripped on a root and fell, face first into the brush at the base of a tree. He came up red faced and angry. I had no intention of a prolonged fight with this man. He is a professional, extremely fit and trained to kill using anything, everything, or nothing. Killing me was first and foremost on his mind.

Stupid me, I let him get up, brush himself off and gather his wits. Turning to me I could see the flame in his eye and murder in his heart. I decided to end it now and not give our audience the long fight they were hoping for. Fit and trained he may be, but he had a temper and I was going to use his temper to end this engagement.

Roaring like a bull, he ran forward with his arms spread, acting like he was going to get me in a bear hug. I had seen this move before and was ready for it. His plan was to make me brace and defend the move, at which time he would change his stance in mid stride and launch his body, feet first into my mid-section. He did exactly that, sidestepping him, I brought my elbow into his face as he landed beside me. Blood splattered everywhere as his nose flattened against his face, stunning him. Landing stretched out, I immediately placed a knee in his chest, pinning him. With my left hand poised to strike a killing blow, hitting the broken nose with the heel of my hand in a fashion that would drive the broken bone into his brain, ending the fight and his life, I looked into the Captains eyes.

"Captain, I won't kill him if you agree to tie him up until we are out of the picture." I said in a matter of fact tone.

Turning to two of his men he motioned toward us. Stepping forward, they ran to us and reached for the Sergeant. Stepping out of the way, I was a bit surprised they took him away and not me.

"Agreed, now I want you to agree to something." He responded.

"I am listening." I answered, intrigued at what it might be, especially since we were at a big disadvantage.

"I will keep him restrained if you promise not to interfere with our retrieval of the contents below us." He said in an even tone.

"Agreed, help yourself. We will sit under the shade and watch. We will not lift a finger to hinder or help." I said, looking toward my friends for agreement, which I got.

With that, the seven of us made our way to a group of large trees and made ourselves at home in their shade. The way we sat, one man could watch us. The Captain noticed our arraignments and nodded his approval.

For three hours we watched the men bring up crate after crate until the boxcar below was emptied. While some opened the crates and unloaded the gold bars, others started looking for boxcars that might be attached to the one we found. Another two hours went by before the search was called off, no other boxcars were found.

While the men worked reloading the bars into back packs for transport, we noticed the small volume of gold compared to the size and number of crates. We also noticed the crates were mostly filled with ash. It coated the men that were in the boxcar and laid a fine dust on everyone involved in the repacking. We sat up wind and didn't get any on us, which we were thankful later.

At the back of my mind, something kept nagging at me about the ash. Turning to Soledad, I asked, "Honey, in all the material we went through, especially the files we got from Mrs. Whistle Britches, was there any mention of the type of radioactive material that showed up at the Castle?"

"No, I don't believe so, but several Geiger Counter reading showed there had been something radioactive present at one time." Soledad answered with a puzzled look on her lovely face.

"Was or is?' I asked. Seeing a puzzled look on everyone's face, I continued, "The ash, something is nagging at me about the ash. The men coming in and out of the hole are coated with it. They almost look like old pictures of men coming out of coal mines in Kentucky and Tennessee."

Kurt added, "Coal, the brown coal used many parts of southern Germany has very small traces of uranium and other radioactive materials. It's not enough to be harmful but people are warned to keep the ash bins cleaned out and the ash disposed of properly."

"Could the coal ash generated by the furnaces at the Castle, in concentration and enough volume, cause the reading that are in the files? Can it cause the reading we got the other day?" I asked the group.

Gregor said, "I think it could. And if it can, did someone use the fear of radioactive materials to aid them in removing the gold?"

Standing up, I said, "There is one way to test our theory."

Motioning to the man who was guarding us, I walked over to him and told him I needed to talk to the Captain. After eyeing me cautiously, he nodded and walked to the Captain, who was supervising the packing of the bars. They talked for a moment before the Captain turned and walked to me.

"We are almost finished and will be on our way shortly." He said as he walked up to me. "The private said you needed to speak to me?"

"I will get to the point. We think your men are in great danger. If the ash that is all over most of your men is what we think it is, then they certainly are. We have an instrument in the van that will prove or disprove our theory. May I get it and run a few tests?"

"If this is a ploy to try to do us harm or escape, you know what will happen, don't you?" he asked.

"There is no doubt in my mind." I answered.

"Go, get your instrument and run your tests, but be careful, I will be watching as will three of my men." He answered while motioning for his men to follow me.

Quickly stepping to the rear of the van, I opened it, grabbed the box that contained the Geiger Counter and rushed to the Captain. Opening the box, I showed him what it was. He paled when he recognized what I was holding. Running the background test, I got hits of 10-20 CPM, normal back ground radiation.

Turning to the piles of ash left by empting the crates in the search for the gold, the counter went nuts. Upon hearing the Geiger Counter, the Captain ran to my side and held out his hand. Figuring he had more experience in such things, I complied. We went from man to man, taking reading, until we checked every man.

"Captain," I said in a serious tone, "your men need to get out of those clothes and in the river, now. Everyone who has ash on him has to go in. At least the water will dilute it enough as to not be harmful downstream. Then, when you get back home, radiation treatments may be needed."

I turned to our little group and yelled at Kurt, "Get out of those clothes and in the river, the ash is radioactive." I will give our German friend credit. He turned into a streaker in under a minute.

Giving orders as fast as he could, he had his men strip, pile their clothes with the ash and dump it all back in the hole. After as much as could be accumulated was back in the ground, he had them place markers telling of the danger. They weren't much, sticks with paper sheets on them, but at least it was something to warn innocents that may find the hole.

Standing next to me, still wet from a quick bath, the Captain asked, "Why did you warn us about the radiation? You could have said nothing thus letting us get sick and possibly die."

"Sir, we have no ill feelings for you and your men, well, all but maybe one," I replied with a smile, "You gave your word that no harm would come to us if we stayed out of your way. We did and you will honor your word."

"How do you know I will not have you shot before we leave?" he asked with a smile of his own.

Cocking my head to the side, I answered, "If you were going to shoot us, you wouldn't have wasted a man to guard us while you worked, you would have shot us and put him to work. But mainly, I think you are a man of your word, no matter to whom you gave it."

Shaking his head, he smiled and said, "I hope we never meet as advisories again, it would be a shame to kill a man such as you." Then, motioning to his men, they loaded up, some in their skivvies, and headed into the forest, all but the Captain and two men, armed with submachine guns.

For a moment I thought I had read him wrong, that he was going to shoot us anyway. But the men walked to our van and car and emptied a clip each into the engine compartments. The men did a great job of hitting anything that could spew liquids or emit clouds of steam. Turning to us and saluting, the three men disappeared into the forest.

Lae looked at Gregor and asked, "Did you get the insurance coverage when you rented them?"

"No, Glen told me it was not worth the money." He said as they all looked at me.

I caught the glimpse and laugh between Father Aaron and Sister Anna. Soledad joined in, along with Kurt, Lae and Gregor, to make the laughter unanimous. Well, I have always wanted to make people laugh, seems I'm getting pretty good at it.

"Well, it wouldn't have covered machine gun fire anyway." I said as we grabbed a few things, including my Colts and started walking. "Besides," I said as I turned to Kurt, "I'm not the one wrapped in a woman's scarf."

"At least they took pity on me and loaned me clothing instead of laughing at my lack of outerwear." Kurt shot back.

Gregor then exclaimed, "Wait, we did not collect our winnings from the fight!"

He almost ducked the punch Lae threw his way, while the rest of us laughed.

Father Aaron to me and said, "It appears moving day will have to be postponed. When we get back I will let my friend at the Guesthouse know not to expect us."

"Thanks Father, I'm not sure when we will be able to make the move." I responded as we started up the road.

As we walked, I started calculating the amount of gold the Stazi walked away with. If my estimate was even close, it was less than one half of a metric tonne. When we get to our hotel we will need to put our heads together on things, I am coming up with a few new theories. I should have known, as we walked, all of us were thinking along the same lines.

The Sun had set while we walked, darkness was setting in and fatigue was taking its toll. Trying to lift our spirits Gregor started singing a Russian marching song, I countered with an American cadence while Kurt started a German drinking song. The three of us hadn't noticed our friends lagged behind, trying to put a little distance between themselves and three off key vocalists. Within a few miles, a farmer in an old stake bed truck offered us a ride providing we stopped the terrible noise.

CHAPTER 22

We made it to our hotel a little after 2AM. Tired was not a strong enough word for what we felt. Ten minutes after walking in the front door, all four of us men slept where we sat. The ladies made it to the beds in their room, draping themselves over the beds fully clothed.

Surprisingly, all were in attendance for a full breakfast at 10AM. Rested, full and with a great cup of coffee in front of us, we started discussing the previous day's events. The restaurant was almost empty and we sat at a table in the corner. It was as private as it gets.

Sister Anna surprised us all with the first direct question of the morning. "Where is the rest of the gold? Those men did not walk off with five metric tonnes of gold."

"You are so right Sister. It was more like a thousand pounds at the most." Soledad replied.

"I was thinking 800-900 pounds." I said as I looked over my coffee cup at Soledad.

Sister Anna interjected with a huge smile, "I think Soledad is closer than you are Glen. After all women know more about gold than men."

Gregor laughed and said, "But, Sister, men know more about carrying gold for the women."

Lae's wadded up napkin bounced off his forehead and landed in his coffee. Reaching in and removing the soggy mess, Gregor was tempted to toss it back. The look on Lae's face prompted him to toss it into his empty plate.

Kurt leaned forward and said, "Let's use the thousand pounds as a mark. That still leaves four and a half metric tonnes of gold unaccounted for.

Gregor poured more coffee and said, "I want to know about radioactive material that was delivered and later hauled off. Where did it go? Is that what everyone is really after and using gold as excuse?"

"That makes as much sense as anything we have come up with so far. What if the gold was a smoke screen for a large quantity of fusion material that went missing and the agencies are looking for it, not the gold." Father Aaron said, causing all of us to sit up and rethink what we thought we knew.

Sipping more coffee, I said, "Perhaps it is the other way around. Why the ash if there was more dangerous material available? Was this purely a ploy to hide the fact someone was stealing millions of dollars of gold from the SS?"

Soledad summed it up for us, "We have two trains of thought, gold as a decoy to move radioactive bomb making material or radioactive ash to hide the theft of millions in gold. We need to determine which theory is the truth and pursue it until we solve this once and for all."

Lae said, "It is unfortunate the next briefing is Sunday. It could prove entertaining to hit the agencies with our theories."

Gregor and I locked eyes before he said, "I think we should do what we must to settle this before then."

"I agree," I said, "If one of them is hiding something and they do not want us to find anything, they may take actions that are detrimental to our health."

Kurt then said, "You make a good point. Let's go to my headquarters and search through the files once more before we take the next logical step."

Soledad asked, "Which is?"

Smiling, Kurt answered, "The Schloss, shovels and strong backs."

With that, we loaded up and headed back to BND headquarters and more long hours searching files. I whispered to Soledad the idea of a repeat in the file room we checked out earlier, my ribs may be back to normal in a few days.

7 Oct, New Mexico

Franz timed the trip out to the second. His men were in position five minutes before the children would be released from their classes. Franz's new plan did have one compromise. He could take the three younger children and leave the older behind. The older girl would not be released for two more hours thus unattainable.

Cars were lined up on the curb, awaiting the onslaught of children. With the school facing east, the Sun was already casting shadows where the children would come out of the building and about half way to the curb. The distance from the front steps of the school to the curb measured thirty meters, plenty of room for his vehicles to operate. Both vehicles would come in from the north making their attack from right to left as one faced the school. While the van jumped the curb, the sedan would stay in formation on the left side of the van, blocking the van from defensive fire while providing covering fire in case the children's escorts open up on them.

One of the cars sitting at the curb was filled with four, ex-military Navaho whose job was escorting the children home. They were not, however, picking up the children. Ever since the Stazi agents were turned over to the U.S. Department of State, Sani enacted three different scenarios to getting the children home, rotating them weekly. The three unknowing targets left the school building through the gymnasium and loaded up in a four door, four wheel drive, Ford pickup truck. As they pulled out of the school grounds, the car with the four men was to pick up the tail, watching for anyone dumb enough to follow the children.

As the bell sounded and the children rushed from the building, Franz franticly tried to spot their targets. Several looked similar and he almost jumped the gun, but his training held him in place until his targets were identified. Unfortunately for him they never appeared. Confused, he jumped out of the van and approached the sedan, intent to ask them if they saw anyone that remotely looked like their targets.

Just before he arrived, he heard the deep rumble of a big V-8 drive by going south. Looking at the truck, he looked directly at one of the children whose picture was in his hand. He quickly noticed the other two in the seat beside her. Training or not, Franz knew he was running out of time and disappointing the Sturmbannfuhrer would mean death, he started yelling and pointing at the truck. Running back to the driver's door of the van, he jumped in and pursued the truck, the sedan right behind him.

All of his actions were noticed by the four Navaho escorts who quickly followed the sedan. The front passenger of the Navaho vehicle got on the CB radio and informed the driver of the truck of his followers. Calls then went out notifying Police, Sheriff's Deputy's, and anyone else with a gun, of the situation. While the van tried to close on the truck carrying the children, over fifty Law Enforcement Officers and concerned citizens concentrated in the crossroads the truck would pass in an effort to lose its pursuers.

The man driving the 4x4 was a professional driver. His time in the Marine Corps was spent mainly driving Generals around, in peace as well as in war. His partner in the front passenger seat stayed on the radio giving status reports as fast as they passed cross roads and landmarks. At the edge of town was a crossroad that went to a planned development, which wasn't started as of yet. This crossroad is where the first line of defense was to be.

In case they were followed past the cross roads, the plan was to turn on an old dirt road about a mile short of the road that went to the main house. In fact, it was the same road the Stazi operatives took the night they were captured. This was a last resort move. Claymores were set on both sides of the path at an interval that would devastate any pursuit that had the misfortune to be more than two seconds behind the 4x4. The chase did not get that far.

The van had a hard time staying up with the 4x4, not enough horses under the hood. Motioning for the sedan to pass, Franz put his faith in the abilities in the man driving it. In a matter of seconds, the sedan was closing and the front passenger was firing his H&K out of the window, trying to hit the tires on the truck.

So intent was his concentration on the 4x4, Franz did not see the sedan following them until it pulled alongside the van. Glancing down at the passenger as the car passed, he did a double take when he realized the man had rolled down his window and was pointing a pistol at his front tire. Before he could react the man fired two rounds into his front tire causing him to almost lose control of the van. Accelerating past the stricken van, the sedan continued pursuit of the sedan carrying Franz's men. Franz kept the van upright and continued, at a much slower rate, to follow.

Murphy's Law has a way to totally screwing up anything and everything. Today was no exception. As the 4x4 made the last curve, only three hundred yards from the crossroads and a train load of firepower, three of the 9MM rounds fired from the H&K found the right rear tire of the 4x4. That in its self was bad enough, but three more found the deferential housing and shattered the casing, causing the left rear axle to slide out of the housing. Suddenly there wasn't anything holding the rear of the truck off the ground and it slid to a stop, two hundred and fifty yards from safety.

The two guardians made sure the children were on the floorboard of the back where there was protection from gunfire. One tossed a blanket over them in case of flying glass. Both men had 1911 Colts, knew how to use them and were in position to hold off the attackers until help could arrive from the crossroads. The position of the truck blocked direct fire from the crossroads to the sedan and the pursuers, making the crossroad position ineffective.

The four men in the sedan did not hesitate to attack. Sliding to a stop behind the truck they poured murderous fire into the 4x4. The back window disappeared under the onslaught showering the blanket the children were hiding under with broken glass. The tail gate took a terrible pounding as well as the bricks in the bed of the truck. The Senora had plans to build a planter out of those bricks but she will have to get more. The bricks saved the lives of the children, providing a barrier that prevented a single round from penetrating into the lower passenger compartment where the children were hiding.

However in their haste, they all fired at the same time, thus emptying their weapons at the same time, not smart. While they franticly reloaded two things happened that was bad for their health. The sedan carrying four pissed off Navaho arrived on the scene and two equally pissed of Navaho opened fire with the 1911's.

The shock of coming under such unexpected and intense fire broke the men's reserve. Two died as they tried to move into position to fire upon the sedan thus giving the Navaho in the truck clean shots. Another crossed over to the other side when he broke cover and ran toward the 4x4. This gave four of the Navaho clear shots and pissed off Navaho don't miss. The last man lost his nerve and tried to run. He got about thirty yards before a .30 caliber hunting rifle ended his run by taking his right leg out from under him. The Deputy who made the shot had a good story to tell for years, two hundred and fifty yards at a moving target is always a good story. Officers of the Law are notorious of ribbing each other at every opportunity. He was ready to have something else to talk about besides his nose dive in front of the Plaza a few days ago when responding to a shooting.

Franz took this all in as he rounded the curve. Not liking the scene before him, he tried to turn around and escape. The Navaho in the sedan had not forgotten about the van. They piled in their car and gave chase. They were not alone. Police cruisers from three agencies joined them. The damaged van only got a few hundred yards before it was too riddled with bullets to move. The four men in the back who were trying to give cover fire for their escape lay dead. Paul Franz knew what he had to do as the van came to a stop. As the officers approached the wounded van, one last shot rang out.

The children were loaded quickly in a cruiser and taken home. Fortunately they heard the firing but did not see the results. Later that evening, all three demanded to see the men who were in the 4x4 with them. The Senora finally gave in and asked the two men to come to the main house. The two men were sitting in the dining room drinking coffee with the Senora when the children came in.

Kyle walked up and shook their hand in turn then said, "Thank you for protecting my sister and our friend. You know how girls are, needing protection all the time."

One of the men said, "You are most welcome little warrior. We could not have been successful without your help." The other man nodded his approval.

Kyle's face lit up with the praise, swelled his chest and walked to his Great Grandmother and sat in her lap.

Jennifer was next. She just smiled at the men and gave them both a hug before joining Kyle.

Rebecca was entirely another matter. She walked up to the two, looked them up and down before saying, "When my daddy gets back, he will let me prove to you that I can shoot." With that statement she turned and walked out of the room, headed to bed. Kyle and Jennifer hurried along behind her.

After the children left the room, the Senora asked the men, "What was happening with the children during the chase and shootout?"

They looked at each other and laughed before one said, "Jennifer followed instructions and stayed down, Rebecca kept demanding a weapon while Kyle kept telling his sister to put her butt on the floor, shut up and stay down."

The other said, "Your Great Grandchildren remind us of their parents. Rebecca much like her mother, strong willed and adventurous. Kyle is like his father, adventurous in his own right but always protecting the women."

Consuelo could do nothing but agree and laugh along with two of her favorite nephews.

Back in Santa Fe, one person wasn't laughing, he was in surgery to save his right leg. In the waiting area sat over a dozen officers of the Law, a couple of lawyers, a few reporters and two quiet Navaho. Everyone was waiting for him to come out of recovery so he could be interviewed and interrogated. Not necessarily in that order.

Three hours later the suspect was wheeled into recovery. The nurses kept everyone out until the surgeon said it was ok for him to have visitors. The officers had men sit watch until they could go in, their job, keep everyone else out. It almost worked.

Two hours after surgery, a small nurse went in the room and stayed over thirty minutes. The officers were getting s little antsy until the nurse finally left the room, busily writing on a clip board. As the officers settled back down to wait, the nurse rounded the corner at the end of the ward, shuck the white coat and hit the stairs. Coming out the side exit of the building, Sani smiled as he got in his new pickup truck and headed to the Hacienda.

The Senora listened intently to the information Sani produced from the wounded criminal. It was clear to her there was much more at play than she or John thought. When Sani finished the report and left the room, Consuelo picked up the phone and placed a call to a special number in Munich. The first thing John did as he finished talking to his Love was book a flight to Berlin. The second thing was to drive to Soledad and Glen's hotel.

CHAPTER 23

The little girl sitting with her parents across the waiting area from me was trying to keep a straight face. I, on the other hand, was trying to make her laugh. Keeping my head straight, I would look to the left then roll my left eye to the right keeping my right eye looking left until my left eye was facing right then my right eye followed and looked to the right. It gave a strange appearance and made most kids laugh. She was a tough cookie.

I was determined to make her laugh before the rest of our group met me for a late dinner. We were all beat after a day of digging in the archives of the BND and coming up with nothing new. A hot shower and a late dinner, we had decided, should make us feel somewhat better.

My antics to make her laugh ended when John Kirkpatrick walked into the restaurant. The look on his face got my attention immediately and I rose to meet him.

Offering my hand, I greeted him with, "John, this is an unexpected pleasure."

With a half-smile, he said, "It is for us both dear boy, for us both. Where is the rest of your merry little band?"

"They will be here any minute. John, I don't like the look on your face, what's up?" I asked, heart frozen.

"Everyone is fine at home. No bloody noses or scraped shins to report, if that is what you are worried about." John said, his tone softening somewhat.

My heart thawed and started pumping again so I could answer him, "As long as everyone at home is healthy, we can handle anything."

"Handle what?" Soledad asked as she walked past me and gave John a kiss on the cheek. "How are you John, it's been a long time."

"We need to talk." John said in a flat tone that got everyone's attention, the rest of our band walked up in time to hear his statement.

"We need to eat, let's do both. Won't you join us?" Soledad asked with a quizzical look in her eye.

A table for eight was ready for us within minutes, at the back of the dining room. The manager knew of our need for privacy so he held this table in reserve for us. Coffee and appetizers were ordered and consumed, small talk filled the time.

After ordering the entrees, Soledad started the ball rolling, "John, something is amiss. You have our undivided attention."

Boy did he ever. After a ten minute narrative we knew everything that had gone on in New Mexico, what John had done in Berlin, and his new theory, which he planned to prove with another trip to Berlin.

Janet spoke up first, "The children are ok? They are not in anymore danger are they?"

John answered with, "Consuelo has locked down the area. The children will not leave the Hacienda until this is resolved. There is not a safer place on the planet than with her."

Soledad then stated, "You knew of the dangers and yet you allowed the men to get that close to our children?"

Since she was sitting next to John, he was within reach. Thankfully I was as well. A split second before Soledad's right fist started its journey to John chin, I softly reached over and touched Soledad's arm.

"Soledad," I said in a soft voice, "He would never put you or our children in harm's way. He was working with Sani the whole time to keep our kids safe."

"How do you know?" she demanded, glaring at me.

"Because he is your Grandfather." I flatly stated.

She sat there, stunned, looking first at me, then John, then back to me. The clenched fist, which had not been seen by anyone but me, slowly opened and she relaxed.

"I thought you had caught on at my estate when you were in the den looking at pictures. The picture of Soledad's parents kept your attention for several minutes." John said to me.

"You and my Grandmother? Unbelievable!" Soledad stammered.

"In this case it was my son and her daughter. Consuelo and I met years before our children were married. She was just widowed and I had been a widower for several years when we met. Our friendship grew until it is so much more." John said with growing passion in his words.

"Why didn't you marry?" Janet asked?

"She would not leave her mountains and I would not leave government work. However, when this is over, I will once more ask for her hand." John said with conviction.

Soledad has calmed down a bit, saying, "When this is over, we need to talk."

"Of course my dear, of course." John said with a tear in his eye.

Soledad stood, John stood to meet her. Looking into his eyes, Soledad started crying a river. Reaching out, Soledad held a Grandfather she never knew she had. Looking around, there wasn't a dry eye in the room, much less at our table. Our waiters held our entrees until the tears were drying and we were all seated. The food was superb. The conversation turned to the mission at hand.

Cognac is one of the few things the French got right. The aroma and the slow burn of this fine liquor help open the creative parts of the civilized mind. Well, it sounds good anyway. After dinner we adjourned to our room to further our discussions and planning while enjoying the soothing beverage.

John had listened to our adventures and our theories while swirling the cognac and sipping occasionally. Finally he said, "In a few short days, you have learned more, disproved more and opened more questions than all our agencies combined have done in thirty years." shifting in his chair, he leaned over to the table where we had laid out the files and continued, "before me sits the accumulative work of numerous field agents, dozens of analysts, several scientists and more than a couple of politicians. Yet in light of what you have told me, it is rubbish."

We looked at each other, pleased at the compliment he had given us. He then shot us down.

"However, your theories are just that, theories until proven. I will tell you this, my interest in all this was the gold. I knew nothing of the radiation connection until it came to light in the documents brought to us recently. In fact, you were the first to have a crack at them when Frau Hartmann brought them to you." Turning to Soledad he added, "Frau Hartmann is actually one of your cousins my dear, I will be happy to introduce you to Abby later. The real Frau Hartmann died several years ago but her story and documents are all true as far as we know."

John's brow deepened, he took another sip of the cognac before saying, "Someone very powerful and evil has knowledge of weapons grade material being moved through the Schloss during this time frame. Or the same person is using radioactive material to hide the theft of gold from the SS. Both are good theories, the question, which is the correct one?"

Father Aaron spoke up saying, "And, who is The Someone?"

One question gnawed at me so I had to ask, "Why the fake Hartmann? Why not just give us the information with everything else?"

Gregor answered for John, saying, "The more varied the sources, the more believable the story."

John smiled and said, "Quite right dear boy, isn't that always the case?"

We all nodded in agreement as we swirled our cognac. All but Sister Anna, she had one glass of cognac and was asleep in her chair.

7 Oct, Bavaria

Hans wiped the oil off the old rifle, handling the weapon as if it were fragile. His cloth started dry but as it soaked up the oil, it turned soggy and slightly red. Hans noticed the red and grimaced in shame at letting this old friend rust away. With shaking fingers, he reassembled the weapon, taking care to assemble it the way his old sergeant trained him to do so long ago. Setting the rifle on the table, fully assembled he reached for the ammo box that was stored with the rifle. Opening the box, he counted out his stores of ammo, sixteen 7.92 cartridges. Not enough to fight a war, but perhaps enough to defend a Schloss.

Looking at the clock on his table, Hans decided he needed the few hours sleep he could get before meeting Willie and Fredric at 5AM for breakfast. As he placed his head on his pillow his thoughts drifted to his friends ammo count, he hoped they had more than sixteen rounds or it could be a short defense.

In their respective rooms, Willie and Fredric went through the same ritual as Hans. Overall, the old warriors had three Karabiner 98k rifles, thirty three 7.92 rounds for their rifles, two rusty bayonets and a foggy pair of binoculars. Not much in modern warfare, but perhaps enough to turn the tide during a skirmish.

7 Oct, East-West German border

The Sun disappeared below the mountains as Dieter Koch sat on pins and needles waiting for his commando team to arrive at the forward command post. For years the East had a route in the area that allowed passage back and forth, unchallenged. That route came in very handy for operations such as this. Having never served in the field, he was shocked at the appearance of Captain Lange and his men. The men were dirty, ragged and some only partially clothed. The only causality seemed to be one man with a swollen, battered face.

Koch's men were relieving the commandos of their packs, placing them in the back of a truck for transport, supposedly, to East Berlin. As the trucks tail light disappeared, Koch approached the Captain.

"You did well Captain, my superiors will be pleased." Koch said with a smile, extending his hand. Lange ignored his hand, turned away and with the shuffle of an exhausted man, joined his men in the small chow hall.

Koch couldn't wait to place the call announcing his success at recovering the gold. Stepping into the command bunker, he ran everyone out and placed his call on a secure line.

The phone was answered in one ring, the voice at the other end was the correct one, but Koch always dreaded talking to the man. He was scared to death of him.

"Koch, this better be you and you had better have good news." The voice on the other end said without preamble.

"Yes, my team has recovered the gold. It is in transport now to your designated location." Koch said with a bit of a stammer.

"Tell me how it happened, leave nothing out." The voice demanded.

Koch took five minutes and told everything he knew, as he finished the voice on the other end exploded.

"You fool! Fifteen men cannot carry the gold in question, nor could fifty. I leave one simple task for you and you are too incompetent to fulfill.

Trying to calm the other man down, Koch said, "I will send them back to get the rest, we will make sure we get it all this time."

"You will do as I say or you will not see another sunrise. Tell the garrison commander these men are traitors and your orders are to have them shot immediately. I will take care of the gold myself." The voice screamed.

"Shot, I cannot do that!" Koch stuttered.

"You will or you shall join them." the voice said in a cold manner.

"Yes sir, it shall be done. I will then return to Berlin and await your orders Herr Sturmbannfuhrer." Koch said to a dead line. Staring at the hand piece, Koch wondered again how he had gotten involved with this crazy, but powerful, old man who insisted on holding on to a rank bestowed on him by a long dead regime.

The Sturmbannfuhrer was visibly shacking as he placed the hand piece on the cradle. Things were not going according to plan, not at all. The team he had sent to kidnap the American children had not reported in, they were three hours late, now this. With the loose ends taken care of at the Stazi, or will after Koch dies before dawn, he decided to use his own resources to recover his lost goods.

Koch rushed to the commander of the garrison that made this check point home and gave him orders to kill all the commandos who came across the border a few moments ago. Staring at him in disbelief, the young Captain took a moment to gather his thoughts before obeying, but obey he did.

His face hurting, the sergeant left his brothers and went looking for the aid station and something to make his face feel better. As he rounded one of the buildings he saw the garrison commander rush out of the command bunker carrying a rifle yelling at his men to assemble.

The darkness came to his aid, allowing him to get close enough to hear the Captains orders, arrest the commandos then execute them as enemies of the State.

Thirty seconds later the sergeant was in front of Captain Lange telling him everything he heard. Not wasting any time, Lange had his men outside and headed toward the mountain trail they had just used to get into East Germany, now they were headed back to the West and hopefully safety.

The garrison troops arrived at the building that housed the commandos only to find it empty, the young Captain correctly assumed where they went. He was not experienced in combat however and his men paid for it.

As with any retreating force, you leave a rear guard to slow any pursuit. Lange placed four men, led by his Lieutenant, in key positions to buy time needed to get the rest across a dangerous pass. After crossing, the main force could cover the rear guard as they went through the pass.

Young and inexperienced, his Lieutenant made a key mistake. Wanting to assure his men were in position, he exposed himself, only for a moment, to the lead elements of the pursuit. Just as he was getting back to his position, three 7.62 rounds tore into the young man, throwing him against rocks at the top of the pass.

While one of the men went to help his Lieutenant, the other three poured murderous fire into the hapless garrison troops who were standing in the open on the trail. The commando threw the wounded officer over his shoulder in a fireman's carry and hightailed it across the pass and under the defensive fire of his brothers. Taking the wounded man from his transport as soon as they crossed the pass, two commandos started working on his wounds while the remainder of the men poured fire into the ranks of their pursuit.

Lange placed his hand on the man that had carried the young man to safety is a gesture of gratitude. The commando smiled at his Captain, turned and added his weapon to the onslaught. After what seemed like an eternity, the remaining three commandos made it across the pass. Not wasting any time, Lange had his men several kilometers from the border and outside a small West German village within a couple of hours.

They young man was not doing well and needed major medical treatment as soon as possible. Handing his weapons to his sergeant, Lange knew what he had to do, after all, this village would not have the help needed, but it would have a telephone.

Koch saw the troops returning from the pass, far fewer men were returning than left in pursuit. Asking one of the soldiers where his Captain was, all he got was a blank, bloody stare as the man pushed past him without saying a word. No officers or senior NCO's were among the men who returned. No one knew what happened just that many were killed or missing. Seeing he was not going to get anything out of the returning men, he went to his car planning to leave the mess behind.

His driver stepped out of the car and walked around to open his door as were the norm. Too late Koch saw the sidearm in the man's hand. Sightless eyes watched the car disappear into the night.

CHAPTER 24

It was just past 8PM and we decided to adjourn for the evening and have dinner. I don't know why we were taking the time to look at the menu. Everyone knew it well after eating here as much as we have.

Sensing someone beside me, I looked up and saw the hotel manager next to me. Leaning over he whispered in my ear, "I hate to disturb you. However you have an urgent call. You may take it in my office if you like."

Thanking him, I followed him to his office where he closed the door behind me thus giving me privacy. The manager was standing there when I came out of the office.

I turned to him and asked, "Do you know of a surgeon staying here or know of one close? We have need of one immediately."

He led me to a table by the window that was occupied by a lovely old couple. She was dainty but sat with her back straight, chin up and a lively twinkle in her eye. The gentleman next to her was not much bigger than she. The biggest thing about him was his handlebar moustache, I thought, as it turned out it was his heart.

"Excuse me, Mein Herr, may this young man have a word with you?" the manager asked the gentleman.

Motioning to a chair next to him, he turned to me and said, "Sit young man and tell me what is on your mind. My wife and I are not getting any younger."

Nodding thanks to the manager, which he smiled in return as he walked away. Turning to the older man, I said, "We have an emergency and need a doctor as soon as possible. I am afraid it is a couple of hours from here and it may be tomorrow before we return."

Watching them both as I spoke, I noticed concern cross the lady's face. For a minute, I thought I was barking up the wrong tree and needed to cut this conversation short. The man took a sip of his wine, set the glass on the table and stroked his moustache.

Finally he said, "Son, tell me straight, what is the nature of the emergency."

Deciding I needed to level with him if there was a chance he was going to help us, I replied, "Three 7.62 rounds in the right torso of a young man who is in too bad a shape to be moved."

He looked at his wife and waited for her reaction. She smiled, nodded and motioned toward me.

Ten minutes later we were loaded and flying low. These BMW's will haul ass when you need it and right now we needed it. In the car with me was the vacationing Physician from England, Gregor and Father Aaron. Following as best they could was the rest of our merry band.

Less than two hours later I started slowing down as we were reaching our destination. Just before we entered the village, two men stepped onto the road way and directed us to a small barn. Captain Lange greeted us with a handshake and a proclamation.

"We must get inside immediately. A few of the Border Guards followed us into the West and snipe at us occasionally. My men have established a perimeter so we should be safe once inside."

The English doctor wasted no time in attending the wounded young man. Fifteen minutes went by as we all stood in silence, awaiting any news of the man's condition.

Motioning to us, the Doctor said, "Your men did a marvelous job on the boys wounds, but he needs blood badly or the lad doesn't stand a chance. I have the rudimentary items needed for a transfusion but I need a donor of the same blood type. Do you know his blood type?"

Lange answered, "Yes, he is O positive."

I pulled up my sleeve and sat down.

While we were occupied in the barn, the rest of our group caught up with us. Lae and Soledad along with Sister Anna checked on the rest of the men. A couple that was part of the rear guard had minor wounds from the fight in the mountains, which the ladies treated while the men protested that they were all right. Soledad was cleaning a leg wound made by a ricochet, not much more than a nasty cut. Lae was using a sewing needle and thread to close a cut on another man's arm.

"We need fresh water." Sister Anna called over her shoulder while cleaning a shoulder wound.

Within seconds a canteen appeared next to her. Looking up to thank the man Sister Anna was surprised to find the Sergeant standing there. The Sister nodded her thanks. The man replied in kind and walked away, checking on the rest of his men.

Soledad said to Lae and Sister Anna, "Will wonders never cease? After what Glen did to his nose and his ego, I didn't expect help from him."

Lae replied, "He may be an ass, but he is a soldier. He will take care of his men no matter who he has to use."

The Doc finished with me as one of the commandos sat down, sleeve already rolled up. The man nodded his thanks as he took my place. Looking behind him as I walked by, another man waited in case another pint of blood was needed.

Rigging his contraption on an old sawhorse, the Doc's setup was crude but effective. As I walked by it, one of the legs jumped as slivers of wood flew off it. The ranging fire by the East German snipers was getting annoying. The Doc shook his head as he restructured his transfusion apparatus. The Doc seemed to be a tough old bird, he didn't flinch.

Turning to me, the Doc said, "If they get lucky they may hit one of us, I don't have enough supplies to set up shop."

"How long before he can travel?" I asked.

"We have to get him stable before he can be loaded for transport. I'd say a couple of hours, maybe longer." He said with frown.

"We will make the firing stop." I said as I rolled my sleeve down and went looking for Gregor. I didn't hear the Doc when he said something about being a pint low.

I found Gregor talking to the Sergeant about the snipers. They were behind a low rock wall just north of the barn. A white flash appeared on the side of the mountain close to the trail the men had come down. Everyone ducked and waited to see where the bullet landed. It was easy to spot, chips of rock showered over us.

"The Doc said we need at least a couple of hours, maybe longer before the Lieutenant can be moved. I don't like letting them take pot shots for that long." I said as I looked over the wall.

"Nor do I my friend, shall we?" Gregor asked, looking at me with a smile.

"We shall." I answered with a smile of my own.

"What are you planning?" the Sergeant asked, with an incredulous tone.

Looking at Gregor then at him, I replied, "We are going to stop the sniping."

He shook his head as we disappeared into the night.

We were glad we both had on dark clothes as we started working our way through the out buildings of the little farm. Gregor spotted a water trough to our left so we stopped long enough to use the water to help muddy our faces. Within fifteen minutes we had worked over two hundred yards up the mountain. The terrain was in our favor, as well as the stupidity of our targets. We found a small stream that cut through the mountain west of the trail. On top of that, their firing drew us to them. Five minutes later we heard talking to our right.

Gregor peered over a rock ledge, directly above three men. We took a few minutes surveying the area. The waning moon and the cloudless night gave us good visibility from our perch. The cold mountain air also made it easy to pick up their conversation. Two of the men wanted to get back across the border. The third wanted to shoot at the barn until he ran out of ammo. He apparently out ranked them because they finally got quiet. I noticed they were wearing caps instead of helmets, this gave me an idea. As he settled down to fire again, I steadied my aim and hit him on the head with a thrown rock about the size of a grapefruit.

His lights went out with a grunt. The other two, unsure what had happened didn't rush to his aid. Gregor and I smiled at each other and waited. It took several minutes for one of them to check on the unconscious man. When the man's hand touched his friends head and came back bloody, he called to the other man.

Their conversation was funny as hell. Mistakenly they though he had been shot. They thought since the barn was so far away, they didn't hear the report. One wanted to leave him and get back to camp, the other almost agreed. Finally gathering him and their weapons, they started up the trail into East Germany. We sat there for another ten minutes to make sure the threat was over. All was quiet so we headed back to the barn.

Captain Lange filled in Kurt and Joseph on the happenings of the night. After a fifteen minute monolog, Kurt and Joseph excused themselves and walked away to have a private conversation. Lange made the rounds looking after his men.

"Joseph, you are far more experienced than me in these matters. That the hell are we going to do?" Kurt asked

Joseph smiled and said, "You sound like Glen, I think he is rubbing off on us all." After a few minutes of deep thought, he continued, "It is a given the West German government will not tolerate an armed group of Stazi operators roaming the countryside. The question is where our fifteen friends can call home for a few days while we get things settled?"

"We take them home with us." I said from the dark as Gregor and I walked up in time to hear Josephs comment.

"Are you serious?" Kurt asked, surprised at my appearance.

"Why not? We leave their weapons locked up in the van, put them four in a room except for the wounded man. Put him with Lange and the sergeant so they can keep an eye on him." I explained.

"Glen, you come up with some of the wildest ideas." Joseph said with a smile, "But it sounds good to me. Do you think the good doctor will check in on the boy for a few days?"

With a laugh I answered, "Whose idea do you think it was? Well…
the staying at our hotel part was the Doc's, the rest was mine."

Lange listened to our idea, hesitantly he finally agreed. That settled
we loaded up as many as we could carry and headed to Munich.
Lange, the Doc, Sister Anna, Father Aaron and Kurt stayed behind
with the wounded Lieutenant along with seven of the commandos. It
was a tight fit but this way we could get everyone in two trips.

It only took seconds for the manager to get us the rooms needed.
They were all on the same floor, close to each other. While Soledad,
Janet, Lae and Joseph got the men settled, Gregor and I drove back
for the next load. Before we left, I asked the manager if we could
use one of their shuttle vans for a few hours. He agreed immediately,
tossing the keys to me without hesitation. Leaving the BMW behind
and taking the second van gave us room for the Lieutenant to lay
prone while the Doc attended him.

Twenty minutes after our arrival to the barn, we were loaded and
ready to go. The Lieutenant was settled in, the Doc had room he
needed and all was great. That is until we opened the barn door to
drive out.

Standing before us was a farmer with a double barrel shot gun.
Pointing the weapon around and shouting at us was a little comical,
except he had the hammers back on the shotgun.

Kurt stepped out of the van, walked up to the farmer and said as
he flashed his identification, "The Government thanks you for the use
of your barn. You will be receiving a check for the time we used
your facility. I know money is not the issue, the fact we did not ask
permission before hand is. Please accept our apologies and accept the
check in the spirit it is offered."

The farmer ranted a moment about the worthlessness of the
government but agreed to take the money as a lesson to the government.
Kurt drew applause and laughter as he stepped back in the van.

Lange sat in the front passenger seat of the van I drove. A few
miles down the road he said, "Thank you for what you are doing. It is
far more than I expected. I would not have asked for help but for my

Lieutenant, if anything happens to him, my wife and daughter will not be pleased."

"Well, we can't let anything happen to him then. I wouldn't wish a pissed off wife and daughter on anyone." I replied with a smile, "Besides I have been betrayed by my superiors, I know how it feels." After a moment of silence, I asked, "What are your plans Captain? What is your next step?"

"I have been thinking about that. Several things are extremely irregular with this situation. As members of the Felix Dzerzhinsky Guards, we are trained in covert operations and all types of combat. Our superiors would never order us killed out of hand. They have too much money invested in us. Had that order been from my Regiment, we would have had a short trial and executed before an audience to drive home obedience. Someone outside my chain of command ordered our execution." Lange said in a tired voice.

"Didn't you say the man who gave you the orders was a senior agent in the Main Administration for Reconnaissance?" I asked.

"Yes, Koch is his name. He is in charge of Main Administration for Reconnaissance. We were assigned to run this operation for him." Lange said with a deep frown and a worried look.

"We know who placed those order then. He probably told your boss you had all been killed in the operation. It proves you can't trust a spook." I said, exasperated.

"I am unsure of the depth of trouble I have buried my men." Lange said as if speaking out loud. After a moment of silence, he continued, ", I officially offer my services to aid you in your operation. I give my word to serve you and your team until such time as those services are no longer needed. As to my men, I will present my decision to them and let them make up their own mind and follow their own convictions."

I was shocked, looking at him, then the road and back to him, I said, "Captain, I accept your offer, however I am in the same boat as you. I will have a meeting with my people while you meet with yours. Afterward, if the meetings are a success, we should have a joint meeting to get everyone acquainted."

"Agreed," He replied then said, "Call me Ernst."

The Sun was making an appearance as we drove into the parking lot of the hotel. The sunlight spread across the sky in golden rays with hints of purple, heralding another beautiful fall day.

Taking the service entrance and elevator, we quickly got the Lieutenant set up in his room with the Doc checking him out before catching some sleep. Closing the bedroom door where the wounded man rested, the Doc came over to Ernst and me, took off his glasses, cleaned them, and placed them on his face.

With his stall tactics depleted he finally said, "Boys, with rest, care and good food, the young man will be fine. My wife has plans for us to travel again in two days. I shall check on him from time to time but feel free to fetch me anytime you may need me. I do however advise him to see his doctor on a regular basis to make sure his wounds are healing properly. The other men have been tended and will be good as new. " Turning to go he stopped, turned and said, "Thank you gentlemen, for allowing me to ride once more into the breach."

While shaking our hand, he noticed our puzzled looks his statement caused. Smiling he said, "We have not been formally introduced, Colonel William Smyth, retired of course, formally of Her Majesties Black Horse."

That drew smiles from us both, Ernst said, "Captain Ernst Lange, formally of the Felix Dzerzhinsky Guards, presently aiding the West German BND."

Turning to me the Doc asked, "And you young man?"

Smiling, I replied, "I'm Glen Williams, here to buy a car."

"Indeed? Quite so, quite so." He said with a smile as he turned to walk down the hall.

"Colonel, one more thing before you go, if I may?" Ernst said as he reached out and touched the doctor's arm.

Turning, the Doc said, "Of course son, what is it?"

Looking at me then back to the doctor, Ernst said, "My men and I were exposed to radioactive material yesterday. What can and should we do."

Frowning, the Doc said, "Tell me everything."

After a five minute narrative, including input from me, Ernst finished and waited for the doctor's response.

Smiling, he said, "Not to worry, not to worry. Low levels such as the 1,500-2,000 CPM you read, even for several hours, are not fatal. In fact you will not suffer any ill effects unless you experienced over 10,000 CPM for several days."

Seeing the relief on our faces, the Doc smiled, patted Ernst's arm and said as he turned to go, "Boys, you have nothing to fear from the radiation. Captain, I would worry more about who betrayed you and your men."

As the old Doctor walked down the hall, Ernst turned to me and said, "After every one is settled, I will meet with my men, if I can find a place to do so."

Smiling at him, I replied, "Come with me, I think something can be arraigned."

We found the manager in his office. He was very accommodating, giving Ernst the key to a small meeting room next to the one we had been using. When I asked him about using our room that morning, he laughed and said that room was ours, no one is allowed in it but his staff when setting up the room for our briefings. Ernst and I agreed to meet with our people within the hour. Afterward he and I would get together and confirm a joint meeting, if our people were receptive to our idea.

It took me a few minutes to gather our group, and get them together. When I told them about Ernst's offer I was met with silence.

Gregor broke the silence, "If he is serious, we could use them, if we can trust their loyalty."

"Did you see the way his men looked at us when we loaded them up and came here? I think they were more in shock over our help than the betrayal of their people." Soledad added.

Lae pitched in, "I think we should meet with them, if they agree and see what they think about the idea."

Janet yawned, stretched and said, "This is getting stranger by the minute. I agree with Lae and I think I speak for my sound asleep husband back there." she said as she looked around at Joseph, who waved his hand in agreement.

Kurt shook his head, stood and had two very resounding comments, "Let us meet with them. After we eat that is."

Father Aaron and Sister Anna said "Amen" and headed to the restaurant.

An hour later, Ernst and I got together for a short meeting. I told him we were willing to meet and discuss the situation.

With a slight grin, Ernst said, "One of my group was not as eager to meet."

"Let me guess, the one with a sore nose." I replied with a smile of my own.

"You are correct. He has one stipulation, a private meeting with you." Ernst said, obviously unsure of my answer.

"Across the street is a small park bench, if the meeting goes south there it won't get us kicked out of this hotel. Tell him to meet me there in five minutes." I said with a laugh.

I went straight to the bench so I could watch him as he approached. He had to wait for a couple of cars to pass before he could join me. The delay gave me more time to study him. As he sat on the bench next to me, he seemed a different man than the one I had met earlier. I waited for him to speak first, it took a few minutes.

Finally he asked, "Why did you not kill me when you could have so easily?"

Turning to face him directly, I thought about my answer long and hard. When I responded it was directly in his eye, "Sergeant, I told myself a long time ago that I would trust my instincts when serious matters are at hand. Not long ago I had to take the life of one of your agents. He was firing at me while I stood next to my wife and friends, I could not allow that. When you placed your hand on my wife, I couldn't allow that either. The difference was, he was using his weapon, and you were not. Besides, I thought you too good a man to kill."

Staring at me for a moment, he sat back, rubbed his face and said, "I hope you accept my apology for grabbing your wife. I do not understand how you could know what kind of man I am, considering the short time we were in proximity of each other before I touched her."

"Your Captain holds you in high regard. I saw his face when you went down and the concern in his face when I held you down ready to strike the killing blow. I liked Captain Lange when I met him. I figured if he thinks highly of you, there must be a good reason." I told him, continuing I said, "Also, the apology has to be to my wife, not to me."

He stared into my eyes for a moment, stuck out his hand and said, "I will make a formal apology in front of everyone. I offer my services as I know my Captain has already done."

Shaking his hand, I said, "Glad to have you on board Sergeant."

"Call me Max." he replied as we started across the street. Half way across he said, "So, it was you who killed Steiner. We heard about his death just before this assignment. He was a man who needed killing. The world has not seen such an evil man in years. I am relieved you can tell the difference between him and me. I would hope I had not slid that close to the bottom of humanity."

Fifteen minutes later both groups were seated and ready to hear what each other had to say. The first order of business according to Max was his apology to Soledad. Max walked up to where Soledad sat, stood at stiff attention, clicked his heels and bowed before her in the finest Prussian manor.

"Frau Williams, I stand before you to ask forgiveness for placing my hand on you in a most ungentlemanly fashion. It was unprofessional as well unforgivable in my mother's eyes. If she were still with us, her rebuke of my actions would be most severe for I was not raised in such manor. I will fully understand if this plea falls on deaf ears."

I don't think he drew a breath while waiting on Soledad's response. Sitting in front of him, barely looking at him, I thought she was going to give him a stroke. Finally she let him off the hook, a little anyway.

"I dare say I would agree with your mother." Soledad said as she stood. Max winced slightly, still standing at attention after coming out of the bow. To his credit, he stood there and took her comment.

"However, how can I not accept such a well presented and heartfelt apology?" Holding out her hand, she said, "Let the friendship of your people and mine begin here."

Taking her hand, he bowed, kissed the back of her hand, stood at attention, clicked his heels, did an about face and rejoined his men. The cheers and laughter, with the tension broken, was loud and universal, everyone was laughing.

Several minutes went by before we got down to business. We filled the men in on everything we found, thought we knew, the old theories, everything. Their questions and our answers lasted several hours before all were satisfied we left nothing out. One of the main things we all agreed on, the Schloss was the key. Father Aaron said he could find quarters for everyone that would be out of the way and close to the Schloss, but needed to get back to the village to set it up.

Gregor and I tried to loan the Father our rental, but he wouldn't take it. As he and Sister Anna drove off in the junk pile he called a car, we said a prayer for their safety.

When they were out of sight, Soledad said, "I don't know about everyone else, I'm beat and going to bed and catch some sleep."

All agreed and to our rooms we went. Much to my dismay, Soledad did mean sleep.

CHAPTER 25

Father Aaron turned the ignition off in his poor old car a little after 11 AM. Sitting for a moment to gather his thoughts, he wondered how to approach one of the oldest families in Bavaria with a slightly illegal favor. He knew they had an old hunting cabin at the eastern edge of the estate. It would be a perfect place for a base camp. It was large enough to house the commandos and in the edge of a secluded forest with plenty of privacy. With his thoughts in a row, he said a quick prayer and opened the car door, shaking slightly at the thought of what he was about to ask.

The door opened after the second knock. The man who answered was not the friendliest sort. However when he recognized the visitor as the Priest from the village, he smiled and let him in. The man asked him to wait in the parlor while he went to the owner. Seconds later the Lady of the house made an appearance.

"Good morning Father, what a pleasant surprise. Will you join me for tea?" Elsie von Beitel asked with a broad smile.

"Yes, I believe I would, thank you." His voice not as shaky as he was afraid it would be.

With a few minutes of small talk behind them, Father Aaron finally broached the subject of his visit. "Frau von Beitel, I find myself in the unusual situation of needing your help."

"Just ask Father, I will help in any way I can. You seem stressed, are you ill?" she asked, genuinely concerned.

"No, thank you for asking, my health is not the issue. I would like to borrow your old hunting cabin for a few days. I have several friends that need a quiet, out of the way place to stay." He said, relieved he did not stutter when he asked.

"Of course Father, it is yours as long as you and your friends need it. I am afraid though, it has not been very well maintained. It is solid enough but a bit dirty." She said with a slight frown.

Smiling, Father Aaron said, "Thank you for your generosity. Besides they can give it a cleaning while they are there."

"That would be fine Father. When do you expect them to move in?" she asked softly.

"Would today be too early?" he asked, hesitantly.

"Today is not a problem. They can move in and stay as long as they need." Elsie said as the tea was served.

With that out of the way, the rest of the visit was of the village and the delicious scones served with the tea. After only an hour in Elsie's home, Father Aaron had accomplished his mission, said his good byes along with his thanks and headed to the church.

Elsie watched him drive off with fear in her heart.

8 Oct, Munich

The water felt wonderful, so much in fact she took a longer shower than normal. It gave Soledad time to think and what went through her head scared the hell out of her. The attempt on Glen's life then the attempts to kidnap the children proved there was substance to the rumors of gold in the area. She didn't know what scared her the most, looking for the gold or finding it.

Looking at her reflection in the mirror as she brushed her long dark hair, Lae ran the happenings of the last few weeks through her nimble mind. She milled over several ideas and came to a conclusion. Dressing quickly, she quietly checked on Gregor, as he lay sleeping, on her way out.

Soledad stood by the bed watching Glen sleep with a gleam in her eye. A little after 2 PM and he had not moved since his head hit the pillow. Lying on his right side with the sheet just over his lower body, most of him was exposed. She could see the small scar on his left cheek, left by some moron with brass knuckles. The rest of his face was the way God made it, beautiful. She couldn't get enough of looking at him, especially when he is unaware. The muscles of his upper body spoke of hard work, good food and a natural gift of size. She was glad he did not go for body building, toned she liked, hard and ugly, in her mind, was not for her, although some women liked that look.

Following his body to the cover and the curve his hip made gave her warm feelings in several places. His left leg was completely exposed to his cheek giving her a glimpse of his firm rear that raised her blood pressure a couple of points. Her gaze stopped at the small scar on his left calf, placed there by a Pathet Lao fighter with an AK47 and the desire to take her man's life. Glen's aim was better. The almost matching scar on his right leg was made during a fire fight when Glen went after a Ranger who was wounded and needed carrying. What she used to bandage his leg, Glen has never lived down. The duct tape wasn't the issue, but the Kotex brought a lot of teasing and laughter from everyone. Before her lay her perfect man, warrior, gentleman, great father, kind, gentle, generous, handsome and oh dear God what a lover!

With thoughts of pleasure that would have to wait, she turned and headed to the door. Just before her hand grabbed the door knob, there was a soft knock. Opening the door, she smiled at her visitor. Lae stood there with a serious look on her face. Holding a finger to her lips for silence, Soledad eased out of the door and softly closed it.

"Let's go find Kurt." Lae said as they walked to the elevator.

"You read my mind." Soledad said as she pulled a pencil and notepad out of her pants pocket and started to write. The two created a list on the way to Kurt's room.

The look on Kurt's face as the two women walked in his open door was pure puzzlement. They woke him up and stuck a piece of paper in his face and demanded the items by nightfall. He nodded, they smiled, thanked him and left. As the door closed behind them, he glanced at the list, shook his head, smiled and picked up the phone, placed a call then went back to bed.

Soledad and Lae went to the restaurant for a late lunch. Sitting at one of the tables that had a view of the city, they sat in silence for a few minutes after drinks were served. Both had a lot on their mind that they wanted to share with their friend, but were hesitant to start the conversation. As they sat there, Janet joined them. The waiter brought her a drink and all three women sat in silence.

Finally Lae said, "You realize our men want us out of the way."

Janet took a sip of her tea and said, "You are right as rain Lae. Joseph hasn't said anything, but I know he is thinking it."

"Glen knows better than to suggest it but it doesn't keep him from thinking it." Soledad said in agreement.

Lae added, "One thing we do not want to do is fail to follow instructions if this turns ugly."

"She is right," Janet said, "if shooting starts we need for them to know where we are and what we are doing. They may not like our plans but they need to know them."

Soledad grinned at her friends and said, "Oh, they won't like our ideas but they will have to accept them."

The next three hours were filled with discussions, plans and occasional laughter. As their brainstorming session came to a close, the three friends had a moment of sobering silence. Talking, planning and ideas were one thing, reality is quite another. There are men out there that want to do them and their friends harm and these three formidable women were determined not to let that happen.

8 Oct, Munich

Rosenheimer Street held special meaning for the Sturmbannfuhrer, in fact for all Nazis. Down the street from where he sat was the beer hall where Hitler started the Beer Hall Putsch. Unfortunately, the Burgerbraukeller Beer Hall was showing its age. In fact there was talk of tearing it down in the name of progress.

The small eatery where he sat was not exactly the Burgerbraukeller, but his plans were not as great as his late Fuhrer. The three young men sitting at the table with him were not of the quality of the party of old. They did have one thing he needed, men.

"Gentlemen, thank you for joining me and listening to my problem. As you can see it is imperative we act in secret, no one must know our objective." The old Nazis told the younger men.

"Of course we understand mien Herr. We can have fifty armed men ready to go in two days who are loyal to the cause. Will that be sufficient?" one of the young men asked.

Handing him a card with his contact information, the older man said, "That will be perfect. Call me at the number on the card in twenty four hours and you will have your final instructions."

Taking the card, the three stood, nodded and walked away, talking among themselves, anxious to prove their worth to the Party. Shaking his head at the gullibility of the young people, the evil old man went to the pay phone and placed a call.

"The fools will be ready in two days, they are so anxious to prove their worth they have no idea what they are getting into." He said in a low voice, not wanting other patrons to overhear.

"Good, I will have our men ready Herr Sturmbannfuhrer. Are you certain twenty men and five trucks will be sufficient?" the man said on the other end.

"I am certain. In three days we will be wealthy men on our way to a warm climate and a comfortable life. Make sure your men maintain their surveillance. We must know where and when they make the find. Good day, my friend." He said as he hung up the phone.

The old Nazis smiled at the thought of what he had told his protégé. Warm weather will be good for his old bones. It is unfortunate his partners will not live to enjoy the climate. But for now, he hailed a taxi to his hotel and a lunch served with a delicious wine followed by a nap. After all, he had nothing to do until dinner when the Americans would make an appearance and entertain him while he dined.

A thought nagged at the back of his mind, what if his gold is not uncovered in time by the Americans? Everything he had lined up called for an attack on them on the evening of the 10th. No, his planning is correct, he told himself. Everything he fed them to aid their investigation, the files that appeared at the American Consult, and the new files that mysteriously appeared at BND Headquarters coupled with their own lucky findings should have them close to discovery.

He hoped so. The metric tonne of gold he had smuggled out of the area before the rest of it vanished is almost depleted. His lifestyle was expensive to maintain and his funds were getting dangerously low.

Picking up the phone again, he placed one more call.

It seemed everyone waited on everyone else to answer the damn phone. Finally, Inspector Mann picked up the receiver.

"Hello, Bundesgrenzschutz, how may I help you?" he said in his grumpiest voice.

"Good day, this is Colonel Steinmann. The 10th Armored Division will be holding joint exercises with American units in southern Bavaria over the next few days. If you get reports of invasion or terrorist activities, it is us." The voice said with a laugh.

Mann laughed back, "Thanks for the call Colonel, I will spread the word. I expect the written notification in our office by end of the day."

"Thank you, you will have it, and please make sure the G9G are notified, I would hate to have our new recruits go up against such fine Police as G9G." the voice said as the laughter died down.

Have no fear, your children are safe." Mann said as he hung up.

Placing the phone on the hook, the Sturmbannfuhrer smiled. Good, that call should keep the Police out of the way while he retrieved his property.

8 Oct, Bavaria

Captain Lange watched the Sergeant get the men settled in. The old hunting lodge was built like a fort, strong walls and high windows. The forest around the lodge was overgrown with brush and fallen limbs, the lodge needed a few repairs. Lange smiled at the thought of how he would keep his men busy. After a few days the lodge and grounds would be in first class shape. It was the least they could do for the hospitality they had been shown.

"Captain, the men have been settled and are starting guard rotations." The Sergeant reported with a salute.

"Max, we are no longer in the Guard, call me Ernst." Ernst said with a smile.

"With all respects sir, you are my Captain. I will address you as such." Max said, still standing at attention.

Reaching out, Ernst placed his hand on Max's shoulder, leaned over and said, "You are the best NCO with whom I have had the pleasure of serving. You have followed my orders to the letter. Do not fail to do so now. We have worked together for several years as soldiers. Let us now work together as friends."

Softening his stance, Max said, "Ernst, I have considered you a friend from the first day we met. I find it an honor you consider me one."

Ernst studied his friend for a moment, then said, "In front of the men, we will maintain military discipline, however in private, you are my equal and my friend, always speak your mind. Agreed?"

Smiling, Max replied, "Jawohl!"

The two men walked the perimeter, inspecting the placement of the guards, while discussing the predicament they find themselves. Afterward, Max turned in while Ernst sat on the porch, staring into the night.

8 Oct, Munich

Just after 7 PM the Doc stopped by and checked on the Lieutenant. Surprisingly, his wife was with him. Lae was sitting with him at the time and reported there were no changes.

Lae stood back and let them check his bandages. His wife did the exam while the Doc watched.

Noticing Lae's interest in her exam, the Doc stepped up to Lae and said, "She was my assistant for almost fifty years. Until our retirement she was the finest nurse in Her Majesties service."

Lae watched her for a moment before saying, "It appears to me she has not lost her touch."

Overhearing their conversation, she turned and said, "Dear, we can't go off and leave this boy until he is better. Let's postpone our departure for a week and keep him under eye."

Smiling at her and winking at Lae, he said, "Yes Dear, you are right as always."

At that moment Lae knew what he was up to, he wanted to postpone their trip so he could keep an eye on the wounded man, but wanted it to be her decision. His plan worked. As they said good night, they promised to return in the morning. Lae smiled as she watched them walk arm in arm down the hall gazing into each other's eyes.

Noticing the time, Lae headed to her room to get ready for dinner. They had agreed to dine around 8 then hit the sack for an early start in the morning. Entering the room, she heard the shower running. Quickly disrobing, she joined Gregor, much to his surprise.

As she wrapped her arms around his neck, she said, "My Love, you have thirty minutes to ravish me before we must get dressed to meet the others." Then with a gleam in her eye she asked, "Are you up to the challenge?"

Gregor's response was a huge grin and a deep kiss.

Soledad had the same idea, except for the shower part. She came out of the bathroom wearing nothing but a smile. Fully clothed, I sat on the sofa, frozen in place, immersing myself in her beauty. She walked up to me as I started to stand. Placing her palm on my forehead she pushed me back. As I settled into the sofa, she straddled me, kissed me and gazed into my eyes.

After a deep sensual kiss, she whispered in my ear, "Glen, my thoughts have been of you all afternoon. I stood by the bed and watched you sleep earlier and my pulse rate has yet to come down."

All I could do was groan with the pleasure building in me. Starting at the side of her neck, I kissed down her throat, across her shoulder. Slowly she sat back a little, giving me access to her magnificent breasts. Taking one nipple in my mouth, I drew it deep and used my tongue the way she likes, drawing a deep moan from her. Kissing the valley between, I moved to the other breast as she rubbed the back of my head, running her fingers through my short blonde hair.

Several minutes went by while we enjoyed each other's essence. A knock at our door changed things. Soledad jumped up and was in the bedroom before my mind registered the knock. As I watched the bedroom door close, I heard the knocking at the door. Since I was fully dressed it only took me a minute to answer.

Looking through the peep hole, I was surprised to see Kurt standing in the hall with a woman I had seen at BND Headquarters. Looking my clothes over, I made sure I was presentable before opening the door.

As the door opened, Kurt said, "I am sorry to bother you while you are getting ready for dinner, but this could not wait." Turning to the woman he introduced us, "This is Rachael, she works with us at Headquarters. Do you remember the file you gave Otto that was stuck together? Rachael got the pages apart. Not only did she separate them, she used her abilities and restored most of the words. You will not believe what she found."

A fully recovered Soledad joined us, asking, "What did she find that prompted her to bring it over tonight?"

Turning to the young lady, Kurt said, "Rachael, this is Soledad. Please tell them what you told me."

After shaking Soledad's hand, Rachael said, "I know where the gold is, at least some of it."

"Where?" Soledad and I asked together.

Smiling a big smile, the young lady said, "Under the stables. The north wall has a trip lock that opens a trap door. Below the stables is a large storeroom that had thought to have been filled in, it has not. That has to be where the gold is hidden."

"It sounds plausible to me." I said, looking over at Soledad.

She stood there with a funny look on her face. Suddenly she turned and went to the table that was stacked with the files we had been scouring over for days. Digging into the stack, she seemed like a woman on a mission. Several minutes later she found what she was looking for.

Turning to us, open file in hand, she read from our notes, "There were references of Calvary horses being taken care of and groomed where they "rested on mountains of gold". Another clue in John's journal spoke of a "cave lined with gold that reflected on the horses polished bridals." Both of these supposedly came from diaries of men who were at the Schloss and died of their wounds. John seemed to think they were ravings of feverish, ill men." Closing the file, she looked at us and said, "Damn, you may have it right. Care to join us in the morning?"

Rachael smiled a bashful smile and said, "No, I do research, not field work. However, please let me know what you find."

Kurt answered for us, "You will have a full report, I promise."

After saying good bye, Kurt escorted Rachael to her car and sent her on her way.

Dinner was a bit animated. Even though we tried to keep our voices down, our excitement was hard to control. Finally we finished dinner and adjourned to our room to continue our discussion.

Evil eyes watched us leave the dining room. The Sturmbannfuhrer couldn't believe our enthusiasm. His mind started running over different scenarios that would account for our speedy departure. We usually stayed at our table, having coffee, for an hour or so after our meal. Only one scenario made sense to him, we thought we had found the gold. A sense of urgency came over him. Hurriedly he settled his check and went to his room. Three calls later he felt better having moved his time table forward. Instead of Monday, he and his men will be in position by 3 PM tomorrow. All he knew for certain, they had better find the gold tomorrow, all his remaining fortune was riding on them being as good as he hoped.

Cognac flowed into seven glasses. After everyone was served, a toast was proposed.

"May we find what we seek!" Gregor said as he raised his glass.

We all followed with a here, here and took a sip of the liquid silk. For a few moments, we were as quiet as I have seen us as a group. Several things were running through each of our minds, none of which we seemed anxious to discuss.

Finally Lae spoke up, "Do you think the men who have caused problems at home will continue to do so?"

"The kids are safe, at least as safe as they can be. According to John, before he flew back to Berlin, Consuelo has an army guarding the Hacienda. John also left two of his best men to bolster the defenses. I think the problems back home are over. I'm also thinking we need to cancel the move to the Bed and Breakfast in the village and remain here. I don't want to put the owners in the line of fire, if it comes to that." I said as I swirled the golden liquor in my glass.

Gregor and Joseph started talking at the same time. Both paused and Joseph continued after Gregor motioned him to do so, "I fear the emphasis will be placed on us, more so than before. I dare say we are surely going into harm's way tomorrow, if we are being watched as close as we all think we are. Therefore I think you are right Glen, our competition as enough targets without involving anyone else."

Gregor nodded and said, "Our British friend is correct, therefore we have come to a conclusion." Taking a deep breath, Gregor turned to Lae and said, "I want you on a plane in the morning. I want you home and safe."

I turned to Soledad as Joseph turned to Janet. However we did not get a chance to say a word. All three women stood, came together, crossed their arms and, as one, said one word, "NO."

Soledad then said to Kurt, "Did you get what we asked for?"

"Yes, Rachael brought it when she brought the files." Kurt said, keeping his eyes on the women.

Holding her hand out, Lae said, "Well, where is it?"

"In my room, I shall be right back." Kurt said as he hurried from the room and away from three pair of male eyes that bored into his back.

Joseph, Gregor and I started to speak at the same time. Soledad's loud whistle shut us up. This particular silence was not golden. In fact it was downright uncomfortable. It was short lived, thank God. Kurt returned with a duffle bag within minutes, slightly out of breath since he ran to his room and back.

Taking the seemingly heavy duffle from him, the ladies adjourned into the bedroom of the suite. When the door closed, all of us looked at each other, shrugged, sat back and sipped our drinks in silence.

Gregor was the first to speak up, "I do not think they are going to listen to us."

Joseph and I looked at him and then each other. We actually held our laughter for all of fifteen seconds, after that we exploded. Kurt joined us and Gregor sat there looking at the three of us laughing our heads off, wondering what he had said. Slowly a smile spread across his face and he joined us.

Joseph said as our laughter died down, "I needed that. There is nothing like a good laugh to break the stress in an uncomfortable situation."

"We all needed it. Now, if we can hold our laughter when our women emerge from the bedroom, I have a feeling laughing at them would be a huge mistake." I said, finishing my drink.

Kurt smiled and said, "I know you are correct Glen, laughing would be a mistake of major proportions."

We all froze when we heard the doorknob turn on the bedroom door. Soledad was the first out, followed in turn by Lae and Janet. They looked ready for war. The composite tactical vests they wore fit them like a glove, contouring to their womanly figures. The vests had built in holsters under each arm and multiple pockets for clips. The holsters and pockets were filled. I did not recognize the pistols and couldn't wait to check them out. There were two large pockets in the lower front which were filled as well, but I couldn't see what was in them.

They came in like they were models, turning and posing. All three had determined looks on their faces that told us our argument about them going home would fall on deaf ears.

Holding my hand out to Soledad, she instantly knew what I wanted. Pulling one of the pistols from its holster, she popped the clip, opened the slid until it locked and handed it and the clip to me. Gregor and Joseph joined me as I studied the weapon.

I read the side of the pistol out loud, "Sig P220, this must be new, I haven't seen one before. Damn, it's a .45ACP." turning to the women I asked, "I know Lae can handle a .45 because I have seen her shoot Gregor's 1911's. Soledad has hit pretty good with my Pythons which have more recoil. What about you Janet?"

She looked her husband and then me straight in the face and said, "I grew up shooting my father's Webley, which was a .455 caliber. We all can handle the .45 and you three damn well know it."

"Looks like you have ten extra clips. From the size of them, what do they hold? 7-8 rounds?" Joseph asked as we went to our women to study their new accessories closer.

Kurt answered, "8 in the clip and one in the chamber gives them a lot of fire power before reloading."

Gregor balanced one of Lae's in his hand and said, "Nice balance, and they are lighter than my Colts."

Lae smiled up at Gregor and said, "Less than two pounds with clip and is very accurate. I think we have found the pistol I want to keep for my own."

Soledad laughed and said, "That goes for me too. But I will keep my Walther in an ankle holster. Glen, you and Gregor will have some competition on your firing range when we go home. Lae and I plan on kicking your butts in tactical shooting."

"How good are the vests?" I asked Kurt over my shoulder.

"It will stop auto pistol ammo at close range. However the larger more powerful rounds my break a rib or two. Long range rifle fire will not penetrate it, close range it might deflect an angled shot. Straight on, up close, military ball rifle ammo will cut through it like butter." Kurt replied while we all listened closely.

"Ladies, remember the cardinal rule about getting shot, DON'T." I said in a loud voice.

Soledad grinned and said a resounding, "Yes Dear."

Tapping the filled large pocket on her vest, I asked Soledad, "What's this?"

Giving me her sexiest smile she replied, "We each have two flash bang grenades."

Damn. Gregor, Joseph and I looked from our wives to Kurt, shook our heads and went to refresh our drinks.

8 Oct, Berlin

Vodka in hand, John stood at a window in his room on the eighth floor of his hotel. After several minutes admiring the rebuilt, well lit, Berlin skyline, his focus changed to his reflection in the glass. What he saw was not a surprise. Looking back at him was a tall, distinguished, older man with grey hair, grey moustache and slim build. The reflection was uncannily clear, his eyes were as clear as any mirror. In those eyes he saw the inevitable, growing old. A decision he had been putting off for years became clear as the liquid fire in his glass. He had told Soledad earlier he planned on asking Connie for her hand, again. Smiling at the man in the glass, he knew how he would present both his retirement and proposal.

Turning to the desk by the bed, he picked up a report that was less than an hour old. Dieter Koch was found shot dead at a border post. This saved John three bullets that had been ear marked for Koch. But, who ordered the hit? The report also told of Koch placing a phone call, after which he ordered a squad of Guard Commandos shot as enemies of the State. The Stazi Guard squad had crossed into East Germany carrying gold bars, which was loaded on waiting trucks and driven into the night, destination unknown. Before the orders to execute could be followed, the squad escaped over a mountain pass back into West Germany. The Border unit that pursued them was shot to pieces, losing seventeen of their pursuing troops along with twenty one wounded.

Sitting in the recliner next to the bed, he planned on starting the wheels turning in that experienced mind of his. However, age, fatigue and vodka took their toll and he was asleep within minutes.

CHAPTER 26

9 Oct Munich

Dawn found us in the restaurant devouring a large breakfast. Instead of ordering, we told the waitress to bring scrambled eggs and anything else that she thought we would eat. She did not disappoint us, the food was outstanding.

After eating everything she brought, we settled back with coffee. Again we were quiet, especially for us. It was if we all knew we were coming to the end of our quest. We also knew we would be going into harm's way if we were watched as closely as we thought we were. Someone out there was quick to kill anyone who got in their way and in their way was exactly where we were going.

Soledad broke the silence with one word, "Ready?"

That one word sent us to our rooms for our gear. Ten minutes later we loaded into our two vehicles and hit the road, full of determination and resolve to finish this once and for all.

As we pulled out of the hotel garage, I realized the old man, who had been at every meal, was not present this morning. Wondering where he was for only a minute, my mind went to more pressing issues, like, what's for lunch?

9 Oct, Bavaria

That particular old man was already on the road and was pulling into Elsie's driveway. Elsie almost had a stroke when she saw the car pulling up to her door. The minion opened the door for the

Sturmbannfuhrer and stepped aside. The evil incarnate didn't bother knocking on her door. He barged in and took over.

"We will have visitors by mid-day. You will have food and drink ready for forty men. At 4 pm twenty men or more will arrive and will need refreshments as well. Do as I say, you will see the sunset. Fail me and you will be shot. Do you understand what I have said?" he said to a scared Elsie.

Vowing to herself not to show fear, Elsie said simply, "Yes." Turned and walked into her kitchen.

Her staff would have to start the cooking if food was to be ready when the men arrive. Both of her men were already there, having seen the car drive up. Her instructions were short and to the point, do as the Sturmbannfuhrer says, with one exception.

9 Oct, Hunting Cabin

Ernst enjoyed the sunrise as he sipped coffee on the cabins porch. Looking into his cup, he must thank the private who made it for him. It was superb, as was breakfast. His men were up and working on the cabin and grounds. By the time their stay was over, however long it was, Ernst planed on having brought this property back to life before they left. It was the least they could do for the Lady and her hospitality.

9 Oct, Munich

The young men who made promises to the Sturmbannfuhrer were scrambling to gather their promised forces. Their orders had been changed. They were now to arrive at a villa north of the Schloss by noon today instead of Monday. Knowing they would be hard pressed to gather the forty men promised, they set a departure time and would leave in time to arrive when they were ordered, no matter the number.

9 Oct, Bavaria

Having left before dawn, the five trucks carrying twenty three heavily armed mercenaries were making good time. Their leader rode in the lead truck and was pleased at their progress. They would be in position well before the allotted time of 4 PM. He and his men were experienced thugs, for the lack of a better word. Among them were thieves, murderers, con artists and all were ex-military. The common bond they shared was the love of money. They had performed missions for the old crazy Nazi in the past and were paid well for their efforts. He expected this particular mission to pay very well. Taking gold away from young Nazi wanna be's would be like taking candy from a baby. It did not bother him that they may have to kill the young men to accomplish their mission, nor would it bother his men.

9 Oct, New Mexico

Consuelo watched the clouds as they raced across the moon. Standing on the veranda, her thoughts went to her family that was starting their day in Germany. The call from Soledad, followed by the call from John, had her stomach tied up in knots. At this moment they are beyond her reach and aid. She did not like the feeling it gave her. The children are as safe as she could make them. Needless to say, anything short of an invasion couldn't get close to them. Saying a prayer for all, she turned and went to bed, the longing for John's warmth beside her kept her awake until well after the moon had set.

9 Oct Bavaria

East of the Schloss, on a knoll about three hundred meters from the blacksmiths shop, two pair of binoculars watched us drive up. The men holding them were the recon team the mercenary leader had sent ahead to keep an eye on us. They would be in a good seat for things to come.

Sunday mornings were quiet at the Schloss, as was our experience earlier, however today seemed much quieter. It was if the forest knew something was unusual happening. The old gate keeper just waived us through the gate and returned to his cottage.

We parked on the south side of the blacksmith's shop and stables. Within minutes we had our gear unloaded and were ready to proceed. Soledad, Janet and Lae went into the building to look for the trap door trigger while the men did the same outside. The notes didn't say where exactly the trigger was hidden.

After several minutes of searching and some digging along the wall, we gave up and went inside to join the women. The look on their faces told us they were having the same luck we had, none.

"Glen," Soledad said when she saw us come inside, "We don't have any idea what we are looking for. The papers only said there was a trigger that would open a trap door. Not what the trigger was or how it worked. The only thing we noticed was the carvings on several of the stones. Someone spent a lot of time craving Knight's Crosses on them."

Looking at the stones she pointed out, I said, "Looks like Iron Crosses to me."

"If it was easy, anyone could have already found it." Kurt said to Soledad with a bit of a smile. Then turning to the carvings he said to me, "The Iron Cross is remarkably like the Knight's Cross, except the Knight's Cross has a slightly longer lower leg."

Studying the carving closer, I could see what Kurt was talking about. The work was very well done and had held up to the ages. The lower leg was slightly longer than the other three.

The seven of us walked the wall, stables and open floor looking for anything out of the ordinary. I spotted new hay on the floor in a couple of places and wondered where it came from. Standing by one of the clumps of hay, I studied the ceiling. Gregor walked up to me and started laughing. Kurt and Joseph came over and looked up at the same area, trying to determine what I was looking at.

I looked at Gregor, trying to understand what he was laughing at when he motioned to the others standing beside me, looking up. It hit me what Gregor was thinking and I could not contain my own laughter.

"What, may I ask, is so bloody funny?" Joseph asked with a puzzled look on his face.

Gregor couldn't keep quiet, saying, "We were on a trip into Colorado to attend an Outdoor Guide conference when we started discussing human nature. Glen told me he could prove that humans were easily manipulated. I bet him lunch he could not. Never bet the man a meal, you will lose every time."

Joseph turned to me and asked, "What did you do?"

Smiling at him I said, "Nothing much, I pulled over on the shoulder of Highway 9 between Silverthorne and Kremmling, got out of the car and started staring up the mountain."

Gregor picked up the story, "Within minutes another car stopped. The people got out with cameras and started studying side of mountain. They never came over to us to ask what we were doing."

Continuing I said, "After five minutes, three cars had stopped. We got in ours and drove off. But we didn't go far. In fact we stopped only a mile away, waited fifteen minutes, turned around and went back. There were at least a dozen cars stopped. People were gathered in groups pointing cameras, binoculars and fingers up the mountain. We walked among them, asking what was going on."

Gregor pitched in saying, "When we asked, people said there were sightings of several bear. Another man said it was a cougar, not a bear. One odd looking woman said it was a Sasquatch sighting."

Kurt then asked, "What did you do?"

Grinning at him, I said, "Got in our car and drove to Kremmling in time for lunch."

As we finished the story, I heard birds flying in the hay loft and more hay fell to the floor. Satisfied birds caused the hay to fall, my attention returned to the laughter our story prompted from our friends.

Two hours went by and no trigger. Gathering together to discuss our findings, or lack thereof, I leaned against the north wall of the stable. The cool rock of the wall felt great against my back, and I said as much. Soledad sat next to me, leaned back and sighed. Sipping cold water from a couple of thermos bottles, we relaxed and started to discussing our options.

While we talked, Soledad kept looking at Lae. I couldn't see what Lae was doing from where I sat but Gregor could.

"Lae, what are you studying on the wall?" Gregor asked as he stood and leaned over her.

Soledad slid over and started staring at the section of the wall that had Lae's attention. Turning to me she said, "Glen, Kurt, you guys, come look at this. It's a Knight's Cross engraved into the stone. At first it looks like the rest but there is something odd about it."

Janet was quick to spot the difference. "Guys, is not pointed at the floor like the rest, it's pointed to the left."

She was right. The Cross was carved in a stone that was about four feet above the floor. We looked along the wall to the left and found another pointed the same way, again four feet above the floor as were the rest. There were more Crosses carved into the wall at four foot intervals, vertical as well has horizontal, all were carved correctly. Following the Knight's Crosses that were carved to the left, we worked our way past the door that went into the living quarters and the black smith shop.

Roughly halfway between the door and the west wall of the building a Knight's cross had the correct orientation, long leg down. The next Cross to the left had its longer leg pointed to the right, opposite of the Crosses we had been following. Just above the floor, directly below the properly oriented Cross was another improperly oriented Cross, its longer leg was pointing up. Looking left and right of it we found Crosses every four feet, all properly oriented.

Turning our attention to the two crosses that were pointed at each other, Soledad was the first to notice another irregularity. The Cross that was four feet off the floor, the bottom leg had a slightly wider base than the others. Leaning into it, Soledad blew some dust away reviling a thin rectangular hole, like a slot, through the rock. Getting on her knees, she did the same at the longer leg. Since it was closer to the floor, she had to dig a little to remove packed in dirt. Taking my offered pocket knife, she made short work of the dirt. This Cross had the same style hole through the rock.

All of us studied the two crosses and the slots in their long arm bases. Now the question is, what do we slide in them and what will happen when we do? Searching the stables, we tried everything we could find, which wasn't much, nothing worked. After almost an hour, we had exhausted every possibility.

My stomach told me noon had arrived so we stopped and decided to go into the village and have lunch with Father Aaron and Sister Anna. Mass was over and they would be free to join us for the afternoon. Fifteen minutes later we were cleaned up and sitting in a nice eatery with food ordered. Father Aaron and Sister Anna wanted to be filled in on everything, which we happily obliged.

During the course of the meal, I saw Soledad studying her table knife with a funny look on her face.

Turning to Kurt, she asked, "Kurt, what kind of knives were around when the original Castle was built."

Thinking for a minute, he replied, "Most every kind you can think of. However, besides swords, stilettos were very popular as a personal weapon."

"What if that's what we need to slide in the crosses?" Soledad asked with a smile.

Father Aaron said, "I have a collection of antique as well as replica blades. Perhaps we can find two that will work?"

We all looked at each other, rapidly finished our meals and headed to the Church for the blades.

Thirty minutes later we stood around the Crosses and watched Soledad slide a stiletto into one of the Crosses. It slid to the hilt with no resistance and no reaction. Father Aaron handed her another with a longer blade. With two inches to the hilt, the blade stopped. Soledad looked around at us, took a deep breath and pushed harder. A loud click was heard as the hilt hit the rock. Nothing happened.

Father Aaron handed her another long blade and stepped back, we all did. I held out my hand for the knife but Soledad shook her head and slid it to the hilt with one quick move. A loud click followed by the sound of dry gears grinding against each other. I grabbed Soledad and pulled her away from the wall, not taking any chances with my Heart.

Slowly, along the wall between the door and the west wall, the floor started sinking as a 4 foot by 4 foot opening appeared. Shining a light into the dark hole, we saw a ladder against a rock wall. Before I could start down this rabbit hole Gregor pushed past me and started climbing down.

Within minutes, we all were standing in a large room, in the dark, except for our flashlights. The size of the room surprised us. It was the same size as the stables above. The ceiling was made of heavy timbers, at least twenty inches square. Every twenty feet stood a column made of rock and mortar supporting the ceiling. From the amount of dirt that fell when the opening appeared, I guessed there was at least a foot of dirt on top of the timbers, creating the floor in the stables. The wall that held the ladder was a match of the one above it. The other three walls were of wood, probably the same timbers that made up the ceiling.

The air was surprisingly fresh. It was not stale and musty like we expected. There must be a good ventilation system built into the structure. From the looks of the place, it was part of the original building, all except what Gregor found. Lights, though dim, came on suddenly, blinding us for a moment.

The lighting was right out of an old war movie. Wires strung along the ceiling connected the numerous sockets that were nailed to the timbers. Over half the bare bulbs worked, filling the area with dim but manageable light. Along the walls were several drawings, paintings and old snap shots. The art was quite good. In fact, several of the pieces were very good. The old photos were of soldiers standing in front of the blacksmith shop dressed in cold weather gear.

On the east wall, in the corner with the rock wall to the north, sat a small forge. Above it was a chimney that disappeared into the rock wall. Blacksmith tools were sitting where they were left years ago, seemingly waiting to be picked up and used. On the floor around the forge, debris of all kinds littered the area. Sitting on a table, covered in years of dust, sat seven clay blocks.

I picked one up and studied it for a moment. A minute later it dawned on me what they were. Taking a side in each hand, I pulled until it separated into two exact halves. They were molds. The one I held in my hand was of an Angel with spread wings. Within minutes I had all seven apart and laid out on the table. Noticing someone beside me, I was surprised to see Sister Anna staring at the molds.

"Are these what I think they are?" she asked in a whisper.

"If you think these are some of the molds used to make the figurines at the Church, I think you would be correct." I responded with a smile.

Lae and Soledad joined us as Sister Anna said as tears started down her face, "Oh my, then this is where they created all the beautiful art they gave to the Church. Here, in this awful place."

Soledad and Lae stepped to each side of her and started their own soft conversation, trying to console her.

Getting out of the way, I noticed Gregor, Kurt and Father Aaron standing around a large cluster of debris on the floor across the room. As I walked up, I heard them discussing their theories as to what it was doing there.

"It looks like someone had been building coffins and this is scrap." Father Aaron said as I walked up.

Kurt leaned over, grabbed a piece of wood and said, "Not just coffins, but crates as well." Holding up the piece of wood he continued, "This looks like the same material as the crates we found on the train."

"I believe you are right. Not only about that but the coffins as well, look at the carving on the large piece of wood sticking out of the side." I said, joining them.

While we looked through the pile of scrap, the ladies remained huddled around the forge and molds. That is until Soledad stepped around one of the rock columns to get to the other side of the forge and fell down.

No one likes to trip, Soledad is no exception. Saying a slightly unlady like word, she got up, dusted herself off and said very loudly, "Well hell."

Lae and Sister Anna were at her side rather quickly to make sure she was unhurt. As they looked at where she pointed, their exclamations were as loud as Soledad's.

As one, they all said, "GOLD."

Interest in the wood died as we ran to where the ladies stood, staring at the back of a column. Seconds later, seven surprised people gazed at a stack of gold bars that were four bars wide and ten bars high. Gregor stepped out of the group and walked to the next column south of where we stood. He glanced down and walked to another to its west, and then another. After walking the length of the room, he returned and stood silently, waiting for someone to ask him about his walk.

Able to restrain his excitement, Gregor said in a somber voice, "There are two more stacks like this one, behind the two closest columns along the south wall."

The next hour was full of counting gold bars and calculating their worth until we could reach an agreement on the value of one hundred and thirty gold bars. With the weight of the bars at twenty seven and a half pounds each, over one and a half metric tonnes of gold was hidden behind three columns, and no one knew, for over thirty two years.

Gregor noticed I was squatting on my boot heel using the floor and my knife like paper and pen. He walked over and watched me go through my calculations, waiting quietly for the outcome.

After three times checking my work, I stood and said, "Ladies and Gentlemen, before you, and behind the other columns, rests over $7 Million in gold. I figure the gold that was taken into East Germany was part of this stash, if so, this accounts for two metric tonnes of the five that were reported as having passed through the Castle in '45."

Soledad was the first to ask the question that was on everyone's mind, "Where is the other three tonnes?"

Silence answered her. Ten minutes later, seven of the bars were brought out of the room and into the light for the first time in over thirty years.

CHAPTER 27

Max walked into the forest for the 15:00 (3 PM) check on his men who were guarding the perimeter when he heard several motors in the distance. Max quickly went a knoll that gave him a view of the Estate on which the cabin was part. He did not like what he saw. Three canvas covered trucks pulled up to the door and at least thirty armed men piled out. As he watched, a small man met the newcomers on the walk and started pointing toward the Schloss to the south. Five minutes later he reported what he saw to Ernst.

Ernst did not waste any time, "Max, we must help defend the Schloss. Our new friends are there conducting their investigation." Turning to the rest of the men, who had joined them when Max came running back, "To arms gentlemen, I do not want to kill anyone unless absolutely necessary, however I do not want our friends harmed in any way."

With a resounding "Jawohl Herr Kapitan" the men scrambled for their gear and were ready to move out in under five minutes.

Stepping out of the cabin, Ernst stopped on the porch, his attention on a man that two of his men brought before him. "What do we have here gentlemen?"

"Sir, he was running through the forest in a direct path here. He says the Lady of the Estate sent him to warn us." the soldier said as he held a firm grip on the man.

Looking the man over, Ernst asked, "Warn us of what, the thirty men who arrived a short time ago?"

The man didn't back down nor cower, looking Ernst straight in the eye, he said, "My Lady said to tell you they plan on killing the Americans and taking anything they find. There is an old crazy Nazi running the operation and has made our home his headquarters."

"When do they plan to attack?" Ernst asked, slightly warming up to the man.

"Their orders are to wait until they see evidence of a find. When that happens, if it happens, they are to rush in killing everyone in the blacksmith shop. Also, if they haven't seen any sign by 5:30 they are to abandon the raid and come back to the Estate." He said in an even tone.

Ernst studied him for a moment and came to a conclusion, "You were a soldier, correct?"

The man stood as straight as he could with two men holding his arms and said, "Jawohl! I had the privilege to serve with the 5th Mountain."

Motioning his me to free him, Ernst said, "They were a fine unit. I have read of their exploits in the Balkans, Russia and Italy." Pausing for a moment, deep in thought, Ernst continued, "Do you have a weapon?"

"My compatriot and I are the only men that My Lady has on staff and sadly we are unarmed." He said as he nodded to the men who had held him.

Ernst asked, "Was he a soldier as well?"

"Yes Sir, we served together." He said.

Turning to one of his men, Ernst said, "Bring two side arms with three extra clips each and give to our friend."

"Jawohl!" the young man said as he hurried to fulfill the order.

"You may need them to defend your Lady if things get out of hand." Ernst said as he extended his hand.

Shaking Ernst's hand, the man smiled for the first time and asked, "Who do I have to thank for the weapons and the hospitality?"

Smiling, Ernst, said, "Lange, Ernst Lange. And you?"

"Wolfgang Meyer." He said, trying to keep a smile off his face. Seeing the surprise on Ernst's face he continued, "I see you recognize my name, I was your father's aid."

"When time permits, we must talk." Ernst said as the surprise faded. "But for now, we have a situation that needs our attention. Please thank Frau von Beitel for her hospitality and her warning. It is best you return quickly and protect her."

The young soldier returned with the weapons and ammo. Taking them, Wolfgang nodded to Ernst and hurried back to the estate.

Turning to the young man who brought the weapons, Ernst said, "Go to the blacksmith shop and tell our friends our situation. I do not want them alarmed if firing erupts. Then meet us on the ridge."

With a quick nod and a salute the young man was on his way.

Having planned for outside intervention, Ernst led his men into the forest to positions he and Max had determined would give them an advantage over anyone coming from the north. Within twenty minutes of the watching the men unload from their trucks, he and his men were in place.

The Estate of Frau von Beitel was four kilometers north of the Schloss. Roughly half way between the two, a long ridge ran east to west and had light undergrowth in the forest. Ernst and his men owned the ridge therefore owned the approach to the Schloss. Since the Estate was on a mountain slope, it was higher than the ridge where the commandos waited. It gave the Sturmbannfuhrer a clear view of the blacksmith building and the immediate area around it when looking out the second story windows. The forest along the ridge hid the rest of the Schloss as well as the commando's positions.

9 Oct, Ridge North West of Schloss

Sitting in their concealed positions, the two mercenaries could see movement in the forest but did not know what was going on. Looking at each other and shrugging, they sat back and waited as per their orders. A few minutes later their radio came alive. The convoy carrying the rest of the mercenaries was minutes from their staging area. While one communicated with their leader, the other watched the Americans as they brought shiny bars out of the blacksmith shop.

9 Oct, Elsie's Estate

The Sturmbannfuhrer was furious at the tardiness of the young men. Pushing them to move into the forest along a ridge just north of the blacksmith shop, they rushed into a dangerous situation. Instead of sending a couple of men out on point to scout their path and fanning out to proceed to the ridge, they started walking in a group.

9 Oct, the Ridge

Max looked at Ernst and could not suppress a laugh, "Look as those idiots! They would not last three minutes in combat. What are your orders?"

Ernst had decided what he would do as soon as he saw the way the men were deployed, turning to Max he said, "Have three men deploy on their left and three men on their right. Tell no one to fire unless I give the order. If I have to shoot one of these fools I do not want a blood bath."

Max did not like it but he understood the need for such an order, "Ernst, do not get yourself shot because you do not want to kill these idiots."

Smiling at his friend, Ernst pated Max on the back, then stood and started walking toward the group of young men. When he was fifty meters from his men, Ernst leaned against a tree and waited for the close knit pack of idiots to reach him.

The leader was within ten meters before he realized Ernst was there. Surprise only lasted for a second. Swinging his assault rifle into position to cover Ernst, he was surprised again when Ernst didn't act scared.

Wanting to act in control in front of his men, the young Nazi said, "Do not move or I will cut you in half."

Ernst smiled and said, "I have no intention to move. However I do have a question." Without giving the young man a chance to respond, Ernst continued, "Why so many men and so many weapons for a stroll in the forest?"

Sneering at Ernst, he said, "Our presence is not your concern. What should concern you is what we are going to do to you. We cannot let you leave and give us away."

As the young Nazi made that statement he nodded to the man to his right. The man responded with a sneer of his own as he sat his rifle down and drew a large knife. Walking toward Ernst with the blade pointed at his intended victim, the man wasted no time reaching the commando.

Without much movement on his part, Ernst shifted his weight onto his left foot. With thirty men at his back the man was slightly over confident and walked right up to Ernst. With little effort Ernst right boot rearranged the man's genitals. The knife hit the ground just before the man sunk to his knees as he proceeded to lose his lunch. While the group's attention was on their comrade, Ernst pulled his side arm and shot the Nazi leader in the right foot.

Dropping his weapon and grabbing his foot, the young Nazi forgot his mission as the pain shot through him. The rest of the Nazis didn't know whether to come to the aid of their stricken leader or shoot the man responsible for his wounding, therefore neither was accomplished. They did manage to point their rifles at Ernst.

Knowing Max and his men, Ernst raised his left hand and made a circler motion. Within seconds, commandoes appeared in the forest in a half moon configuration completely blocking the Nazis from any further advance. The shock of commandoes appearing out of the forest with automatic weapons aimed at them was too much for the wanna be bad boys. Slowly they started dropping their weapons and stepping away from them.

Speaking loud enough for all to hear, Ernst said, "You will gather your leader and proceed to your trucks, load up and go back to whatever rock you crawled from under. You will do so quickly and without argument. My men will follow you with orders to shoot any man who does otherwise. Am I understood?"

"Yes, yes we understand!" the wounded man screamed, "Hurry, get me to a doctor before I bleed to death."

Two of the men helped the wounded man up and started back to the estate and their trucks, the rest followed without saying a word. Ernst had ten of his men follow them back to their trucks to make sure they leave as instructed. The rest of his men gathered the dropped weapons with plans of taking them to the hunting cabin.

CHAPTER 28

Gregor and I froze when we heard a single report echo off the mountains. We had brought some of the bars outside and were studying them in the sun light. The marking on them were consistent with Nazi molded gold bars, a Swastika present in the top middle.

The gunshot brought Kurt outside to confer with us, "That sounded like it was to our north and very close."

Before we could reply, a young man ran up to us from the north east. We all recognized him as one of Ernst's commandos.

The young man ran up to me, saluted and said, "With my Captains compliments, there is a large group of men on the way here from the Estate of Frau von Beitel. Captain Lange is leading our men in an attempt to stop the advance."

Gregor asked, "What was the cause of the gunshot we heard a few moments ago?"

Smiling slightly, the young commando said, "Knowing my Captain, he was successful in diverting the advance."

"Thank you and thank the Captain for the warning and the help. Please ask him to keep us posted." I said.

As the young man turned to go, a procession of trucks came down the old forest road and stopped at the edge of the forest. Three men got out of the lead truck and started walking toward us. We could see automatic weapons under the coats the men were wearing. So far they hadn't touched them. However, our weapons were under our jackets, out of sight. When the man spotted the bars he smiled and sped up his pace. Stopping ten feet from us, he smiled and motioned toward the gold.

"Thank you for finding the gold so quickly. I was afraid you would not come through and find it at all." He said with a leer on his face.

"Really, and who might you be?" I asked in an even tone.

"Who I am does not matter. The fact that we are going to relieve you of your find does." He said as a mischievous grin spread across his face.

As he said that, the man on his right shifted his submachine gun to cover us while the man on his left motioned for the men in the trucks to join them. None of us had moved, though we were all armed, knowing we could not be faster than the man who had his weapon trained on us. Suddenly the man on the left turned to us with his submachine gun at the ready as well.

The leader reached under his coat, palmed the grip on his weapon and said, as he brought it to bear, "We have heard too many stories about each of you to let you live. In another time or place, I would have enjoyed having a drink with you and hearing the stories first hand. Oh well, such is life."

Those were his last words. As he brought his weapon up, three shots rang out behind and above us. All three men were drilled through their rotten hearts, dead before they hit the ground. The men coming from the trucks thought, at first, those shots were their people getting us out of the way. The misconception only lasted seconds. Diving through the windows of the blacksmith shop we were micro seconds ahead of the hail of automatic fire they brought down on us.

The commando raised the submachine gun he carried and let loose a burst in the general direction of the men. Gregor had both 1911's in his grip as I palmed the brace of Pythons. Kurt looked at each of us in turn then stared at his Walther .380. Shaking his head, he smiled, raised the pistol and fired several shots through the window. In the mix was the sound of rifle fire coming from above us.

Gregor crawled to the far window on the right while I did the same to the left. When we were in position, Kurt and the commando fired through the center windows to draw fire. This move gave us the chance to survey, even if only for seconds, our assailants. The concentrated fire at the center was overwhelming, showering Kurt and the young commando with chips of stone.

Working our way back to them Gregor spoke up, "I count eighteen combatants with automatic weapons. There were also seven bodies, I think."

"I think you nailed the count, both dead and alive. The question is who the hell are they?"

"Our enemy." The young commando said with a smile.

Gregor motioned toward the ceiling and asked, "Who saved our pork?"

"Bacon, who saved our bacon." I answered with a huge grin.

Frustrated, Gregor said, "Whatever part of pig, who saved ours?"

"Don't know, but it sounds like the fire is shifting from us to them. The hay loft is wood and won't stop the rounds like stone." I said as I worked my way to the door that led to the back of the shop where the ladies and the ladder to the loft were. I met Joseph at the door.

"What the bloody hell is going on?" Joseph asked as another burst went through one of the near windows.

"We have a large group of heavily armed individuals who want to relieve us of the gold as well as our lives. We also have persons unknown with rifles in the hay loft who seem to be on our side. I'm going up there and see who we have to thank for the assistance." I replied as the ladies joined us.

Joseph nodded to me, turned to the ladies and said, "Stay down there and guard the gold, we will take care of the party up here."

Janet pushed past him saying, "You need our help and you know it."

Before he or I could say anything else, our three women had weapons in each hand and were joining the fight. Kurt saw them enter the room on their hands and knees and understood the situation immediately. Turning to us he gave thumbs up and started placing the ladies at every other window. Joseph patted me on the shoulder, nodded and went back to help. Knowing the ladies were in good hands, including my Heart, I started up the ladder to the loft.

As I reached for the trapdoor at the top of the ladder, the little voice in the back of my head started screaming at me. Since it seems to always to be right I went down the ladder, grabbed a shovel that was hanging on a tool rack. Back at the top of the ladder I used the shovel to push the trapdoor open. The little voice was right again. Three holes appeared in the center of the door tearing it to shreds.

"Whoa there! First you save my hide then you try to put holes in it? I'm on your side and we don't have time to waste so I am coming up.!" I yelled in German at the opening, praying they could hear me.

Slowly I climbed the last few rungs and peered over the flooring of the loft. It only took seconds to spot three rifle bores pointed at my head. Behind those bores sat three dirty, bloody old warriors. When they recognized me they lowered the rifles and sat back. Several feet behind them the north wall of the shop looked like Swiss cheese. The automatic weapons used by our adversaries riddled the area just above the rock wall showering the men with splinters of wood and chips of rock.

Crawling to them I gave them a quick look over and asked, "Are you wounded? Can you travel?"

The smallest of the three spoke up, in English, "No, we have not been hit, just scratched from flying debris. Yes, we can travel and I suggest we do so as soon as possible. We have but one bullet between us and will not be of any further help."

"May I?" I asked reaching for a rifle.

The man on my right passed his to me saying, "This one is loaded. The sights are dead on at one hundred meters."

The rifle he handed me was a fine specimen of a Karabiner 98. The rifle had great balance and felt good in my hands. Looking at the other weapons I was slightly surprised the other two were the same type. Studying the men it dawned on me, they probably served together and knew something about what was going on, why else the interest in putting up a defense of the old shop? I had a ton of questions for them but now was not the time.

"Gentlemen, let's get out of here and find a healthier environment. Go out the door and get down the ladder. When you hear me shoot…" I stopped as I noticed one of the men raise his hand, as if in school.

"We can show you and your friends a way out of the shop, if you like." He said in an anxious voice.

The other two nodded in agreement.

Gregor surveyed the area in front of the shop again. As he watched, two men moved between trees on their left, getting closer to the blacksmith shop with every step. One of the men peered around a tree trying to get a good look at the shop. It was the last thing he did in this world as a .45 slug from Gregor took his life. From what Gregor could tell there were now at least 12 bodies down in the forests edge and in the area between the forest and the shop. However as he watched, three of the "bodies" crawled a little closer then slumped down again.

Turning to Kurt, Gregor said, "Not all of the men on the ground are dead. Several of them are crawling slowly toward us."

The young commando looked out a window for a second and said, "At the rate they are moving, they will be close enough in a few minutes to throw grenades into the windows, if they have them."

Kurt replied, "If they have grenades and get close enough to use them, we are in serious trouble."

Soledad fired out her window and caused one of the crawling men to jump. Her action caused a violent reaction as over a dozen automatic weapons tore into the old shop tearing the opening and back wall to pieces.

Lae and Janet were holding their own as well. Both had fired almost fifty rounds and accounted for at least three enemy causalities. The added firepower the ladies brought to the party prevented them from being overrun. However three women and three men armed with handguns, except for the commando, could only do so much against a heavily armed, experienced, dedicated foe.

Kurt turned to Gregor and said, "I am going to check out the back and look for a way out of here."

Gregor nodded as he fired at another of the crawling men thus drawing fire away from Soledad.

Working his way to the door leading into the stables, Kurt couldn't help but wonder where the authorities were. The local Bundesgrenzschutz should have been on scene right after the shooting started. With the amount of firing, Kurt would expect a G9G unit to respond, but so far, nothing. Running across the stables, Kurt cracked open the door leading to the Schloss. Two automatic weapons persuaded him to retreat back inside. Damn, they were boxed in.

Several miles away the local Bundesgrenzschutz office was receiving calls about the fighting. Everyone on duty had been briefed about the exercise between the 10th and the American units thus making it easy to reassure the locals there was not a Soviet or East German invasion. Unknown to Kurt at the time, help from the authorities would never come.

Standing in front of the old men, I couldn't believe what he said. They knew a way out of the old blacksmith shop, thank God. His declaration changed my plans. Explaining to the three what I wanted them to do only took a few seconds. As the trap door closed behind them, I went to the edge of the loft and readied my weapons.

Kurt was surprised when three old men climbed down the ladder from the loft. The three were unarmed and looked like hell. Staring at Kurt and his raised pistol, the men froze for only a second. The smallest of the three got his nerve first and walked up to Kurt. Within one minute Kurt had the story and the plan. Telling the men to wait there, Kurt ducked down and went back into the blacksmith shop.

Crawling to Gregor, Kurt said, "We are boxed in, I almost got my head handed to me when I looked out the back of the stables. However, Glen has a way to disengage this fight and more importantly has found someone who can get us out of the trap we are in."

Frowning, Gregor asked as he fired two rounds out of his window, "Did you get this information from Glen?"

"No, from three old men who were in the loft." Kurt replied as he fired two more rounds at their attackers.

"How do we know they are on our side and not leading us into a worst situation?" Soledad asked as she approached the two, stopping to fire through a window.

Turning to Gregor, Kurt said, "One of the men told me, Glen said we would be suspicious, so Glen sent a message."

"What message?" Gregor asked as he popped off two more rounds and had the satisfaction in seeing a man go down.

Kurt smiled and said, "Glen told them to tell the big pissed off Russian, 'We are who saved your pork.'"

Laughing out loud, Gregor said, "That sounds like Glen. Ok, what is plan?"

As the others gathered around him, each taking turn firing out of various windows to keep the enemy down, Kurt laid out Glen's plan. When finished he looked directly at Soledad and waited for her to explode. Much to his surprise she didn't.

Noticing the attention, Soledad said, "Glen knows what he is doing. If anyone can pull this off, it's him."

Making eye contact with everyone, Kurt said as he looked at his watch, "Get ready then, Glen is expecting us to be ready to move in two minutes."

Soledad looked over at Lae and Janet and said, "Ladies, pass out our flash bang grenades, perhaps six of these babies will buy us some time."

With nods all around, everyone got into position to set the plan in motion.

9 Oct, the Ridge

When he heard firing at the Schloss, Ernst rallied his remaining men and started to come to our aid, he didn't get very far. When the young Nazis heard the shooting, mistakenly thinking they were being reinforced, they proved to be more resourceful than anyone thought. Approximately half pulled handguns out of their clothing and engaged Max and the commandos that were following them. Within seconds three of the commandos were down and the rest were pinned. Outnumbered two to one, Max knew he had to disobey Ernst orders about killing if his men were going to survive the next few minutes.

Ernst led his few men in the direction the young Nazis had taken back to the estate. After the first outburst of firing, all was quiet except steady firing coming from the Schloss. He had gone about a kilometer when he spotted Max moving from position to position talking to his men. Ernst accurately sized up the situation and Max's response to the attack from the young Nazis. Ernst knew Max planned to attack and remove the threat to his men.

The Nazis were inexperienced to say the least, they were bunched up and trying to overpower the commando position. However Max and his men were experts in this type of combat and had deployed to start a counter attack that would bring havoc to the young men. Ernst liked the way Max had positioned his men and moved to their right flank to provide support. It was as if Max knew what Ernst was thinking, he looked over his right shoulder and spotted Ernst immediately. All he did was nod and the plan of battle was ready.

9 Oct the Schloss

Holding the old rifle in my hands, I got ready to reduce our opponents' number by one. My two Colts were fully loaded and ready. The path to the trap door was clear. Looking out one of the holes in the side of the loft I picked my target, he was standing by a tree giving orders. Anyone giving orders makes a prime target for a sniper and a sniper I had become. Sniping was not my style of combat. If I have to take a life, I had much rather face my enemy, both of us armed and ready. There are always exceptions, and this was one.

The second hand on my watch touched 12, one second later we had one less antagonist. Dropping the rifle I dove for the floor as high velocity rounds chewed up the wall of the loft.

With the sound of the single rifle shot, the firing from the forest shifted to the loft. Adding the six grenades to the mix it gave our group a chance to get to the stables and down the ladder. Gregor was the last to go down.

"Gregor!" Soledad yelled, "He knows what he is doing! We have to shut the door." Punching Gregor on the leg until he looked down at her, she said, "I don't like leaving him either but he expects us to follow instructions."

As Gregor turned to respond, two men came rushing into the stables from the rear. Thankfully Gregor spotted them before they spotted him. The loud reports of twin .45's ended that threat. Seconds later the trap door was closed and locked. It would take more than small arms to punch a hole in the door. Hopefully the enemy doesn't have any C4.

With Colt Pythons filling my hands, all I could do was lay flat holding them over my head protecting myself from falling pieces of wood. Damn, they guys are laying it on thick. Knowing I had to continue to draw their fire until our people got underground, I crawled to the edge of the loft and fired a couple of rounds in the general direction of the attackers. The fire shifted to that spot, good thing I moved immediately after firing.

Three long minutes had gone by. The loft and roof of the old building was getting torn to shreds. It was time to vacate the premises. I hope. Studying the old chimney I was beginning to doubt my plan. The damn thing was built like a fort. The stones had to weight over two hundred pounds each. They were massive, for a chimney. Crawling to where it came through the floor, I gave one of the stones a kick. Not smart, I thought, as the pain shot up my leg. I had thought the issue might be the internal diameter of the chimney being big enough for me to slide down to the underground room, not the inability to gain access to the tube.

Shaking off the pain I had inflicted on myself, it dawned on me the firing had stopped. That could only mean one thing, our attackers were in the building. I prayed the trap door going underground was secure and that these bozos did not have grenades. A soft thud on the floor blew that hope. Ducking behind the chimney I opened my mouth and held my ears. The explosion blew gaps in the roof and side of the loft but the chimney prevented my taking shrapnel.

With both Colts pointed at the opening, I was ready for some unfortunate bastard to stick his head into the loft. Leaning against the chimney for support, I noticed an unusual placing of the stones on the back side of the chimney. Following the stones up to the roof I couldn't believe what was in front of me and a new plan started to form. Two more grenades caused me to put my new plan into action.

Soledad watched in amazement as one of the old men went to one of the support columns and studied it about four feet above the floor. Suddenly smiling, he pushed a finger into a small hole in the column. On the other side a small rod was pushed out of the stone. One of the other men did the same thing at another column. With rods in hand, they went to the rock wall that was lined up with the identical wall above them. After a few minutes studying the wall they found what they were looking for. Each started pushing the rods they found into small holes in the wall. As both rods were driven home a small crack appeared in the wall. With a slight push, the crack opened into a door. Willie was all smiles as Hans and Frederic triggered the ancient door.

Frederic said something in German to his compatriots and motioned for them to hurry into the opening.

Soledad turned to Gregor and asked, "What did he say?"

With a straight face, Gregor replied, "He said our diversion is no longer effective, it will not be long before they find the door leading here. We must hurry."

Paling, Soledad raised her hands to her mouth and muttered, "He means Glen, doesn't he? He means Glen is no longer effective."

Rushing to the opening above the fire pit, Soledad looked into the darkness praying for Glen to appear as was his plan. The chimney was dark and quiet, much to her dismay. As she raised her hands to her mouth preparing to yell into the abyss, a violent explosion rained dirt on them all. The attackers had found the door and were attempting to breach it. It withstood the first blast. How much more could it take?

Lae grabbed her arm and said, "Glen will find a way, we must go so that we may be alive to greet him."

Soledad looked at her friend, nodded through the tears and followed Lae into the darkness.

9 Oct, Elsie's Estate

Having seen the rout suffered by the young Nazis, the Sturmbannfuhrer called for his minion to grab as many rifles as he could carry from his car. He then motioned for the minion to follow him as he rushed to stem the retreat. As he reached the first of the young men, they heard the firing from the Schloss. The old Nazis had never been a ground combat commander but he knew how to put fear into men. He knew the young men feared him, you could see it in their eyes. Therefore, he used their fear and an old MP40 submachine gun to get their attention. As he reached the retreating Nazis, the Sturmbannfuhrer fired a long burst into the ground in front of them.

"Get out of the way old man! We are not going to die for you." The wounded leader shouted at him.

Three 9mm rounds silenced his tongue forever. The others slowed and stared at their fallen comrade. The small stature of the Sturmbannfuhrer made the MP40 look huge in the eyes of the scared young men. Needless to say he got their attention.

"You fools, do you not hear the shooting coming from the Schloss? The rest of my men are attacking from the rear. Join them and your brothers who stayed and are fighting your fight. Let us crush the defenders and take the gold! We will all be rich men by nightfall!" the old Nazi screamed as he pushed through them waiving his weapon in the direction of the Schloss.

As he made that statement his minion caught up with him and started passing out the rifles he carried. He did not have enough for everyone but that didn't matter, most of the young men started pulling pistols from under their clothes. With renewed vigor, they rejoined their comrades in an effort to crush the commandoes and take the Schloss.

One kilometer from the estate Ernst and his men were in a fight for their lives. Seconds before the order was given to attack the Nazis, they were reinforced by the Nazis who ran, led by an old man with an old weapon. They were out outnumbered two to one when Ernst and Max joined forces and the rest of the Nazis joined their brothers.

The odds had not changed much after fifteen minutes of fighting. The commandos had four men down, all alive but seriously wounded. This left a total of nine effective combatants. The Nazis suffered far worse with four dead and five wounded. However they still had twenty two fighters and one crazy commander.

"Ernst, the firing behind us has slowed. Do you think the Americans have fought their attackers to a standstill?" Max asked as he crawled to Ernst position.

Squeezing his friend on the shoulder, Ernst said, "They are an amazing group. I believe they are capable of withstanding the attack. However to help insure their survival we must not let these crazy bastards through."

As two of their men joined them, Max smiled and said, "Captain, the only place these idiots are going is to hell."

9 Oct, the Church

"Stupid son of a bitch!" Sister Marie yelled as she slammed down the phone.

"Sister, such language!" Sister Sara said, scolding her for the outburst as she sat at the Fathers desk.

"Well, they are! Everyone I talked to at the Bundesgrenzschutz station I called is either a moron or a stupid son of a bitch. They said the shooting we hear is an exercise between the 10th Division and an American unit. What are we going to do?"

Sister Sara looked at her friend with a scowl and said, "Sister Anna and the Father are up there where there is shooting, and a lot of it. When they left after Mass they did not say anything about an Army exercise. I think there is something terribly wrong up there. But since the authorities say there is nothing wrong, what can we do?"

Sister Marie started to let lose a string of curses when she bumped the table that sat across from the Fathers desk. Setting up the pictures she had knocked over, she paused as she stared at one. Sitting it down she turned to Sister Sara and said, "Quick, hand me the Fathers rolodex and the phone."

9 Oct, the Schloss

The double blast of the last grenades blew most of the remaining roof off the middle of the loft. Dirt and wood filled the air as I climbed the back of the chimney to a trapdoor that led to the roof. The door opened easily and I was on the roof in a second. Working my way to the southwest end of the building, I looked for a way down that would keep me out of the attacker's sights.

A submachine gun burst from one of the holes in the roof convinced me to hurry. Sliding to the edge of the roof I paused for only a moment before jumping the fifteen or so feet to the ground. Hitting the ground in a crouch and rolling I avoided injury. My next move was hauling ass into the trees, chased by another long burst.

After running about fifty feet into the forest, I stopped behind a tree. However none followed that I could see. The only thing that I could think to do was to go back and prevent them from following our group underground. Filling my hands with the Colts I prepared to return and take as many of the bastards with me as possible to protect my friends.

"Excuse me." a voice said from the forest.

Looking down the sights of the Colt, finger on the trigger, I stared into the eyes of a stranger. He didn't flinch as he looked past the bore of the Colt and into my eyes. His hands were empty and open, his stance relaxed. Taking this in, I decided to find out who he is and what he is doing here.

"You have ten seconds to tell me why I don't want to pull the trigger." I said in a low tone.

"John said I shouldn't surprise you. Said you would fight a chainsaw when surprised. I should have listened." The man said in an even tone, smile spreading across his face. "He also said to tell you Jennifer, Becca, Lupe and Kyle are doing fine and Consuelo has them locked down tight. He then called you his grandson-in-law. Are you?"

Lowering the hammer and holstering the Colt, I said, "Well, you must be one of John's or you wouldn't know about our relationship. Thanks for the update on the kids. What are you doing here?"

"I am a tourist and a bird watcher enjoying the countryside. I am also John's eyes and ears on your little endeavor. And, if you should need assistance, I am to offer mine. It appears you are in need. Should I unpack my camera or something a little noisier?" he said with a straight face.

Starting to like the guy, I asked, "I am a little surprised John picked you to bird watching in a German forest."

"Why? Because I'm Black? What better cover? Who would think an American operative in Germany would be an African American? I'm hiding in plain sight." He said with a laugh.

Laughing as well, I said, "Sounds crazy enough to work and looks like John found someone crazy enough to try it." Offering my hand, I asked, "What is your name, you already know mine."

Shaking my hand, he said, "Anthony Smith at your service." Seeing my smile, he continued, "Well, Anthony is right anyway." He said with a smile.

"Anthony, we need to get back into the blacksmith shop and prevent some unpleasant men from breaching a door into an underground room. You ready?" I asked, anxious to get back into the fight.

Reaching into his back pack, he unloaded a camera and supplies. Smiling at me he reached deeper into the pack and pulled out two Ingram Mac 10's with extended clips. After pocketing extra clips he handed me two grenades and pocketed two in his jacket. Stashing the camera and pack he stood and motioned for me to lead the way.

Unholstering the Pythons I smiled, turned and started backtracking to the shop. I was feeling better about stopping the men since my jump off the roof, after all my force had doubled in size. Our pace quickened when we heard muffled explosions coming from the shop.

Inside the stables, by the trap door leading into the underground room, the mercenaries shook their heads in disbelief. They had used up to four grenades at a time trying to penetrate the trap door. The door was damaged but it held firm. As the smoke and dust cleared from their last attempt, one of the men noticed a hole in the floor next to the door. Wedging three grenades in the hole, they stepped back, hopeful of success. Their perseverance was rewarded as the blast tore the door from it hinges and gave them access to the room. Wasting no time, four went into the underground room, firing as they went.

They wasted their bullets, the room was unoccupied. Quickly the rest of the men joined their comrades in the room, all but two who stayed behind as guards. After a quick search, they were concerned at not finding the Americans. That concern went right out the window when stacks of gold bars were found behind support columns.

The new mercenary leader was ecstatic at the amount of gold. Thinking he had found all they came for, he quickly ordered his men to bring it to the surface and load it on their trucks. In his haste he made a major mistake. Except for the men driving the trucks and the two men he left on the surface as guards, he brought all his men into the room to give them instructions and start the removal of the gold. His plans were disrupted when he heard the sound of two shots and the noise caused by the body of one of his guards as he fell through the trapdoor.

Anthony and I were surprised at the ease of reaching the stable door. It was if we were suddenly alone. Peering quickly through the door I spotted two men standing by the damaged trapdoor. They were probably guards but were not very good ones. Weapons ready, Anthony and I walked into the stables at a fast walk. We got to within fifty feet of the men before we were spotted.

As the echo of our shots faded, Anthony turned to me and said, "Mine hit the ground first."

"I put mine through the door, he had further to fall." I threw back at him with a smile.

Watching all the doors, Anthony said, "Now what?"

"I am going down there. That is where my friends went, I will follow. " I replied.

"Well then lead with grenades my friend." Anthony said as he pulled one out of his pocket.

"Can't, my friends are in the room." I said as I stepped close to the opening, trying listen to any movement down there. My shadow in the opening caused a reaction as three bullets came through the hole and smacked into the ceiling.

"Just how the hell are you going to accomplish that and stay alive?" Anthony asked as he watched dirt and wood fall from the ceiling.

Looking over his shoulder, an idea came to mind as I studied the chimney. I couldn't get into the chimney from the loft, perhaps I could from the stable. Stepping over to the chimney, I pulled the two grenades Anthony had given me, pulled the pins, placed them on a rock ledge on the back side and ran toward Anthony. Both of us hit the floor a second before the explosions. The dust hadn't settled before I was at the chimney and started kicking at the opening the grenades made. Anthony covered the trap door, firing a round into the wood of the floor at the opening as a reminder to the men below that someone unfriendly to them was in the stable.

After a minute or so, I had a hole big enough for me to climb into the chimney tube. As I peered into the opening the thought of leading with a grenade sounded good, but I could not risk hurting my people. Before I went into the dark tube, Anthony came over.

"Glen, the trucks have pulled up on the north side and the drivers are piling out of the trucks armed and headed this way. I can hold them off but you better hurry." Anthony said as he shifted position to cover the opening going into the blacksmith shop.

Nodding, I holstered the Colts and went to the east wall where I had seen several ropes. Quickly grabbing a coil that looked long enough for what I had in mind, I threw it over a rafter closest to the hole in the chimney. Tying one end around my waist, I gripped the rope and started repelling down the chimney. The sides of the tube were rough with small rock outcroppings every few feet. Those outcroppings were a great help. Using them to control my decent, I went as fast as I dared into the dark tube.

As I reached the light at the end, I leaned over and peered into the room in an attempt to locate and identify all the occupants. After a quick look, I realized the only people in the room were our attackers.

They were busy staging the gold bars near the stairs which gave me time to lower myself into the fire pit. Within seconds of untying the rope, all Hell broke loose above ground.

Automatic weapons fire caused the work to cease and the men to gather at the base of the ladder, weapons ready. This gave me the chance to get a good count. An even dozen men with automatic weapons stood at the base of the ladder. I'm good, but I would need luck as well to survive a 12 to 1 fight. If I did not survive, there would be nothing to prevent them from finding whatever my friends used to escape the room and follow them. Another thought came to mind, we can't trap them here, they would surly find the way out and, again, follow my friends. Damn, the only option is to let them escape and join their comrades that were currently keeping Antony busy. I don't give a rat's ass about the gold, but I object when people try to harm my friends and my Heart.

As I reached my decision to join Anthony and let these bastards out of this hole, one of the men spotted me. Hesitating for only a second, reminding myself these men had tried to kill me and every one of us, and would so again if given a chance, I pulled the pins on the other two grenades Anthony had given me before I went down the chimney and tossed them among the men. The man saw them bounce and yelled a warning.

They scattered and I went up the chimney, climbing as fast as I could. I was out of the chimney in seconds and on the stable floor in time to see two men come through the back door. Taking in the situation, I knew Antony was being flanked and didn't see the two men. Filling my hands with the Colts, I screamed like a Comanche and ran toward them, firing as I went. My actions diverted their attention from Anthony's back and made them focus on me. Both opened up with their H&K Submachine guns firing from the hip, which was stupid, spraying 9mm rounds in my direction.

I felt a tug at my right side and then a hammer hit my right leg causing me to stumble for a second. As I recovered from the hit, my left Colt found its mark and put down the man on the left. Switching aim to the man on the right, I fired the two Colts at the same time striking the remaining man in the chest with both rounds.

Running to Anthony, who was still engaged with the three men in the front, I grabbed his arm and said, "Let's blow this Popsicle stand, I'm running low on flavors and there are more unwanted guests coming to the party."

"How many more?" Antony asked as he fired a burst from one of his Mac 10"s and rose to join me.

"An even dozen upset party goers with automatic noise makers." I said as we cleared the back door and sprinted into the forest.

We stopped after only a few steps into the forest and checked our back trail, no one followed. One of the men peered out the door in our direction but he must not have seen us. After only a few seconds he was gone.

"Anthony, let's move to where we can see their trucks. I want to see how long before they appear with the gold and make a head count. I also want to make sure they did not try to follow my people." I said as we started moving through the forest.

"Glen, you are leaking." Anthony said as he pointed to my right leg and side.

Looking down, all I could think of was my jeans and shirt were ruined. But Anthony was right, I had taken two hits. The one in the side was purely a flesh wound. In fact it almost missed me. The one in the leg was about half way between my knee and hip, and a harder hit. I wasn't bleeding badly therefore the artery was intact, as well as the bone. But I was bleeding and we needed to plug the holes before I lost too much blood and lose my effectiveness.

Anthony rushed to his camera bag he had left in the forest and pulled out a med kit. In minutes he had treated and bandaged my wounds. Five minutes later we were sitting in a good spot to watch the blacksmith shop and the trucks. Now we wait.

CHAPTER 29

The door closing behind Soledad had a feel of finality that shook her to the bone. She hated the idea of leaving Glen behind, but she was following his wishes. She hoped and prayed he knew what he was doing. Running into Lae shook her back to the situation at hand.

"I'm sorry Lae, I didn't see you, it's so damn dark." Soledad said as she steadied her friend.

"It is too dark to do anything except run into things and each other." Lae responded.

A light suddenly appeared. Sister Anna smiled at them, passed a small flashlight to Lae and Soledad and said, "You do know we have pockets in our Habits, don't you?"

Father Aaron laughed and said, "I had forgotten you always carry those small flashlights as well as matches. Thank God."

Kurt and Gregor stood side by side, listening to them as they studied the walls of the cave they found themselves. Without saying a word, Gregor reached for the light in Lae's hand. When she saw the look on his face she passed it to him without hesitation. Father Aaron, Sister Anna and Soledad saw the exchange and turned to see what had caught the attention of the two men.

It took several minutes for the ladies to understand what they were looking at, the men knew immediately, they stood in a crypt. The caskets lined both sides of the cave and seemed to go further than the light. Shining the light on the exposed ends, they noticed writing on each.

Father Aaron shined his light on the three old men and said, "This is where you buried your comrades. This is why we never saw a grave. They are all in this cave."

Willie spoke up first, "Ja, where else would they be? Besides we did not want to give the SS the satisfaction in watching us bury our friends. We also had other items to bury." He said as he pointed at a casket ten feet down the tunnel.

Shining his light on the casket, Kurt read the inscription out loud, "Geld von Kinder."

Soledad hadn't picked up any German, even though Gregor and Glen spoke it to each other to stay in practice. Turning to Gregor she asked, "What does that mean?"

"Money for children." Gregor answered as he studied the casket. Turning to Willie and his two partners, Gregor continued, "How much gold is buried here?"

The three old warriors looked at each other for a second before Fredric said, "Over five metric tonnes, however a few people have been pulling from here to maintain their families. There is probably three metric tonnes or so still here."

Soledad looked at Kurt and said, "That amount makes the amount of gold to over eight metric tonnes? That is far more than the evidence shows."

Laughing, Hans spoke up for the first time, "There was more than one shipment of gold. In fact there were three."

Willie added, "We were not the only ones who plotted to steal the gold." turning to the other two, he said, "Do you remember the crazy SS Major? You know the one. He had the Frankenstein monster for a driver?"

Hans said, "I remember he was stuck on his rank. He only wanted to be called Herr Sturmbannfuhrer. I do not remember hearing his name."

Fredric threw his two cents in saying, "Remember how he had us load all the ash from the furnace into boxes marked dangerous?"

Hans answered, "Yes, he also had us place a quantity of gold bars in the ash. I still have not understood why."

Gregor interrupted the three, saying, "I know we all want to hear your stories, but we must get out of this tunnel before we are trapped here with your comrades and the gold. Is there another way out?"

Frowning, Willis answered, "An escape tunnel would not be much good without two ways in and out, would it?"

"Besides," Fredric said, "How do you think small quantities of gold have been removed over the years?"

Stepping aside, Gregor motioned for Fredric to take point. The little group followed the old warrior into the darkness.

9 Oct, the Ridge

Ernst and his men were gaining ground on the young Nazis. After less than thirty minutes of heavy fighting, the experience and training of the commandoes was taking its toll on the other group. Even with seven of their number wounded and out of the fight, the commandoes had the upper hand. Ten of the Nazis lay dead and seven more were wounded. In addition to the causalities, their crazy commander had vanished. With only a dozen or so active fighters, they were losing the momentum they had gained a short time ago.

Dirt flew into Ernst's face as he ducked behind a fallen log. His move prevented him from catching a long burst from one of the Nazis submachine guns. The commando he joined behind the log returned fire to give his commander cover.

Ernst nodded at the young man, took a quick look over the log, and said, "Not very friendly guests, are they."

Smiling at his Captain, the young man replied, "No sir, they are not, however there are fewer inhospitable guests out there. Sir, if I may? I do not want to be out of line."

Ernst nodded at him to continue.

"Our advisories have taken severe punishment. I think if we hit them along the entire front their will to fight will shatter and they will retreat back to where ever they came from."

"You may be right. However we only have five men to carry out such a plan since one must stay behind to care for our wounded." Ernst said as he looked over the log and studied the situation.

"Sir, we have you and four men you have trained to be the best fighting men in the world." The young man said with steel in his voice.

Placing his hand on the young man's shoulder, Ernst said, "Be ready in five minutes to hit them with steady fire and be prepared to move forward." As he started to rise, Ernst continued, "Thank you for reminding me who we are. Always speak your mind to me. You will never be out of line."

As Ernst moved from behind the log to put their plan in action, the young commando prepared to implement his part of the attack. As he readied his ammo, he smiled with pride of his unit and of being a part of such a fighting force. He vowed to himself to follow Captain Lange where ever he leads, in whatever army, for whatever country.

Within a few minutes, Ernst had delivered the new plan to his remaining men. Three of his wounded insisted on joining the attack, including Max, who was he to argue? To a man they were ready to push the Nazis off the mountain. They were more than ready when Ernst started the ball rolling with a yell and steady firing of his submachine gun.

Coming off the ground and from behind embankments, the commandos attacked with the ferocity berserkers of old would be proud. The sudden counterattack took the Nazis by surprise and finished off their resolve. Leaving their fallen comrades where they lay, the survivors faded into the forest, running back to their trucks and escaping the slaughter.

Max worked his way to Ernst's side, being gentle with his wounded arm. Pausing for a moment to catch his breath he finally said, "Your orders Captain, shall we pursue or let them go?"

With a tired laugh, Ernst replied, "Pursue with what? We have more wounded than unscathed. Let us keep an eye on them while we care for our men, I would hate to lose anyone to these thugs after what we have been through. I will take two men and follow them to make sure they leave the area. Please search their positions for any wounded and treat them with our own, well after disarming them." He said, smiling at Max.

Max winced as he moved his arm, when his breath returned he said, "I wish we had that old British doctor with us. He is a good doctor and a damn good man."

Looking at his friend, Ernst said, "Perhaps we can, please send two men to me." an idea forming in his tired mind.

9 Oct, the Estate

Elsie stood in her foyer, facing the man who had tormented her for thirty years, his anger as tangible as the pistol in his hand.

"My plans have been thwarted by those American fools and their inept friends. I am forced to withdraw and find another way to recover what is rightfully mine. You, on the other hand, I have no further need." The Sturmbannfuhrer said as he raised his pistol.

Wolfgang said from a side door, "Drop your weapon or we shall kill you."

The old Nazi turned his head and was shocked to see two pistols pointed at his head. When he got his tongue, he screamed, "How dare you threaten me! Drop your pistols or I will kill your mistress."

Reaching up with his thumb, Wolfgang pulled the hammer back on the Walther in his hand and said, "We shoot in three seconds, one, two…"

He didn't get to three. The old man lowered his weapon and ran to his waiting car. The minion didn't get a chance to open his door. The old man was shouting all the way from the house for him to get in and go, quickly.

No sooner than the Sturmbannfuhrer disappeared down the road, the young Nazis came running out of the forest and into their trucks, following their old leader.

Wolfgang turned to Elsie and said, "There were far fewer leaving than arrived earlier."

Elsie smiled and replied, "I noticed. However, I fear the commandos will be fewer as well. Let us gather medical supplies and get ready to come to their aid if needed.

9 Oct, the Ridge

Within minutes, two of his men had their instructions and were headed to the von Beitel estate. Taking a route that would keep them away from the retreating Nazis, the two young men covered the distance at a dead run. As the came upon the estate, they stopped to study the Nazis. The young commandoes didn't need to worry about them. The only evidence of their presence was the dust in the air raised by their speeding trucks.

A call from the house stopped them at the edge of the porch. Explaining their reason for being on estate grounds took only a moment. After Frau von Beitel agreed to their request, they started to turn away. A call from Elsie stopped them. Within minutes they headed back to their wounded comrades with sorely needed medical supplies and three extra pair of hands.

Ernst and two men took the same route the Nazis had taken thus taking longer to arrive at the estate. Therefore, they did not see the small group leave the house and head to the ridge. Ernst did notice there were no vehicles around the house. He expected to see some kind of a car that the crazy old man would have driven, but there was nothing. Shaking his head, he smiled at the thought of catching the old man and interrogating him.

Satisfied the fight was over and his men out of danger, Ernst returned to the ridge to care for his wounded. As he entered the small copus of trees they were using for a field hospital, he was surprised by what he saw. Before him were Frau von Beitel, Wolfgang and another man helping treat his men. The old Lady's arms and front of her dress was covered in his men's blood. The look on her lovely face was sheer determination. Wolfgang and his comrade had the same look on their faces as well. They must have brought the supplies they were using from the estate. There was no other explanation of the quantity and quality of the dressings and medicines.

Walking through the wounded, praising each man for his heroism, Max did what he could to maintain the high moral this unit was known for. Pride in these kids brought tears to his eyes that he tried hard to hold. As he came to the more seriously wounded, he almost lost the battle to hold the tears at bay. Several of the men tried to get him to get his wounds treated. Max told them he would when he had a chance. He was determined not to get treated before all of these kids were tended to, not a minute sooner, his men came first.

Pausing to catch his breath and reposition his injured arm, Max turned and saw his Captain and friend standing at the edge of the trees, tears flowing freely down his tired cheeks.

9 Oct, the Forest

Anthony tapped me on the shoulder and pointed to the far edge of the blacksmith shop and said, "Glen, here comes four more men, looks like all sixteen are present and accounted for."

"Sixteen? There should only be fifteen." I said as I shifted to get a good look at the new comers. It only took a second to recognize the sixteenth man, turning to Anthony I said, "Damn it, he is the grounds keeper of the Schloss."

"Well, he is not one of their favorite people. They just slapped the hell out of him. It looks like they are interrogating him. They probably want to know how the rest of your people got out of the blacksmith shop unseen." Anthony said as we shifted locations to get a better look.

I was prepared to let these jerks drive off with the gold, good riddance to both. If they let the old man go, they still can. But Anthony was right, blood was flowing from the old man's nose. Then they hit him again, driving him to his knees.

"Anthony, if he hits him again, or pulls a weapon, I going to stop him." I said, looking toward my new partner.

"I'm with you Glen, I don't like this either." Anthony said as he checked the clips in his Ingram's. Continuing he asked, "What's the plan?"

"Simple, you keep the men loading the trucks busy while I grab the old man." I said with a smile.

"I was afraid that would be it. Oh well, I didn't have anything to do this afternoon." Anthony said with a soft sigh.

"Wait for my signal then shoot the hell out of those trucks." I said with a smile on my lips and a gleam in my eye.

"What signal?" he asked.

"You will know it." I said with a smile.

Looking back at the men who held the groundskeeper, I knew what I would have to do. Nodding to Anthony I stood and walked out of the forest and headed straight to the old man. I was forty feet away before I was spotted.

There was a man on each side of the old man and the new leader of these assholes stood directly in front of him, his back to me. The leader had pulled a sidearm and was balancing it in front of the old man's eyes. Tough as nails, the old man didn't blink.

When one of the men spotted me, he pointed at me over the leaders shoulder. As the man started to turn I palmed the Colts and drilled him through the heart with both. Quickly turning the Colts on the two men holding the old man I put them down as well. Running to him I grabbed his arm and all but pulled him after me. We rounded the corner of the blacksmith shop as 9mm rounds tore at the stone. As we cleared the corner I heard the full auto bursts from Anthony's Mac 10's.

Surprising the old man by not turning into the building but running into the forest and sliding into a small ravine, he looked at me, smiled and said, "Good thinking young man, they will expect us to hide in the building, not the forest."

"Sir, we aren't stopping yet, unless you can't run a bit further." I said with a smile. My side had opened and my leg hurt like Hell.

"Son, to get away from those bastards I would run a marathon." He said with a smile of his own, not mentioning the blood on my shirt and my limp.

"How would you feel about fighting back?" I asked him as I handed him one of my now fully loaded Colts.

Hefting the magnum in his hand, his face lit up. Turning to me he said, "I can not get a shot at the bastard who kept hitting me, you took care of him. But his cohorts are just like him so lead the way."

Smiling my thanks, we turned and started toward the sound of firing. As we ran through the forest my thoughts were of Soledad and the rest, where were they? Are they safe? Hell, are we safe? Laughing out loud, my thought was definitely not.

9 OCT, THE TUNNEL

Willie stopped, after what seemed like forever, to rest. The air was closing in on them like a hot, humid blanket. Soledad and Lae tried to count the caskets they passed, they both gave up somewhere over two hundred.

As they started to press on, Fredric said, "Willie, I believe we only have one hundred meters to go before the shaft that takes us out spurs off to the right."

Han answered for him, "You are right my friend, we are almost out of this hell hole."

Ten minutes later they were at the fork, only there was only a straight tunnel and a cave-in on the right, rocks and boulders filling the old fork.

"Gregor eyed the cave-in and said, "We do not have equipment to dig through this. What is ahead?"

Fredric said, "About two hundred meters of nothing, then a massive steel door."

Willie asked, "Why did the old tunnel cave in? I know of no one who would intentionally do so."

Father Aaron spoke up, "What about the new office building complex that was built northwest of the village. Could the construction cause the cave-in?"

Hans replied, "It could, and I haven't been in the tunnel in over ten years."

Kurt said, "Construction blasting can cause cave-ins for kilometers around, which is probably the answer."

Losing patience, Gregor said, "I do not care what caused it, only that it happened and blocked our escape." Turning to Fredric, he continued, "You were unable to breach the door?"

"That is correct. We do not know what is behind the old door. Several times we tried to breach it to no avail. But we had to be careful not to make too much noise and raise the suspicion of the SS." Willie said as he exchanged glances with the other two old warriors.

Gregor eyed the group and all nodded, onward they go. After all, behind them was an armed group hell bent on killing them. Thirty meters from the old fork, the tunnel narrowed and digging was required to continue. As time went on, their spirits dampened as much as the air.

9 Oct, the Estate

The hospitality of Frau von Beitel was unbelievable. Making use of every bedroom, she turned her home into a hospital. Elsie and her two men seemed to be everywhere at once. She was amazed at how the training and experience she received during the War came back to her. It was as if it were only yesterday that she cared for the wounded at the Schloss. Wolfgang made it a point to keep the two parties separate, including armed guards where the Nazis were bedded down. Ernst noticed the arraignments and nodded his approval to Wolfgang.

With his Lieutenant in Munich, Ernst had a total of fourteen men, counting himself and the young man he had sent to the Schloss, all but three were wounded, some still sporting wounds from the fight at the border. Of the wounded, four were critical and needed better care than Elsie could give them. Four others had limb wounds, arms and legs, like Max. The others had slight body wounds that were more superficial than anything. No fatalities, thank God.

Having made the rounds, Ernst was looking forward to sitting down, at least for a few minutes. His rest would have to wait, a call from outside prompted him onto the porch. Coming down the road at a rapid clip was a hotel van followed by a bobtail truck. As the van skid to a stop, a familiar face climbed out and smiled up at Ernst.

"Colonel William Smyth and Company reporting for duty!" The old doctor said with a blustery shout and a grin almost as big.

Ernst was off the porch and had the doctor in a bear hug in a split second. After regaining his composure, Ernst stepped aside and turned the Colonel and Company over to a patiently awaiting Elsie. Following them inside was a group of well supplied young men and women who went to work immediately on the men in need.

Ernst turned as the driver of the van walked up to the porch. Surprised to see the manager of the hotel, Ernst extended his hand in thanks.

"May I ask where the good doctor came up with his Company?" Ernst asked as they turned to enter the house.

The manager smiled, then laughed, saying, "There is a medical school convention in town and these students are staying at our hotel. After we got your call, the Colonel interrupted one of their work sessions and convinced them to join him."

"How on Earth did he do that?" Ernst asked.

Holding back a laugh, the manager said, "I watched from the doorway, the good doctor has a way with words, a flamboyant style and a flair for the dramatic. He said, and I quote, "Ladies and gentlemen, do you want to read books and study your life away? Or do you want to live the life of a healer? There are good men in need as we waste away in a hotel meeting room. Come with me and you will understand the true meaning of being a doctor! Now, who is with me, once more into the breach?"

"That worked?' Ernst asked, beside himself.

"Oh he was very persuasive, after the first couple of students joined him, the rest almost ran him down." the manager said with another bout of laughter.

Laughing together, the two men followed the students and the doctor, into the breach.

Standing just off the porch, Max had taken everything in that had just transpired. He was worried, very worried. Ernst Lange was a man who controlled his emotions, normally. Over the last few days Max had seen more emotion from his friend than the rest of the time they had known each other. Vowing to keep a sharp eye on Ernst, Max made his way to his sentries and started his rounds.

Ernst finally found an unused chair and sat down, stretched his legs out and melted into the chair. It was short lived, no sooner than he totally relaxed Max rushed into the room.

"Captain, heavy fighting has once again erupted near the Schloss. Automatic small arms fire from at least a dozen weapons are involved." Max said as he slid to a stop in front of Ernst.

Standing on tired feet, Ernst smiled and said, "To steal a phrase from the good doctor, once more into the breach."

9 Oct, the Forest

The old grounds keeper was in better shape than he looked. We made great time getting back to Anthony's position. I should say last known position for he was nowhere to be found. From the looks of things, the men below came after him. Starting at the trucks there was a trail of bodies that led to where we stood.

Turning to the groundskeeper, I said, "My friend is outnumbered seven to one and is probably running low on ammo."

With a frown, he asked, "How do you know there are seven?"

Pointing at the trail to the trucks, I replied, "There were twelve."

Looking at the forest floor, I picked up Anthony's trail and motioned for my new partner to follow.

Looking at me with a strange expression, he had to ask, "Are your tracking? Who do you think you are, a Red American Indian?"

All I did was smile.

9 Oct, the Tunnel

The old warriors were right, there was a massive steel door blocking the way. Exhausted, the small group sat where they could to catch some much needed rest.

Ten or so meters from the door, the tunnel opened into a large room. Scattered about the room was evidence of human occupancy throughout the ages. Shields, swords, battle axes and various pieces of armor were piled into one corner. Across form the medieval collection was more modern evidence. Ammo crates and broken rifles littered the wall to the right of the door. There were other various items scattered about the room, crosses, goblets and a broken up church pew.

Sitting on a small table on the left side of the door were three candles, which was a good thing. The flashlights which Sister Anna had pulled from her Habit were getting very dim. Pulling matches from her Habit, Sister Anna lit the candles and joined Janet, Lae and Soledad in looking for more.

While the women searched for light, the men studied the door. The thing was massive. Eight feet in width and eight feet high it was very imposing. Joseph, Kurt and the young commando studied the right side while Gregor and the Father concentrated on the left. Willie, Hans and Fredric poked and prodded the center, looking for a way to open it.

There were blast marks all over the door and around the edges where it was recessed into the rock. From the looks of it, everything was placed against the door. No drills were used to plant explosives.

The young commando made note of the lack of effective attempts by saying, "Gentlemen, it looks to me as if all the attempts through the ages were done by amateurs and not demolition experts."

Glaring back at him, a ticked off Gregor asked, "I suppose you are an expert, whatever your name is."

Smiling at Gregor, he said, "My name is Elias Cortez and I am highly trained in demolition."

Kurt looked at the young man and asked, "Elias Cortez? But you are an East German?"

Smiling at Kurt, Elias said, "Yes, I was born just outside Berlin. My father had been part of the Spanish consulate in 1939 and stayed throughout the war. When the war was over he stayed to help rebuild Germany. My Grandmother worked for him which is how he met my mother."

Gregor got them back on the subject at hand, "Elias, can this be blown with what we have?"

"No, it cannot." Elias said in a soft tone.

Father Aaron turned to the ladies and asked, "Any luck finding more candles or anything else we can use?"

As one they turned and shook their heads. It appeared this large room had been raided several times through the years and anything useful was long gone, other than the three candles they were currently using.

Looking down the long dark tunnel they had just come down, Sister Anna said, "I do not want to go back, there must be a way?"

"We have to do something. The air here is getting worse by the minute." Joseph said as he kicked the door.

Coming together around their meager light, the twelve trapped allies discussed their situation, trying to find a solution. Unfortunately the only resolution they could see was to return the way they came and pray their attackers were gone, if the oxygen would hold out.

Soledad summarized their predicament for the group. Saying, "The way I see it, we have no choice but to return to the room and, if need be, fight our way out."

"I hate to admit it, but you are right. If we have to fight, we fight." Lae responded.

Kurt said, "We better be ready for anything. Let us check our weapons, ammo and get ready to pull out in five minutes." Pointing to their light, he continued, "The candles are getting dimmer."

After a check of their remaining ammo, they were a little disappointed at the outcome. The ladies each had a total three full clips, one in each of their pistols and one extra. Gregor was in a little better shape with full clips in his 1911's and an extra for each. Elias had a total of two clips for his H&K and did not have a sidearm. Kurt had two clips for his Walther.

With the final check behind them and a tally of ammo, Elias said with a crooked smile, "With less than two hundred rounds, we will have a short fight."

Willie pulled an old bayonet, motioned for one of his cohorts to do the same, and said, "We can help if they get close enough."

Fredric spoke up and said with a laugh, "Speak for yourself Willie, you and Hans have the only bayonets. I just have my bare hands and perhaps this brass rod I found in the corner. If I sharpened the end I can stab one of them." He said as he held up the heavy rod.

Soledad studied the rod in his hands for a moment, turned to Lae and Janet and said, "Ladies, it is time for us to study the door. Perhaps we might see something the boys missed."

"We really do not have time for this, the air is almost gone." The Father said, pointing to the dimming candles.

The ladies were ignoring him. All three took pieces of their clothing and started rubbing the door and the adjoining wall, wiping off layers of dust, dirt and blast marks. The men stood back, wondering what the ladies were looking for. Hans caught on first.

"Where did you find the rod?" Hans asked Fredric.

"It was leaning in the corner, by the pile of ammo boxes." He replied.

Looking quickly around, Hans almost ran over Willie and Father Aaron getting to the corner. Disappointment clouded his face after a few moments. The rest of the men suddenly caught on to what they were looking for and started looking for another rod.

Lae found what the ladies were looking for first, "Hey, I found a Knights cross like the one in the wall, it has the long leg pointing down and has a hole at the bottom."

Soledad took the rod and came to her side. Holding her breath, she pushed the rod into the hole. It was a tighter fit than the small rods used to trip the lock on the door in the other room, but it slid in without a problem. After slightly more than a foot of the rod disappeared into the wall, a soft click was heard. Nothing else happened.

Janet went to the other side of the door and started rubbing the wall, about the same height, as the Knights Cross Lae had found. Within seconds the second Cross appeared. Everyone shouted with joy, but it was short lived as Gregor pointed out the lack of a second rod.

Over the next several minutes of searching in earnest, the group had accomplished nothing but the use of oxygen. The ladies started collapsing with the lack of fresh air, followed by the Father and the three old warriors.

Kurt sat down and with shallow breaths said, "Elias, Gregor, they are all breathing, but only just, we must find a way out of here and quickly."

Nodding in agreement, Elias slid into unconsciousness. Kurt laughed a shallow laugh at Elias as he too fell face first onto the floor. Gregor looked around the room in disgust. The thought raging through his mind was 'We are not dying here! Not like this.'

Pulling himself off the floor, Gregor staggered to the corner of the room that held the discarded weapons and ammo crates. Picking up one of the Mauser rifles with a shattered stock, an idea came to his oxygen deprived mind. Taking the rifle by the breach, he swung the barrel against the wall, repeatedly. Finally shattering the wood forearm, Gregor crawled to the door and tried to slide the barrel into the hole. The front sight prevented the entry.

Cursing in his native Russian, Gregor slung the barrel across the room. In the dying light he saw it land on another Mauser and caused the end of the barrel to bounce up. It took a moment for Gregor to understand what he saw. Crawling hurriedly to the other rifle, he grabbed it and headed to the hole in the wall.

Pulling the cleaning rod from its sheath underneath the barrel, Gregor slid the steel rod into the hole. A little over a foot into the wall, Gregor heard a soft click. Immediately after the click, the door moved slightly into the wall beside Gregor. Standing, and with the last of his strength, Gregor pushed against the door with everything he could muster. Suddenly the door gave and Gregor fell past the open door, unconscious, into another dark room.

9 Oct, the Forest

Ernst and three men came upon the blacksmiths shop from the east. Halting two hundred yards out they studied the scene through binoculars. Much to their surprise there was nothing going on. North of the shop sat several trucks, steam coming out from under their hoods and several had flat tires. There were also bodies. Ernst and his men checked the bodies quickly and reconnoitered the area within minutes, including the shop and stables.

"Gentlemen, I fear we have come to the party much too late to aid our friends. That said, I have a question, since there are none among these unfortunate individuals, where are they? " Ernst said to his men, worry in his voice.

One of the men spoke up, saying, "Captain, a group of men ran into the forest in line with the trail of bodies. They were apparently in pursuit of someone. Two others went into the forest heading west, one of which is wounded."

Without hesitation, Ernst said, "We pursue the pursuers."

In combat spread formation, Ernst and his force of three commandos entered the forest in hopes of finding their friends, alive.

9 Oct, the Forest

After three hundred meters at a rapid pace, we slowed our advance in fear of overrunning our enemy. Good thing too, I hurt like hell. My side was leaking at an alarming rate. I was having trouble keeping it wrapped. The leg wound was seeping through the bandage but was not leaving a trail like the other wound.

Pausing to catch our breath, I said, "Sir, if I may, how have you stayed in such shape all these years? I know several younger men you could run to ground."

Smiling through gritted teeth while holding his side, he said, "I can thank the Desert Fox for drilling into my thick skull the importance of being fit." With a bigger smile, he continued, "Had I not been able to run fast when Montgomery chased Rommel's Afrika Corps across North Africa, I would probably be dead."

"That explains it, another soldier, I should have known. Almost every man I have met in this country, over the age of 50 was a soldier." I said with a smile of my own. Continuing I asked, "I understand Rommel was a great commander and soldier but he was also a good man."

"In my opinion, you have it backwards. He was a good soldier, but a great man." He said as he extended his hand. "I am Herbert Gerhard."

Shaking his offer hand, I said, "Glen Williams, it is very nice to meet you Herbert. I am sorry for getting you involved in this mess but it is nice to have your assistance."

Laughing, he said, "Call me Herb. But my uninformed young friend, I have been involved since 1944."

As I sat there with my mouth open, automatic weapons fire erupted slightly to our north.

Herb continued, "After we save your friends, I think a beer and a story is in store for us both."

Rising to our feet, side by side we advanced to the sound of the fighting.

With a controlled final burst, Anthony reduced his pursuers to six. Afterwards, they divided into three pairs and proceeded to try and flank him. One pair circled to the left while one circled to the right. The apparent leader and the other continued up the trail in hopes of flushing Anthony out in the open.

Anthony was in a bit of a pickle. Having expended the clips for his Mac 10's, all he had left was a Kbar fighting knife, his wits and his little bag of magic tricks. Fifty pound test mono fishing line had many uses outside of catching a meal. Two of Anthony's pursuers found out one of the uses, much to their dismay.

Standing straight up and smiling, he caught the leader's attention. When the man pointed to him, Anthony took off in what the other men thought was a dead run in an attempt to escape. Anthony ran hard, for thirty feet then went to ground. Crawling back to his mono filament trip wire, he waited for the men to arrive.

Running as fast as the forest allowed, the two men covered the distance between them and the man they wanted desperately to kill within a minute. Suddenly, something grabbed their feet and head over heels they went. Anthony was on them before they stopped bouncing, clubbing the leader at the base of his neck with the handle of the Kbar, knocking him unconscious. The other man recovered much too quickly and was bringing his weapon to bear. Concentrating on his target only ten feet away, the man was surprised to feel a kick in his chest and was more surprised to look down and see the handle of a Kbar sticking out of his chest.

As the man sagged to the ground, Anthony was relieving the unconscious man of his weapon when he heard a click. Looking up, Anthony's life flashed before his eyes as he stared up pasted the bore of a submachine gun and into the eyes of a very pissed off mercenary.

Herb and I topped a small rise in time to see two men cross the trail we were on and move into the brush. Their movements suggested they were trying to sneak up on someone. That someone could only be Anthony. Motioning for Herb to move to my right, we proceeded into the brush behind them.

Within fifty feet we heard a commotion to the men's front, they heard it too. Picking up our pace to match theirs, we spotted Anthony and two others on the ground in seconds. The men didn't hesitate to raise their weapons. Herb and I did not hesitate either, the big difference between them and us, we pulled the triggers. The heavy magnum rounds threw the two men on top of Anthony, he immediately voiced his displeasure.

"What the hell? Why did you make these two assholes land on me?" Anthony said as he crawled out from under the two men.

Smiling, Herb and I bent down to help him up and all hell broke loose. To our right two submachine guns opened up on something to our left. A couple of submachine guns answered their fire with long bursts of their own. Hugging the ground and trying to see what was going on was a bit difficult. All three of us rolled toward the trees in our front, trying to get out of the line of fire and figure out what caused the sudden activity. As quickly as it started, it was over.

Holding the Colts at the ready, Herb and I surveyed the forest, ready to shoot the first thing that moved. To our right there was movement then a voice called out to us.

"Glen, I have seen what those Colt Magnums can do to a man. I prefer you not blow large holes into me or any of my men." Ernst said in a loud, booming voice.

Recognizing his voice, I stood and said, "Ernst, it's great to hear your voice. What are you doing here and who were you shooting at?"

Stepping out of the brush with one of his men, Ernst pointed to where the other fire came from. As he pointed two more of his men came out of the brush shaking their heads.

"Captain, there were two and they are both dead." One of them said in a tired voice.

"Damn, I wanted one of them alive to question. Who they are, who sent them and why, are questions I would like to have the answers." Ernst said vehemently.

Anthony stood, pointed to the unconscious man and said, "Well sir, here is a live one with a knot on his head."

The man had not moved, but his eye movement told us he heard everything we said. Not taking any chances, two of Ernst's men covered him with their weapons while I grabbed one arm and Anthony got the other and stood him up. As he came up his eyes popped open and he resisted until he saw the two submachine guns pointed at him.

Walking up to him, Ernst looked him in the eyes and said, "I think I know who and what you are, but I want to hear it from you."

Ernst did not flinch as the spittle ran down his cheek. The silent man smiled as Ernst wiped the mess off his face with his sleeve.

"Silence, I expected nothing less." Turning to us, Ernst continued, "Several years ago a small heavily armed group robbed a holding company outside of Berlin. After brutally killing everyone in the building, they got away with millions in bearer bonds. They vanished until a few years later, the same group, we suspect, pulled a similar stunt in Paris. There have been two other robberies that were unsolved due to no witnesses. The villains killed everyone, every time."

Pausing for a second, placing his submachine gun under the man's chin, Ernst said, very bluntly, "One of the people killed outside of Berlin was a dear friend of my family. If you were involved, I will kill you myself."

Smiling an evil smile at Ernst then at us all, the man finally spoke, "Kill me then, I was there. I was at all you mentioned, and more that you know nothing about."

I couldn't keep my mouth shut, surprise, surprise, "Why fight to the last man? Who sent you and why?"

Looking at me was a face from the Devil's own table, "The crazy old Nazi said there was millions in gold to be had. Besides, the more of us you kill, the bigger the take for the rest of us, it is simple math. There is also the fact of our vehicles being disabled, we could not run."

Herb spoke up for the first time, saying, "Vermin like you should be executed at any rate."

Snapping his head around and preparing to spit on Herb was the last thing he did on this earth. As Anthony and I lowered the body to the ground, Herb handed my pistol to me.

Turning to Ernst, Herb said, "He enjoyed the beating they gave me a little too much."

Anthony looked the scene over, shook his head and said, "When that idiot gets before Saint Peter I can hear what old Peter will say to him, "What were you thinking, planning on spitting on an old man holding a loaded weapon?"

The momentary laughter was broken by Ernst, "That appears to be the last of them, but we will continue to be cautious. The group that attacked us from the estate has been defeated as well."

Looking around, I nodded and said, "That leaves one question, where is Soledad and the others?"

CHAPTER 30

Slowly Gregor was aware of a hard object digging into his side. Shifting slightly he realized it was the edge of the open door. Behind him he heard movement in the dark and was relieved to hear familiar voices. There was light moving around in the room in front of him. It finally sunk into his clearing mind what was going on. The others had come to before him and were exploring the newly found room.

"Gregor, are you all right?" Lae asked as she bent over to check on him.

All she got was a grunt and a nod. Patting him on the back, she joined the others in their exploration. Gregor looked around as his head cleared and was surprised to find everyone in the room. The three old men, Kurt and Joseph were studying a door across from where he lay. Father Aaron, Sister Anna, Soledad, Janet and Lae were across the room by some shelving. The young commando was watching the tunnel for pursuit.

The air was surprisingly fresh for a closed underground room, even for a room the size of this one, which Gregor estimated at twenty five meters square. After a moment or two surveying the room in dim candle light, Gregor spotted the reason, a fireplace was in the corner next to the unopened door. The chimney must help provide an air current. If so, the chimney might be their way out if the other door can't be opened.

"Gregor, please take a look at this." Lae called to him.

Rising with a grunt, he walked to her, the movement helping clear his head further.

Before her was a long shelf lined with small objects covered by cloth and dust. Sister Anna reached over and removed the cloth from one of the objects. Shiny gold, bright blue enamel and the shape of the thing shocked Gregor. Picking up the egg, he knew he was holding history in his hand. Upon seeing his reaction, the others walked down the shelf removing some of the coverings. Each shelf section had five shelves. The shelving was twenty feet long. This meant there was one hundred feet of shelves covered with artifacts of all types.

Behind the shelf, several large crates, stacked four high, filled the space to the wall, packed tight but leaving walkways between the stacks. On the other side of the room were crates that looked like the type used to store paintings. A quick count put the crates at over one hundred, the painting crates at a little more. In a space closest to the fireplace by the unopened door sat a desk and five four drawer file cabinets. On the desk sat desk pad, an old ledger, pen set and a lamp. Gregor reached over and pushed the switch on the lamp, it came on.

The look of surprise was on everyone's face, well almost everyone. Willie, Hans, and Fredric looked at each other and shrugged. Soledad caught the looks and the motions.

Walking up to the three, she said, "You three knew about this place and what is here, didn't you."

Father Aaron and Sister Anna stepped beside Soledad and waited for the three to speak up. Hans was the first.

"Yes, we did. We helped smuggle these things into the room while patients at the hospital." Hans said as he walked over to the unopened door. Continuing, he said, "Obviously, we also knew how to open the trap door leading into the tunnel. However they never showed us how to open the massive door that guarded the art, even though, as it turned out, opened the same."

"Since the other entrance to the tunnel was on the hillside, giving us access to the gold when needed, we did not care about the art." Fredric added.

"Everyone who was involved made a pact to only take gold when needed for our families. Then not take enough to raise suspicion as to where the money came from." Willie said as he leaned on the desk, fatigue showing in his aged face.

"How many people know about this?" Father Aaron asked, surprise in his voice.

Willie looked at his two comrades before answering, "Where the art is concerned, besides the three of us, three men from the Vatican and the Priest that Father Aaron replaced in '43. As you know, the old Priest died, his death brought Father Aaron here. We do not know about the three from Rome."

Han took over, saying, "As to the gold, there are several involved, the three of us and four others are all that is left."

Fredric laughed and said, "Do not forget the crazy SS Major who stole the gold before we stole it from him."

Sister Anna asked, "But where are we? The chimney of the fire place comes out somewhere and what about the door, not to mention the electricity?"

Father Aaron added, "This room is a mystery to me. How was it built and no one in the village knew about it?"

Laughing out loud, Hans said, "What makes you think no one knew about it? The three of us, along with a few others, helped build it. It was pretty easy after the tunnel from the Schloss to the Church was discovered. All we did was expand the first part of the tunnel to make this room. " Pointing to the closed door, he continued, "Where do you think that door leads?"

"There have been rumors of the Church hiding valuables and art from the Nazis. I never dreamed our Church had been one of the chosen places." Father Aaron said as he looked around the room. Turning to Hans, he said, "It goes into the Church, doesn't it?"

Sister Anna interjected, "I know every door in the Church. This door cannot lead into the Church."

"Has anyone tried to open the door?" Gregor asked, joining in the conversation.

Sheepishly, everyone looked at each other, some shaking their heads.

"Well hell." Gregor said as he walked over, grabbed the door knob and opened the door without as much as a squeak.

Every one stepped up to see what was on the other side. Much to their disappointment a plaster wall filled the doorway.

"Damn!" Gregor said as he doubled his right fist and hit the center of the wall as hard as he could, venting his frustration upon the plaster.

He was lucky. His fist went between the studs and through two layers of plaster. As he pulled his fist out of the hole his anger produced, a surprised female face appeared in the hole, unladylike words coming out of her mouth.

Sister Sara and Sister Marie had decided to go to the Schloss and find out what was going on up there. Every call they had made fell on deaf ears, including the one to the BND who informed them Father Aaron's friend, Otto, was not in. With the weather getting colder, Sister Marie went into the store room in the basement to get heavy coats for the two. She had just draped the two coats over her arm when a fist appeared right in front of her.

"Son of a bitch!" Sister Marie said as the fist pulled back into the wall.

"Is that you Sister Marie?" Father Aaron called out, knowing full well it was. Turning to the rest, he said, "She learned that American phrase a few years ago and likes the way it sounds. I cannot get her to stop saying it."

Overhearing what the Father said, she replied, indignity in her voice, "Father, it only slips out when I am mad or surprised, you know that."

Looking back and forth to the Father and the Sister, Gregor's impatience got the best of him. Stepping back and squaring his shoulders he said, "Please step back, I am going to open this door."

Without another word, Gregor did.

Reaching down to take my offered hand, Anthony helped me to my feet, looked me in the eye for a moment and said, "Thank you, my wife and mother might agree."

"Agree to what?" a familiar voice said from the forest.

Turning quick enough that Anthony had to help me stay up, I saw, standing next to a tree, my Heart.

CHAPTER 31

Elsie's formal dining room can seat thirty comfortably, we filled it. Besides our group, Gregor, Lae, Kurt, Janet, Joseph, Father Aaron, Sister Anna, Soledad and me, we were joined by almost everyone involved. Ernst, Max, John Kirkpatrick, Anthony, the two KGB agents, the two CIA agents, Dov and one of the other Mosad agents joined us. Sitting at the end was Willie, Hans and Fredric. Across from me sat Otto, Kurt's boss, Wolfgang and the other man who lives at the estate. I still don't know his name. Sitting next to Elsie was Herb, the grounds keeper of the Schloss. Finishing the diners was Colonel William Smyth and his lovely wife.

The food was exquisite both in presentation and flavor. Her elegant décor spoke of history and old money, both were an illusion as we were about to find out.

As the food disappeared and after dinner drinks were served, Elsie stood and presented a toast, "Here is to a promising future, old friends as well as new ones."

After a round of nods and everyone took a sip of their cognac, Elsie continued, "Everyone here is interested in what went on at the Schloss in 1945. There are people here who will tell what they know in hopes of putting it all to rest."

Willie spoke up, "Ladies and gentleman, it is very simple. The Nazis were moving large quantities of stolen objects as well as quantities of gold out of the region. With help of several people here and others who are gone, we diverted as much as we could."

"Diverted yes, stole, not really, except for some of the gold, everything we were able to take is here." Hans added.

Fredric stood and addressed the table, "Before you ask, we were sworn to secrecy by the Church. We were not to divulge anything about the art and artifacts found in the underground room next to the Church. We assumed when the Church was ready to bring them to light, they would."

"Apparently, those who knew about the items have passed on and did not pass the information along." Willie said as he looked over at Elsie.

Nodding to Willie, Elsie stood and said, "I was a nurse at the hospital in the Schloss, not a Baroness or any other royalty. With some of the gold I bought this estate and made up my linage. The plan was to stay close and guard the secrets until such a time to reveal came about." Pausing and looking at her confederates for a moment, she continued, "Unfortunately the Sturmbannfuhrer suspected many things, one of which was my involvement in the disappearance of the gold."

Wolfgang spoke up for the first time, "Elsie saved my life and the life of my brother," he said, pointing to the other man, "Able and I were both so severely wounded the doctors had given up on us. But not Elsie, she took care of us in her spare time and we survived. I fully recovered. Able lost his hearing and his ability to speak, but he lives. Because of her dedication to our survival, we will never leave her side."

Ernst kept looking at Herb, studying him. Finally his hand went up too. Still looking at Herb, he asked, "May I ask sir, what is your interest in this affair?"

Herb blushed and looked over at Elsie. Willie, Hans and Fredric broke out laughing. Able smiled and Wolfgang answered for Herb.

"Mein Herr, his interest is solely in Elsie. He fell in love with her while a patient in the hospital. He has been courting her for years but she is playing hard to get." Wolfgang said between his laughter.

Looking at the group, Ernst asked, "What is funny about love?"

"He's been courting her since 1945!" Hans said as the entire table joined them in laughter.

Elsie reached over and took Herb's hand, smiled at him and said, "I think it is time for me to say yes."

Herbs face broke out in a huge smile while the rest of us applauded the proclamation. Congratulations were given and pats on Herbs back probably made him sore but he took it all with a smile, his eyes locked on Elsie.

Waiting several minutes and for the festivities to die down, Soledad raised her hand, wanting to ask a question but did not want to interrupt the happy mood. Elsie nodded for her to proceed.

"Who is this Sturmbannfuhrer? How does he fit into this?" Soledad asked.

"The Devils spawn." Elsie said in a low voice. "He is an insane, cruel, murderous, twisted spawn of the Devil himself."

"Devil he might be, but a smart one he is. He sent a load of gold north by train and issued orders that got it shot up by the Luftwaffe. After he and his cronies retrieved the gold, they cleaned up the site so well it was as if it never happened." Herb said, speaking up for the first time.

Gregor, Kurt and I looked at each other. That explained the site we found north of Munich.

Kurt interjected, "He must be of the Devil if he could send his brethren of the SS to their deaths by his design."

"What SS? The troops escorting the first shipment were from a Wehrmacht unit that had been pulled from the line in the Eastern Front." Willie replied.

"He tried that again on a train heading south, but the Americans foiled his plans. Fighter-Bombers blew it off the tracks into a river. Heavy rains moved in later the same day and the rail cars disappeared." Fredric added.

That explained the rail cars and gold we found to the south. One thing kept bothering me so my hand went up.

"We found reports of radioactive material being transported. We also found radioactive bullets in the trees to the north of the blacksmith shop. Do you know anything about that?" I asked.

Smiling at either me or my question, Herb answered, "The Sturmbannfuhrer hatched a plan to keep people out of his away. He started rumors, issued orders and provided fake documents alluding to the presence of radioactive material. The fact of the matter, the only radioactive material in the area was the coal and coal dust, and it was slight."

Willie smiled at us and said, "We did hide our weapons and ammunition in the coal bins and dust troughs. That might explain the reading of the bullets you found."

Fredric sat up straight, frowned and said, "The bullets you found were from a fight we had with the SS. Eleven of our brothers sacrificed their lives to give us time to hide the last of the gold in the underground shop. They did not have to die but the SS were butchers."

"Butchers, and stupid, they never figured out how we escaped the blacksmith shop." Hans said as he slapped Fredric on the shoulder, trying to bring him out of his somber mood.

Sitting quietly until now, Lae asked, "What about the crosses we found in the tree? All had names on them. Who buried them in the tree and put the plate over them?"

Hans answered, "It was crazy old Ott. He made the crosses after the fight with the SS as we hid the last if the gold. He said someone in the future would find them and they would be monuments to those who died saving the art and gold from the Nazis."

The three old warriors raised their glasses and waited for the rest of us to join them. As the last glass was raised, Willie said, "To Ott and all our brethren who could not be here tonight."

We talked well into the night. Questions were answered, Cognac was consumed and bonds were formed.

11 Oct, Munich

Breakfast was as wonderful, the cooks out did themselves. As the table was cleared and more coffee poured, it was time to discuss our new BMW's. The appearance of John, Anthony, Max and Ernst delayed that conversation.

"We thought we would fill you in on our arraignment before we left for the States." John said as he sat down.

"Let me guess," I said as I looked at Ernst, "You now work for the CIA."

Smiling, he said, "Yes, we have found a home. However, we will not operate against our old country, anywhere else in the world but not the DDR."

"How are your men?" Gregor asked as he sipped his coffee.

"We were very fortunate to have the services of such a fine doctor as Colonel Smyth. Several will remain here recovering from their wounds while the rest of us travel to America. The important thing is we lost no one. It was truly a miracle no one was killed." Ernst said with emotion.

"The Colonel did a fine job on my leg as well as my side. When he finished he patted me on the wounded leg and told me to stop being a crazy son of a gun." I said as I glanced at Anthony, who chose to ignore the comment.

"John, how did the BND react when you recruited Ernst and his men?" Soledad asked her Grandfather.

Ernst answered for him, "We got his blessing after a deal was struck between Otto and John."

"What kind of deal?" I asked.

"We will return occasionally to help train anti-terrorist commandos." Ernst said with a smile.

"Yep and I have a new assignment, Ernst, Max and the rest are going to get well versed in American culture." Anthony added. Glancing at me he said, "Take care of yourself you crazy son of a gun."

"I will, if you take care and watch your back better." I replied as we shook hands.

"Deal crazy man." Anthony said to me before turning his attention to Soledad, "I don't know where you found him but you have a good man there, a good man but crazy as hell in a fight."

That got a laugh from everyone. After saying their good byes, Ernst, Anthony and John bid us farewell and headed to catch their flight. Across the room, Dov and his men raised their coffee cups in salute and went about their business. The CIA and KGB agents haven't been seen since dinner at the estate. Gregor thinks they are now concentrating on each other, things never change. Kurt, Janet and Joseph flew back home early this morning and promised a full report of the children when they arrive.

I noticed Max hanging back during our brief conversation. As the others walked away he came to my side of the table stood straight as a ramrod and saluted. As I started to rise, he brought his hand down and offered it to me thus preventing me from standing. Taking his hand I looked up into his eyes and was surprised by what I saw. They were watery.

"Herr Williams, I want to thank you and your family for all you have done for us and more importantly my friend. I was worried about Ernst the last few days. He was showing so much emotion I was afraid he was having a breakdown. However I have come to realize it was not a breakdown he was having, it was the return of his humanity. He has always been a great leader and a good man, but the Stazi have a way to take our humanity. Thank you for the return of his, and of mine."

Standing, trying not to grimace from the pain, I said, "Max, I told you earlier that you were too good a man to kill. I am glad you finally realize it. Take good care of Ernst, your men, and yourself."

Surprising him, I grabbed him in a hug. As the surprise wore off he returned the hug. Stepping back he nodded at me, everyone at the table then turned to go. We all saw the tears.

After Max left, Otto appeared and filled us in on the decisions made by the powers that be. The governments of the agents involved and the Vatican came to an interesting conclusion, a bit strange but interesting, concerning the gold and the treasure. When we were let in on their decision, Soledad and Lae applauded the move. Gregor and I looked at each other before busting out loud laughing our butts off.

However we whole heartedly agreed with the solution. With pressure from Otto and John it was decided that the locals involved would be rewarded for finding the lost art and gold. Elsie, Herb, Abe, Wolfgang, Hans, Fredric and Willie will have more than enough money to live comfortably the rest of their lives.

Checking his watch, Gregor said, "One more day and I will drive my new BMW." With a gleam in his eye, he turned to me and said, "Too bad Soledad will be driving yours first."

That drew another laugh from everyone.

12 Oct, New Mexico

Consuelo saw the rental car as it stopped on the drive. Her heart skipped a beat as John climbed out of the driver's side. She reached the door before he did. Throwing the door open she rushed into his arms, holding him as if for dear life.

After several minutes silence, John cleared his tired throat and said, "I have flown all night to deliver a letter to you my Love."

"What kind of letter?" Consuelo asked in a soft voice.

Handing the envelope to her, John stepped back and let her read it. She read it through three times before looking at John, who was no longer standing before her, he was kneeling.

"Oh John, yes, oh yes!" was all she could muster as he stood and took her into his arms. As their kiss deepened, Consuelo let John's letter of retirement fall to the floor.

12 Oct, Bavaria

They were beautiful. In front of us sat three, 1978 BMW 733i sedans, one bright red and two black. Gregor still sat in his after driving it off the end of the assembly line. I think the smile on his face is permanent.

After finishing the final paperwork and promising to have them back by midday tomorrow for shipping, we headed to the Church. Soledad took to the big sedan like a fish to water, looks like I lost my BMW before I got to drive it. Lae was having a blast driving the red one. We may be getting more before heading back.

We parked ours across the street, out of the way. The red one we parked right in front of the Church. Soledad and Lae went inside to get the Father while Gregor sat with me on a bench.

Father Aaron is one of the finest gentlemen I have had the privileged to know, reserved and dignified. The reserved part went right out the window when he saw the red BMW. His eyes lit up and the smile on his face went ear to ear. All of that paled in comparison when he found out the car was his, well, the Churches. Calling for the Sisters, he was in the car in a flash, turning knobs, opening compartments while talking a mile a minute, explaining to the Sisters the features of the car.

"We done good." I said to Gregor.

"Is that a proper sentence?" Gregor asked with a smirk.

"Nope." I said with a smile. "We done good. The Father deserves it. By the way, did you make the arraignments for his other car to disappear? We really don't want him to continue to drive it and save the new one do we?" I whispered to Gregor.

"It has been liberated and is on the way to becoming razorblades or whatever they do with scrap metal here. Sister Anna said she would help him adjust to the loss." Gregor said with a soft laugh.

"My friends, I cannot possibly accept such a gift. However Sister Anna informs me it is a gift to the Church, therefore I cannot refuse. Who am I to argue with a Nun, especially this one?" Father Aaron said with a beaming smile as he looked over at her.

Leaning toward Soledad I whispered, "I'm telling you, he needs to become a Lutheran and take her with him."

All I got in response was a look and an elbow in my ribs. Thank goodness I was standing on Soledad's right and she hit my left side. I don't think my right would have taken the jab.

"Come, everyone, inside, we have prepared a small feast to celebrate the wedding announcement of Elsie and Herbert and to bid our new friends farewell." Father Aaron said as he ushered us inside.

Three short hours later we said our good byes to Father Aaron, the Sisters and villagers who attended the luncheon and prepared to head back to Munich. Stopping at the doorway separating the Chapel from the foyer, we all marveled at the beauty of this fine building and the love that went into its construction. This is truly a beautiful Church. Before I could turn around to continue out, Soledad grabbed my left arm and squeezed. Following her eyes into the foyer, I froze.

Standing in the entrance was an old man, small in stature, but there was nothing small about the Walther in his right hand. While his clothing spoke of money, his posture of a military background. Standing there pointing the Walther at us, waiting for our acknowledgement of his presence, he looked menacing as hell. I then look into his eyes and I knew exactly who he was, the Devils spawn himself, with rattlesnake eyes.

"What can we do for you Major?" I asked in a civil tone, using the American rank equivalent to Sturmbannfuhrer in an effort to judge his state of mind. It worked. My words also brought everyone's attention to the foyer.

"I am a Sturmbannfuhrer you American idiot. You will address me as such." He replied in a voice that got higher in pitch as he spoke.

Call him what you will, fruity as a loon, bat crap crazy or goofy as hell, this man was deadly and we need to watch our step. He's armed, we aren't.

"What do you want Herr Sturmbannfuhrer?" I asked in a soft tone.

"I want what is mine! I worked hard for the gold and I want it back. Members of this village stole it from me in 1945 and I will have what is mine. All my plans, all my time and effort wasted unless I get it returned. I will not hesitate to kill all of you to get what is mine." He said in a rant.

"Do you realize you said "I", "mine" and "my" a combination of ten times in the same breath?" I asked in an even tone as I moved to our left, trying to draw the weapon away from the group. It worked.

Soledad's eyes burned a hole in my back as I kept moving away. She is going to be mad at me for this but here goes.

"Major, I think you are just a thief and a bad one at that. You may be a great planner but your execution is lacking." I said, maintaining my even tone and easy move to the left. "If you were as good as you believe you would have made full Colonel, not stuck as a mere Major."

That struck a nerve. The old man started to shake but the pistol never wavered, it was pointed at my midsection.

While I poked at the man, Gregor slowly moved in front of the ladies and eased them into the Chapel. If shooting started they could duck behind the doorway and out of the line of fire. I could tell Gregor was beginning to lose his patience so I better get the old man moved more to the left.

"Major, you are like a lot of crazy short men throughout history, trying to act bigger than you are. You should be playing an elf in a movie or play so you can keep pretending you matter. Because you don't matter and never have, History has proven men like you never change its course." I said in a rant of my own as I moved even more to the left.

Shaking even more, he raised the Walther and took it in both hands. Gregor chose that moment to make his move. When I saw Gregor shift I let out a Comanche yell which startled everyone, not just the old man.

The Devil's spawn saw Gregor's move and mine a split second later. My wounds slowed me down and delayed me getting to the old man before he fired. Gregor spun to the right as the bullet hit him high in the right shoulder. As he spun, the old man fired into him again. Turning his weapon on me, he didn't get the chance to pull the trigger.

The Devil's spawn lay in a small pool of blood caused by a small head wound, a statuette of Mary lay beside him. Sister Anna held her hand at her mouth, not believing what she had done. While the old crazy man was concentrating on Gregor and me, Sister Anna moved to the shelf of statuettes and figurines. When the shooting started, she grabbed the largest statuette she could reach and threw it at his head. Her aim was true and the throw had the force of a 90 mph fastball. The impact knocked him through the door onto the steps and unconscious.

Before he stopped bouncing on the steps, we heard a motor start up and a car rapidly drive away. The old man driving it could only be the crazy man's driver and minion, as Elsie called him.

While I relieved the unconscious man of his weapon, the ladies rushed to Gregor. By the time I got there, he was sitting up looking at the hole in his shoulder. It only took me a second to spot the impact of the other bullet. Along the back of his left shoulder was a streak of blood, the bullet entered just under the skin, and at the angle it hit, bounced off his shoulder blade and out six inched from where it entered.

Looking up at me, Gregor noticed the look on my face. Frowning he said, "I am glad you find my wounds amusing."

Through the smile on my face I said, "I'm just thinking you won't be able to drive your new BMW again until I can drive mine. But I am sorry brother, I was too slow."

"You are mean Glen, funny but mean." Lae said as she and Soledad treated Gregor's wounds.

Gregor looked at me and said through a smile of his own, "Not to worry brother, we shall heal together while our wives tend to our every need." Soledad and Lae punched his good shoulder at the same time.

Within thirty minutes, the authorities had statements and our promise to stay around while they finished their investigation. The old man was in custody and on the way to the hospital, along with Gregor accompanied by Lae.

Sitting on the steps, my wounded leg extended as it hurt like hell and my side not much better, I noticed an odd look on Soledad's lovely face. Looking over my shoulder I saw what had her attention. Standing at the top of the steps was Sister Anna, holding the statuette of Mary, tears running down her face.

Soledad walked up to her and placed her arms around her. After a few moments, Soledad said, "You saved us by what you did. Don't be sad about it, we certainly aren't."

Sister Anna replied, "I'm not crying about what I did. The damage I caused to the statuette is unforgiveable."

Releasing the Sister, Soledad said, "Let me see, perhaps it isn't so bad."

Sister Anna handed the statuette to Soledad and pointed to a bend in Mary's arm. The damage was on the back of the arm where Mary's red robe draped across the arm. There was a dent and some of the red enamel had chipped off. Soledad's breath caught as she saw the material under the enamel.

Looking into Sister Anna's eyes, Soledad placed her finger to her lips and said, "Shish."

Reaching in her pocket for the small makeup bag Soledad always had with her, she pulled out a small bottle of red nail polish. Handing the statuette to Sister Anna, Soledad performed cosmetic surgery to Mary's arm. The red polish almost perfectly matched the enamel and sealed the wound completely. Stepping inside, they placed the statuette back in its place of Honor. Soledad then took Sister Anna's hand and led her outside.

THE END